MW00327351

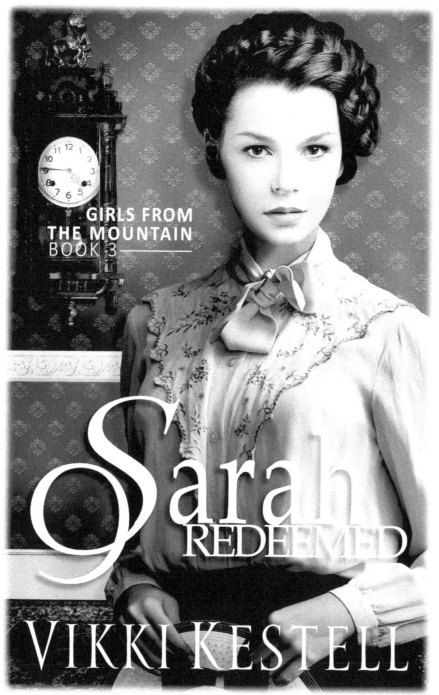

GIRLS FROM
THE MOUNTAIN
BOOK 3

$\mathcal{S}$arah
REDEEMED

VIKKI KESTELL

*Faith-Filled*
*Fiction*™

www.faith-filledfiction.com | www.vikkikestell.com

**Girls from the Mountain, Book 3**
©2018 Vikki Kestell
All Rights Reserved
Also Available in eBook Format

## BOOKS BY VIKKI KESTELL

### GIRLS FROM THE MOUNTAIN
Book 1: *Tabitha*
Book 2: *Tory*
Book 3: *Sarah Redeemed*

### A PRAIRIE HERITAGE
Book 1: *A Rose Blooms Twice*
Book 2: *Wild Heart on the Prairie*
Book 3: *Joy on This Mountain*
Book 4: *The Captive Within*
Book 5: *Stolen*
Book 6: *Lost Are Found*
Book 7: *All God's Promises*
Book 8: *The Heart of Joy—A Short Story* (eBook only)

### NANOSTEALTH
Book 1: *Stealthy Steps*
Book 2: *Stealth Power*
Book 3: *Stealth Retribution*
Book 4: *Deep State Stealth*

𝒮ARAH ℛEDEEMED
Copyright ©2018 Vikki Kestell
All Rights Reserved.
ISBN-10: 0-9862615-0-5
ISBN-13: 978-0-9862615-0-3

## Girls from the Mountain, Book 3
by Vikki Kestell
*Also Available in eBook Format from Most Online Retailers*

Martha Palmer, the generous benefactor of Palmer House—*a most extraordinary refuge for young women rescued from prostitution*—has died. Denver society turns out in strength to honor the elderly woman, as do many of the young women who have lived, at some point during the past decade, under the roof of Palmer House and under the steady and godly leadership of Rose Thoresen.

For Sarah Ellinger, Rose's trusted right hand, an invitation to the reading of Martha's will raises the possibility—and the fervent hope—that Martha has endowed Palmer House with funds to keep the ministry running. However, Sarah expects to receive nothing from Martha for herself. She is as stunned as every Palmer House girl present at the reading to hear:

"To every young woman who lives or has lived at Palmer House and remains unmarried at the time of the reading of this will, I bequeath the sum of five hundred dollars as a bridal gift, payable upon her marriage. To those girls who have already married, I bestow the same amount, payable upon the execution of this will. If, however, a young woman who has lived at Palmer House remains single, I bequeath the same sum, five hundred dollars, payable upon her thirty-ninth birthday."

Five hundred dollars was a fortune many a Palmer House girl would never in her lifetime see again in a lump sum; it could enable a newly married couple to begin their marriage debt-free, perhaps buy a little piece of land or leverage a mortgage to purchase a home.

While the girls of Palmer House, current and former, wept and rejoiced aloud, Sarah did not. She slowly shook her head.

*Oh, Martha. You left me a wonderful gift, for which I am most grateful. However, I cannot claim this gift unless I marry—or until I am quite near middle-aged. Why, Martha? Why did you arrange your generous bequest this way? I shall not be able to claim your gift for nearly eleven years . . . because I shall never marry, whatever the inducement to do so.*

## ACKNOWLEDGEMENTS

**I give up!**
In every way I can imagine,
(except, maybe, via the gift of a Hawaiian cruise),
I have offered thanks and appreciation
to my esteemed teammates,
**Cheryl Adkins** and **Greg McCann**.
You give of yourselves selflessly
to help me make each new book
the most effective instrument
of God's grace possible.
I love and appreciate you.
I always will.

## COVER DESIGN

Vikki Kestell

## TO MY READERS

This book is a work of fiction,
what I term Faith-Filled Fiction™.
While the characters and events are fiction,
they are situated within the historical record.
To God be the glory.

## SCRIPTURE QUOTATIONS

The King James Version (KJV)
Public Domain

## GIRLS FROM THE MOUNTAIN

The full stories of a select group of women introduced in the little mountain village of Corinth or later at Palmer House in Denver, the mile-high city (hence the series title, **Girls from the Mountain**).

*Tabitha, Tory,* and *Sarah Redeemed* are three such stories—the testimonies of fallen women redeemed by God's amazing grace, led out of darkness to become lights in this sinful world. Each book can be read as a standalone volume but having already read **A Prairie Heritage** may increase your enjoyment.

~*~

## DENVER, 1909

Joy was thoughtful. "You said something just now ... You called them *girls from the mountain.* I rather like that."

"Certainly less degrading than 'former prostitutes.'" Grant smiled his endearing half-smile.

"Perhaps that is how we should refer to them from now on. Of course, when the Lord gives us women from Denver, the phrase will no longer apply."

"Denver is surrounded by mountains. I don't see a problem with it. It could be our own little code for the young ladies of Palmer House."

Joy nodded. "I like that."

—An Excerpt from *The Captive Within*

GIRLS FROM THE MOUNTAIN
  Book 1: *Tabitha*
  Book 2: *Tory*
  Book 3: *Sarah Redeemed*

# PART 1

*Be ye angry, and sin not:*
*let not the sun go down upon your wrath:*
*Neither give place to the devil.*
*(Ephesians 4:26–27, KJV)*

# CHAPTER 1

## DENVER, COLORADO
## AUGUST 1919

The trolley shuddered and jerked to a stop in the center of the roadway. Sarah stood and stepped down onto the street with two other passengers on their way to their respective places of employment. The threesome, although not formally acquainted, waited together as they often did for the line of oncoming vehicles to thin before crossing from the middle of the street to the sidewalk.

Exchanging cordial nods, the passengers parted ways. Sarah Ellinger, with a brisk stride, moved in the direction of *Michaels' Fine Furnishings*. By the time she reached the shop, she was overly warm, and the thin fabric of her simple muslin blouse clung to her back. The bright summer morning promised another day of sweltering heat—and the only relief to be found within the walls of the shop was a single oscillating fan. The fan moved stuffy air about the shop but did little to lower the temperature.

"Oh, my." Sarah used a handkerchief to pat the back of her neck where she had gathered her dark mane and braided it up one side of her head, across the top, and down the other side. The braid lifted her heavy hair from off her neck and fashioned a shining russet coronet across the top of her head—a crown that framed a widow's peak set above a smooth forehead. She carried her straw chip hat in her hand for, in the oppressive heat, she preferred a breeze (what there might be of one) rippling across her upswept braid to the stifling confines of a hat.

*Perhaps we shall be blessed with a cooling rain today*, Sarah suggested to herself. She was hoping for a monsoon thunderstorm, a heavy afternoon rain shower common from mid-July through mid-September.

Before Sarah unlocked the shop door, she paused to study the window displays, one on either side of the entrance. Ornate black-and-gold paint scrolled across the window glass, from the outside corners of the window casing and along the glass edges. But, instead of the displays within the windows, she caught sight of her own reflection in the shining glass.

She was always surprised at the image staring back at her, for she thought little of her appearance. No longer in the first flush of youth but not yet thirty years old, she disdained frivolous tokens of femininity in favor of expediency. The overall impression of the image in the window, then, was that of a practical, pragmatic woman. The soft cleft in her chin gave way to a rounded but firm jawline and a wide, reserved mouth. Her grave, dark eyes only added to the impression that she was no one's fool.

Her mouth opened in a sigh when she saw that the bow of her blouse— forever a nuisance—was askew yet again. The brows over those serious eyes drew together into a frown.

"Oh, bother," she remarked to no one.

Peering beyond her reflection, she studied the window displays. They were pleasant and enticing: a stylish boudoir occupied the left-hand window; an artfully composed parlor comprised the right. A skillful arrangement of dried roses adorned the parlor's side table.

"I suppose it is too early for fall flowers," a voice at Sarah's shoulder considered aloud, "but my roses have quite faded in this heat."

Sarah spun about and smiled. "No matter how lovely you make our displays, you are never satisfied, Corrine."

Sarah was glad to see her friend and co-worker after her three-week absence.

Corrine laughed. "I suppose you are right."

Sarah fit the key to the lock and swung open the heavy entrance door. The gust of air that greeted them was but marginally cooler than that outside.

"Ugh. I reckon we shall suffer the heat today," Corrine grumbled as they closed the door behind them. "I already miss the coolness of Lake Louise." In contrast to Sarah, Corrine was all softness and femininity— auburn hair, gently rounded figure, plump cheeks and dimples, and a composed expression, perfected by a cheerful demeanor.

"My, yes; temperatures in the daytime have been miserable, and nights have been near unbearable. Even with the windows open, the upstairs bedrooms at Palmer House are stifling. It is difficult to sleep soundly."

"Oh, how I remember! And how is everyone at the house?"

"We are well, but we miss you, of course. Welcome back, by the way. And how fares everything at the Johnston residence?" The corners of Sarah's eyes crinkled with undisguised mirth.

Corrine blushed and giggled. "Do not tease me, Sarah."

"Ah, but it is not every day my dear roommate abandons me to marry and embark upon a Canadian honeymoon for a fortnight and a half, is it?"

The two women laughed together then.

"Who would have dreamed?" Corrine shook her head, smiling her happiness. "It is still such a miracle, a miracle that Albert loves me, that he loves me despite my . . . past."

The words, "despite my past," were unnecessary. Sarah and Corrine understood each other without them. A full decade had elapsed since a contingent of U.S. Marshals and Pinkerton detectives had arrested those who ran the two "elite gentleman's clubs" situated in Corinth, a little mountain village above Denver. The arrests had liberated Sarah, Corrine, and a number of other young women and girls who had lived—and labored—in those houses.

It was true that Sarah and Corrine had been prostitutes, but hardly by choice. They and the other girls had been deceived, most of them lured to Denver by false promises of employment. Once in Denver, they had been abducted, beaten, and starved into submission; forced into a life of ongoing degradation; watched and supervised continually; and imprisoned in their rooms each night.

Sarah had been a prisoner in the Corinth brothel for more than a year when a stranger arrived in the village, a young widow who introduced herself as Joy Thoresen. With her own money (rumor had it), the widow—herself but twenty-six years old—purchased a disused, two-story log house, made it over into a mountain guest lodge at great expense, and began receiving paying lodgers.

Then, risking her safety and that of her few but loyal companions, this Joy Thoresen also began receiving escapees from the two brothels—and she dared to take them in, hide them, bind their wounds, and smuggle them down the mountain to Denver—and to freedom.

By defying the man who owned the brothels, Joy's actions had cost her dearly: His men had set Corinth Mountain Lodge ablaze in the night and burned it to ashes. Joy and her friends escaped the inferno, only to be captured and herded to the town center. However, in the closing chapter of Corinth's heinous gentleman's clubs, the U.S. Marshals and Pinkerton men had arrived to save Joy, her friends, and fifteen young prostitutes.

Weeks afterward, an elderly Denverite, Martha Palmer, had given Joy and her mother, Rose Thoresen, the keys to a neglected, three-story Victorian house. Joy and Rose Thoresen moved to Denver—taking with them Sarah, Corrine, and those girls from the two brothels who chose to accompany them. In the years since, Sarah had resided at Palmer House—a most extraordinary refuge for young women rescued from prostitution.

Sarah understood all too well what Corrine referred to when she said with wonder, "It is a miracle that Albert loves me."

"The greater miracle is the blood of Jesus that has washed away our sins and removed the stain of what we once were," Sarah whispered. "No more shame."

"No more shame," Corrine echoed. Without another word, she and Sarah reached for each other, embracing in the fellowship of their shared sufferings and mutual salvation.

"I find my little room at Palmer House barren without you, Corrine," Sarah confessed. "Ten years is a long time to have shared so many joys, trials, and confidences, only to have lost you now. When I awake in the night and do not hear your gentle breathing from across the room, I feel quite bereft."

Corrine gave Sarah another squeeze. "I understand, my dearest friend."

With a final comforting hug, they parted and set to their morning tasks: Sarah withdrew a money bag from her reticule, sorted the bills into the shop's cash register, and began to wipe down the register, countertops, and the shop's china. Corrine dusted the window displays and the shop's furniture before picking up a broom to sweep the walkway outside the shop.

Having set the shop to rights, Sarah and Corrine declared themselves ready for the day's customers. Corrine turned the sign hanging against the door's glass from "Closed" to "Welcome."

"Will Joy be in today?" she asked Sarah. The shop belonged to Joy Thoresen Michaels (now Joy O'Dell), the same woman whose brave actions had led to the downfall of those who operated the houses of evil in Corinth.

"I believe she will be. She wishes to assure herself that the accounts and inventory are in proper order before she takes leave. And now that you are home from your honeymoon and have resumed your duties, she will not fret that I might be alone in the shop while she is homebound."

The pleasant tinkling of the bell over the shop's door interrupted them. Sarah and Corrine smiled and greeted their first customer of the day.

~*~

ACROSS TOWN, EDMUND O'DELL pulled his aging Bergdoll touring car to the curb before a fine mansion constructed of dressed stone. The estate and its expansive lawns were encircled by a wall built of the same stone. He shut off the motor, jumped from the driver's side, turned around, and held out his arms.

"Come to Papa, Matthew."

A tot four months shy of two years, whose dark hair and eyes marked him as O'Dell's son, bounded from the seat into O'Dell's waiting arms. "See Liam, Papa? See Liam?"

O'Dell had answered that particular question at least ten times during their drive. "Yes, my son." He carried Matthew to the other side of the motor car and opened the passenger door. "Now, give Mama a kiss, Matty."

Joy O'Dell reached for the boy to draw him onto her lap, but O'Dell held him fast.

"Mind what Dr. Murphy said, my love. Matthew is too heavy for you in your condition, which is why he sits between us and not on your lap. Let him hug and kiss you while I bear his weight, if you please."

Matthew deposited a sloppy kiss on Joy's cheek. Then, his attention otherwise preoccupied, he slipped from her arms and strained to free himself from O'Dell's grasp. O'Dell set the boy on the sidewalk but retained his hold on the boy's hand.

"Have a lovely morning, Matthew!" Joy called.

With nary a backward glance, Matthew tugged his father toward the gate in the estate's wall. "See Liam, Papa?"

O'Dell tossed a teasing grin in Joy's direction. "Matty misses you terribly."

Joy laughed. "Oh, yes. The evidence is compelling."

When O'Dell and Matthew passed through the gate and O'Dell had latched it after them, he released Matthew's hand. The little boy raced toward the house on stubby legs, shouting, "Liam! Liam! I here!" as he ran. O'Dell followed at a more sedate pace but caught up as Matthew reached the stone steps leading up to the house's entrance.

"Liam, I here!" Matthew hollered as he labored up the porch's six high steps.

O'Dell let Matthew navigate the steps under his own steam but positioned himself to catch the boy should he fall backward. Anyone who may have observed the man's expression as he shepherded his son up the porch steps would have recognized the love written there.

As Matthew managed the last step, the entry door swung inward, revealing a woman whose titian hair hung down around her shoulders and shimmered with fiery hues. The O'Dells' friend, Tabitha Carpenter, clasped the hand of another toddler. The boy bounced up and down, his excitement too much to contain. A wealth of strawberry blonde curls bounced with him.

"Maaah-eeee! Maaah-eeee!" The boy could not manage his "t"s yet, but no one doubted the meaning of what he screamed with such delighted abandon.

"Liam!" Matthew shrieked in return.

Tabitha released Liam, and the two boys, in their mutual enthusiasm, raced toward each other, collided—and rebounded. Down they went onto their padded backsides, astonished one second, roaring with hilarity the next. The boys struggled to their feet, hugged with the fervor only children know, joined hands, and—pushing past Tabitha's skirts—raced into the house.

Elated screams echoed from the interior.

O'Dell arched one brow in Tabitha's direction. "I regret Matthew's reluctance to spend the day with Master Liam, Mrs. Carpenter."

"And I apologize for Liam's want of welcome, Mr. O'Dell."

The faux formality fell away as Tabitha and O'Dell chuckled together in the easy friendship of years.

"We are still beyond happy to have you and Mason back in Denver, Tabitha, and to have you return with such a beautiful, ready-made family? Even a greater pleasure. Thank you for taking Matthew today. It will bless Joy not to have to chase him all day long."

Tabitha and her husband, Mason, had both served in the Great War, Tabitha as a volunteer nurse for Britain in Queen Alexandra's Imperial Military Nursing Service, and Mason as a volunteer pilot, training younger men to fly reconnaissance for the British Army's Royal Flying Corps at a base on the coast of England.

When a German squadron had attacked the inexperienced and unarmed trainees of their flying school, Mason had taken to the sky in an armed fighter plane and mounted a counterattack. After he had levied considerable damage on the attacking German *Fokkers*, he led them away toward the coast of Belgium. Other British pilots followed after the German planes and fought a great air battle over the water. During that furious battle, Mason's plane was shot down and had crashed into the sea.

He was declared killed in action.

Unbeknownst to Tabitha or the British Army, Mason had been rescued by a German ship searching for its own survivors of that clash. He languished for more than a year in a German prisoner-of-war camp—until the signing of the Armistice in November 1918.

Tabitha was nursing returning prisoners on the blood-sodden fields of France following the German surrender when Mason stumbled into the tent hospital where she was serving. He was in poor health when he arrived and was sent to a British Army hospital in England to convalesce. Tabitha accompanied him.

Tabitha and Mason remained in England following the war's end while Mason regained his health. During that time, having witnessed the scores of children orphaned by the fighting and the deadly Spanish Influenza, they initiated paperwork to adopt two such orphans. They had only returned to Denver in May, bringing with them a daughter, Sally, near six years old, and a son, Liam, fourteen months of age.

"We thank the Lord daily for bringing us safely home and for filling our arms and our hearts with Sally and Liam," Tabitha whispered. "Speaking of Sally—"

A thin face filled with large blue eyes and surrounded by hair as red as Tabitha's pushed aside her mother's skirt.

"Yah, Mum?"

"Hello, Miss Sally." O'Dell's greeting was charged with playfulness.

She popped out from behind Tabitha. "Hullo, Unca E'mund. Ya brung Aunt Joy w' ya?"

Sally retained the broad accents of the London streets where she had lived before being orphaned and sent to the Colchester orphanage where Tabitha had met her.

"I did, but I left her in the motor car."

"Wot! Why ever did ya leaves her there?"

"Manners, please, Sally." Tabitha was gentle in her reminder.

"Sorr', Mum." But Sally smirked at O'Dell, expecting an answer.

O'Dell grinned. "Matthew will have a new baby sister or brother soon, so I am taking particular care of your Aunt Joy until the baby comes."

"Aye? A new babe? Bu' how—"

Deducing where Sally's inquisitive mind was headed, Tabitha stepped in. "I would be happy to explain it to you after your Uncle Edmund leaves, Sally."

O'Dell nodded his agreement. "Er, yes. I must take Aunt Joy to her shop now. See you soon, Miss Sally."

"'Bye, Unca E'mund!"

~*~

WHEN O'DELL ARRIVED AT Joy's shop, he ran around the vehicle to the passenger side and threw open the door. He doffed his trademark bowler hat and offered his hand to his wife.

"Do take care to find the walkway with your foot before you step down, Joy."

"Take care to find the—" Joy gathered the fullness of her skirt into one hand and attempted to peer around her bulging waistline. Try as she might, she could spy neither her feet nor the sidewalk, curb, or gutter below.

Joy sighed her frustration. "Merciful heavens. I cannot find my foot, Edmund, let alone find the walkway with it. Of course, it must be down there . . . somewhere, but it may as well be—"

O'Dell stooped down, took hold of her boot, and guided it to the sidewalk. "There. Now, here is my hand. I shall, um, assist you to stand." He had come perilously close to blurting, "I shall haul you to your feet," but had stopped before uttering that inadvisable turn of a phrase.

His wife was well into her last month of pregnancy, already sensitive about her size and lately prone to tears. Despite her protests to the contrary, O'Dell knew she felt about as graceful as a tightrope-dancing pachyderm.

O'Dell held her arm while she steadied. When she was safely away from the curb, Joy sighed her satisfaction. "The up and down portion may prove 'a wee bi' tricky,' as Breona might say, but once I am standing, all is well."

With an expression that conveyed, "Dearest, I do not quite believe you," O'Dell answered, "Nevertheless, I shall accompany you to the door."

"I am fine, Edmund, really."

"Of course, darling—and I shall accompany you to the door."

"Really, Edmund!"

"Yes, I really *shall* accompany you to the door."

"Oh, fiddlesticks." *Sigh* "Very well."

"And you will telephone me the moment you have concluded your business. I shall drop what I am doing to fetch you home."

"You are fussing over me, dear."

"That I am. And this afternoon, you shall have a nice nap until I bring Matty home for dinner."

"Oh, my. A nap does sound lovely."

Sarah swung open the shop door. "Good morning, Joy."

"Good morning, Sarah." Joy spied Corrine behind Sarah and fixed her with a grin. "Ah, and good morning, Mrs. Johnston. What? Home from the honeymoon already?"

"I have been gone three weeks—as you well know."

Joy laughed. "Yes, and I cannot say how glad I am to have you back, actually. I am finding it harder to move about. This babe seems twice as large as Matty was."

Sarah looked around with raised brows. "Speaking of Matthew, did you not bring him?" She loved having the toddler at the shop—as chaotic as his visits turned out—and was disappointed not to see him.

"No; no, I did not. I confess, he can run faster than I can at this point. And he runs from daylight to dark. I am worn to a nub just watching his inexhaustible supply of energy."

Holding his hat before him in a pleading gesture, O'Dell injected himself into their chatter. "If you ladies will excuse me?"

"Of course, dearest," Joy answered. "Have a lovely morning."

As O'Dell departed, Sarah asked, "Did you leave Matty with Miss Rose?"

"No. Tabitha offered to have him for the day. He and Liam will keep company together."

"I suppose that makes sense, but we do so love having him about."

Corrine chuckled. "*You* enjoy having him, Sarah. You spend half your time singing to him, telling him stories, chasing him up and down the aisles, and cuddling him—when he will let you."

"Well, I enjoy children," Sarah retorted in good-natured fun, "and it is high time you and Albert provided me with a few babies to play with."

Corrine blushed a deep red. "Us? Why, we have been married less than a month!"

Sarah ogled her with wicked meaning. "Ah, then! I shall expect to offer my congratulations shortly."

"Pshaw! What nonsense. I have work to do." Corrine, with her exceedingly pink nose in the air, stomped off to unpack a crate of newly arrived linen tablecloths.

Joy smiled with Sarah. "I see we must pray the Lord to send you a godly husband soon, Sarah, so that you and he can fill your home to the rafters with little ones of your own."

Sarah blinked, and one corner of her mouth drooped. "No, please do not pray that for me, Joy. I am content to love the children of my friends."

"What? You do not wish for your own family, dear Sarah?"

The smile that Sarah returned was tinged with regret. "I truly would wish to have a child of my own to love and raise but . . . I confess, the price to get one is more than I am willing to pay."

Then it was Joy who blinked. "The price?"

"You know. Marriage. A husband."

Sorrow beset Joy's expression. "Do you not wish for love, Sarah?"

"Love?" Longing took hold of Sarah's heart and squeezed. The pain, her old, familiar companion, ran deep, down into the marrow of her bones.

*Oh, that I might know love, that I might find a special someone who would never hurt me or use me.*

She shook her head. "Never mind me, Joy. I was only thinking aloud."

~\*~

SARAH STAYED LATE AT the shop that afternoon to catch up the books. Corrine had been gone for an hour when Sarah locked the shop door and walked to her trolley stop.

As she stepped aboard, she noticed that the car had fewer passengers than her usual, earlier car. Just five individuals rode with her—two shop girls, a bored businessman, and a well-dressed young couple.

Before she had taken her seat, the couple caught her attention—for the man had been speaking in a loud voice and had broken off as she entered the car, only to recommence his harangue once Sarah had seated herself across the aisle and looked out the window.

"I told you I would not stand for it, Willa, and I meant it. Looking at every man who passes. Smiling and wagging your hips like a harlot!"

Sarah shifted in her seat and stared at the man, her mouth open in dismay. She realized that the two shop girls and the bored businessman were looking elsewhere—anywhere but at the public display of abuse to which they could not help but be witness.

Sarah, however, did not look away. She fixed her eyes on the man, then, quite deliberately, on his hand gripping the woman's arm. The woman's white face told Sarah that she was both terrified and in pain.

The man noticed Sarah's attention. "What are you staring at?" he shouted at Sarah.

Sarah did not immediately reply; neither did she look away.

"I said, *what are you staring at?*"

Sarah glanced forward, toward the driver. She caught his eyes watching in the mirror above his seat before he turned them back to the street ahead. Sarah turned her head toward the angry man.

"I am looking at you, sir."

"You mind your own business." He wrenched the woman's arm, and she cried out.

"Shut up, you worthless, no-good whore. Don't know why I married you anyway."

Sarah did not decide to stand; she simply found herself on her feet—just before she found herself matching the man's volume and shouting, "No, *you* shut up, you cowardly lout!"

He rounded on her with raised fist.

Instead of flinching, Sarah leaned toward him. "What? Do you think to strike a woman? And in a public conveyance? Why, you are nothing more than a *spineless bully.*"

She whirled forward and found all eyes within the trolley upon her. "You, sir! You, the driver! Do something!"

The driver, put on the spot, brought the trolley to a juddering stop. He stood and roared at the man, "Get off! Get off m' car!"

This was not the solution Sarah had in mind, but it was the conclusion of the confrontation. The abusive man yanked his wife toward the rear door where she stumbled down the step after him.

As the trolley shuddered and resumed its journey, Sarah's last view of the young woman was of her crying and pulling, trying to free herself from the man's grip—and the man backhanding her.

Sarah jumped to her feet, thinking to push the door open and leap out, to do something—*anything!*—to help the poor creature.

But what could she do? Futility struck her, and she collapsed.

*I can do nothing. Nothing.*

Sarah slumped down in her seat and wept tears of anger and frustration. She did not care that every ear in the car could hear her. She was still sniffling when one of the shop girls stood to disembark. She paused in the aisle near Sarah.

"You are very brave," the girl whispered. "I wish I were brave like you."

Then she was gone.

Sarah ground her fists into her eyes. *What good is it to be brave? Did I stop that man? No! And if his wife were brave, could she escape from him? No—he will likely kill her before long, and all the courage in the world will not have saved her.*

Sarah pulled her hankie from her reticule and wiped her face, determination drying her tears.

*That is why I shall never submit to such bondage.*

*No, not I.*

*Not ever.*

# $\mathcal{C}$HAPTER 2

## SEPTEMBER

Sarah dreamed she was in the shop, folding rich, ivory brocade napkins and tablecloths, one after another, stacking them in their proper places. However, no matter how many she folded, customers appeared at her side to pick through them and take them away. As quickly as she placed the linens on the shelves, greedy hands claimed them, while customers behind her clamored for more.

Held fast in a deep sleep, Sarah heard the shop telephone ring. On and on it rang, unabated, from na far distance. She fretted over its unanswered persistence, but she could not leave off folding the cloths and napkins: Too many hands and voices insisted that she fold faster to add to the depleted supply of table linens.

As the telephone continued to ring, Sarah shouted for Corrine to answer it, but her voice was no more than a whisper; it did not carry over the urgent demands and grasping hands of her customers. Eventually the ringing ceased, and Sarah gave the whole of her attention to folding the never-ending supply of tablecloths and napkins to meet the needs of her anxious customers.

Then, the scene in the shop faded, and she woke to a soft tapping on her bedroom door. Muzzy-headed, Sarah threw back the covers. Her room was hot and sultry, her nightgown damp. When the tapping came again, she fumbled for her alarm clock.

Half past one o'clock in the night.

Yet another tap sounded on her door. She padded across the room and found Rose standing in the hallway. She was clad only in her nightgown; her hair hanging over her shoulder in a single braid.

"I am sorry to bother you, Sarah, but Mr. O'Dell has telephoned. Joy's labor has begun. The doctor says she is early in her pains, so Mr. O'Dell is taking this opportunity to come and fetch me."

"What do you need me to do, Miss Rose?"

"Thank you, Sarah. I did rouse you to ask a favor. When Mr. O'Dell comes to get me, he would like to bring Matthew with him and place him in your care."

"But of course. I would be happy to watch him."

"Bless you, dear. There is no need for you to get up. I shall dress and pack a light bag; when Mr. O'Dell arrives, I shall bring Matty up to you. We can hope that he will sleep through until morning, allowing you to do the same."

Sarah crawled back into her bed and drowsed until another soft rap at the door stirred her. When she opened her door, Rose offered the bundled boy to Sarah with a smile. "Mr. O'Dell carried him up the stairs for me. He says Matty did not even stir when he put him in the motor car."

"Ah, what a good boy."

As Rose transferred the toddler to Sarah's arms and placed a bag inside the door, she smiled again. "God willing, Matty will have a little brother or sister later this day."

"I shall pray for a safe delivery for Joy."

"Thank you, Sarah. Our trust is in the Lord."

Sarah tucked Matthew into her bed and laid down beside him, her face near his. His gentle, whiffling breath was sure and steady. She inhaled the sweet smell of his skin and hair.

*O Lord, I do not envy Joy the many heartaches she has already endured in her life, but I am so very glad for her that you have given her this precious boy and this new baby. Thank you for blessing her and Mr. O'Dell and for seeing their child safely into the world.*

She did not give voice in prayer to her own longing for children. She accepted that children were beyond her reach.

~*~

A FEATHER-SOFT OBJECT brushed against Sarah's nose. She sighed in her sleep and turned her head away from the annoyance. But when a damp, pokey thing tried to pry her lips apart, Sarah jerked awake—and found herself face to face with a dark-eyed toddler—who chortled when she startled.

He prodded one of her nostrils. "Nose," he announced.

"Um, yes, it is. Good morning, Matty." She blinked her eyes at the clock; it read a quarter to six. "My, you are an early bird, are you not?"

He grinned larger and pushed a finger between her lips. "Mowff."

"Mouth. Yes."

Sarah nibbled his finger. "Teeth," she said.

He laughed, a great belly laugh, and Sarah laughed with him. She pointed to her eye. "What is this?"

"Eye."

She indicated her ear. "And this?"

"Ear!" he shouted—inches from said appendage.

"*Ow*. Indeed, it is." Sarah pushed the covers back. "Shall we get up, wee boy?"

Matty clambered from the bed. As he stood, he looked around, confused. "Mama?"

"Your mama is at home. You get to spend the day with me. Will that be fun?"

He pointed at her. "Sar."

"Yes, Matty. I am Sarah."

"Where Mama?" A finger slid into his mouth, a mouth trending toward tremulous.

*Oh, dear. I had best think fast.*

"How would you like a cup of milk, Matty?"

He stared around, still confused, but he nodded.

"There's a good boy. Do you need a dry nappy first?"

SARAH THOUGHT SHE AND Matthew would be the first in the house to rise this early on Sunday morning, but she found Mr. Wheatley, the wild tufts of his hair scruffier than usual, seated in the kitchen, sipping on a steaming cup of coffee.

"Why, what have we here?" he asked with mock concern.

Matthew ran to him and scrambled onto his lap. "Milk," he demanded.

"Say, 'Milk, please,' Matthew." Sarah was already pouring milk into a tin cup with a sturdy handle.

"Milk, pease."

Mr. Wheatley patted Matthew's hand. "Good man."

Matthew patted him back. "Goo-man. Milk, pease."

He took hold of the cup Sarah placed on the table and gulped down half of it in a go.

Mr. Wheatley beamed with unfeigned pleasure. "I take it Miss Joy is about the business of bringing Master Matthew's new brother or sister into the world?"

Sarah had her own cup of coffee now and drew on it before answering. "She is, Mr. Wheatley. Mr. O'Dell fetched Miss Rose near two o'clock in the night and brought Matty for me to watch. If we receive no news by ten this morning, we shall take Matthew to church with us."

By eight, the house was waking up to its Sunday morning routine. Breakfast on Sundays was at nine, later than usual, allowing everyone— but especially Marit, Palmer House's cook—an extra measure of sleep and a more relaxed start to the day.

Marit entered through the back door, leaving baby Toby with her husband Billy, but bringing her two older boys, Will and Charley, with her. However, when the boys discovered Matthew in the kitchen, they could not contain themselves. Marit shooed them all outside to play.

"Would you like me to watch over Matthew, Miss Sarah?" This offer came from Blythe, Palmer House's newest addition. The fifteen-year-old girl, a cloud of bright curls swirling about her head, had arrived at the house in Breona and Pastor Carmichael's care two weeks prior. She had been found, wandering alone and not quite in her right mind, during the church's street ministry. Blythe had been in poor health when Sarah met her, so weak and painfully thin that her eyes swam like overlarge pools of midnight blue in her slender face.

Sarah did not know Blythe's story. Her name implied a happy, carefree being, and she may have been so at one time, but it was apparent to everyone that the sweet girl was fragile—wounded in both body and spirit. The day Blythe arrived, Rose had spent an hour sequestered with the Carmichaels in the parlor before they took their leave. When Rose reappeared, her eyes were red from weeping.

After she had recovered herself, Rose showed Blythe to the room she would share with Pansy, another relatively new girl. Then she had asked Pansy and Ruth to draw a bath for Blythe and find her some clean, comfortable clothes from the donations gathered by the Christian women's group that helped support Palmer House.

That evening at dinner, Rose had introduced Blythe, although, by then, most everyone had already said hello to her. Without placing too much emphasis upon the newcomer's delicate state, Rose had murmured, "While Blythe is adjusting to life at Palmer House, she will be keeping company with Marit and Olive during the day and helping with whatever occasional light tasks they find for her."

Olive was Palmer House's housekeeper. She had lived in the house for nearly as long as Sarah had. When Breona, their previous housekeeper, had married Pastor Carmichael, she had continued on in the housekeeping position until she was expecting her first child. Midway through her pregnancy, she had trained up Olive to take her place. With Corrine's marriage and departure from Palmer House, Sarah considered Olive her closest friend in the household.

Rose's comments regarding Blythe's unexacting duties signaled to the family at Palmer House that Rose's first concern was for Blythe's health. To everyone gathered at the table, it was evident that Blythe needed rest and healing before she undertook any strenuous responsibilities.

They knew, too, that Marit would take Blythe under her wing and urge extra bits of food on the girl between meals.

When Sarah first set eyes on Blythe, she had experienced a visceral need to shelter and protect the girl. Blythe, in response, had attached herself to Sarah's side like a shadow clings to a body at midday.

As Sarah considered Blythe's offer to watch over Matthew and studied her hopeful expression, she felt a wave of compassion for the girl. She knew Blythe was not fit enough to chase after a two-year-old tornado, but she saw Blythe's willing, eager heart. More than that, Sarah recognized how Blythe longed to "fit in" and belong to Palmer House's unconventional family.

"Shall we watch him together?" Sarah offered with a smile. She threaded her arm through Blythe's thin one and drew her outside. Under the warm late-summer sun, they trailed behind the threesome crew of boys to "keep an eye" on Matthew, who was considerably younger than Billy and Marit's boys and unaccustomed to their rough and ready ways.

"He is such a beautiful lad," Blythe murmured.

"That he is," Sarah agreed.

"I-I hope—that is, Miss Rose suggested that I might . . . that I might someday marry and have a baby. A family."

It was impossible to miss the yearning in Blythe's soft voice; Sarah even understood Blythe's desire for a child to love.

"If it is God's will, dear one, I am certain the right man will come along."

"But how do we know what God's will is, Sarah? Miss Rose talks a great deal about Jesus, but I do not understand half of what she says."

Sarah led Blythe to a stone bench in the shade of a tree where they could watch the boys. "Shall we sit here, Blythe? I shall try to explain."

Blythe was keen to comply. "All right, Sarah."

Sarah pursed her lips. "Let me see. Where to begin. Well, do you know that God, our heavenly Father, has made everything? Everything we can see and everything we cannot see?"

Blythe's eyes widened. "So much? Even the sky?"

"The sky, the sun, the moon, the stars—God made it all. And he made us, each one of us, in his image and likeness. People are the only thing in all of God's creation made in his image—which is why he calls us his children and himself our Father."

"I have never had a father," Blythe whispered. "Only Uncle Jack. I wonder what it is like to have a father."

Sarah did not respond to Blythe's pensive reflections: She had not had a father either and experienced her own difficulties trying to visualize God as her loving heavenly Father.

*What do I know of fathers, loving or otherwise?*

She preferred to think of Jesus instead—as either a babe in the manger or as he hung on the cross—helpless. Much easier to visualize.

A tug on her sleeve brought her attention back to the present.

"Sarah?"

"Forgive me, Blythe. Where was I? Yes, because God made us in his likeness, we are, each of us, special to him. Still, even though God loves us very much, each of us strays from him. We sin against God and against others. We wander far away from God until we are lost, so very lost, and cannot find our way to him. Do you know what it feels like to be lost, dear one?"

Blythe grew still, her expression frozen and hunted. "Oh, yes. I think I have been lost forever."

Moisture glistened in the girl's eyes. "I do not want to be lost anymore, Sarah."

"And that is why God the Father sent Jesus, his Son. Jesus died upon the cross to pay for our sins; then he rose from the dead, so we could have the hope of the resurrection when we die, too."

"But if I am lost, how do I find my way back to God?"

"Ah, that is where I am going, my sweet girl. Jesus said he came to seek and save those who are lost—lost just like you and lost just like me. In fact, God our Father sends Jesus to find each of us. If we are sorry for our sins and call upon Jesus, he will come to us and wash us clean."

"Jesus will come to me? To me? How?"

"His Spirit will come and live within you. You will feel him inside, forgiving you, healing you, taking away all of your guilt and shame."

"H-he will take away my shame?"

There was something so urgent in Blythe's voice that Sarah turned toward the girl.

"Yes, Blythe. Jesus will take away your shame. All of it."

Blythe exhaled and leaned against Sarah. "Please, Sarah, I want to call upon Jesus."

"Then we should pray, right here, Blythe, for Jesus is willing to save you, at this very moment."

Sarah and Blythe slid from the bench to their knees. Blythe clasped Sarah's hand as if it were the only lifeline between her and heaven. "O Jesus," she wept. "O Jesus!"

"Jesus, please forgive all my sins—I am so sorry," Sarah prayed.

"Yes, Jesus! Please forgive me. I am so sorry. I am so ashamed."

"Jesus, please come into me by your Holy Spirit and wash me clean."

"Jesus, please come into me and wash me clean."

"Take away my shame, Lord Jesus, and make me wholly yours."

By now, Blythe was overcome and could scarcely speak. "T-t-take a-away my sh-shame, Jesus! P-please take it a-away. Please."

"Make me completely yours, Jesus," Sarah whispered.

"Make me yours, Jesus. All of me. Please, Jesus."

Sarah let Blythe cry herself out, and the girl repeated again and again, "Th-thank you, Jesus, for t-taking away my shame. Th-thank you."

A little while later, as Blythe was wiping her eyes, something damp poked Sarah's cheek.

Sarah laughed softly. "Why, Matthew O'Dell."

~*~

THE NEWS DID NOT COME until late that Sunday afternoon when Rose telephoned. Sarah, sitting on pins and needles in Palmer House's great room with most everyone else, jumped when the telephone jangled at last.

Sarah picked up the receiver. "Hello?"

"Joy and Mr. O'Dell have another baby boy!" Rose's voice overflowed with happiness. "They have named him Jacob. Both he and Joy are doing well."

"Praise be to God," Sarah whispered.

"Yes. To God be all the glory!"

Sarah mouthed to the girls gathering around her. "A boy!"

Her announcement generated smiles and cheers of thanksgiving.

"Sarah," Rose continued, "I know you must work tomorrow and that you require a good night's sleep tonight. Mr. O'Dell will come fetch Matthew home after dinner this evening."

"I would so love to see the new baby."

"Perhaps we can arrange that, if Mr. O'Dell is amenable to another trip."

When Sarah hung up, she gathered Matthew into her arms. "Guess what, Matty? You have a baby brother."

He slid his finger into his mouth, not at all sure what she meant.

~*~

IT WAS NEAR SEVEN o'clock when O'Dell's knock sounded on the door to Palmer House. Mr. Wheatley let him in.

"Congratulations, Mr. O'Dell, sir. We are all as pleased as punch for you and the missus."

O'Dell, elated but short on sleep, grinned. "Thank you, my friend. I have come with orders to fetch our older son home to meet his little brother. Where might he be?"

"Matthew is a-sleepin' on Miss Sarah's lap in the great room. Wore himself out today a-playin' with Will and Charley but refused a nap when we all could see he needed one in the worst way."

"No, Matthew does not care for naps."

"Gave Miss Sarah a run for her money, the little man did. Her trying to put him down for a sleep t'was like tryin' to put socks on a rooster, I calculate. Leastwise 'till he passed out over his plate at supper."

O'Dell found Sarah as Mr. Wheatley has promised, glued to her chair by Matthew's sleeping weight.

"I am here to take Matthew home. If you are willing, you may come along, and I promise to bring you back before ten o'clock."

"Oh, yes, please. I am sorry Matthew is sleeping, and I do hope he will not be up all night as a result of his late nap. He simply refused to go down earlier, but I could not keep him awake through dinner."

"I understand. Let us stir him now so that he will be alert enough to meet Jacob when we get home."

They managed to rouse the boy, but he sat, groggy-eyed and listless in Sarah's arms during the drive. However, when Matthew caught sight of the house O'Dell and Joy rented and recognized it as his home, he bounced up and down on Sarah's lap. "Mama! Mama!"

O'Dell took him from Sarah, then helped her from her seat and set Matthew on the stone path that led to the house. Rose stood in the front doorway, waving to him.

"Gramma! Gramma!"

"Come to Gramma, sweetheart," Rose called.

She swept him up in her arms, but after a quick hug, Matthew wanted down.

"Want Mama."

Rose set Matthew on his feet, and O'Dell squatted beside him, holding him still. "Matthew, listen to Papa. Mama is in bed, and you mustn't climb on her. She needs to rest a little."

"Mama sick?"

Sarah heard the panic in his voice.

"No, she is only tired," O'Dell answered. "You have a new brother, Matty. His name is Jacob. Can you say Jacob?"

"No. Want Mama."

"Would you like to see the baby?"

"Baby?"

"Yes, your baby brother, Jacob."

"'Cub?"

"Yes, Jacob. Would you like to see the baby?"

His eyes widened. "Yes, Papa. See baby."

Sarah followed O'Dell and Matthew into the bedroom. She saw that Rose had used several pillows to bolster Joy into a sitting position. Although Sarah noted Joy's fatigue in the dark half-moons under her eyes, her face was freshly washed, and her hair combed and braided. In the middle of the bed, tucked against her side, Sarah spotted a small, flannel bundle.

Matthew had eyes only for Joy.

"Mama!"

Sarah was likely more excited to see the baby than Matthew was at the moment, but she would not have missed witnessing the boy's first glimpse of his brother for the world. She slid around the side of the bed opposite Joy where she could watch. Rose joined her there.

O'Dell held Matthew over Joy, allowing his little arms to wrap around her neck without putting any weight on her. Joy hugged him back and kissed him repeatedly.

"Oh, Matty. Mama is so glad to see you."

O'Dell pulled a chair up to the bedside and sat down, Matthew on his knee. Matthew had not noticed the tiny bundle snugged against Joy's far side—not until Joy lifted the babe, placed him in the crook of her arm closest to Matthew, and turned back a corner of the flannel bunting, exposing a plump but miniscule face topped with spikes of black fuzz.

Matty went still; he stared and stared, his eyes wide with wonder. Then he looked up at O'Dell and giggled.

"What do you think, Matty? This is your baby brother, Jacob."

Matty clasped his hands together and leaned forward. "Baby?"

"Yes," Joy said. "Your baby brother."

Joy lifted a flannel fold, exposing the tiniest pink fingers Sarah had ever seen. Joy reached for one of Matthew's hands.

"Give me your finger, Matty," she instructed. She held his hand with his chubby index finger extended and brushed his finger over the baby's hand.

Matty shivered with excitement. "Baby!"

"Yes." She released her hold on Matthew's hand. "Touch him gently, my dear."

Matty stroked baby Jacob's Lilliputian hand and shivered again. And when the baby's diminutive fingers unfurled under Matty's touch, Matty leaned closer and cooed. "Li'l baby. Li'l baby 'Cub."

At that moment, the babe's eyes opened and stared, as though looking for the source of the cooing. Matthew, tears standing in his eyes, looked to his mother. "Mama. Want baby. Want baby, Mama."

"You want to hug baby Jacob?"

"Hug baby, Mama."

Joy lifted the newborn into O'Dell's arms, and he held the babe against Matthew's chest. "Be gentle, my son," O'Dell cautioned.

Matty, his expression flushed with solemn reverence, gathered the baby to himself and held him close. "Li'l baby. Luf you, li'l baby."

After an interlude, O'Dell whispered, "Very good, Matty, my son. Let us give Jacob back to Mama now so he can go night-night."

Before Matty relinquished his hold, he bent his face close to the baby and placed a kiss on his forehead. "Nigh-nigh, 'Cub."

Sarah was undone: It was the most pure and beautiful thing she had ever witnessed. She tried to stifle the sob that welled up in her throat and chest, but she could not keep it in.

Fortunately, Rose, Joy, and O'Dell were struggling with their own happy tears and did not notice Sarah's.

# CHAPTER 3

I t had been a typical day at Michaels' Fine Furnishings. For several years, Joy had managed the shop with Sarah, Corrine, and Billy at her side. In the last two years, however, sales had lessened. They were good enough to ensure that the shop turned a healthy, albeit modest, profit—but not enough to keep Billy employed, as well as Corrine and Sarah—and Billy had a growing family to support.

So, Billy had gone off to a moving company whose owner took one look at Billy's impressive height and muscled frame and hired him on the spot. Now, in all matters to do with the shop, Sarah was Joy's second-in-command and Corrine Sarah's lieutenant. And, with Joy's time often occupied with family, Sarah and Corrine were frequently alone together in the shop.

Sarah and Corrine lived by the tinkling of the bell over the shop door, signaling the entrance of a prospective customer. Their clientele was composed, primarily, of women and married or engaged couples shopping for their homes. Rarely did a gentleman or a pair of gentlemen enter without female companions.

The shop closed at five o'clock each evening when the throngs of downtown shoppers headed home to their dinners. Sarah and Corrine had not had a customer in over thirty minutes. They were refolding linens in one of the shop's display rooms, tidying up in preparation for closing, when the shop door opened and the bell over it jingled.

Corrine left Sarah and hurried to greet the prospective customers. She was mildly surprised to spot three well-heeled young men pausing inside the door, laughing together, staring around. Something in their conduct made her slow.

One of the young gents, however, caught sight of her. "Woul' you look a' tha'?"

He pointed at her, then staggered some, jostling his nearest companion. His friends glanced in Corrine's direction.

"Beaut," he remarked. "Let's ask her ou' fer a drink w' us. Hey, miss. I'm Jeff and this here's Rob an' Ed. May we buy you a drink?"

Corrine halted. Why, the three loiterers were intoxicated!

She glanced behind her toward the side room where Sarah was working. Raising her voice, she attempted to sound authoritative. "I am sorry, gentlemen, but the shop is closed. I must ask you to leave at once."

Instead, the man who said he was Jeff tottered toward her. "Shop closed? Why, tha's fine luck for all. C'mon wi' us, then. We'll trea' ya t' a good time."

"Real goo' time." Ed echoed.

Jeff, having crossed the room, staggered. He lunged at Corrine to keep his balance, but she evaded his grasp and ran behind the counter to the register. From beneath the register she retrieved a short wooden baseball bat—kept handy at O'Dell's insistence. With the bat in one hand and her other upon the receiver of their wall telephone, she said, much louder, "Gentlemen, this shop is closed. Please leave at once, or I shall call the authorities."

Unfortunately, her voice trembled.

Emboldened by her show of uncertainty, Jeff picked himself up and swaggered her way. "Thin' you're better than us, do ya? Tha's no' wha' we hear. Heard you was a whore once. Well, we go' money, lots a' money. Money t' spare. We can pay—owwww!"

Sarah had heard Corrine's raised voice; she strode up behind Jeff, a second bat extended—a bat placed strategically in the back of the shop for just such a need—and jabbed him in the kidney. Hard.

Jeff rubbed his back. "You hurt me, you whore!"

"How dare you spew such insults in our shop? Get out. Get out, I say!" Sarah had shed every vestige of ladylike comportment. Her eyes flashed with fury. Her mouth was set in a hard, resolute line.

Jeff sneered at her, inching forward. "Now, there's no nee' t' get yer knickers in a knot, missy. Just conductin' a bit o' business—"

Jeff grabbed for the bat, but Sarah pulled back in time and swung down. The bat clipped the grasping hand with an audible crunch. Jeff shrieked. Clutching his wounded appendage to himself, he screamed curses at Sarah.

Sarah was unfazed. "For shame; you are drunk. Get out of our shop before we call the police."

When she lifted the bat to strike again, one of Jeff's friends rushed to his aid. "Stop! Stop, I say!"

As he approached, Sarah pointed the bat in his direction. She was perspiring. Her face was red, the end of her braid had come unpinned, and her lungs heaved. Moreover, with her recent encounter with the young couple on the trolley before her eyes, she had given herself over to a perfect fit of fury.

"Stay back. You had better stay back, you inebriated hooligan. Come an inch closer, and I shall give you a beating, too."

Rob quailed before her. "Wait. Please. We will go—we will go, I promise. Just . . . just let Jeff come away over to me, and we will be off." He stepped back. "Jeff. C'mon, now."

"She broke m' hand, Rob! She broke it!" He spit another curse word at Sarah.

"Shame on you. You call yourself a gentleman and use such language to a lady? I would like to bash your head in, I really would. I would teach you a lesson."

Sarah's threats hardly recommended her as the lady she claimed to be: Corrine was every bit as shocked as Jeff and Rob were.

Sarah again pointed the bat at Rob. "Remove your friend from our shop while he can still walk, for if you or your drunken friends take another step toward me or my associate, I shall break your legs. By God, I swear it."

Ed, the dismayed third in their group, seeing Jeff hobble toward Rob, did not wait on his mates. He stumbled out the shop door and beat an erratic path down the sidewalk. A minute later, Jeff and Rob followed in the same direction.

Sarah dropped the bat on the shop floor and wiped her face. "Are you all right, Corrine?"

"Y-yes. But are *you* all right?"

"Certainly. Why do you ask?"

"You were so upset, Sarah. You said such awful things and you . . . swore, using God's name in vain."

"Awful?" Sarah's anger flared. "*I* said awful things? After what they did and said? What they intended? No, do not chide me for those actions, Corrine, for I declare to you that I refuse to cower before another man in this life. Never again will I. *Never.*"

~*~

A WEEK LATER, TWO men entered *Michaels'* together. Sarah waited on them but, with her most recent experience with male "customers" quite fresh in her mind, she was leery and aloof in her greeting.

"May I help you, gentlemen?"

The taller of the two men smiled at Sarah. "Thank you, yes. I am interested in seeing your bedroom suites."

"Of course. This way, please."

She led them to the four suites on the shop's floor, and they busied themselves examining the pieces and discussing what they considered the features and attributes of each while Sarah stood ready to answer their questions. The same man, while he and his companion looked over the pieces, glanced back at Sarah every few moments.

Once, when their eyes met, he smiled. Sarah did not return his friendly overture.

After he seemed to come to a decision regarding the furniture, he addressed her. "I have recently arrived in Denver and have rented an unfurnished house. My friend, George, here has been gracious enough to squire me around to the best shops."

"I see. Thank you for visiting *Michaels'*. I hope we can accommodate your needs and tastes."

Favoring her with another smile, he bowed. "Bryan Croft, at your service, miss. I hope you do not think me forward, but as a newcomer to your city, I am grateful for each new acquaintance, Miss . . ."

Sarah blinked at the realization that he was attempting an introduction, hoping to gain her name. Moreover, she noted, he was considering her with frank appreciation while his friend looked on. As she glanced at his companion, the man smiled and nodded—and his lips twitched with restrained humor.

*Ah. You "gentlemen" think to amuse yourself with me, do you?*

A cold flame ignited within her. *I think not.*

Chin raised, body stiff, Sarah answered, "Have you found any of the bedroom suites to your liking, sir?"

Croft's brow furled at the abrupt alteration in her manner. "I beg your pardon?"

An icy edge crept into her voice. "Have you made a selection, sir?"

Suitably rebuffed but mystified, he bowed again and cleared his throat. "Yes. These three pieces, if you please."

"As you wish, sir. If you will step this way, I shall have my associate ring up your purchase and arrange for its delivery."

Sarah removed the tags from the furniture and walked toward the register. She handed the tags to Corrine. "Please see to their purchases."

Without another word, she went into the office and closed the door behind her. Corrine stared after her, wondering at Sarah's icy instructions. A moment later, the two gentlemen approached the counter. Both, but particularly the taller one, appeared somber.

Corrine offered them a bright smile. "Good afternoon, gentlemen."

"Good afternoon. Bryan Croft at your service, miss."

"You have made your selection, Mr. Croft? These three pieces?"

"I, ah, yes, I have chosen these pieces. However, I am concerned, miss, that I have offended your associate, that I perhaps gave her a wrong impression?"

"Oh, dear. I-I cannot say."

"I would very much like for her to join us. If I have offended her, I would like to extend my sincere apology. Please."

Corrine swallowed. "I see. I can . . . ask."

She slipped into the office. She and Sarah had been friends for a long time. She did not always understand what set Sarah off, but she did know that once she had been angered, only time seemed to cool her temper.

Corrine did not hold out much hope for the gentleman's apology.

"Sarah?"

Her friend sat in unyielding silence.

"Sarah, I am speaking to you."

Sarah sighed. "Yes, Corrine?"

"The customer you were attending wishes to speak to you."

"Does he, now?"

"Why, yes. He said he gave you the wrong impression and would like to offer his sincere apology."

"Sincere? I have my doubts."

"But what did he *do*, Sarah?"

"It does not matter. Please tell him I am unavailable."

Irritated, Corrine folded her arms across her breast. "No, I shall not."

"What?" Jolted from her anger, Sarah stared at Corrine.

"You *are* available, and I shall not lie to him for you. It is not right. If this man offended you, then he owes you an apology. Moreover, if, as you say, the offense 'does not matter,' then you should have no difficulty receiving his apology. In either case, it is our job to serve our customers, and your behavior reflects poorly on this establishment."

"Oh, fiddledeedee!"

Corrine was obdurate. "Mr. Croft is waiting on you, Sarah."

Sarah's face reddened. "Fine."

She huffed and added, "Waiting on me? Piffle!"

On rigid legs, with Corrine following behind, Sarah returned to the register. She glared at Croft and said nothing.

"Miss, I have evidently offended you—which was never my intention. I offer you my most profound apology. Please say you will forgive me?"

"But of course," Sarah answered without a stitch of emotion.

She took their payment and delivery information. "Delivery will be Tuesday next week. Thank you for your custom. Good evening, sir."

Croft looked a question to his companion who shrugged. Croft sighed and nodded to Corrine and then to Sarah. "Thank you, and a good evening to you, ladies."

The bell jingled as they departed. Sarah walked to the front and flipped over the sign.

"Closed. And good riddance," she muttered.

"Why, Sarah Ellinger! I have never seen you exhibit such abominable manners."

Sarah did not reply, so Corrine drew near and placed her hand upon her friend's arm.

"Please, dear one. You must tell me what that man did that so upset you."

"If you must know, he told me some tale of being new to Denver—and used that as an excuse to attempt an introduction."

"An introduction? Is that all? Truly? But times have changed, Sarah. Introductions are much less formal. Many genteel people do not take exception to such an innocent gesture."

"Innocent? You should have seen his companion—*sniggering* behind his back. I saw through their sham."

Corrine frowned. "They impressed me as being true gentlemen."

Sarah shrugged. "It was a ploy, an effort to achieve familiarity. New to Denver—what drivel."

"But he did purchase a bedroom suite. Does that not confirm Mr. Croft's assertion that he is new to the city?"

"Oh, Corrine. I do not know—neither do I care. What I do know is that men are ruled by their baser instincts and, in my estimation, they are not to be trusted."

"Surely you do not mean all men, Sarah? Do you not know many godly men such as Mr. O'Dell, Mr. Carpenter, and Pastor Carmichael? What of Billy and Mr. Wheatley?"

Sarah's mouth tightened. "And yet, we cannot see into a man's heart or behind closed doors, can we? All looks well on the outside, but within, do not even Christian men make unconscionable demands upon their wives? Do they not expect their wives to surrender their wills, to submit to them in every way?

"Last month, I observed a man slap his wife—on a public street! And not a person beside myself thought to intervene. Women are but chattel, possessions in a man's eyes, and marriage the means of securing a woman as his sole property."

Corrine's lips trembled. "I am not Albert's property, Sarah, nor does he treat me as such. He is an upright man, a godly man. We respect and honor each other as fellow believers in Christ."

"Have you forgotten how such 'upright' gentlemen used us in Corinth and how many of these 'gentlemen' prided themselves on their church affiliations?"

"Forgotten? Certainly not. But those men were liars and hypocrites. My Albert is not a liar. He is not a hypocrite!"

The wounded expression on Corrine's face pricked Sarah's conscience, but her anger would not allow Corrine's feelings to sway her course.

"I believe my familiarity with men is longer than yours, Corrine. You say you had a loving father at one time, a father who—you contend—cherished and protected you. And that, had he and your mother not died unexpectedly, you would never have been cast into the world to make your own way at a young and vulnerable age. You would not have had to seek employment far afield from your home. Likely as not, you would not have answered an employment advertisement in the newspaper and been tricked into coming to Denver—but *you were*, Corrine.

"Perhaps, as you say, Albert is different but, of the men in my experience, the vast majority are not. They have used me, sold me, and enslaved me."

Sarah straightened and stared at Corrine, her face set in resolve. "I shall never again permit a man to have power over me."

"But—"

Sarah held up her hand. "We are dear friends, Corrine, and so I do not wish to speak further on this subject lest we damage our friendship. It is time to close the shop. Please go home . . . to Albert. I shall lock up."

She opened the door and waited, silent and stoic.

Corrine, a sheen of unshed tears glassing her eyes, walked to the office, gathered her hat and handbag, returned to the front, and departed.

When she had gone, Sarah fit the key to the door and locked herself inside. She went to the register, removed the cash from its drawers, placed it in the moneybag, and tucked the moneybag into her reticule. Nothing remained but for her to leave the shop and lock the door behind her, but she did not move.

Instead, she sat down hard, and her thoughts slipped away from her. Memories she had run from for two decades flooded over her, sweeping her back, back, back.

Back to a time and place far off, and to the gently waving stems of a thousand tulips . . .

~*~

# ALBANY, NEW YORK
# 1899

"DO NOT WORRY, SARAH, my precious, darling girl. Everything will be all right. You will see. Richard will take care of us. He will take care of you . . . after."

Sarah could not stop trembling. Even in her best dress, her near-black hair freshly washed, combed, and plaited, with shiny blue ribbons tied into bows at the end of her braids . . . even with her mother gripping her hand so hard it hurt—and despite her mother's desperate reassurances—Sarah knew everything would *not* be all right. In some deeply primal and instinctive part of her being, Sarah intuited that *this moment*, standing outside the judge's chambers, waiting to be called inside, marked the finish of "all right."

Sarah's mother was ill.

For more than a year, her health had been declining. Her illness was a coughing, hacking, wasting disease that sapped the breath from her lungs and stripped the flesh from her bones. Soon—not this month, and perhaps not next month, but *soon*—the disease would steal the soul from Edwina Ellinger's body.

As her beloved mother weakened, Sarah's fears multiplied. Her father—a shadowy figure more the shape of her mother's sorrowful recollections than of Sarah's actual memories of him—had died of pneumonia when Sarah was but two years old. He had left Sarah and her mother alone in the world. For all of her eight years, the only family Sarah had actually known consisted of her mother and a few distant cousins who had migrated to the Canadian plains two years past.

Her mother had inherited her parents' modest but adequate estate—a lovely three-story townhouse with bow front windows overlooking State Street—and enough income (if managed prudently) to sustain a comfortable, respectable lifestyle.

But as Edwina's illness had progressed, she had fretted and worried over her young daughter's future. Sarah had often heard her mother's whispered plea, "O God! If only you would grant me a few more years to see Sarah safe and happy to her husband's house. If only . . . Please, God."

But Sarah was far too young to marry, and the harbinger knocking at Edwina's door far too avaricious. Edwina had survived the latest of Albany's long, wet, freezing winters, but she knew she would not endure through the next. She cast about with what little strength she had remaining for a safe harbor in which to moor her only, her beloved child and found nothing.

Then, in the coveted warmth of spring, they had met Richard Langston.

Edwina was no longer able to walk with Sarah through the nearby park, so each afternoon, after Sarah had completed her studies to the satisfaction of her governess, Miss Zahn, and practiced her piano lessons for an hour, their man servant, Nevis, would roll the wheeled rattan chair down the townhouse steps and out the gate to the sidewalk. He would then carry Edwina to the chair, and Sarah would tuck a soft blanket about her mother's legs.

Nevis would push Edwina's chair across State Street to Washington Park and follow the park's winding paths until they reached the small lake. There he would leave Sarah to navigate her mother's chair along the lakefront paths for an hour before he returned to see them home.

On that warm spring day, the park was awash with a profusion of tulips in full bloom, bending and waving on their tall stalks. Forevermore, Sarah would associate tulips with the day Richard Langston had inserted himself into their lives.

Sarah had drawn her mother's chair alongside the water's edge, so they might feed the ducks. Edwina particularly enjoyed dropping bits of bread for the ducks to snap up, so Sarah never failed to bring along whatever crusts remained of the previous day's baking.

Richard Langston had been strolling through the park himself that afternoon, but it was not the first time Sarah had seen him. She had noticed him twice in the previous week—and something about him had bothered her. Today, while Edwina's weak hands painstakingly tore the bits of breads into smaller pieces, Sarah monitored the man's movements out of the corner of her eye.

He seemed to be watching her, studying her. His attention would flick to Edwina as though assessing her, then back to Sarah . . . and the skin along Sarah's arms prickled.

"Mama, the afternoon is warm; let us go over to that tree and rest in its shade." Once she had her mother's chair underway, Sarah intended to push it far from the man surveilling them.

"The warmth is what I need, child," Edwina murmured. "It seemed all winter as if I would never get warm again. We shall stay here in the sun."

Stymied, Sarah stepped between her mother and the man's regard and put her back to him. After a while, she began to relax—which had been a mistake.

"Pardon me, madam," a well-modulated voice spoke. "I cannot help but notice that the ducks and their little ducklings come near enough to feed from your fingers. Are you well acquainted with them?"

Sarah stiffened and did not acknowledge the greeting. His question was the shabbiest of excuses for initiating a conversation—not at all a proper way to suggest an introduction. Her mother, however, smiled and lifted her head.

"Sarah, do please step to one side," she murmured.

Sarah moved aside—what else could she do? But she did not turn; she kept her back toward the man.

Edwina answered, "My daughter and I are here daily, so the ducks have come to know and trust us, Mr. . . . ."

*No, Mama!*

"Langston, ma'am. Richard Langston, at your service."

"Mr. Langston, I am Edwina Ellinger. This is my daughter, Sarah. Sarah, please say 'good day,' to Mr. Langston."

Gritting her teeth, Sarah muttered, "Good day, Mr. Langston."

"Good day to you, Miss Sarah."

He offered her a tulip he must have plucked from the park gardens. He presented it along with an ingratiating smile.

"No, thank you," Sarah murmured.

"Well, if I cannot give a flower to the pretty little girl, then I shall give it to her lovely mother, so obviously the font of her daughter's beauty." He sketched a gallant bow and extended the buttery yellow flower to Edwina.

Edwina blushed and took the tulip. "How very kind of you."

As easily as that, Richard Langston made an acquaintance with Sarah and her mother. Every day thereafter, he "happened upon" them on their daily walks. Initially, they exchanged only cordial smiles, nods, and "hellos," but Sarah sensed it would not be the extent of their contact. So, when Nevis left them in the park each afternoon, she would wheel her mother along unfamiliar paths, telling her she wished to explore other views of the lake, often against her mother's protests.

It made no difference.

Wherever they meandered, even if it took nearly the entire hour they were in the park, Richard Langston would find them. Sarah stood aloof from Langston. She rebuffed his every attempt to engage her in conversation. She knew that *he* knew she was leery of him, so he was careful to give his attentions primarily to Edwina, regaling her with bits of New York history or tales from his travels.

However, whenever Sarah cut her gaze in his direction, she found his eyes upon her, studying her, appraising her.

Worse, Sarah saw how her mother lit up when Langston made his presence known. Edwina began to accept that they would meet Langston on their walks, and she looked forward to his conversation.

He took over pushing Edwina's chair and engaged in attentive—and somewhat flirtatious—banter with her . . . all while watching Sarah.

Eventually, Langston began to meet them where Nevis left them, thwarting Sarah's efforts to avoid him. Edwina took more care with her hair and dress; she referred to him often throughout the day, quoting his anecdotes or little jokes, referring to him as "dear Mr. Langston."

Sarah realized she had lost the battle when her mother invited Langston to dinner. Within another fortnight, Edwina announced, "Sarah, Richard has made me an offer of marriage. He may not have much in the way of possessions or wealth, but he is a gentleman and . . . and he declares that he loves me . . . and you."

Now, on this ill-fated day, despite Sarah's many objections and pleas, Edwina would stand before a judge and be married to this man. So much worse, she would, at the same time, appoint Richard Langston Sarah's legal guardian in the event of her death.

"My heart is comforted, Sarah, knowing that after today, should something . . . happen to me, you will not be alone in this world."

Tears ran from Sarah's eyes, down her cheeks, and onto the lace collar of her dress. The inevitability of facing life without her dear mother terrified Sarah—but not nearly as much as the prospect of being alone in the world . . . under Richard Langston's guardianship.

WHEN SARAH CAME BACK to herself, shadows had lengthened within the empty shop, and she was shivering. She wondered how long she had sat there . . . remembering what she had somehow forgotten.

# $\mathcal{C}$HAPTER 4

Olive pulled Sarah aside before breakfast and slid her arm about Sarah's waist. "Sarah, did you not sleep well last night?"

"Why do you ask?"

"Oh, my dear. You have such dark smudges under your eyes."

"Do I?"

"My, yes. Is everything all right? You do not seem quite yourself."

Sarah shrugged uneasily. Olive had touched upon a nerve, for Sarah had not slept well. Instead, she had tossed and turned, fretting over her argument with Corrine and the strange memories that had followed. When she finally did nod off, the disturbing scenes she recalled the previous afternoon had stymied her attempts to sleep.

Even now, she was distracted, her thinking troubled and agitated.

Unwilling to reveal the harsh words she had said to Corrine, Sarah instead answered, "I-I had some bad dreams last night."

"Dreams?"

"Worse than dreams. Memories from my childhood. Awful things. Things I had forgotten."

"Remembrances from your childhood?"

"Yes. From when my mother became sick and . . . when she married my stepfather and left me in his care after she died. I do not know how it is that I forgot those terrible happenings or why, yesterday, I suddenly remembered them, but they were so—" Sarah could not finish.

"Your stepfather? Was he . . . did he?"

"I cannot bear to speak of it, Olive."

"Perhaps you could talk to Miss—"

"No. No, please do not tell Miss Rose. I do not wish to dredge up what is in the past. Let it stay there! Promise me you will not say anything to her, Olive? Please?"

Looking a little uncertain, Olive nodded her acquiescence.

"All right. But I shall pray for you, Sarah. I do not like seeing you so peaked."

They went into the dining room for breakfast then, but Sarah dreaded going to work that morning and facing her friend. She wondered if their disagreement of the previous day would come up or if they would both treat it as water under the bridge.

~*~

WATER UNDER THE BRIDGE? It was not to be.

When Corrine arrived at the shop, Sarah was forced to admit to herself how deeply she had wounded her friend: Corrine was not her normally cheerful self. She was reserved. Careful. And withdrawn.

A cloud hung between the two women.

*It is my fault*, Sarah conceded. *I was unkind and outspoken. Cruel. And I do not understand why I would be cruel to Corrine, because I love her as a sister. She is my dearest friend.*

"I-I wish to say that I am sorry, Corrine," Sarah finally whispered after an hour of uncomfortable strain between them. "I am sorry for what I said yesterday. I . . . I allowed my emotions to get the better of me. I should be more careful of what I say."

Corrine, usually so quick to forgive and cover over the little failures of others, considered Sarah, and Sarah was discomfited with what she saw reflected back.

When Corrine answered, she said, "I know you are sorry, dear friend. I know you do not mean to be harsh."

"And yet?"

Corrine nodded. "Yes, I wish to say something."

Sarah licked her lips. "All right."

"I prayed for you last evening, Sarah. I said nothing to Albert, of course, but after supper, I spent the evening alone in our room, praying for you, trying to understand what happened yesterday, asking our Lord for his help and wisdom. I think, that is, I *believe* he may have whispered a word to me. For you."

"Oh?"

Corrine took Sarah by her hands. "I love you, Sarah. Nothing I say is intended to wound you."

Sarah's nerves jangled a warning. In the many years she and Corrine had been friends, Corrine had never been as serious as she was at this moment.

Corrine began, "Scripture tells us that our mouths speak what our hearts are filled with. I do not believe the problem to be so much what you said yesterday or even what took place between you and the two gentlemen, but rather what those events revealed, dear Sarah."

Sarah did not answer, but her chin began to tremble. She did not relish Corrine poking about in her private, inmost parts.

Corrine pressed her point. "The passage I speak of is found in Luke 6:45. It tells us, *A good man out of the good treasure of his heart bringeth forth that which is good; and an evil man out of the evil treasure of his heart bringeth forth that which is evil: for of the abundance of the heart his mouth speaketh.*

"Sarah, it is what is in our hearts that comes out of our mouths. The hurtful things you said? They came from your heart."

"I-I do not understand."

Corrine put her head to one side. "Do you mean you do not understand the verse or are you saying that you do not understand what is in your heart?"

"That. M-my heart." Sarah's insides were churning; she felt as if her lungs were being squeezed and would soon burst. "Are you . . . are you saying my heart is *evil?*"

"I know that Jesus has saved you, Sarah, just as he has saved me. We came to Jesus together, and he has made us new creatures in him. It is possible, nonetheless, as Christians, to hold back pieces of our heart from Jesus, aspects of our lives we refuse to surrender to him.

"This verse says we store up treasure in our hearts—either good treasure or evil treasure. Well, what do people do with their treasures? Do we not guard them? Keep them hidden? Protected? Safely locked away? But, no matter how hard we try to keep our treasures locked away, those things fill our hearts to overflowing until they come out of our mouths. If our treasures are good, then good words come out of our mouths; if our treasures are evil, then evil comes out in our words . . . words that injure others.

"When I was praying for you last night, I felt the Lord whisper that you have locked something away in your heart that is part of your old life, your 'old man.' I do not know what it is. Perhaps you do not know what it is either, but Sarah? It is an evil thing.

"I have known you a long time, my sister, and this is what I have witnessed: Given the 'right' conditions, you are easily affronted, easily angered. And when you are angered, this evil thing lurking in your heart rushes out of your mouth, wounding whomever is near, even your dearest friends, but wounding yourself, too. I would say, in fact, that you suffer the most harm—for although you tamp down the anger after each incident, it does not leave, it does not go away. Rather, it continues to grow . . . and strengthen. As your friend, I must speak the truth in love: I have observed this behavior worsen lately."

Sarah's breath came in great gasps, and her eyes streamed tears.

Corrine drew Sarah to herself, wrapped her arms about her, and held her tight. *O Lord,* Corrine prayed. *Please speak through me.*

She whispered, "I am afraid for you, Sarah. Whatever you are holding onto in your heart, it is poisoning you—and I do not think it will be satisfied until it has destroyed you. Please. Please seek the Lord. Ask him to reveal this ugly, destructive thing to you so that you can surrender it to him, so he can free you from its hold."

Sarah clung to Corrine; she seemed to crumple in on herself. *Lord? Is Corrine right? Am I harboring something evil in my heart? Lord? What is it? What am I to do about it?*

~*~

CORRINE'S GENTLE BUT DEVASTATING exhortation affected Sarah deeply. She was troubled in her thoughts far into the evening. Leaving her window up to allow a breeze in, she had, at last, fallen asleep when a strange rattling intruded.

Heart pounding, Sarah sat up. "What is that noise?"

She again heard sharp taps and tings—the sound of small objects striking and glancing off glass, other objects missing glass but thudding nearby. Inside her bedroom. "What? Is someone throwing pebbles at my window? Through my window?"

Sarah threw back her covers and crept to the sill. She leaned forward and looked below.

A dark figure called to her. "Sarah?"

"Mr. O'Dell?"

"Yes. Please come down, Sarah."

Sarah pulled on her robe and ran, barefooted, down the staircase. She unlocked and opened the front door. "What is it? What is wrong?"

"Joy is sick. A high fever. The doctor is with her, but he cannot stay all night, so I left Joy with him and came to fetch Miss Rose—and you, if you will come. I did telephone, but it rang and rang and no one answered."

"Mr. Wheatley is the only one on the ground floor, and he is quite deaf while asleep, I am afraid. Miss Rose is typically the house's lightest sleeper; however, I fear she is overtired at present."

O'Dell looked at his feet. "I know she is; she worked tirelessly after Jacob's birth, letting her responsibilities here pile up. It troubles me to burden her further, but Joy is calling for her mother. When I telephoned, and no one answered, I decided to drive here and awaken the entire house, if need be."

His smile was apologetic. "I saw your open window, so I tossed gravel at it to rouse you rather than pound on the front door and disturb everyone. I hope I did not distress you too much?"

Sarah uttered a soft snort. "You surely did startle me, but I am recovered now. Do you wish me to awaken Miss Rose? And did you say you came to fetch me, too?"

"Yes. Mother Rose will not have the strength to attend to Joy and care for Matthew and Baby Jacob at the same time. I can and will help, of course, but I must be in the office early tomorrow morning for an important meeting. I had hoped you would come to watch the children? Matty is quite attached to you."

"I cannot leave Corrine at the shop on her own all day. That would not be prudent."

"We shall close the shop tomorrow, if necessary."

"Very well—but for one day only. Let me go up and awaken Miss Rose."

She knocked softly on Rose's door three times before Rose answered. As Sarah suspected, Rose was slow and bleary-eyed.

"What is it, Sarah?"

"I am sorry to disrupt your sleep, Miss Rose, but Mr. O'Dell is here. Joy is running a fever and is asking for you; the doctor is with her, but he must be in and out as he attends to other patients. Mr. O'Dell asks that you come help nurse Joy, and that I come to care for the children."

"I shall dress and pack a bag. What of you?"

"I told him I would come, but what of the shop? Mr. O'Dell proposed we close it for the day, but I would hate for Joy to lose out on any sales."

Rose thought a moment. "Arouse Olive and ask her if she is willing to leave her duties here to assist Corrine tomorrow. If she is agreeable, we shall leave the key and money bag with her. Then please dress and pack a light bag."

Sarah did as Rose asked. Fifteen minutes later, she was in the rear seat of O'Dell's motor car, and they were speeding into the night. While they drove, she prayed. *Lord, your Son, Jesus, healed many fevers during his ministry on earth. He even healed Peter's mother-in-law of a fever. I come to you now, in Jesus' name, and ask that you heal Joy of her fever. Thank you, Lord.*

When they arrived at the O'Dell home, Rose told Sarah, "I shall bring Jacob to you as soon as I can convince Joy to let me take him."

When Rose and O'Dell slipped into the bedroom, leaving her alone, Sarah entered the kitchen, filled the tea kettle, and set it on the gas stove to heat.

Five minutes went by. The kettle sang, and Sarah turned the burner down to keep the water hot. She looked through Joy's well-ordered cabinets and found what she needed to make herself a cup of tea.

Ten more minutes passed before Rose appeared with the baby.

Sarah stood to take the sleeping infant. "How is Joy?" she asked.

"Her fever is quite high; she is agitated and in great discomfort."

"What does Dr. Murphy say?"

"Dr. Murphy was unable to come, so he sent his new associate. The doctor examined Joy and believes that a portion of the afterbirth remained within her and is putrefying, causing infection and fever. He said it is imperative that this piece of afterbirth come out."

"What can he do for that?"

"At present, he is massaging Joy's lower abdomen to stimulate cramping, hoping her body will expel the portion on its own. It is quite painful. I could not bear to watch it any longer."

Sarah pursed her lips. "And if the afterbirth does not come out?"

"The doctor said he would attempt to remove it . . . manually."

"A surgery?"

"Yes. To . . . to scrape it out."

Sarah shuddered. "Miss Rose, we should pray."

"Oh, yes. Thank you, Sarah."

With Jacob cradled between them, Sarah and Rose cried out to the Lord for his help. Sarah prayed specifically that Joy's body would expel the infected tissue as it was meant to and that the doctor would not find it necessary to perform a dangerous surgery.

Afterward, Sarah made Rose a cup of tea and left her sipping it to look in on Matthew. She carried Jacob with her. When she found Matty in a sound sleep, she tucked Jacob into the bassinet opposite Matty's little bed and returned to the kitchen.

Possibly an hour later, a haggard O'Dell entered the kitchen. "The doctor believes he was successful. Given a day or so, he believes her fever should abate."

"Thank the Lord," Rose breathed.

"Yes. Thank you, Lord!" Sarah agreed.

"The doctor is packing up. He will return later; however, Joy requires a change of linens."

"Let me," Sarah responded. "Miss Rose, perhaps you could lie down with Matty on his bed? You need your rest."

"No, no. I shall help you change Joy."

"No, please, Mother Rose," O'Dell said in all gentleness. "I shall assist Sarah. Please do as she suggests. You will be wanted in the morning."

Rose nodded. "Very well. Sarah, I shall show you where the basin and washcloths are first."

"And I shall gather the fresh linens," O'Dell added.

The doctor was gone when O'Dell and Sarah entered the bedroom. Joy, flushed with fever, appeared to be sleeping, until she moaned and thrashed in pain.

"I realize it is unconventional for a married man and a single woman to do this work together," O'Dell murmured, "but I could not ask Miss Rose to do more until she has slept. I did not realize how worn she is. Perhaps you could bathe Joy and then I could help you change the bedding?"

Sarah laughed under her breath in dark humor. "Without putting too fine a point upon it, Mr. O'Dell, I was rather compelled to overcome such social conventions in my youth."

"Ah, quite so. Still . . ."

"We shall do as you say, Mr. O'Dell. If you will find an unsullied gown for Joy, I shall bathe her and call you when I have finished to help me change the bed."

The earliest hint of dawn had crept through the curtains when Sarah and O'Dell completed their chores. O'Dell slipped off to snatch an hour of sleep before he left for the office. Sarah was putting the stained linens into ice water to soak when a high, thin wail caught her ear. She washed her hands and rushed to fetch the baby before he awakened Rose and Matthew.

She returned to the kitchen with the fussing infant and smiled into his angry, red face. "Listen to you, little man! What a racket you make. Shall we change your nappy and see if that satisfies you?"

She changed his diaper and gown, wound him snugly with a blanket, and sat down to rock him close to her heart. For a minute, she cooed little nothings to him, and he stilled. He was less than two weeks old but so alert! Sarah watched, completely engrossed, as he listened and looked for her.

"What a good baby," she crooned. "What a good little angel you are."

She yawned, and her eyes drooped. Together, she and the baby slept.

~*~

SARAH WOKE WHEN A wet finger poked her neck. She was growing rather accustomed to being awakened in this mode. She cracked one weary eye, and the wet finger retreated into a little mouth.

"Good morning, Matthew O'Dell." Sarah yawned. "Goodness. I guess I fell asleep."

Matthew pointed with a slobbery index. "'Cub."

"That's right. Baby Jacob. Would you like to sit in my lap with your brother?"

Matthew proved his adept climbing skills by clambering up the front of the chair. Sarah tucked him into the crook of her free arm. As Sarah set the rocker moving back and forth, Matthew nestled his head against her shoulder, and Sarah put her cheek to his soft hair.

*Lord, is this what heaven is like?*

~*~

AN HOUR LATER, JACOB O'Dell awakened.

Hungry.

Screaming.

Like a wild banshee.

"Oh, my goodness," Sarah groaned. "How can such a big noise come from such a teeny body? And I am so very sorry, Master Jacob, but I do not have what you need. Please be patient just a few minutes."

The household was up now. O'Dell flew out the door, Rose took Jacob in to Joy to nurse, and Sarah fixed a small pot of creamed wheat cereal for Matthew's breakfast. When Rose returned and sat down to help Matthew with his cereal, Sarah—behind Matthew's back—tipped her head toward the bedroom, asking an unspoken question.

"She is in less pain, thank the Lord, and her fever is coming down."

"Oh, I am glad!"

"As am I."

~*~

IN THE MAIN, ROSE left Jacob with his mother throughout the day, so she could nurse him. Rose removed the baby to change him as needed, allowing Joy to rest in bed and heal. However, Rose was content to let Sarah manage Matthew, declaring that the toddler had "more jump and bounce than six frogs in a bucket."

So, while Rose cared for Joy's needs, Sarah kept Matthew occupied. She read him stories, took him on walks to the park, and played tag with him in the O'Dells' little yard behind their house. She loved every moment of it.

As much as she enjoyed caring for Matthew, the high point of Sarah's stay with the O'Dells was the conversation she and Rose had during Matthew's nap. They were sharing a cup of tea and a quiet respite when Rose ventured to confide in Sarah.

"While it is our desire that all of our girls at Palmer House learn good and wholesome work skills, become independent, and are able to leave us and move on with their lives, I must tell you, Sarah, how much I cherish your ongoing and stabilizing presence in our home. With both Joy and Breona married and occupied with their families, you must know how much I lean upon you, Olive, and Marit."

Sarah flushed with pleasure. "Miss Rose, it is my honor to help you any way I can. I admire you so much." She looked down. "And I have been wanting to be an assistant at Palmer House for some time."

Rose cupped Sarah's cheek with her hand. "The Lord bless you, my daughter. I consider you so already."

Sarah leaned her cheek into Rose's hand, soaking up the love she extended so freely. "Miss Rose, you are such a strong and godly woman. I think one of the things I admire most about you is that you do not require a husband to complete you. You are a whole person on your own."

Rose sighed. "Thank you, Sarah, but I would not have you believe that is completely true."

Sarah looked up and saw a great sorrow within Rose's soul. "It is not?"

"No, my dear. While it is true that each of us, when Jesus saves us by his blood, are complete in him, Scripture also tells us that the Lord has said, *It is not good that the man should be alone; I will make him an help meet for him.* God, our Creator, tells us that being alone in this life is difficult. If we are called to singleness—as the Apostle Paul was—then the Lord's power and grace will enable us to bear our singleness. However, I know from experience that the burdens of this life are lighter and sweeter with a husband's love and strength."

Sarah whispered, "I-I may be called to singleness, Miss Rose. I do not desire a husband's love."

Rose drew back and studied Sarah. "I wonder . . . how one can say she does not desire what she has never experienced? You told me once that you never knew your father's love, Sarah. The lack of a father's love can wound a woman's heart, even twist it out of its natural shape.

"What I can tell you is that I have lost two husbands in my lifetime, Sarah, and I mourn them both to this day. Yes, I am strong in my faith, but I do not want you to think that it is easy, this being a widow, being single— it is not. I would not trade the joy of those years of marriage for the world."

She hesitated before finishing her thought. "All that being said, I have determined to make my latter years count for the Cross. I have set my heart and will to be fruitful for God."

"That is what I want, also, Miss Rose."

~*~

LATE THAT AFTERNOON following his nap, Sarah took Matthew to visit Joy and Jacob. Joy was weak from the pain and fever, but she was visibly improved. She allowed Matthew to sit on the bed next to her. While she helped him hold and examine Jacob, Sarah brushed out her long, blonde hair and braided it down her back.

"You have no idea how wonderful it feels to have you run the brush over my scalp, Sarah. Every inch of my skin—even on my head—throbbed when the fever was at its peak. Now my skin aches and itches."

Sarah set the brush aside and gently massaged Joy's neck and shoulders. "You must be weary and sore from lying abed."

"How right you are. I am anxious to regain my strength and return to caring for my family."

"You must not overtax yourself just yet, Joy. This was a serious infection; your body needs time to recover."

Rose poked her head through the doorway. "Pardon me, but the doctor is here. He wishes to check in on Joy before he retires for the evening."

"Please send him in, Mama."

"I shall withdraw," Sarah murmured. "Shall I take Matthew with me?"

"Yes, please. I do not know what we would have done without you while I was so sick, Sarah."

Sarah ducked her head. "It was my pleasure to help. And I am so happy for you—two healthy baby boys. What a blessing." She tickled Matthew and scooped him off the bed. "Shall we go see your toys, Matty?"

"Yes, pease, Sar."

Joy blew him a kiss. "Mama loves you, Matty. You are such a good boy."

Sarah paused at the bedroom door when Rose reappeared with the doctor. She had forgotten that Palmer House's longtime physician, Dr. Murphy (now a stately old gent) was not attending Joy. Sarah was shocked when a tall man of significantly younger years followed Rose into the room. Sarah set Matthew on the floor and moved farther to the side, chin down, waiting for the doorway to clear so she could make good her escape.

"How are you feeling this evening, Mrs. O'Dell?"

"Much improved, Doctor Croft, thank you."

Matthew pulled on Sarah's hand. "Toys, Sar."

His unexpected demand drew all eyes to him, including those of the doctor.

"Ah, this must be young Master O'Dell." He stooped down. "Hello, Matthew. What do you think of your new baby brother?"

Matty nodded with vigor. "'Cub."

"Jacob. Very good, Matthew."

As he stood up, his gaze passed over Sarah. And stopped.

Dumbfounded.

Not as stunned as Sarah had been when he entered the room. Her lips had parted in amazement. And mortification. Now, hot color blazed up her neck into her cheeks.

For just an instant, as he recognized her, she saw candid appreciation flicker in his eyes—the same admiration she had seen at the shop. He recovered quickly, however, shuttering his countenance and assuming an air of formality. He bowed. "Dr. Bryan Croft, at your service, miss."

Sarah did not answer; she was tongue-tied.

Joy broke the awkward silence. "Dr. Croft, this is our dear friend, Sarah Ellinger. Dr. Croft has taken partnership with Dr. Murphy, Sarah. He is quite new to Denver."

*New to Denver.*

Nothing Joy said could have stung Sarah more.

As for the man's response to their second meeting? Outwardly, his comportment was impeccable. Dispassionate and professional. What neither Rose nor Joy could see—what only Sarah saw—was the sardonic light in his narrowed eyes.

And how he bit his bottom lip in an effort to control its twitch as he held out his hand to her.

*Is this man laughing at me?*

*Insufferable scoundrel!*

Sarah's chagrin gave way to indignation. She ignored his extended hand. "Pardon me. I was taking Matthew to his room."

Realizing he had blocked her egress, Dr. Croft stepped aside. "I see. Do please forgive my *second* oversight."

Sarah growled, stood tall, and shepherded Matthew from the room. The sweetness of the day was gone, swept aside by the exasperation smoldering in her breast.

Dr. Croft sighed and nodded to himself before turning to Joy. He set his bag on the side of her bed. "I should like to take your temperature and listen to your heart and lungs, Mrs. O'Dell."

"But, Dr. Croft, before you do, I cannot help but notice our friend's discomfort in your presence. May I ask, were you already acquainted with Miss Ellinger?"

"I beg your pardon. I visited your shop a few days past and somehow offended your friend. I apologized for distressing her, however . . ."

He shrugged and did not finish his thought, but Rose and Joy were as mystified as he was at Sarah's behavior.

Rose, for her part, turned inward. *Lord, this is unlike my daughter Sarah. Should I be concerned for her? Perhaps I shall ask Olive if she has any insights into Sarah's actions of late. Whatever is perturbing her, Lord, I ask that you help her by your Spirit to overcome it.*

&#x2766;&#x273B;&#x2767;

# $\mathcal{C}$HAPTER 5

T he jingle of the telephone on the wall of Palmer House's great room disrupted the morning's pleasant quiet. Rose Thoresen lifted her eyes from the sums she was working to the telephone. Newly returned from nursing Joy in her illness and then staying on to help with the children and cooking as Joy recovered, she was weary and behind in her tasks.

Managing the household sums was not Rose's only duty; the house's finances could, in actuality, be considered but a small piece of her responsibilities. Rose led the girls in Bible study each morning after breakfast, kept track of the girls' comings and goings, and met with them individually on a biweekly basis to counsel them, pray with them, and often simply love on them while they wept over their sorrows and difficulties.

The difference between life in a whorehouse and life at Palmer House was extreme. A girl fresh from a brothel required gentle schooling in appropriate, non-provocative dress. Rose, too, provided ongoing coaching to help them moderate their accustomed language to something less "salty."

In addition to all these efforts, Rose strove to maintain a stable and wholesome environment for the newborn and growing Christians in the home. Although Sarah often helped Rose sort out small squabbles, praying with the quarreling girls and helping them to mend fences and friendships, this "preserving of the house's peace" was a balancing act that required a great deal of Rose's care and discernment—even the meting out of discipline.

Although the labors of the past week were behind her, Rose was spent. Sighing, she put down her pen, rose from her desk, and lifted the telephone's conical hand receiver. "Good morning. Palmer House. Mrs. Thoresen speaking."

She did not immediately recognize the voice on the other end of the call when it replied, "Mrs. Thoresen? Stephen Sedgewick here. I am very glad to have reached you at home."

*Oh, yes. Martha Palmer's grandnephew.*
*Her departed sister's grandson.*

"Good morning, Mr. Sedgewick. How are you today?"

He was silent for a moment before murmuring, "I am grieving, Mrs. Thoresen."

As his words sank in, Rose's throat tightened. "Mrs. Palmer?"

"Yes; I am sorry to inform you that my great-aunt passed away in her sleep last night. Her staff rang me not more than thirty minutes ago. I know how devoted you were to her, and how she esteemed you and your work. I wished to be the one to deliver this sad news to you."

"I thank you, Mr. Sedgewick, and I am sorry for your loss. This is a very hard blow. Mrs. Palmer was dear to all of us at Palmer House. Will you please keep us apprised of the plans for her funeral?"

"I shall, Mrs. Thoresen."

Rose hung the receiver on its cradle and sank into her chair, her figures and sums forgotten. In her mind's eye, Rose pictured the old woman with the shock of white hair, bent nearly double over her cane, twisting her head at an impossible angle in order to look up into the faces of others.

*O Lord, our God, how grateful I am for Martha's sake. She is now in your presence—standing tall and upright, healed in both body and spirit, lifting her head and hands in worship to you! How happy she must be.*

And Rose remembered the first time they met.

~*~

"MRS. THORESEN, MIGHT I have a word with you?" The question had come from near Rose's elbow. She turned, looked down, and found the thin, elderly woman with a wizened face, stooping over a cane.

"How do you do?" Rose extended her hand. The elderly woman trembled and leaned her left side more heavily on her cane so that she could reach Rose's outstretched grasp. Her skin was dry and fragile, but soft, like raw spun silk.

"Mrs. Chester Palmer. Please call me Martha. P'rhaps we could set in that corner for a moment?"

When they had gone aside and sat down together, Martha said, "I shall not take much of your time, Mrs. Thoresen, but I felt so impressed by the Spirit to speak to you . . . and I did not want to let the moment pass by."

"Of course," Rose had answered.

"The thing of it is," Mrs. Palmer began slowly, "I b'lieve I have your house."

Rose had been taken aback.

"I must warn you," Mrs. Palmer continued, "the house is in poor shape. Once it was a beautiful place, but it has been empty and has not been maintained for nigh on ten years."

She turned her head down and fidgeted with a hankie up her sleeve. "It is large, though. Very large. Has a sizable spot of prop'ty with servant quarters and a carriage house in the back."

She turned her head and looked up at Rose again. "I want to give it to you."

And she had. Martha had given her old home—neglected, disused, and filled with painful memories—to the ministry of rescuing women from prostitution and healing their wounded souls.

"MARTHA," ROSE WHISPERED. "Thank you for your kindness to us and your obedience to the Holy Spirit. You left behind a great testimony of your faith in Jesus. Can any of us do more?"

Rose reached again for the telephone. "Operator? Keystone 4672, please."

Joy answered. "The O'Dell residence."

"Joy, this is Mama. I have some sad news to report."

When Rose finished speaking with Joy, she repeated the same announcement to others who knew and loved Martha Palmer: Breona and Pastor Isaac Carmichael, Mei-Xing and Minister Yaochuan Min Liáng, Mason and Tabitha Carpenter, Emily Van der Pol, Grace Minton, Viola Lind, and the family at Palmer House.

AROUND THE DINING TABLE that evening, conversation was only about Mrs. Palmer and the many instances of her generosity.

"She always sent over the nicest Christmas packages," Olive reminisced. "Beautiful electrical Christmas lights for our tree, boxes of chocolates, peppermint candy canes, bags of oranges all the way from Florida—"

"The most vunderful hams," Marit interjected, "cured vit maple sugars."

"Mmm," Pansy enthused. "I do love ham."

"Ham!" little Toby crowed.

Will had his own favorite memory. "Ice cream was best. She sent us chocolate ice cream on Independence Day."

"And strawbr'y," Charley shouted. "I likes strawbr'y bestest."

Blythe had not yet spent a holiday at Palmer House and felt it altogether her misfortune—and somewhat inconsiderate of that sainted woman—that Mrs. Palmer should choose to die only months before Christmas. "What else, please? What else did she do at Christmas?"

"One year she gave every one of us girls hankies edged in French lace," Olive said. "I cannot bring myself to use mine. It is too exquisite."

Sarah's smile was dreamy. "I think I loved the flowers best of all. At Easter Mrs. Palmer always sent a dozen pots of white lilies. Their perfume would fill the house for weeks. At Christmas it was poinsettias—dozens of them."

Memories of Martha Palmer's many kindnesses besieged Rose, too— until an unwelcome realization set in.

*Lord? The needs of Palmer House have stretched us to our limits for a decade. You have sustained us all these years partly through Martha Palmer's liberal financial gifts. I know your mighty hand is not dependent upon her generosity, but still . . .*

Rose's appetite departed. Long after dinner ended, her heart lay heavy in her breast.

~*~

FOR SARAH, THE NEWS of Martha's passing had been hard to bear, but the remembrance and sharing of her many thoughtful gifts had been, somehow, even harder. They signaled not only the cessation of those loving gestures, but also the conclusion of an era. Sarah could tell that Miss Rose was disturbed, too. She was subdued when they left the table and for the remainder of the evening.

Later, as everyone settled in for the night and the house quieted, Sarah knelt on her bedroom floor and leaned upon her mattress, her hands folded in supplication.

"Father, with the loss of every individual Miss Rose has leaned upon— first Flinty, then Mei-Xing, Tabitha, Breona, Joy, and now Mrs. Palmer— with each loss, Miss Rose carries more of the weight of Palmer House upon her own shoulders. Even Marit and Billy, with three children to raise, cannot help Miss Rose as much as they did when they had only little Will. And dear Mr. Wheatley is so frail these days."

The notion that they might lose Mr. Wheatley in the not-so-distant future—that sole man to whom Sarah had ever bared her soul—struck her with particular force.

"Oh, my Lord! I love and respect Miss Rose so very much, but the burden of this ministry is too much for her alone. Please, Lord. Will you not send her help? And could it be me?

"Will you allow me to assist her more? I do not know how—I give most of my salary from the shop toward the house's upkeep as it is—but I am willing to do more, Lord. Please show me?"

Sarah let her petitions linger upon her lips as she slid between her bedcovers, but she slept poorly that night. Perhaps the collective emotions of the past weeks—the difficult conversation with Corrine, the news of Martha Palmer's death, and Sarah's concerns for Rose and Palmer House—would not allow her mind to settle. For whatever reasons, her sleep was uneasy, disturbed by dreams that were partly night visions and partly memories—ugly memories, recollections that reopened the most painful chapter of her life.

~*~

AS EDWINA'S HEALTH deteriorated, Richard's overtures toward Sarah intensified. He never failed, when circumstances gave opportunity, to touch her: a gentle pat on her arm here, a caress of her cheek there. And whenever he touched her, Sarah would shiver or tremble, and her breath would catch in her throat. If he managed to secure her hand—generally when they walked through the park—he would hold it fast and stroke her skin with his thumb.

He was particularly partial to lifting a strand of Sarah's dark hair and curling it about his fingers, rubbing its silky softness. "You have such lovely hair, Sarah. From the moment I first laid eyes upon you, I wondered what it felt like."

Whenever Richard took her hair in his hands, Sarah felt as though a chain had trussed her to him. In desperation, she fell upon a solution: While he was holding her hair, she would grasp the tress near her scalp and, in one swift movement, yank it from Richard's grasp. Usually, she would feign a yelp of pain so that her mother heard her

When she had secured her mother's attention, she would reproach her stepfather, saying, "Richard, you hurt me! Please do not pull my hair. Mama, do tell Richard not to pull my hair."

Richard soon caught on to Sarah's ploy. Thereafter, he kept to his other devices—never neglecting an occasion to catch Sarah alone in a room so he might touch her. As Edwina began to spend more time abed, Sarah grew more vigilant. She learned to keep obstacles such as furniture and doors between herself and Richard. She made it a habit to step out of his reach whenever he came near, and she kept company with her mother hours on end each day in order to avoid him.

But all these tactics were but delay. Sarah knew her mother was dying—and when she was gone, no one would be able to protect her any longer.

Sarah understood full well that Richard was a predator.

And that she was his prey.

~*~

"MRS. THORESEN? STEPHEN Sedgewick here."

"Yes, Mr. Sedgewick?"

"I am calling to provide you with the details of my great-aunt's funeral service. The service will be held on Saturday, September 28, 10 o'clock in the morning, at her church, Trinity United Methodist."

"Everyone at Palmer House would like to attend, Mr. Sedgewick. Would that be all right?"

Rose knew the beautiful stone church would be filled with Denver's moneyed social elite, some of whom had come alongside Rose and Joy to establish and furnish Palmer House, but also those who had criticized Martha Palmer and others for their association with fallen women.

"Actually, I have given instructions to the funeral home to mark off the entirety of the first three pews on the Gospel side of the sanctuary for you and your girls and any girls who have previously lived at Palmer House."

"Why, you are most kind, Mr. Sedgewick. Thank you."

"You are welcome, Mrs. Thoresen; however, you should know that it was Aunt Martha's particular request in the written directions she left with her attorney for her service, that her Palmer House friends be accorded this particular honor."

Rose's throat threatened to close upon her next words. "How like Martha."

"Indeed, indeed. Her will also stipulated that all present and former residents of Palmer House be invited to attend her graveside service and the family luncheon after." He snorted a dry but humor-filled laugh. "I and my wife and children are Martha's only remaining blood relations but, I think we can admit that, in her heart of hearts, Aunt Martha considered you and your girls her true family."

"You are very understanding, Mr. Sedgewick."

He laughed softly again. "We feel no slight at all. Great-aunt Martha had more than enough love to go around. But that does bring me to my aunt's last instruction: Her attorney requests that you remain after the luncheon for the reading of her will."

Rose's breath caught in her throat. "I . . . I understand. Thank you."

~*~

EDWINA ELLINGER PASSED away on a bitter wintry night.

Richard had not permitted Sarah to remain by her mother's side until she drew her last breath, but Sarah had stayed awake in her bed, knowing Death was coming and, by the servants' scurrying footsteps and muted voices, the hour in which it arrived.

Sarah had lain under her covers, shaking with grief and with fear until the early hours of morning—because her dear mama was gone, and no one could protect her any longer. Then she experienced a wild, exhilarating idea: *I shall run away.*

Sarah got up and, in the waning darkness, tugged a little valise from the shelf of her wardrobe. She filled it with clothes and necessities, then dressed herself in warm outerwear. She picked up her little purse and perused its contents: three dollars and twenty cents. Practically a fortune.

When she was ready, she stood at her window on the second floor and looked out into the last of the night. Snow lay upon the ground. Icicles hung from the eaves. The streets were deep with ice and dirty slush.

A harsh reality struck her. *Where could I go? How would I live?* Sarah knew only the immediate surrounds of her home, in particular, the park.

*But I cannot live in the park. I would freeze to death.*

She slowly unpacked her bag, undressed, pulled on her nightgown, and crawled back into bed. She lay there shivering until it was light enough to be morning.

When she crept to her mother's room at dawn, before the house stirred, Edwina's body had been washed and dressed and her hair brushed and braided. She was laid out in an attitude of repose, her hands crossed below her breasts, one upon the other, but what Sarah saw was an empty, inanimate husk, not her mother.

She reached for Edwina's hand—it was cold. Hard.

*Mama is not here. She is gone. I am alone.*

Sniffling but resigned, Sarah went back to her room to wait until she was called.

~*~

AT BREAKFAST, THE DAY following Edwina's funeral, Richard made an announcement. "Your mother's illness has taken a toll on our finances," he stated.

Sarah stared at her plate. For months she had taken her meals in her mother's room. She had not wanted to come down to breakfast this morning, had not wanted to eat or be alone with him, but she was also afraid to stay in her room, fearful of what would happen if he came upstairs to fetch her. She kept her eyes downcast, terrified to meet Richard's gaze.

"Sarah, please look at me when I am speaking."

Sarah's eyes blinked rapidly, and her breath came in shallow pants. She managed to lift her chin and fix her gaze on a mole on Richard's cheek.

"Did you hear what I said about our finances?"

"Y-yes."

"I would like it if you answered, 'Yes, Daddy.'"

The spit in her mouth vanished; Sarah thought she would choke and throw up.

"I suppose we can ease into that," Richard added as an afterthought. "However, our straitened circumstances require that we economize. I regret the changes to the household I am forced to make today."

Sarah blinked again. Changes? Had her mother's death not been change enough?

"I must let some of the staff go, Sarah, beginning with Nevis."

*Nevis? No! He is our household's only male servant, the only one who would stand up to Richard if . . .*

Sarah could not put the accusation into words, because she had no vocabulary to explain the fear that Richard's presence engendered. She only knew that Richard represented an evil that pressed down on her, that she was certain was coming.

"I have already informed him that today is his last day. After all, his primary service was to lift your mother from bed to chair and back, then turn her when she was no longer able to move under her own power."

Richard's aversion to her mother's illness—his loathing of her body as it was racked with coughs, as she spit up blood and phlegm, when her incontinence kept the nurse and maids busy cleaning her and changing linens—had been evident. The sickroom smells had repulsed him, so Sarah had clung to her mother's side, knowing she was safe with her, that Richard would not seek her out there.

All that was over. The nurse was gone, the room cleansed and aired, and now Nevis—

"Your education will continue to be overseen by Miss Zahn, but she will no longer live here. She will come in each morning for three hours to conduct your lessons."

Another pillar of safety and strength crumbled beneath Sarah's feet.

Before the week was out, the household's five servants and one governess had been reduced to a single maid, their longtime cook, Mrs. Whitten, and a part-time governess—none who would "live in" any longer.

It was after dinner, when the house was devoid of servants, that Langston made his move.

"I have bought you a new dress, Sarah."

Richard was excited, nearly giddy. He gestured to her bed where he had placed a dress box. He waited with expectant elation.

Sarah's confusion overrode her normal caution. "I-I thought you said we needed to economize."

The skin on Richard's face took on a mottled quality. "Are you being ungracious, Sarah? Thankless? Unappreciative? You never struck me as an ingrate."

Sarah backpedaled. "No, I-I, no, of course I am not."

In a sudden move that made her jump. Langston flipped the box off the bed onto the floor.

"Oh, yes, we need to economize—all the more reason I should expect *some measure of gratitude* for the sacrifice this gift represents!"

When she did not immediately answer, his rage quickened. He kicked the dress box; it skidded across the polished floor and hit the wall. "I did not think your mother remiss in teaching you common courtesy. Is your conduct so lacking, so deficient as to disgrace her memory?"

Sarah quailed before his anger. "I am sorry. Please. I-I, um, thank you."

"Thank you, *Daddy*. You *will* call me Daddy."

Sarah stuffed down the terror making her feel faint. "Th-thank you . . . Daddy."

As if a summer squall had passed and the sun had reappeared from behind a scudding cloud, Richard's countenance cleared. "Say it again, Sarah. It would make me happy to hear you say it again. Say, 'Thank you, Daddy.'"

"Thank you . . . Daddy."

He sniffed. "Pick up the box and place it on the bed."

Sarah did as she was told.

"Look at me and say, 'I am sorry, Daddy.'"

Sarah stared at the wall behind Richard's head and parroted his words. "I am sorry, Daddy."

"Now, you may open the box and take out your new dress."

"Yes, Daddy."

The dress was a gorgeous concoction of pale pink and ivory petticoats, frills, and bows—a party dress with a wide band of ribbon for a sash.

A child's dress.

A *little* child's dress.

Sarah was now nine, going on ten—not five or six.

"I would like to see you in it, Sarah. Would you like me to help you try it on?"

The implications of his offer turned Sarah's blood to ice. "No, thank you, Daddy. I can manage."

He pursed his lips and studied her. "Very well. I shall expect you downstairs in no more than ten minutes." At the door, he turned. "Do not disappoint me."

When Sarah crept down the stairway exactly ten minutes later, her heart stuttered in her chest. The dress fit her in every way except the length. The skirt, already too short, stood out even farther, undergirded by ruffled petticoats—but her legs were bare from her short pantalets to her anklets.

She felt naked. Exposed. Defenseless.

"Come. Let me see you." Richard's eyes held a strange light, and his breathing was heavy. He held out his hand to her and beckoned her to where he was sitting.

He pulled her onto his knee and wrapped his arm about her waist, pinioning her arms. She squirmed and tried to pull away, but his arm tightened, and he held her immobile.

"No," she whispered. "Please."

"I only wish to touch you, Sarah. It is all right for me to touch you. I am your Daddy, after all."

As he pulled her closer, Sarah whimpered and went limp. She made herself go far away in her mind . . . back to springtime in the park, where acres of tulips waved their colorful banners and she and Mama were safe and happy.

# CHAPTER 6

The funeral of Martha Palmer was to be held at the church of her longtime membership. She and her husband, Chester, had been part of the building committee for the stately Gothic-inspired stone church, finished and dedicated in 1888, some thirty-one years past. Because Trinity United Methodist sat on the corner of East 18th Avenue and North Broadway, some distance from Palmer House, friends had arranged transportation for the household. Edmund and Joy O'Dell arrived to lead the little motorcade. Sarah and Rose rode with them to the church; Matthew sat between them, clutching a little wooden soldier; Joy held Jacob on her lap. Three additional motor cars for the remainder of the house followed behind.

Sarah leaned forward in her seat as they neared the church. Denver police were on hand to manage the flow of vehicles disgorging their passengers on North Broadway at the church entrance. O'Dell stopped alongside the curb and helped the women out. While he went to find a parking spot, Sarah stood with Rose, Joy, and the children, waiting for the remainder of their party to arrive—Billy, Marit, their boys, Mr. Wheatley, Olive, Ruth, Pansy, Frances, Tilda, Dinah, and Blythe.

Others gathered with them outside the church: Breona and Pastor Carmichael, Mei-Xing and Minister Liáng, Mason and Tabitha Carpenter, Corrine and Albert Johnston—and a long line of Palmer House alumni, their names and faces stretching over a decade: Gretl, Flora, Nancy, Maria, Jenny, Alice, Marion, Jane, Gracie, Trudy, Edna, Vivien, Della . . .

Even as Sarah noted the many former Palmer House girls gathering with them, she knew a number would be missing. A few had moved away and could not make the journey and, sadly, not every soul who had resided for a time under Palmer House's roof had bowed to the Lordship of Christ. Rose and Joy had sown good seed, but a few hearts had been like rocky ground where the seed did not penetrate and take root. Other girls had "gone forth" from Palmer House as Christians, but the seed of the Gospel had "fallen among thorns" and had been "choked with the cares and riches and pleasures of this life."

*Lord,* Sarah prayed, *bring these young women back to you. Break up the fallow ground of their hearts so that they are able to receive your word with gladness and so you might rain righteousness upon them. I am asking in Jesus' name: Restore their souls to you, O God.*

At five minutes before the hour, Rose and Sarah, side by side, led the girls of Palmer House, past and present, down the center aisle of Trinity United Methodist Church to the three empty pews waiting for them at the front of the church. At the head of the first pew, Rose and Sarah turned, faced the back of the church, and watched the two columns of young women file into the pews. They were followed by Billy, Marit, their children, and Mr. Wheatley, then O'Dell, Matthew, and Joy, carrying Jacob.

Sarah felt Rose's hand on her arm tremble; Rose smiled and nodded as each woman turned into the pews. Sarah knew each woman, too, some whom they had not seen in years. She found herself teary-eyed as the fruit of Rose and Joy's labors passed before them: These were strong, upright, godly women, healed inside and out, transformed from destroyed souls to healthy womanhood under Rose's care. It was a proud moment but humbling in its magnitude.

*To you be all the glory, Lord,* Sarah prayed silently. She knew Rose would be offering up the same sentiment.

Sarah and Rose took their seats last, and Sarah let her gaze wander around the sanctuary that was so vastly different from Calvary Temple's repurposed warehouse. This edifice was lined throughout with costly carved wood, polished and gleaming; it was hung with tapestries of red velvet. The thick carpet throughout was the same deep red. Inspiring stained-glass windows filtered the daylight with color. An organ, its majestic pipes soaring high into the vaulted ceiling, focused all eyes to the front where lay, in a simple pine casket, the body of Martha Palmer.

The church's sanctuary, including its choir loft on both sides of the organ and its balconies stretching along three sides of the church, was filled to capacity with the cream of Denver's society—shoulder to shoulder with the residents and friends of Palmer House. All had come to pay their respects and honor to this woman who had shaped so much of Denver's history, culture, and growth.

Even Pastor Jamison—retired for the past five years—came out of his retirement to officiate. He stepped to the raised, marble-topped lectern and said, "We have come together today to celebrate the life of an extraordinary woman—extraordinary because every accomplishment was the result of a life surrendered to God."

~*~

ONLY "FAMILY" HAD BEEN invited to the burial service. With the many children of the mourners also attending, the graveside service was mercifully short. After Martha had been laid to rest, Sarah and Rose rode back to the church with the O'Dells for the family luncheon.

Lunch was a lively affair, despite the reason for their gathering. The sumptuous meal was catered by a nearby restaurant and could not have been more of a family reunion than it was for those who had come down the mountain from Corinth in April, ten years past. Sarah, Rose, and Joy hugged Gretl Plüff repeatedly and broke off only when Marit and Breona sought to hug her, too.

"It has been too long, Gretl. Tell us how you are doing?" Joy asked.

"To God be the glory, Miss Joy. As you know, I am the Senator's cook and we live in our nation's capital when the Senate is in session, then return to Boulder the remainder of the year."

"You must see many wonderful things in your travels," Joy answered.

"Yes, but to be here, today? With all of you? I would not trade this for the world." She leaned forward to whisper around a grin. "A far cry from being cook to Corinth's Gentleman's Club, eh?"

Sarah was chatting with Tabitha and Breona while the two women's children plus Shan-Rose, Will and Charley, and little Matty O'Dell ran the length of the fellowship hall, laughing and largely expending the energy they had derived from the lavish lunch. Rose and Joy stood close by, talking with Mei-Xing and Victoria Washington of *Victoria's House of Fashion*, known to her friends as Tory.

Sarah observed a man approach Rose.

"Mrs. Thoresen, I believe?"

"Yes, I am Rose Thoresen."

"Able Forsythe, ma'am. I am Martha Palmer's attorney."

"Oh, yes. You wished to see me at the conclusion of the luncheon?"

"In point of fact, ma'am, when the caterers have cleared away the lunch things and I have dismissed them, I shall address everyone here."

Rose's brows lifted. "All of us?" She glanced at Sarah and saw that she had heard, too.

Forsythe's smile widened. "Yes, all of you, with the exception of the children. Since our business will be of an official nature—and somewhat tedious for young ones—I have arranged for the children to be watched over in the Sunday school wing where they can play to their hearts' content."

When he excused himself, Sarah and Rose exchanged hopeful glances; Sarah knew she and Rose were thinking and hoping the same thing—that, if it were God's will, Martha had endowed Palmer House with enough funds to continue its work.

At Rose's request, Sarah circulated among the gathering and spread the news that Mr. Forsythe had requested that everyone remain for the reading of Martha's will. True to Forsythe's word, when lunch was over, two young women from the church gathered up the children and led them away. The caterers cleared away the lunch things, took down the long tables where lunch had been served, set up a small table at the head of the hall, and arranged chairs in rows in front of it. When they completed their tasks, the caterers departed.

Then Forsythe stood by the small table and invited everyone to take a seat. When the audience of around forty adults (including Stephen Sedgewick, his wife, and two grown sons) had settled, Forsythe addressed them.

"My name is Able Forsythe, attorney to the late Martha Palmer. I thank you for honoring a great woman today, and I thank you for staying at my request. We are gathered here for the formal reading of Mrs. Palmer's will. The fact that you are here, indicates that, to one degree or another, you have been mentioned in Mrs. Palmer's will."

Sarah shivered, and a murmur rippled through the ranks of Palmer House girls. Sarah found her fingers being gripped in Rose's hand.

"I, Martha Ann Palmer, being of sound mind and body, on this date, the twenty-fifth of January, in the year of Our Lord, nineteen hundred and fifteen, do declare this to be my Last Will and Testament. My sole surviving relations are my grandnephew, Stephen P. Sedgewick, lately of Colorado Springs, Colorado, the grandson of my late sister, Agatha, and two great-grandnephews, Norris and Raymond Sedgewick, the sons of Stephen Sedgewick. I have no other living relatives.

"To my grandnephew, Stephen, I bequeath my love and appreciation and the sum of ten thousand dollars. To my great-grandnephews, Norris and Raymond, I bequeath the sum of one thousand dollars each."

The Sedgewick family nodded and murmured among themselves. Sarah supposed they were already acquainted with the specifics of Martha's will.

After listing the pensions and provisions Martha had made for her household staff, the attorney continued, "To Mei-Xing Liáng, as dear to me as the daughter I lost, I bequeath the amount of one thousand dollars. I furthermore give leave to Mei-Xing and her husband, faithful minister of God, Yaochuan Min Liáng, to live in my home on Palisades Avenue as long as you choose. At your deaths, I bequeath the house to your children as their shared property to use or dispose of as they jointly determine."

Sarah swallowed hard as Mei-Xing sobbed on her husband's shoulder.

Forsythe went on, "The remainder of my estate, inclusive of all monies and the proceeds from the sale of real property, is to be held in an interest-bearing trust and disbursed by my attorneys in the following manner:

"To Mr. Earnest Wheatley, I bequeath a monthly stipend in the amount of seventy-five dollars for your care and comfort until you join us in heaven. Thank you, Mr. Wheatley, for your years of friendship to our girls and to me.

"The property known as Palmer House was gifted to that ministry in 1910. I pray its use for God's purposes will continue unabated as long as the Lord wills. For the household upkeep of Palmer House, I bequeath a monthly stipend of two hundred dollars. For repairs and material upkeep of the house and its grounds, I bequeath an annual disbursement of five hundred dollars."

Rose's hand gripped Sarah's hand so hard that she winced. Rose was crying silently, but she was not the only one. Every beating heart in that room connected by the common thread of Palmer House's ministry was affected. Sarah heard muffled sniffs, sobs, and thanksgiving to God. She had to wipe her own eyes again and again.

*Oh, thank you, Lord! Thank you for speaking to Martha's heart. Thank you for using her gifts to take the strain from Miss Rose's heart and shoulders.*

Forsythe did not speak again until his audience had regained its composure. During the lull, Sarah saw him nod to Rose and smile. Stephen Sedgewick, too, turned to smile his approval in Rose's direction.

Then Forsythe recommenced. "*Ahem.* Regarding Palmer House, the will further stipulates: The monthly and annual stipends will be disbursed to Mrs. Rose Thoresen and used for their stated purposes so long as Mrs. Thoresen chooses to manage Palmer House. At the time of her full or partial retirement from this blessed service, it is my counsel that the following individuals serve as or elect a board of directors to oversee the ministry of Palmer House: Isaac and Breona Carmichael, Yaochuan and Mei-Xing Liáng, Edmund and Joy O'Dell, and Mason and Tabitha Carpenter.

"For Palmer House to continue to receive the listed stipends from my estate, the board of directors will serve in uncompensated capacity. They will select new management for the house and approve the disbursal of said stipends to the acting management. In the event this ministry, as conceived and directed by Mrs. Thoresen, ceases to function, monthly and annual stipends drawn from the trust will end. I suggest that proceeds from the sale of Palmer House be gifted to Calvary Temple of Denver or to another worthy ministry as the board determines."

Sarah could see Rose turning the conditions of the bequest over in her mind, nodding and agreeing with Martha's wisdom. But Forsythe's next words shook Sarah.

"To every young woman who lives or has lived at Palmer House and remains unmarried at the time of the reading of this will, I bequeath the sum of five hundred dollars as a bridal gift, payable upon her marriage. To those girls who have already married, I bestow the same amount, payable upon the execution of this will. If, however, a young woman who has lived at Palmer House remains unmarried, I bequeath the same sum, five hundred dollars, payable upon her thirty-ninth birthday."

Five hundred dollars! It was a fortune many a Palmer House girl would never, in her lifetime, see again in a lump sum; it could enable a newly married couple to begin their marriage debt-free, perhaps buy a little piece of land or leverage a mortgage to purchase a home.

The girls of Palmer House, current and former, wept and rejoiced aloud.

Not Sarah. She blinked back her astonishment and focused upon the stipulations of Martha's gifts to the girls of Palmer House.

*Her generosity will enable many of our girls to marry well. With such an incentive, a decent man might take a bride with a checkered past, even a frail thing such as Blythe. But our girls could be selective; they could afford to wait for an advantageous offer. But for me? A bridal gift, payable upon marriage?*

Sarah slowly shook her head. *Oh, Martha.*

"Ladies and gentlemen? If I could have your attention once more?"

The clamor stilled, and all eyes returned to Forsythe. "Finally, I bequeath the residual of this trust in its entirety to two individuals in equal shares. The trust will be paid out in annual increments, beginning on their respective twenty-first birthdays, to Shan-Rose Liáng and Edmund Thoresen Michaels."

Amazed silence met his announcement.

Shan-Rose was Mei-Xing's first daughter, a great favorite of Martha's. She was nine years old; twelve years would pass before she would receive any benefit from the bequest.

However, her name was not the cause of the hush.

The second beneficiary, Edmund Thoresen Michaels, was Joy's first child, the son of her marriage to Grant Michaels. He had been named Edmund after Grant's best friend, Edmund O'Dell. Grant had suffered from viral congestive heart failure and had passed away in late April 1911 . . . four months after his son was born.

Only weeks prior to Grant's death, the infant had been abducted.

Despite the conduct of a joint manhunt by U.S. Marshals and the Pinkertons—spearheaded by Edmund O'Dell—the trail of baby Edmund and his kidnappers had gone cold outside Pueblo, Colorado.

No trace of him had been found since.

~*~

ROSE, SARAH, AND THE O'Dells were subdued on the return drive to Palmer House. Martha's last bequest had triggered a fresh wave of grief in Joy and a sense of failure in her husband. O'Dell gripped Joy's hand, and they whispered together during the drive.

Rose was aware of her daughter and son-in-law's struggles and kept to her own thoughts, also grieving the absence of her first grandson. Matty, tuckered out from a long, unusual day, slept between Rose and Sarah, tucked under Rose's arm.

Sarah was glad for the quiet, grateful that Matthew was sleeping. It gave her time to inspect her own feelings and try to understand them.

*Oh, Martha. You left me a wonderful gift, for which I am most grateful. However, I cannot claim this gift unless I marry—or until I am quite near middle-aged. Why, Martha? Why did you arrange your generous bequest this way?*

She fretted over the conditions of Martha's will. *The likely topic of conversation at Palmer House for weeks ahead will be of nothing else but Martha's generosity and of finding a suitable husband as soon as possible—while I shall be required to wait. Oh, Martha! I shall not be eligible to claim your gift for nearly eleven years . . . because I shall not marry, whatever the inducement to do so.*

Irritation rippled through her. Sarah tried to pinpoint its cause. The closest she came to a name for the feeling was *resentment*. A nagging voice insisted, *Why? Why must society insist that every woman marry, even when she has no inclination to do so? What is so wrong with remaining single?*

When the motor car arrived at Palmer House, the afternoon was late. O'Dell offered Sarah his assistance: Flushed with frustration over Martha's will, she brushed his hand away.

Rose untangled herself from Matthew's sleepy arms, and O'Dell helped her down to the curb. He began to walk Rose up to the house also, but Sarah shook her head and took Rose's arm from him. "No. I will help Miss Rose to the house."

O'Dell shrugged. "As you say, Miss Ellinger."

Sarah could tell that the older woman was exhausted, but as they walked, Rose spoke. "I still cannot take in the many blessings Martha left in her will. Palmer House will do well now."

"I, too, am very thankful for her bequests to the house," Sarah replied. "And because of them, I am hoping that I can soon assist you more."

"In what way, Sarah? You help me so much already."

"I would like to stop working for Joy, Miss Rose. I would like to take over some of your responsibilities here at the house and lighten your load. I could not do so while you depended so much upon my contributions. However, I hope, in the near future, it will be time for me to give Joy my notice."

Rose stopped walking and stared at Sarah. "You would give up your income to help me?"

Sarah laughed. "I have been giving up most of it anyway."

Rose reached for Sarah and embraced her. "You dear girl. You dear, dear girl! You are the answer to my prayers."

They continued up the porch steps, and Rose chose her next words carefully. "I would ask you, though, dear Sarah: Is everything well with you in your heart?"

Rose's question surprised Sarah. "Why do you ask, Miss Rose?"

"It is only that I have noticed that you are not quite yourself these past weeks."

Sarah was immediately on her guard. "In what way?"

Rose canted her head to one side to study Sarah. "Your temper seems a bit frayed. You were short with Mr. O'Dell just now. A few weeks back, you were somewhat rude to Dr. Croft. Is there something bothering you?"

Sarah's answer was clipped. "No."

"Pardon me for pressing you, Sarah. Olive did mention that you were recently troubled by memories of your childhood, and I was concerned for you. If such memories are causing you grief, would you like me to pray with you over them?"

Sarah reddened. "Miss Rose, I spoke those things to Olive in confidence."

Rose drew back. "Oh, Sarah. I had no idea; please forgive me for intruding."

Sarah opened the front door to Palmer House and stood aside for Rose to enter before her. Her lips pressed together, Sarah added, "It is not you who broke a promise, Miss Rose."

~\*~

THEIR CONVERSATION WAS interrupted by the return of the remainder of the household. As Sarah had predicted, no young woman under the roof of Palmer House could speak of anything but the wedding gift Martha Palmer had bequeathed to each of them.

Blythe stole up alongside Sarah and hooked her arm through Sarah's. "Oh, is it not wonderful, Sarah? Perhaps . . . perhaps, as Miss Rose intimated, I, too, can look forward to having a home and a family." Blythe's wan face was alight with hope.

"I see no reason you could not, do you?"

"It is only that . . . even though Jesus has given me a new heart and a new life, I wondered if I would ever find a husband who would be able to truly love me. I thought that a *good* man might not want me because . . . because . . . " Blythe left her statement hanging.

"Because?"

"Well, you know. If he knew . . . about everything."

Sarah clamped her jaws together. Hard.

When she did not speak, Blythe asked, "Do you think I shall ever find a good man? Someone who will forgive me and love me anyway?"

"Forgive you for what?"

"Well, for what happened."

"For 'what happened'? Why? Did you choose what happened to you?"

"Choose? Well, I-I . . ." Blythe shook her head slowly. "But, the thing is, Uncle Jack—that is who I lived with—he wanted his drink and, although it was nighttime, I-I had to go out and get it for him."

"Your uncle sent you out after dark to fetch his drink? Alone?"

"Y-yes. He insisted I go, but if I had not gone out after dark, then maybe those men—"

"Those men? What men?"

"Th-the ones who saw me . . . by myself."

Sarah knew, then, what had happened to Blythe.

Those men.

*Those men!*

Sarah exercised every bit of self-control she possessed to grind out a soft answer.

"You are not accountable for what those men did to you, Blythe, nor do you need a man's forgiveness for it. A 'good' man would know that."

Under her breath she muttered, "A good man? What is that?"

"I beg your pardon, Miss Sarah?"

"It was of no matter, dear."

~*~

THAT EVENING, DUE TO such an emotionally fatiguing day, everyone at Palmer House partook of a light supper and retired earlier than usual—providing Sarah with an opportunity to confront Olive. She knocked on Olive's door and, at her answer, went in and closed the door behind her.

Olive had already shed her dress for her nightgown and was brushing out her hair. "Goodness. Are you as tired as I am, Sarah? What a very long day."

Sarah sat next to Olive on the edge of her bed and turned to face her. "Olive, I must ask you something."

"Yes?"

"Did you tell Miss Rose about my nightmares? About the memories of my stepfather?"

Olive clapped a hand over her mouth in dismay. When she pulled her hand away, she whispered, "Oh, Sarah, I did. I did not mean to—it-it was unintentional. Miss Rose asked me if you were all right and . . . it just came out."

"You promised me, Olive. I trusted you."

Olive dropped to her knees in front of Sarah and grasped her hands. "I did promise—and I broke my promise to you. Oh, Sarah, my behavior is inexcusable, but I declare I am terribly sorry. Please. Please forgive me! I do not know what I would do if I lost your friendship and trust."

Olive's contrition was written on her face in tearful anguish that wrung Sarah's heart.

Sarah thought for long moments about her argument with Corrine, the harsh things she had said—deeply wounding Corrine in the process. She thought, too, about Corrine loving her enough to speak truth into her life while still forgiving her completely.

"I do not want to lose your friendship, either, Olive. I-I was hurt, but not mortally so. I forgive you."

Olive bowed her head to their joined hands. "Thank you, Sarah. Again, I am so very sorry."

"I know you are, sweet Olive. Let us now forget this and put it behind us." Sarah rubbed her forehead where the twinge of a headache was making her eyes hurt. "You know, I am beginning to understand that misunderstandings and mistakes—even sins—between friends cannot help but come, can they?

"As all of us are imperfect, shall we not, at some point, fail or disillusion others? And if we harbor unrealistic expectations of perfection from our sisters and brothers, will not our enemy, Satan—who desires to destroy the love and unity we have in Jesus—use those unrealistic expectations to divide and separate us? I further believe that when we fail a brother or sister, Satan wants us to fear rejection so much that we hide from each other rather than confess our faults to one another. "But if there is no honesty between us, how can we overcome him?

"And if we do not face each other after such a blunder, if we do not admit to our faults, then those we have sinned against have no opportunity to forgive us, and nothing is ever resolved. Rather, we pull further away from the fellowship that is so essential to our growth in Christ."

Olive studied Sarah. "I know what you mean about fearing rejection. I am glad you came to confront me, Sarah. I do not want any offense or hard feelings to ever come between us—only loving truth."

Sarah hugged Olive. "Thank you, Olive. I feel the same."

~*~

SARAH WAS WEARY WHEN she left Olive's room, and her headache was worse. She donned her nightgown and slipped under her covers.

But sleep did not come easily. The enigma of Martha's bequest to the girls of Palmer House bothered and saddened Sarah. *Was marriage the only acceptable future Martha saw for us? Are there no other prospects for us?*

Sarah rubbed her temples, willing the headache away so that she could sleep. Instead, she returned to her recollections of late. She had not thought back to her childhood for many years. It was as though those memories were shrouded in thick, cloying mist. In some respects, she had forgotten the horrors that followed her mother's death and had only recently remembered.

The freshly found memories haunted her. As often and as desperately as she tried to shunt the unwelcome intrusions aside, they returned to play out behind her closed eyelids, like one of those silent cinema films that were becoming so popular.

Except that Sarah's recollections were neither silent nor black and white. No, these long-suppressed memories had come to life in vivid color.

~*~

RICHARD HAD NOT COME to Sarah's room in the night for more than three weeks. Initially, Sarah had been relieved, but as the trend continued, she began to worry.

His alteration toward her had begun around her thirteenth birthday. For her tenth, eleventh, and twelfth birthdays, Richard had taken pains to shower Sarah with gifts and parties, each event more elaborate than the previous—and costing more, Sarah was convinced, than the remnants of her mother's small income could absorb. He delighted in arranging the parties for Sarah and would invite every child of Sarah's acquaintance in the neighborhood.

No, that was not quite right. Richard never invited little boys to Sarah's parties. He invited only little girls, even those with whom Sarah had less than a passing conversance and often girls younger than Sarah. He lavished compliments upon Sarah's party guests and showered them with cake, ice creams, and candies. He pampered them and, in doing so, found opportunities to pat or touch them—always in the most innocuous manner.

Innocuous to all but Sarah. She understood what he was about—even if the doting mamas, who sipped punch and gossiped in the parlor while their innocent daughters played and enjoyed themselves under Richard's supervision, did not.

Sarah frowned as she pondered her stepfather's change in behavior. In contrast to previous birthdays, he had scarcely acknowledged her thirteenth.

She could feel the intensity of his displeasure, too.

*What have I done? What has changed?* She had followed his gaze to where it lingered on her budding figure, on the soft mounding that stretched the bodice of her childish party dress.

The revelation struck her forcibly: *I am becoming a woman—and Richard likes little girls.*

She was acquainted with Richard's periodic dark, brooding moods. Such a humor passed within a few days. This, however, was different. It was no sulking state, no transitory ill disposition. Now when she caught him watching her, what she read in his eyes was similar to the loathing she had seen him express for her mother's dying flesh—the disgust and hostility that he believed he had hidden from her.

Sarah quaked in sudden understanding: *He hates me.*

*What will become of me now?*

TWO WEEKS LATER, Richard called Sarah into the drawing room.

"Sarah, this is Maisie. She has come to live with us."

Sarah stared at the little blonde girl Richard held by the hand. The child was disheveled, dirty, and bewildered. Sarah guessed her age to be five or six.

Sarah's voice cracked when she asked, "Wh-where does she come from?"

"Ah. That is not important. What is important is that Maisie needs a home, and we shall give her one."

He bent toward the child and said, "This is your home now, Maisie, and you will be my little girl."

"But this is *my* home." The objection popped out before Sarah had a chance to think on how Richard might respond. She was shocked when his reaction came.

Dropping Maisie's hand, Richard gripped Sarah by the forearm and dragged her into the hallway, closing the drawing room door behind them. With a wrench that forced her wrist behind her back, he pulled her close to his face.

"Let me be clear with you, Sarah: This house does not belong to you. It is mine. I allow you to live here—and I shall allow Maisie to live here as I choose, as long as I choose. Do you understand me?"

When Sarah did not answer, he twisted her wrist harder.

"Ow!" Sarah sobbed. "You are hurting me!"

"I am waiting. Do you understand me?"

"Y-yes."

"Good. Now, do not forget what I have told you, and do not ever disrespect or disagree with me again."

He released Sarah's arm. "I shall be upstairs. Maisie requires a bath."

Sarah recalled how many "baths" Richard had given her after her mother died. She was under no illusions as to why Richard had brought the girl home.

Her heart broke for the child.

*I must do something to save Maisie from him.*

# CHAPTER 7

The shop had been busy all day with Saturday customers, and Sarah and Corrine were looking forward to closing time and to the end of their work week. "Sunday!" Sarah smiled. "A day to worship. To rest. To just breathe."

"Oh my, yes," Corrine responded. "I think I love Sunday dinner at Palmer House best of all, when we talk about Pastor Carmichael or Minister Liáng's message and share what the Lord has spoken to us through it. Who is coming to dinner tomorrow in addition to Palmer House residents?"

"Hmm. Let me count. Marit said Joy, Mr. O'Dell—and Matty and Jacob, of course. Oh! And Gracie. She is spending the weekend with us. Including you and Albert—pardon me—*Mr. and Mrs. Johnston*, that makes six plus our sixteen.

Corrine giggled. "I am not accustomed yet to being called *Mrs. Johnston*. And goodness! Twenty-two for dinner tomorrow? But what of Mei-Xing and Minister Liáng? Breona and Pastor Carmichael?"

"We see them at our table less frequently than we wish, I am afraid. They are often invited elsewhere for Sunday dinner."

"Our congregation has grown. I suppose they must visit other families in the church—oh, dear. Is that rain?"

Sarah glanced toward the shop windows and the heavy droplets that pelted them. She huffed. "As grateful as I am to have my umbrella, I do lament how dirty Denver streets are when it rains. I shall spend half an hour when I get home sponging my hem and cleaning my shoes."

"And I," Corrine sighed.

"Mm-hmm. Well, let us tidy up. It is near enough to five o'clock."

Sarah was ready to empty the cash register when the shop bell jingled and a trio of young women, laughing in merriment, stepped inside, their hats and hems streaming rain.

"Good afternoon, ladies. I apologize, but we are just closing," Sarah called out.

The tallest of the three, a woman with short brown hair curling out from beneath a jaunty straw hat, answered for them.

"It is we who should apologize. We got caught in the downpour and ducked inside to escape it. Please do say we may stay a minute? We promise not to stray from your mat here."

She and her companions laughed again, sharing the humor of their situation.

Sarah, drawn to their happy abandon, left the cash register and crossed the shop to them; Corrine followed her. "Of course, you may stay. We shall likely wait out the worst of the storm ourselves before leaving."

"Well, we are in your debt," the spokeswoman said. "I am Lorraine Pritchard—although my friends call me Lola." She offered her hand to Sarah. "My companions are Meg and Dannie—short for Danielle, of course."

"Of course," Dannie echoed. She and Meg chuckled together.

"I am Sarah Ellinger, the assistant manager of *Michaels' Fine Furnishings*. This is Corrine Johnston, my friend and co-worker."

While they shook hands around, Sarah took stock of their temporary refugees. Their attire indicated that they were not working-class girls from the factories, but neither were their clothes stylish enough to be shopgirl-worthy—not precisely. Their mode of dress was somewhere—or something—other than stylish, a touch unconventional, even *avant-garde*. Then she noticed two of them carried brown leather cases of differing size and shape.

Sarah realized she was staring—and that Lola's mouth was pursed in a small, amused smile.

"We are musicians," she explained. "Professional musicians. Meg plays trumpet; I play clarinet—among other instruments."

"And I play double bass—meaning you are not likely to see me toting my instrument about town," Dannie quipped.

Her companions laughed. When Sarah remembered how big a double bass was, she laughed with them.

"I do love symphony music," Corrine offered.

Lola replied, "Why, yes. We do, too."

She and her friends laughed again, but under their breath, as though Lola had told a joke only they were privy to.

Sarah felt at once a bit gauche in the eyes of these three worldly women. And Lola continued to study her, as if taking her measure, although for what, Sarah did not know.

*Goodness,* Sarah thought. *Professional musicians? I am quite out of my element.*

Corrine was of no help. She blinked and said nothing further,

Lola was still assessing Sarah when Meg tugged on her arm. "The rain has blown by," she whispered and giggled afterward. "We shall be late for rehearsal if we dawdle much longer."

"A shame," Lola smiled.

She shook herself a little and addressed Sarah. "Perhaps you will come hear us play sometime? I could drop by with an invitation."

"Er, yes. That would be lovely, I am sure."

Meg and Dannie laughed again—the trio seemed to always be laughing at something—and pulled on Lola's arm.

"Thank you for your hospitality, Sarah and Corrine." Meg said. She and Dannie were halfway out the door.

With a last glance behind her, Lola nodded, turned, and followed her friends.

Sarah locked the door behind them and turned the sign from "Welcome" to "Closed." Staring after them, she found she was sorry to see them go.

~*~

AS THEY HAD DONE for nearly a decade, the family at Palmer House walked to church on Sunday. Rose and Sarah led the way; the girls followed behind, two by two, and Mr. Wheatley, Billy, Marit, and Olive brought up the rear. Billy shepherded young Will and Charley along; Olive took turns with Marit carrying little Toby.

Calvary Temple had changed some since its earliest years. The congregation—a broad spectrum of social standing and nationalities, including a thriving flock of Chinese Americans—still met in the old warehouse in which they had begun. However, the members had plastered and painted the warehouse's interior, framed in classrooms for Sunday school and Bible studies, and made curtains for the warehouse windows. The initial mishmash of seating (they had employed whatever came to hand in those fledgling days: castoff benches, mismatched dining chairs, and discarded sofas) was being progressively replaced by pews as the church could afford them.

What had not changed was the vibrancy of the worship and preaching. No one officially led the singing. An organist and pianist began a well-known hymn; a helper near the front held up a chalkboard on which was written the hymn number, the congregation found the correct page in their hymnals (also an addition), and everyone sang their hearts out to the Lord. Often the organist and pianist would play the same hymn twice. Repetition allowed the congregation to memorize the stanzas, set the books aside, and lift grateful hands in worship, singing from their hearts.

This morning was no different. The musicians began, the congregation stood, and worship commenced. Heartfelt, overflowing praise filled the hall, but Sarah fidgeted. She found herself a bit distracted, unable to enter in as she was accustomed to doing. She glanced around and, for the first time, felt as if she were looking from the outside in, gazing upon the scene in the warehouse church, seeing it with fresh eyes.

As the congregation raised its collective voice, Sarah shivered. Nearly three weeks had elapsed since Corrine had spoken to her with such serious conviction. Since then, Corrine's normally generous and cheerful disposition had reasserted itself.

It was Sarah who felt different. She had pondered Corrine's words and the prophetic authority with which she had delivered them—an authority very unlike Corrine's personality, a manner that continued to ring with power in Sarah's heart, but that also left her uncertain. Somewhat agitated.

*I wonder what is amiss with me.*

That was the crux of Sarah's deliberations. Much of what Corrine had said was true: Sarah was easily angered. She did not know why or what triggered it, only that a furious storm lay dormant and undetectable within her—that is, until some unexpected event activated it. And Sarah could not put her finger on what, specifically, elicited an outburst, a response she felt powerless to understand, let alone to control.

Perhaps worse, as Sarah brooded over Corrine's warning, she found herself pulling in, withdrawing into herself.

*I feel myself . . . slipping. Not in any definable or sinful way, but it is worrisome, because I do not know why or how to stop.*

She came back to her surroundings as the congregation finished singing and sat down. Pastor Isaac Carmichael walked onto the platform and began his sermon.

"This is our third week on the study of 'The Overcoming Christian Life.' We began this series by asking the question, 'Why do some believers overcome sin in their lives while other believers are defeated?' We are examining this topic and question from several angles. Today we shall search the Scriptures on the topic of bondage. Isaiah 61:1 reads:

*"The Spirit of the Lord God is upon me;*
*because the Lord hath anointed me*
*to preach good tidings unto the meek;*
*he hath sent me to bind up the brokenhearted,*
*to proclaim liberty to the captives,*
*and the opening of the prison to them that are bound.*

"This prophetic passage was fulfilled when Jesus stood in the synagogue of his home town, Nazareth, took up the scroll of Isaiah, and read these same words aloud. We know that Jesus accomplished this prophesy because as he sat down, he added, *This day is this scripture fulfilled in your ears.* It is not often that we can know, by internal confirmation, when a biblical prophecy has been fulfilled; in this case, we can.

"We, those whom Jesus has saved, often see ourselves as the brokenhearted in this passage: *He hath sent me to bind up the brokenhearted.* Sin has a ravaging effect upon our lives, and we rejoice when Jesus heals our broken hearts. In contrast, we may not as easily see ourselves in the subsequent lines, *to proclaim liberty to the captives, and the opening of the prison to them that are bound.* I wish to focus our attention today upon the words, *them that are bound.*"

For a moment Pastor Carmichael paused, and the gathered believers quieted.

"Think of what 'them that are bound' implies. It implies that some people are tied, unable to move. It implies that they cannot free themselves. The words 'bound' and 'bondage' are closely related. Our 1913 Webster's Dictionary defines 'bondage' as,

*The state of being bound;*
*Condition of being under restraint;*
*Restraint of personal liberty by compulsion;*
*Involuntary servitude; slavery; captivity.*

"Perhaps this definition helps us understand how detrimental 'being bound' truly is. No one wishes to lose their personal liberty. No one desires involuntary servitude, slavery, or captivity—which is why the greatest news in history is that Jesus came *to proclaim liberty to the captives, and the opening of the prison to them that are bound.*

"Now, it is relatively easy to recognize bondages of the physical realm. If I may inquire, how many of us here will testify that Jesus has loosed them from bondage to alcohol?"

Hands lifted and a chorus of unabashed "amens" rang across the room.

"How many has Jesus loosed from bondage to the opium den? To the gambling halls?"

More hands rose, and many heads nodded in acknowledgement.

"We know, too, that among us are those whom Jesus has loosed from bondage to adultery and fornication, from bondage to brothels, pimps, and habitual loose living. And we rejoice and declare, *thank you, God!* Thank the Lord! For God is *well able*, through the blood of Jesus, to free us from *every* bondage. No more shame. No more guilt. No more slavery.

"Friend, if you are here, and you are enslaved in any area of your life, I tell you truly: There is hope in Christ. At the conclusion of the service we shall pray with you to surrender your life to Jesus, because the same Jesus who heals the brokenhearted also releases those who are bound."

Pastor Carmichael again paused, and he walked slowly across the platform, listening for the Spirit to lead him in his next sentence.

"I wish this morning to address not only visible, overt bondages, but also those covert, internal bondages we cannot see, those bondages that are concealed within our hearts, screened from external scrutiny, hidden—*we tell ourselves*—from God himself.

"But can we hide anything from the Lord of the Universe?"

A murmur of dissent rippled through the congregation, and Sarah saw heads shake in the negative.

"No, we can hide nothing from God. Hebrews 4:13 states, *But all things are naked and opened unto the eyes of him with whom we have to do*. So. Answer me this: When we think to 'hide' what is in our hearts from God, are we not deceiving ourselves?"

Something about his question reverberated within Sarah's heart: *Am I trying to hide something from the Lord?*

His next words sucked the breath from her.

"Deceiving *ourselves*. Anything that contradicts God's word is deception—a lie. *Self*-deception, then, is a lie *we* embrace, a falsehood we justify and exalt above God's word."

Pastor Carmichael stopped, stood still, and addressed the congregation.

"My brothers and sisters, please give me your full and undivided attention. I beg you to listen with 'ears that hear,' ears that will receive this spiritual truth: No deception is more powerful than *self-deception*. It is a form of idolatry and must be treated as such—for when we have vaunted our own opinion above the Lord's righteous decrees, are we not lifting our very selves above him? When we have willingly assented to a lie, have we not determined that we know *better than the God of the Universe?*

"Have we decided that our finite minds know more than the One who made us? Is this not vain and fruitless reasoning? The danger of such a rationale cannot be trivialized, for we risk spiritual blindness and alienation from the life of God. The Apostle Paul said it this way in Ephesians 4:

*"This I say therefore, and testify in the Lord,*
*that ye henceforth walk not as other Gentiles walk,*
*in the vanity of their mind,*
*having the understanding darkened,*

*being alienated from the life of God*
*through the ignorance that is in them,*
*because of the blindness of their heart.*

"We see then, that self-deception is great bondage. It is bondage to a falsehood we embrace, a falsehood that contradicts God's word, a falsehood we have exalted over God's word. It is idolatry.

"To briefly summarize, our ongoing study is on 'The Overcoming Christian Life,' and the question we seek to answer is, 'Why do some believers overcome sin in their lives while other believers are defeated?' Our text from Isaiah 61:1, fulfilled in Luke 4:18, tells us that Jesus came *to proclaim liberty to the captives, and the opening of the prison to them that are bound.*

"We may be loosed from the bondages of visible sin, but if we remain the captive of deception, an *invisible* bondage, can we live an overcoming Christian life? No, we cannot. What lurks in the dark corners of our hearts will, in due time, reveal itself on the outside, through our actions and behaviors.

"We shall, in the coming weeks, delve further into what God's word says regarding spiritual bondage, how we can identify such bondages, and how to break free from them. At this time, however, I invite all who know they need salvation—those who wish to receive Christ as both Savior and Lord—to come forward and surrender to the Lord of Lords.

"I also invite any who will acknowledge self-deception in their hearts and repent of the lie undergirding the deception. We are here to pray with you and speak the word of God over your life.

"Come now."

The organist began to play softly and, all across the wide hall, people left their seats and made their way to the front. Sarah sat still, the words Pastor Carmichael had spoken vibrating in her being: "What lurks in the dark corners of our hearts will, in due time, reveal itself on the outside, through our actions and behaviors."

*Lord? You know I love you, but Pastor's words echo what Corrine said to me. Is it true? Have I embraced a deception? Is something displeasing to you lurking deep inside? Lord, please show me. Reveal what is hidden in my heart. Please.*

Sleep was difficult to find again that night. Sarah tossed and turned, visions of the past pressing in on her, demanding her attention. When she did, at last, nod off, it was only to dream, to remember, to relive.

~*~

SARAH HAD CREPT DOWN the back stairs early the following morning. Neither the cleaning maid nor the cook "lived in" any longer, but Sarah knew that the cook, Mrs. Whitten, would be in the kitchen at this hour, preparing breakfast and planning lunch and dinner.

When she pushed open the door at the bottom of the stairs, Mrs. Whitten uttered a gasp. "Child! Ye gave me sech a start. What air ye about, coomin' down here this time o' th' morn?"

Sarah was nervous and scared, but for Maisie's sake she made herself talk. "I need your help, ma'am."

Mrs. Whitten turned from the biscuit dough she was rolling. "What kind o' help?"

"For Maisie . . . and me."

The cook put her fisted hands on her hips. "Maisie? And who might Maisie be?"

"A little girl. Mr. Langston brought her home last evening. She is going to live with us now."

Comprehension bloomed over the cook's face—comprehension followed by anger, then disgust. Within moments, those emotions resigned themselves to regret and caution.

"A little girl, ye say?"

Sarah nodded. "Please. She is so young. He said we are to give Maisie a home here, but . . ." She did not own the words to explain, but she saw that Mrs. Whitten understood her well enough.

The woman dropped her eyes to the brick floor and did not answer.

Sarah whispered, "I thought you might help us? Perhaps tell someone?"

Mrs. Whitten muttered, "I figured what he was doin' t' ye after yer mother passed an' he turned out all th' servants boot me an' Tess. Took our rooms, too, he did."

At thirteen, Sarah, despite the isolation Richard kept her in, had some concepts of justice, mostly derived from books. "Please. Could you tell the police? Will they not help us?"

"Th' police!" Mrs. Whitten slowly shook her head. "Iffen they arrests Mr. Richard, I'll hev no job left. Or iffen he finds out I told on him, he'll toss me that quick, he will. 'Tis sorry I am, bu' I canno' chance losin' m' place here, Miss Sarah. I am bu' a wage day away from losin' m' rooms as 'tis."

The main door to the kitchen flew open under the impact of Richard's boot. When he spied Sarah, he shouted, "Sarah! I went to your room to have you get Maisie up and dressed for breakfast—and imagine my chagrin to find you gone. What are you doing here?"

He looked from Sarah to the cook. "Mrs. Whitten, what is the meaning of this?"

Mrs. Whitten's complexion had turned as pasty as her dough. "Nothin' amiss, Mr. Langston, sir. Miss Sarah coom down just now, askin' for a bit o' dough to play wi'—ist so, Miss Sarah?"

"Yes, Daddy. I woke up early is all."

Richard's mouth flattened into an angry, taut line as he studied Sarah. "All? I doubt it. It is evident to me that you are no longer an innocent child. I can but imagine what newly hatched treachery runs in your veins. And you, Mrs. Whitten? I did not suppose you would be complicit in Sarah's duplicity."

"Bu' Mr. Langston, sir! I ha' done nothing amiss, sir, I swears it!"

He leaned into the woman's face. "Do not give me another reason to doubt you, Mrs. Whitten. I am warning you."

"And you!" He grabbed Sarah by her arm, digging his fingers into it as he yanked her from the kitchen.

"Ow! Daddy, Daddy! You are hurting me!"

Richard rounded on her. "Do not presume to call me 'Daddy' again, Sarah. No, and I am glad you have shown yourself to be as devious and false as all women who have gone before you. Your actions make my decisions much clearer . . . yes, even necessary."

He pulled her along to the staircase. "Because of you, I now have urgent business to attend to. Go up and dress Maisie for breakfast."

Before he released her, he added, "Do not speak to Maisie other than to get her from her bed, dress her appropriately, and guide her to the table. I cannot have you ruining her. Do you understand me?"

"Y-yes, Da—"

He slapped the word from her mouth. "You will call me 'sir' or Mr. Langston. Do you hear me?"

Sarah quailed before him. "Y-yes, sir."

He released her arm and gave her a shove toward the stairs. Sarah ran up them, sobbing as she climbed.

~*~

RICHARD WENT OUT AFTER breakfast and was gone for several hours. During that time, he confined Sarah to her room and placed Maisie in the charge of Tess, the maid.

"Sarah is not to leave her room, even for meals, and Maisie is not to leave your side, Tess."

"Yes, sir." Tess was a slow, plain-faced girl, who never lifted her eyes from the floor in Richard's presence.

When Richard returned that afternoon, he had Tess fetch Sarah from her room and bring her to his study. When Sarah entered, she saw that Richard had a guest. She had not seen the man before. He was, she thought, near the same age as Richard and was, judging by his fastidious dress, a wealthy man.

"This is the girl, Willard. Her name is Sarah."

The man did not rise from his chair. He beckoned to Sarah. "Come here, child."

Sarah stood before him, her hands clasped together in front of her skirts. She glanced nervously at Richard, then back to the man. He was busy studying her, looking her over from head to foot.

"My name is Willard, Sarah. I am happy to meet you."

Sarah dropped an automatic curtsy. Her bob seemed to please Willard, who smiled, his thick mustache lifting to reveal a row of very white, even teeth.

"Nice. Yes, very nice. Tell me, Sarah, are you a pleasant child?"

Sarah blinked in her confusion. "I believe so, sir."

"Are you well-mannered? Biddable?"

"Y-yes, sir."

"Obedient?"

Sarah's eyes misted over. "Yes, sir."

Richard murmured, "I did not misrepresent her to you, did I, Willard?"

"No, no. She is quite lovely. All you said she was."

"Have we an agreement, then?"

"Yes. Quite."

"Very good. I shall have her things sent over first thing tomorrow morning."

"Excellent. Here is the amount we agreed upon." He laid a check on the table beside his chair.

Willard stood and grasped Sarah by the hand. He bent toward her ear and whispered, "Miss Sarah, I am taking you home with me. If you are good and obedient, we shall get on famously. Say goodbye to Mr. Langston and let us be on our way."

Sarah resisted him. "What? No! Daddy! Daddy, do not let him take me away!"

The man pulled her closer. "Now, Sarah, do listen to me: If you fuss or make a scene, I shall have to punish you by shutting you up in a dark room. Do you wish for me to punish you?"

Sarah was near to fainting from fear. "N-no, sir."

"Very good. So. Stand up straight and tall, Sarah, and, with your best manners, say your goodbyes."

Sarah was shaking but, scraping together what courage she could find, she said evenly, "Goodbye, Mr. Langston."

Richard nodded. "Goodbye, Sarah."

WHEN SARAH CAME TO herself, she was shivering all over, partly in fear revisited, partly in vain, futile rage. She was unable to calm herself enough to fall asleep for another hour. Under her breath she whispered an old, familiar mantra.

"I hate them.

"I hate them.

"I hate them.

"I hate them all."

# ℰHAPTER 8

T he calendar slipped from September into October, autumn creeping in with shorter days. Blustery winds and cooling temperatures meant fewer customers to the shop, particularly in the morning and late afternoon. Joy shortened Corrine's hours, so that she arrived at ten o'clock and left an hour before closing. To Sarah's surprise, Corrine was not unhappy with her reduced schedule, although it meant a reduced pay packet as well.

"Keeping our house spick-and-span does not take all my time, but I do appreciate a few more hours in my week to do so," she said, as she left the shop early. "And, of course, I appreciate that my circumstances will change."

"Why, whatever do you mean?" Sarah batted her eyes with all innocence, although she knew exactly what Corrine meant.

Corrine blushed at Sarah's silly drama. "As you alluded to when I returned from our honeymoon, Albert and I wish to start a family. I-I had thought last month . . . but it was a mistaken hope. However, God willing, in the next year we shall have a baby, and then I shall stay home to care for our child."

Sarah's brow crinkled. *Stay home to care for her child? Well, yes, naturally. But how did I not foresee that she would want to resign her position here?*

"Sarah? Does the prospect of Albert and me having a baby not please you?"

Sarah shook herself and laughed. "The prospect pleases me immensely, Corrine, although, if you can believe it, I had not thought it through. I suppose I envisioned us working here together until we were old and gray. Silly of me, to not realize you would want to stay home with your baby, yes? Perhaps I saw myself cuddling your babe all day rather than waiting on customers."

Corrine hugged Sarah around the waist. "Is that so? Well, how does 'Aunt Sarah' strike you?"

"Aunt Sarah! You would grant me such an honor?"

Corrine faced Sarah, her smile both serious and radiant. "To whom else would I grant it? I have many sisters in Christ, but you are the closest thing I have to a real sister, Sarah."

"Oh, Corrine. As you are to me."

~*~

CORRINE AND SARAH ADJUSTED to Corrine's shortened hours. It was on such an afternoon, near closing time, when Sarah was alone in the shop, that the bell jingled, and a lone customer entered. Sarah left the counter to greet the woman. She had taken but a few steps when she recognized the short curly hair and cheery straw hat.

"Ah. Hello. It is Lola, is it not?"

Lola smiled and reached for Sarah's hand. "Yes, and I am glad to see you again, Sarah. Do you recall that rainy day when Meg, Dannie, and I blew into your shop and dripped copious amounts of water upon your carpet? I have thought about you often since then."

"Have you?"

"Oh, my, yes."

Lola retained Sarah's hand between her two, and Sarah stared at Lola's long, lean fingers—strong fingers, fingers accustomed to intricate, repetitive labor. A musician's work.

She switched her gaze from their joined hands to Lola's face. She imagined Lola to be a few years her senior, perhaps thirty years old or a bit more. The woman's eyes held Sarah's with a searching intensity that both startled and intrigued Sarah.

Flustered, she glanced at their hands again, and Lola released her. When Sarah looked up, Lola's lips were curved with good humor.

"I hope you will not consider it forward of me, but when I was last here, I mentioned that I was a musician and hinted that you might like to come hear us play. Do you recall?"

"Oh, yes. I was curious as to the other instruments you play—beside the clarinet."

"In addition to clarinet, I play oboe and piano. Piano is my chief instrument."

"I used to play a little piano. I love Mozart and Chopin. Which composers do you favor?"

It seemed as though Lola always had an amusing secret that played about her mouth. "I am inspired by American pianists, primarily: King Bolden. Scott Joplin. James Johnson. Jelly Roll Morton."

"Jelly Roll Morton. How droll. And I confess I have not heard of even one of these names. How do American pianists compare to the European classicists, do you think?"

Lola considered Sarah's query. "You ask an insightful question, Sarah. Perhaps, in time, American composers of this generation will be as honored as their great predecessors; however, the styles these new composers have spawned are still in their infancy. It may be decades before these musicians are widely received and acclaimed for their genius."

She reached within the pocket of her skirt and withdrew a card. "We are performing at a private party this weekend, Saturday evening. I was hoping you might come?"

"A private concert? How very kind of you to invite me."

"It is not a concert in the formal sense. Consider it a grand *soirée*, an evening musicale for the enjoyment of a select audience. Here is your invitation."

Sarah examined the card. "The, um, musicale does not begin until nine o'clock?"

Another smile. "Many of our engagements begin late."

"Goodness. I am generally abed by ten. This would be quite a departure from my normal schedule."

"Will that be a problem?"

"It is a problem in that I have no transportation at that time of evening. I am sorry. Perhaps when you give an afternoon performance? Do you ever play in the park?"

Lola chuckled. "No, we have not had that honor. But do not concern yourself about transportation. If you will give me your address, I have enlisted the services of a trusted gentleman friend to call for you. I shall be warming up with my fellow musicians, you see, prior to the event; however, I shall be able to see you home myself afterward."

"You are quite generous." Sarah turned the invitation over in her mind, wondering how Rose would view it. At the thought of Rose, Sarah felt the tug of a small concern.

*But Miss Rose would not object to a musical outing, would she? I am confident she will not disapprove.*

"Thank you, Lola. I accept."

"Wonderful. My dear friend, Blake Williams, will call for you. May I have your address?"

Sarah walked to the register, wrote down Palmer House's address, and returned to Lola. "Your friend cannot miss the house—it is the largest on the block and sits on the corner."

"I shall tell him. Shall I tell him to call for you at, say, eight o'clock? Time enough to arrive and get settled before the music begins."

"Yes. Eight o'clock. Thank you again—I am certain to enjoy it."

Lola slipped her arm through Sarah's—as if it were the most natural thing to do—and gently tugged her toward the door. "I must run to a rehearsal, but I am delighted you will come Saturday, Sarah. I look forward to getting to know you better."

"As do I," Sarah answered.

While their arms were still linked, Lola reached out her other hand and touched the heavy braid that crowned Sarah's brow. Her fingers stroked one thick strand. "You have such lovely hair, Sarah. I have been wondering what it feels like—and I am not disappointed. It is wonderfully silky."

Sarah blinked. At Lola's touch, a spark flared between them—as did a disquieting sensation, nearly a memory but not quite clear to Sarah. She inched backward, sliding her arm from Lola's.

Lola laughed and held out her hands in mock contrition "Oh, please pardon my impetuosity. I should not have been so familiar. Do say you forgive me, my new friend?"

Sarah squared her shoulders and smiled. "There is nothing to forgive, Lola. I look forward to the musicale Saturday evening."

"And I also, Sarah."

With a bright laugh and a flick of her hand, Lola bid Sarah goodbye and left the shop.

Sarah stared after Lola's departing figure for many moments. She was left wondering why Lola's touch had stirred her.

~*~

AFTER DINNER, WHEN THE dishes were cleared away and the dining room and kitchen tidied up, Billy, Marit, and their little brood retired to their cottage at the back of Palmer House's lot. Rose, the girls, and Mr. Wheatley gathered in Palmer House's great room to spend a pleasant evening together, reading, mending, playing games, and visiting.

Rose was ensconced in her favorite overstuffed chair when Sarah approached her.

"Miss Rose? May I have a moment of your time?"

Rose stood and hugged Sarah. "For you, my precious daughter, I would give whatever you ask. Shall we retire to the parlor?"

When they had settled themselves in the parlor, Sarah began, "I have made a new friend, Miss Rose. Her name is Lorraine. She and her friends took shelter in the shop during a rainstorm a few weeks past. She dropped by again today just before closing."

"I am happy for you, Sarah. Would you like to invite her to dinner?"

Sarah hesitated for the briefest moment. "Why, yes, I suppose I would sometime soon. However, Lola—for that is what her friends call her—has invited me to a musicale Saturday evening."

"How lovely."

"I think so, too. Unhappily, the musicale does not begin until nine o'clock." She handed Rose the invitation.

Rose studied the card, but her surprise was evident. "Goodness. Nine is quite late to begin. I cannot imagine how you could return home until much later."

"I agree. I could be out until midnight or later."

Rose studied Sarah. "Does your friend, Lola, have a motor car at her disposal?"

"She has arranged for a gentleman friend by the name of Blake Williams to escort me. He will call for me at eight o'clock."

"I am happy to hear you will have an escort, but will Lola not be with him when he calls for you?"

"Not before the concert. You see, she is one of the musicians, and she must rehearse before the start of the performance."

Rose shifted in her chair, and she perused the invitation again. "Where is this concert to be held, Sarah?"

"I forgot to ask, Miss Rose."

"And you have not met this man, Mr. Williams, who will call for you?"

"No, ma'am. However, Lola assured me that he was a trusted acquaintance. A gentleman."

Rose looked into Sarah's face, searching it. "This is quite unusual, Sarah. A man you have never met. A concert with no location. I confess my concern."

Sarah licked her lips. "I would, of course, invite Mr. Williams in to meet you. You may interview him and judge his suitability yourself—I would welcome your opinion and approbation, actually. And he will surely know the concert's location."

Rose continued to seek something in Sarah's eyes. Or perhaps she was thinking or praying, Sarah could not decide—however, she was startled by Rose's next question.

"Will alcohol be served at this event, Sarah?"

Sarah's brows shot skyward. "I should think not, Miss Rose. Alcohol has been prohibited in Colorado for three years. I cannot believe Lola— Lorraine—would have an association with illegal activities."

Rose looked down to her folded hands. "My spirit is unsettled, Sarah, perhaps needlessly, but I have learned to trust the whispers of the Spirit within me. And the lateness of the event does extend hours beyond our curfew."

Sarah was taken aback by the mention of curfew and bristled. "Miss Rose, I am, as you know, twenty-eight years old, no longer one of the Palmer House girls. As one of your assistants in the house, I assumed that I would be exempt from the girls' curfew and be allowed the same liberties as I would have if I lived elsewhere."

A flicker of surprise (and hurt?) crossed Rose's face before the older woman resolved her expression into placid lines.

"You are quite right, Sarah. I have been accustomed to treating you as one of the girls. I apologize. If the gentleman will make himself known to us when he calls for you—and if I know where the concert will be held—my concerns for you should be satisfied."

"Thank you, Miss Rose." But the prick of Sarah's conscience was too sharp to ignore. She sighed. "Goodness. I-I apologize to you for my tone a moment past. It was unnecessary and hurtful. I am very sorry."

Rose patted Sarah's hand. "I forgive you, Sarah. I love you, and I take responsibility for my part in our momentary disagreement. I know you do not mean to wound with your words."

"I love you, too, Miss Rose."

As they stood and embraced, Sarah ran Rose's last comment through her mind: *I know you do not mean to wound with your words.*

*Is that not what Corrine said?*

# CHAPTER 9

P almer House was all atwitter Saturday evening as Sarah prepared to attend her friend's musicale. Sarah was to wear her best dress, an elegant hand-me-down from Emily Van der Pol's women's group—a soft, midnight-blue gossamer gown with exquisite jet beading along the high neckline and around the embroidered bodice.

Ruth and Pansy fussed over Sarah's toilette and buttoned every one of the lengthy line of petite jet buttons down Sarah's back and along her tight gigot sleeves. Blythe and Frances polished Sarah's black boots until they shone like mirrors—then insisted on buttoning them up Sarah's slim ankles for her.

"What will you do with your hair, Sarah?" Frances asked.

"My hair? Why, nothing out of the ordinary, really. I shall freshly braid it and wear it as I always do."

"Perhaps a flower?" Pansy proposed.

"A posy from Pansy?" Sarah teased.

"May I suggest a rose from Rose?" a familiar voice announced in the doorway. "I must credit Mr. Wheatley for this beauty, though. It was he, not I, who cut it and trimmed off the thorns for you."

The girls gushed their approval over the soft yellow bloom.

"It is the perfect color," Ruth pronounced.

Sarah set to work and, within a few minutes, had achieved the raven crown above the striking peak in her hairline. When she had finished, Rose twined the rose's stem into Sarah's thick strands, nestling the yellow bloom within her plaited tresses.

Sarah stared in the mirror. "I am presentable but, sadly, quite out of fashion."

"Well, I do not give a fig for what fashion dictates," Frances retorted. "You will outshine every woman there."

"Oh, yes. You are *so* beautiful, Sarah," Blythe sighed.

Blythe's adoring comment made the girls giggle, but Rose agreed with her. "Sarah is beautiful inside *and* out. True beauty is unfading; it blossoms on the inside and shines forth on the outside."

Sarah beamed at her. "And that is why you will always be a great beauty, Miss Rose."

The girls laughed when Rose blushed. "Heavens. How you turn this old woman's head, Sarah."

When the girls declared Sarah "perfect," she took up her shawl, and they traipsed downstairs together.

Mr. Wheatley, stooped and frail, leaned up against the balustrade, waiting for Sarah to come down. His incorrigible white hair stuck out from his head in fluffy clumps; his bushy white brows resembled the two lesser satellites of his tufted pate, but his old eyes shone with approval when Sarah descended.

"A rare one, our Sarah," he mumbled.

Sarah put her cheek to his. "I take only your compliments to heart, my sweet friend."

"We been through a lot together, missy."

"I could not have endured those early days without your shoulder to lean on, dear Mr. Wheatley."

Sarah teared up, and he patted her back. "There, there."

Blythe held out her hankie.

"Do not cry, Sarah. The young gentleman will be here directly."

Pansy giggled. "You do not want to appear with a red nose, do you?"

Sarah sniffed back her tears. "Most certainly not."

SPEAKING OF THE YOUNG gentleman . . .

When Blake Williams bounded up the porch steps and dropped the heavy brass knocker on the solid front door, the sound reverberated throughout what he assumed was the house's foyer. He was perplexed, then, as he languished several minutes with no response.

*Could my knock have gone unnoticed?*

He had his answer when a grizzled octogenarian with a head of uncommonly wild hair hauled the door open at a tedious rate and—just as tediously—examined him from head to toe.

"Good evening, young sir."

*Young sir? Who says that these days?*

Besides which, Blake could read the old man's thoughts like a book: *A dandy,* Blake was confident the butler had concluded from his protracted evaluation.

Blake sniffed. *Dandy, indeed. I shall take that as a compliment— coming from an old geezer such as this.*

Blake was confident that he was outfitted in the latest of evening fashion: snowy-white dress shirt topped by charcoal-gray sateen vest, black evening coat with tails, and scarlet tie. White spats over glossy black shoes peeped from beneath the hem of his charcoal trousers. He removed his sleek top hat and placed it in the servant's hands.

"Good evening. Blake Williams calling for Miss Sarah Ellinger."

"This way, sir."

Blake entered the house, waited *an eon* for the aging butler to close the door behind them and lead the way, then he followed the man—at an injured snail's pace—through the wide entryway, then to the right into the house's great room . . . where at least a dozen appraising faces turned their focus on him, all female with the exception of one male.

Blake could not know that Marit, after tucking her children into their beds, had declared she would not miss viewing the gentleman caller "for the vorld," nor could he know that her husband (not to be left out of such exciting doings) had accompanied her. The unsuspecting Blake only knew that around twelve sets of eyes stared without comment or expression at their polished—and quite bemused—visitor.

A slender, plainly dressed matron, with calm eyes and a sweet smile, stood and greeted him. "Good evening, Mr. Williams. I am Mrs. Rose Thoresen. Welcome to our home."

Blake executed a perfect bow. "Blake Williams, at your service, Mrs. Thoresen. It is a pleasure to make your acquaintance."

He scanned the room and its unpretentious furnishings, taking in the bevy of young women (as modestly attired as Mrs. Thoresen), and wondered with idle curiosity with which of these simple *naïfs* he had been saddled. He attempted to identify his objective unobtrusively but failed in spectacular fashion—as the amused exchanges between the girls announced.

"Mr. Williams, will you sit with us?"

Blake jerked his attention back to the matron. She indicated a chair of bulging springs and dubious origin—a chair to which Blake was loath to trust his freshly pressed trousers.

And he had not intended to dally about; however, he could find no well-mannered way to decline her invitation—an amiable enough request—which was not, in patent actuality, a *request* he could refuse.

"Thank you, madam."

As Blake assumed the indicated seat, he suffered an uncomfortable revelation: He would not be leaving in the expedited fashion he had planned on. No. He was about to be questioned.

*Questioned?* He swore under his breath while preserving his smile. *Interrogated, I should think! This old biddy will press and prod me like a Christmas goose—while the taxi's meter runs unabated, into the bargain. Thank you kindly, Lola.*

"Er, you have a charming house, Mrs. Thoresen."

"You are kind. It is a pleasant home for our family."

*Family?*

Perplexed, and experiencing a sensation much as a bug under glass might, Blake skimmed the room once more. Oh, without a doubt: Every eye was fastened upon him.

He coughed politely. "I see. You are Miss Ellinger's mother, then?"

Giggles warbled among the watching women, but the penetrating gaze of the sole man in the room (other than that decrepit old husk of a butler still holding his hat) skewered Blake with blatant distrust.

Blake swallowed. *I do hope that clod is not Miss Ellinger's brother. Ye gads! He is half the size of a mountain. I should not wish to cross him.*

The matron smiled and repeated his question. "Am I Sarah's mother? Not directly, no. However, Sarah is the daughter of my heart."

Blake nodded. "I understand." *What? No, I do not understand.*

"You see, we live as a family here at Palmer House, although none of us are related by blood."

"Ah, of course." *The devil, you say—I have stumbled into a commune. A cult!*

"Mr. Williams, would you tell me something of yourself?"

"Myself?" Blake's mind momentarily shut down.

"Yes, if you please."

Again, not a request to be passed over.

"Certainly, madam." *Mind how you go, Blake, my boy. Do not make a hash of this.*

"I was born and raised in Denver, Mrs. Thoresen. My family made its fortune in timber, but we now operate a number of financial institutions. Perhaps you have heard of us? Williams Savings and Loan?"

"I believe so, yes."

"Ah, good, good. Well, I studied business for two years in Boston and now work in the family enterprise."

"How nice. And you are Miss Ellinger's escort for the evening?"

"I—" *Careful, Blake.* "Miss Ellinger is, technically, Lola's—that is, Miss Pritchard's guest. But as Miss Pritchard will be performing, I have hired a car and have agreed to escort Miss Ellinger to the, er, performance."

"The invitation did not provide a location."

"It is the private home of a well-known family. I should be happy to write out the address if you wish, madam?"

"Yes, thank you. That would be very kind of you." *Surely, you jest.*

But she did not. He dutifully took paper and pen from her and scribbled the address.

"And you will also be bringing Miss Ellinger home?"

"Either I or Miss Pritchard will hire a car to bring her home."

"And what time shall we expect you, Mr. Williams?"

*Blast it all, Lola!* But he smiled amiably and nodded.

"Do you have a preferred time, madam?"

Because, what else could he say?

"I think midnight appropriate, but only given the late start of the concert."

*Concert? Late start? Do play along, Blake. The taxi's meter is running.*

He inclined his head. "Of course. As you wish, Mrs. Thoresen."

The matron stood and extended a handshake. "It was very nice meeting you, Mr. Williams."

Blake stood, took her hand, and bowed over her fingers. "Again, it was my pleasure, Mrs. Thoresen."

"And may I introduce Miss Ellinger?"

*Heavenly days. At last!*

He unbent and discovered a raven-haired beauty at his elbow. For a moment he was struck dumb by her loveliness and her simple, tasteful—albeit *dated*—attire.

"Blake Williams, at your service, Miss Ellinger."

"How do you do, Mr. Williams?"

"Quite well, thank you."

Every eye in the room watched with vicarious enthusiasm.

*Good grief; what an exposition.*

"Shall we be on our way, Miss Ellinger?"

"Yes. I am ready."

"And do you have your invitation, Miss Ellinger?"

"I do, thank you."

Blake retrieved his hat from the doddering old butler and took Sarah's arm. He managed to maintain his composure as they waited for the "dry old stick" to totter to the door and wrench it open with the last of his strength.

When Blake was assured the elderly man would not, from the effort, fall dead at his feet, he escorted Sarah down the long walkway and beyond the gate. There, he released her arm and held the door for her to climb into the taxi's back seat. Then he joined her.

Blake Williams held his middle, chuckling, then laughing aloud as the cab pulled away. "Well! What an ordeal and a spectacle that was. It was good for a hoot, but I am relieved to have it behind me."

Sarah could think of no response, so an uncomfortable silence followed. She studied him out of the corner of her eye. After minutes had passed, she ventured to speak on what she hoped was a safe topic. "How long have you known Miss Pritchard, Mr. Williams?"

"Please call me Blake. Mr. Williams is my father. And by the by? No one calls Lola 'Miss Pritchard' or even Lorraine."

Sarah cleared her throat. "I see. Ah, can you say how far our drive is . . . Blake?"

"Not far. Perhaps another twenty minutes. I am certain you are familiar with our destination—the Polk-Stafford mansion?"

"Oh, my goodness. We are going there?"

"Sure. Justin Stafford hosts such 'dos' most Saturdays."

"Dos?"

"Yes. Private parties."

"By parties, you do mean musicales, yes?"

He chuckled again. "I suppose one could call them that." He slid an ornate case from his breast pocket, clicked it open, and offered the case to her. "Cigarette?"

"No, thank you." Sarah frowned. Nothing Blake Williams said or did—now that they were out from under Miss Rose's scrutiny—seemed what it had been inside Palmer House. Nothing felt 'right.'

*What in the world have I gotten myself into?*

He removed a cigarette for himself, tapped it on the case, and studied her as he lit it. "I must confess, you are every bit the looker Lola said you were—shining hair like black silk, a fine figure, and a come-hither gleam in your eye. I can imagine how you drive men wild simply by walking into the room. Why, if I were—"

"Mr. Williams, I believe I have made a mistake. Please tell the driver to stop the car immediately. I wish to get out."

But, rather than compliance, her demand was met with laughter and a good-natured pat on her hand. "Sarah, do say you are not serious?"

"I most certainly am." Sarah yanked her hand from under his and rapped on the window between them and the driver. "Stop the car, please. Stop, I say."

Alerted to her request, the driver maneuvered toward the edge of the roadway.

"My dear girl, please calm yourself."

"Do not patronize me, Mr. Williams. I wish to get out."

As the car came to a standstill, Sarah reached for the door and pulled on the handle. Blake forestalled her by reaching across her and jerking the door shut.

"Sarah, you are behaving like a child."

Sarah drew herself up. "Mr. Williams, we are not familiar enough for you to offer such an opinion—you who are years my junior besides."

He chuckled and shook his head. "And yet it seems that I just did. But do hear me out, Sarah: My compliments were honest and sincere. They contained no threat; neither do you have anything to fear from me. To put it plainly, you are not my type."

Sarah pulled the door handle again—and he yanked it shut.

"Let go! Let me out!"

"Listen to me, you spoilt girl: I am doing Lola a favor by escorting you to this party, and I guarantee that she will be quite cross with me if you decide not to come. However, if you still wish to return home, I shall have the driver turn around and take us there, and I shall see you safely to your door. I really *will not* have it said that I left you by the side of the road in the dark."

He let go of the door. "Now. Have you quite finished your fit?"

Sarah's mouth hung agape. She had not been spoken to with such brash familiarity in years.

"Miss Ellinger? Do you wish to return to that oversized dormitory you call Palmer House and the annoying warden who runs it, or will you allow me to escort you to the party?"

Sarah could have given the word for him to take her home; she could have minded the alarms in her head—but she did not. Concerned that Lola would be "quite cross" with Blake if she did not attend the event, she tipped her chin up and stared straight ahead.

"In future, kindly keep your personal observations to yourself."

Blake snorted. "As you wish, princess."

He rapped the window. "Drive on, please."

~*~

THE POLK-STAFFORD MANOR sat upon a low hill, dominating a slice of the Denver skyline. The house was ablaze with lights, and vehicles lined the winding road leading up to the estate proper. Each motor car idled briefly at a guarded gate; when the gate opened, the car continued on up the lane to the house.

As their taxi neared the gate, Blake nudged Sarah. "Give me your invitation, please."

The taxi paused before the closed gate. Blake rolled down his window and handed his and Sarah's invitations to a guard. The guard looked inside their vehicle to count the number of passengers, then examined the invitations.

As he handed them back, he murmured, "Have a good evening, sir, miss."

A second guard rolled the gate aside and the taxi drove through.

"I am surprised that the invitations do not contain more than a date and time."

"Quite an intentional precaution. Those who are given invites know the location. If the wrong sort of people were to get hold of an invitation and it contained an address? Why, unwelcome visitors might crash the party."

His answer confused Sarah: precaution? wrong sort of people? "crash" the party? She found herself so mystified that she kept her further questions to herself.

When they crested the low summit, the driver pulled in front of the house under a well-lit awning. A house servant in evening attire opened the door and assisted Sarah from the car while Blake paid the driver.

Sarah squinted under the bright lights, but her first impression was of dozens of elegantly gowned women and exquisitely dressed men either conversing in clusters or ascending the steps to the house. Her second thought was how out of place she was—and not merely in her outmoded dress.

*I surely do not belong here.*

She had no opportunity to turn back, however. Blake had dismissed the driver; he then took her by the elbow and steered her toward the steps up to the house. At the base of the steps, two additional male servants waited.

"Good evening, Mr. Williams."

Blake nodded and, for the second time, handed over their invitations. When the servant handed them back, Blake told Sarah, "Keep your invitation in your handbag."

"All right."

She tucked the card into her reticule, then he took her arm. Blake was obviously familiar with where they were going: They climbed the steps into the house, walked down a long hallway, turned right, and passed through a set of open, oversized double doors. They stepped into an immense Rococo-style ballroom. The ballroom's ceiling rose high above them in an ornate dome. White pillars, shooting from the floor up to a high ceiling, supported the dome.

Grand murals in light pastels adorned the walls, the ceiling, and the dome's underside; stained glass windows had been set into the dome around its apex. Elaborate curves and scrolling patterns of fish, shells, leaves, and flowers—trimmed in gold—appeared in every wainscot, chair rail, and crown molding.

Sarah had never seen anything like it.

Intimate cloth-covered tables lined the perimeter of the ballroom, leaving the center open. At the back of the room she spotted a stage, elevated perhaps three feet, so that it overlooked the room. The ballroom was already crowded with affluent young men and women—and it struck Sarah that not a soul present could have been over forty years old. A haze hung in the air as many of the attendees—even the women—smoked cigarettes. Waiters circulated among the crush carrying silver platters loaded with tumblers of punch.

Blake had Sarah by her elbow; he steered her with commendable expertise across the room. He stopped perhaps ten feet from a piano sitting upon the stage; he indicated one of the small tables and pulled out a chair for her.

"Lola had Justin set aside this table for you."

A placard of heavy stationery read, "Reserved."

"W-will you leave me here by myself?"

"Not if you do not wish me to. However, I shall be joined by a friend."

Sarah nodded and sat down. She wanted to leave this place and flee down the hillside, but she could not overcome her culpability for the disappointment Lola would be certain to feel should she retire before the ensemble's performance. Besides which, she saw so many people of interest around her.

"Would you care for something to drink?"

Sarah was distracted but thirsty. "Yes, please."

While he was gone, she studied the partygoers, wondering at their eclectic dress and comportment.

When Blake set a tall glass of fruity-looking punch in front of her, Sarah took it and swallowed down a mouthful. It *was* punch, but it had been liberally dosed with alcohol. Sarah had not taken a drink since she left Corinth—ten years ago. As unexpected fire hit the back of her throat, she choked and coughed.

Blake laughed. "Careful. You will need to pace yourself if you hope to last the evening."

Sarah pushed the glass away. "I do not drink alcohol, Mr. Williams. Why did you not tell me they would be serving alcohol? It is illegal!"

"Not illegal to drink. Only illegal to make, import, transport, and sell. See? Nothing illegal happening here."

Sarah sputtered her objections. "But still! You should have told me, should have told Miss Rose!"

"Miss Rose?"

"Mrs. Thoresen."

He laughed again. "Tell that old fussbudget? Nothing doing."

"I shall thank you to speak of her with respect."

Blake shook his head. "Relax, Sarah. Have a good time. I doubt you get out much, based on the grilling I took." He put his head to one side. "Are you truly this naïve? Did you not understand when I told you why the address was not included on the invitation?"

*Quite the intentional precaution. Those who are given invites know the location. If the wrong sort of people were to get hold of an invitation that contained an address? Why, unwelcome visitors might crash the party.*

Sarah reddened. "Unwelcome visitors. You were speaking of the police—and yet, you insisted, 'Nothing illegal happening here.'"

Blake shrugged, then waved at a man he spotted across the room. "Pardon me. I shall return shortly." Sarah's eyes followed him across the floor where he met and embraced the man he'd seen. They talked a few minutes, Blake occasionally gesturing in her direction, until they headed her way, pushing through the throng to reach her.

"Miss Ellinger, may I present my dear friend, Juan de la Vega."

"How do you do," Sarah murmured.

Blake's friend had the dark good looks of a Spaniard, but something about him seemed "off": He was too handsome in a vain, coquettish way, his hands soft and smooth, his affectations careful and coy.

And his lips were stained red.

He smirked at Sarah as though discerning her thoughts and slid his arm through Blake's in a possessive manner. "Your gown is lovely, *señorita,* the beading the perfect *accesorio* to your beautiful raven coronet . . . even if the style of dress did pass out of fashion a decade ago."

"Mind your claws, Juan," Blake chided him. "She is Lola's new friend."

"Oh, indeed?" He swept his eyes over Sarah once more. "This could prove to be an entertaining evening after all."

Blake cut him off. "Ah. The music is about to begin."

An effete gentleman paraded onto the stage to the applause and catcalls of the crowd. He bowed five or more times before he held out his hands for quiet.

"Ladies and gentlemen, welcome to this evening's entertainment. May I present, for your listening and dancing pleasure, *The Pythia.*"

Pythia? Sarah searched her memories for the meaning of the word.

*It is a Greek word, I believe*, she told herself, but she had nothing more to add to its origins.

Wild applause sounded around the room, and Sarah's mouth fell open as the ensemble emerged from behind a curtain. Lola appeared on stage first, smiling, waving, blowing kisses to the crowd. She was dressed in a sleeveless, shimmering sheath of silver; a gauzy blood-red scarf wound around her neck and trailed down past her waist. Meg, Dannie, and a third woman followed her. Meg took up a trumpet, Dannie an upright bass, and the stranger a clarinet.

Lola spotted Sarah, smiled, and blew a kiss in her direction, too. Then she seated herself at the piano and, with her right hand in the air and her left on the keyboard, pounded out a slow, rhythmic bass line that Dannie took up on the bass. Within seconds the crowd recognized the tune and cheered. Lola brought her right hand to the piano with a dramatic gesture, and the song broke into a full, undulating swing.

Couples flooded the ballroom floor, and Blake and Juan wandered off, leaving Sarah by herself. Sarah watched the dancers, fascinated by the glamor and movement. The band moved to its next number, *Some of These Days*, followed by *Memphis Blues*. The intensity of dancing increased when Lola's band hammered out *Darktown Strutters' Ball*.

Sarah lost track of which songs and how many the band played until Lola began to sing, *I Ain't Got Nobody*. She turned her head and glanced at Sarah, crooning the words, *Won't somebody take a chance with me?*

Sarah looked away, blushing—straight into the smirking faces of Blake and Juan where they stood across the dancefloor. Embarrassed and irritated, she stared at her hands.

*What am I doing in this place?*

The band played another hour before ending their set to enthusiastic applause. Moments later, Lola joined Sarah at her table.

"Hello, darling." She placed her cheek against Sarah's before sitting down. From a faux-jeweled handbag she placed on the table, Lola withdrew a package of cigarettes and an ebony cigarette holder.

"I am so glad you came. Well, what do you think of our little 'musicale'?"

While Lola fitted a cigarette to the holder and lit it, Sarah scrambled to find a safe topic. "The name of your ensemble? The Pythia, is it? Does the name hold significance?"

Lola drew on the long holder and exhaled smoke from her nose. "A great deal of significance, I should think. The Pythia was the high priestess of the Temple of Apollo in ancient Greece. She was a prophetess, also known as the Oracle of Delphi. We chose the name for that reason."

Lola inhaled, exhaled, blew the smoke away, and coughed to clear her throat. "For a Greek woman of that time, the role of priestess was a means of holding a respected position in society—on her own merits, you see. She had the right to own property in her own name. She earned her own money, lived in her own house or rooms, and went about freely in public. She was not accountable to a husband's will or defined by his position."

"Why is this significant to you?"

Lola laughed softly. "Do not all humans aspire to freedom? Does a woman wish for less independence than a man simply because she has suffered the cosmic misfortune of having been born female? Or are you, Sarah, one of those women who requires a man to validate her thoughts, her voice, her choices? Perhaps even her emotions?"

Lola's words stunned Sarah—they spoke to many of the unarticulated feelings she harbored within her breast.

Lola smiled. "I see I have awakened something in you. But to answer your question more fully, The Pythia of Apollo was the epitome of female independence in the Greek Empire, and she was attended by three other priestesses. Our little 'ensemble' as you call it, turns upon my leadership."

She shrugged. "You could say that I am The Pythia, and Meg, Gina, and Dannie are my attending priestesses. Only musically, of course."

Sarah's eyes followed Dannie and Meg as they mingled with friends. Dannie's appearance on stage had struck Sarah the hardest. Her short hair was slicked back with hair pomade, and she was dressed, head to toe, as a man in evening wear. Meg leaned into Dannie, and Dannie had her arm about Meg much as a man might hold a woman to his side.

"Do Meg and Dannie have a close friendship?"

"Theirs is an intimate relationship. What is called a Wellesley marriage," Lola remarked.

"I am unfamiliar with that term," but she comprehended Lola's meaning. In the Corinth Gentleman's Club, Sarah had seen two girls turn to each other for comfort, affection, and . . . physical intimacy. They had not, however, dressed or acted as Dannie did.

That would not have been allowed in the male-dominated market.

"I imagine you are unfamiliar with many things in my circle, but I should love to educate you." Lola laid her fingers on the back of Sarah's hand and lightly caressed it.

Sarah stared at their hands, understanding dawning on her. "I-I am not like that, Lola. I am not like you—not how you want me to be . . . with you."

Lola turned Sarah's hand over and her thumb stroked Sarah's palm. "Are you not, indeed?"

Sarah jerked her hand away. "No. No, I am not."

Lola placed her elbows on the little table, rested her chin upon her hands, and leaned very close to Sarah. "And yet I am certain you have no inclination toward the male gender, am I correct?"

"Be that as it may—"

"I am glad you admit to it."

"I am not hiding it," Sarah retorted. "I have told my friends that I shall not marry."

Lola continued to consider her. "When I look at you, I see a freshness, a purity in your mien more suited to a woman some years younger than your age. That wholesomeness is what attracted me to you initially. I see now that you are a much more complex woman. Tell me, Sarah, are you as innocent as you seem?"

Sarah stared back. "No."

*Oh, I could tell you tales that would dash that image of my purity to dust, Lola—but merely asking about my past does not entitle you to my trust.*

"Ah. You have secrets."

Sarah sighed. "I appreciate your invitation this evening, but I should be going. Would you take me home, now?"

Lola seemed surprised. "We have two more sets to play. The party does not usually break up until near three in the morning."

"What? Three in the morning? But Blake assured Miss Rose that you would have me home by midnight."

Lola laughed. "Oh, my dear—what *was* he thinking? I do apologize, but Justin's parties are only warming up at midnight, as Blake knows full well. Perhaps he thought it wiser to ask forgiveness than permission." She gave a little flip of her hand. "Please do not fret yourself. I shall hire a taxi for us and see you safely home after our last set."

Sarah said through clenched teeth, "I am sorry to inconvenience you, Lola, but Miss Rose is expecting me at midnight."

Lola leaned back, placed a fresh cigarette in her holder, and lit it. As she drew on the holder, the cigarette's ember glowed a bright red. She inhaled slowly, seductively, then released the smoke through her parted lips. All the while, she considered Sarah.

"I am a bit perplexed, Sarah."

Mesmerized, Sarah stared at the smoke coiling around Lola's features, how she sucked it back into her mouth and caused it to swirl out her nose once more.

"Uh, perplexed? About what?"

"Why, about you, of course. I had thought you a grown woman, an adult."

Sarah's eyes narrowed. "You are playing at word games, attempting to provoke me."

"Provoke you? No. Plumb the depths of this person known as Sarah Ellinger? Yes. I want to know the authentic person you are, Sarah, and so I probe and ask questions."

Her mouth pulled on the ebony holder. "I said I had thought you a grown woman—an adult who makes her own choices. After all, the mark of maturity and independence is found in knowing one's own mind, making one's own decisions, and living with those choices, is it not?"

Sarah knew what Lola was implying. "I know my own mind, and I do make my own choices. To be clear, I have *chosen* to live within certain limits and restrictions—for my own safety and for my spiritual growth and health."

"Safety? Spiritual growth and health? You have given this Miss Rose a great deal of authority over your life. Forgive me for saying so, but how does this further your independence and happiness?"

Lola again drew on her cigarette and exhaled the smoke. It was a slow and practiced process, one from which Sarah could not take her eyes.

"I do not live for my own independence and happiness, Lola."

Lola caught a signal out of the corner of her eye. She waved her acknowledgement and stubbed out the remainder of her cigarette.

As she stood, she smiled at Sarah. "Dear me. As fascinating as this is, it is time to play again. I hope we can continue our conversation during our next break."

Without warning, she leaned toward Sarah, brushed a kiss across her cheek, then spun on her heel and returned to the stage. The band commenced their next set, and Sarah noted Lola watching her, an enigmatic smile playing about her mouth, her eyes questing, seeking for something.

Sarah swallowed and touched the spot where Lola's lips had met her skin.

# CHAPTER 10

Sarah tore her attention away from the band and from Lola; the room seemed to pulse with music, movement, and raucous laughter. Her head pounded with the noise and chaos. Even her eyes throbbed, and she rubbed them with her forefinger and thumb.

*I want to go home.*

She stood, gathered her shawl and reticule, and began to push and thread her way through the crowded dance floor to the other side of the ballroom where she had last seen Blake. It took her ten minutes to find him, standing behind a pillar with Juan. She turned her eyes away from what they were doing before she spoke.

"Pardon me, Blake. It is near twelve o'clock. Would you kindly take me home?"

Juan, who was glued to Blake's side, pursed his reddened lips and tittered. "Oooh, tell us, dear Sarah, are you the Cinderella to our little *soirée?* When the clock strikes midnight, will you flee the ball and lose one glass slipper? Will your coach turn into a pumpkin and your coachman into a mouse?" He raked his eyes over Blake. "Because I can tell you that *this* coachman is no mouse. No, indeed."

Juan growled low in his throat like a cat, and Blake stroked his cheek. "Patience, my pretty."

Juan pouted. "How can I be patient, darling boy, when you tease me so?"

Sarah forced down the gorge rising in her throat and the nausea that threatened to bring up the contents of her stomach. "Please. Please take me home, Blake."

Blake raised his brows. "As I told your Mrs. Thoresen, you are, technically, Lola's guest. She has said she will take you home." He inclined his head toward Juan, who preened and rubbed his jaw along Blake's shoulder. "As you can see, I have more . . . pressing obligations."

"But Lola will not finish for several more hours."

Blake shrugged. "Then I suggest you enjoy the evening."

"Yes," Juan purred, "enjoy the evening. I know *I shall.*"

Clutching her shawl about her, Sarah turned from them and forced her way past the couples along the edge of the dance floor, making slow progress toward the ballroom entrance. When she had cleared the press of dancers, she searched for one of the house servants.

*There.* Outside the double doors.

She approached him. "Excuse me," she shouted over the noise of the music.

"Yes, miss?"

"Could you call me a taxi?"

"Yes, miss."

Sarah had a sudden recollection of Blake handing the taxi driver a wad of cash.

"No. That is, wait one moment, please." She dug in her reticule, knowing before she reached her coin purse that she had exactly twenty-five cents in it. She opened it anyway.

The servant observed her frantic search and smirked. "Do you still wish me to call a cab, miss?"

"No. Thank you."

*I do not have the money for a cab. What can I do? Who could I call? Lord, please help me!*

One name, one less-than-desirable—albeit, *acceptable*—solution, came to mind, but she dreaded the repercussions.

*You must swallow your pride, Sarah,* she told herself. *You have no other option.*

Sarah straightened and composed herself. Addressing the servant again, she said, "Please show me where I might use a telephone."

"This way, miss."

He led her farther down the hallway to a lobby furnished with upholstered settees and low coffee tables. A man and a woman, locked in passionate embrace, occupied one of the divans.

The servant cleared his throat. "Pardon me."

The couple broke apart, the woman breathless and laughing. Without a word, they sauntered from the room, hand in hand. Sarah could hear the woman giggling as they meandered away.

"The telephone is just there, miss."

He indicated a cozy niche in the corner of the room occupied by a petite table and padded stool. Sarah spied a gilt-and-ivory telephone and exhaled her relief.

"Thank you."

She sat down on the stool and did not raise the telephone's receiver to her ear. Instead, she folded her hands and stared at them.

"Lord, I am sorry I came tonight. Miss Rose was right to feel concerned, and I should have heeded her wisdom . . . I should have heeded *you* in the cab, and I should have gone home then. I am, therefore, in a predicament of my own making, but I am asking: *Please*. Please grant me favor."

Sighing, she lifted the receiver. When the operator came on, she said, "Keystone 4672, please."

"I shall ring that number, ma'am."

From a far distance, Sarah listened to the rings.

One. Two. Three.

The telephone was in the kitchen. Was it loud enough to awaken them? Would anyone answer?

Four. Five. Six. Seven.

The line crackled and a sleepy voice croaked, "O'Dell here."

Sarah swallowed. "Mr. O'Dell, this is Sarah Ellinger. I am very sorry to ring you so late—"

"Is it Mother Rose? Is she all right?"

"She is well, Mr. O'Dell. I am not calling about her. It is I . . . who am in need of assistance."

"Of course. What is it, Miss Ellinger?"

"I-I am in a bit of a quandary, Mr. O'Dell. I find that I cannot get home."

His voice sharpened. "It has gone midnight. Where are you?"

She did not recall the address, so she answered, "The Polk-Stafford estate."

The chastising silence from the other end of the line told Sarah that O'Dell not only knew her location but likely what kind of "quandary" she found herself in.

Very softly, Sarah asked, "Mr. O'Dell? Could you come get me?"

"Yes. It will take me twenty or thirty minutes. Will you be all right until then?"

"I think so."

"Where shall I look for you?"

Sarah recalled the sloping drive and the gate at the bottom of the hill. She did not relish walking down the drive in the dark nor waiting alone outside the gate, but neither would O'Dell be allowed through the gate without an invitation.

"Just outside the gate."

"Is the gate manned?"

"Yes."

"Stay near the guards, Miss Ellinger. Let them know you are there and waiting for me. They will watch over you until I arrive."

"Yes, sir."

Sarah thought he was going to ring off but, following a breathy pause, he added, "We shall talk after I see you home."

Sarah carefully replaced the ornate receiver and stood up.

*Twenty or thirty minutes. I could wait here for half of that.*

*No*, a voice whispered to her. *Leave this place.*

It may as well have been the Lord's voice speaking to Lot.

She did not argue. "Yes, Lord."

She gathered her shawl and reticule and walked down the long hallway, past the ballroom, toward the doors by which she and Blake had entered.

~*~

SARAH WAS SHIVERING WITH cold and pain when O'Dell's Bergdoll came into view.

She had left the house and found her way down the drive in the dark, but had, at one point, been nearly run over when a departing driver careened around a curve. The lights of his motor car had illuminated Sarah just in time, and the driver had jerked his wheel over. Nevertheless, Sarah, seeing the car veering toward her, had leapt to the side of the road and stumbled, twisting her right knee as she fell. When she landed, she had cut her knee upon a sharp rock and torn a hole in her dress—skinning the heels of her hands into the bargain.

Sarah had hobbled the rest of the way to the gate and made herself known to the two guards.

"You are limping. Are you all right, miss?" one asked.

"Yes. Thank you for asking. I took a little fall, but a friend is coming to escort me home."

The other muttered under his breath, "I would not mind escorting you home."

"Shut your filthy mouth, Jones." The first guard jerked his chin toward the open gatehouse. "You can sit out of the wind in there, miss." He handed her a handkerchief and glared at the other guard. "He won't be bothering you none, I promise."

Sarah had tied the kerchief about her knee and taken the chair in the musty gatehouse. She sat for what seemed a long while until her throbbing knee forced her to walk about. Her delicate shawl was no match for the buffeting winds, however, and her teeth were chattering by the time O'Dell arrived.

He pulled to the side of the gate and climbed out. "Miss Ellinger?"

"I am here, Mr. O'Dell."

"You are freezing!"

"I-I shall be a-all r-right."

He helped her into the car, draped a blanket about her shoulders and tucked one across her legs, then took his own seat and turned the motor car around. Sarah studied his profile in the dark, but they were silent until they reached Palmer House and he turned off the engine.

"Miss Ellinger, are you all right?"

Sarah sighed. "I shall be."

O'Dell's observant eyes had not missed the ragged tear in her dress. "Tell me the truth: Were you assaulted?"

"No. I fell while walking down the driveway, and I scraped my knee."

"And can you explain why you were at such a place?"

"I was misled, Mr. O'Dell. I believed I was going to a concert. Well, a musicale."

He snorted. "A 'musicale'? At Jason Stafford's house?"

"I did not know where the event was to be held, nor would the address or location have meant anything to me." She pulled the invitation from her reticule. "My friend said she was a pianist, one of this evening's musicians. She gave me this."

O'Dell glanced at it. "A speakeasy invitation."

"Speakeasy? I do not know what that is."

"Never mind. How did you get there?"

"My friend sent a gentleman to pick me up. He hired a cab."

"Miss Rose allowed you go out with a stranger?"

"Well, to be fair, she did interview him first. He comes from a respectable family, and he seemed proper enough."

"Proper? Was it proper for him to escort you there but leave you to find your own way home?"

*Oh, if you only knew the improper things I witnessed tonight.*

She felt sick with mortification and sighed again. "It was a terrible mistake on my part to accept the invitation." She looked across the dark car. "I thank you for coming out to rescue me. I know you have more questions, but I fear that my knee is bleeding. I would like to go inside and see to it."

He was quiet for a moment before responding. "Very well. I shall see you inside."

"Thank you."

They were silent up the long walkway and up the steps to the porch. Sarah unlocked the front door with as little noise as possible and stepped across the threshold. A soft light shone from the great room: Miss Rose was waiting for her.

"Thank you again, Mr. O'Dell."

He tipped his hat to her. "I am glad you are all right, Miss Ellinger."

She nodded and closed and latched the door behind her. Then she crept into the great room, prepared to face Rose's questions . . . and disappointment. The clock on the mantel read after one in the morning, and Rose lay curled on one of the sofas, her head cushioned on a throw pillow.

"Miss Rose?"

Rose did not stir. She looked older to Sarah in her sleep, and tired. For several minutes, Sarah watched Rose's even breathing, wondering what to do.

*If I were to awaken her, she would insist that I tell her everything— and she would not rest until she had heard me out. However, I can tell that she needs her sleep. It would be wiser to wait and talk to her tomorrow when we are both rested.*

Coming to a decision, Sarah reached for an afghan and spread it over Rose's slumbering figure. Rose did not shift or stir.

Sarah turned off the lamp and crept upstairs. By the time she had undressed for bed, washed her stinging hands, and wiped and bandaged her knee, she had begun to hope she might avoid a difficult conversation with Rose altogether.

*If she fell asleep before midnight, she may think I arrived home on time and that I allowed her to continue sleeping. I can but hope so! If she knew what all I saw, she would be deeply grieved. And I would not want to be the cause of her disappointment. Perhaps I can spare her the details of this wicked evening.*

As she drifted to sleep, a more truthful rationale raised its head: *And perhaps you are only trying to spare yourself.*

~\*~

THE HOUSE WAS FULLY AWAKE when Sarah yanked her covers aside. As she put her feet on the floor and tried to stand, she found she could not bear to put any weight on her leg nor could she bend her knee. Not only could she not stand, but a sharp throbbing recommenced immediately—as did every rueful memory of the previous evening.

She perched on the edge of her bed and lifted her gown: The makeshift bandage she had wrapped about her knee was crusted with dried and oozing blood; her knee was swollen to twice its usual size. Black and blue streaks crept from beneath the bandage.

"Oh, bother."

Someone rapped on her door. "Oh, Sarah! Breakfast, dear." It was Blythe.

"Blythe? Would you come in, please?"

Blythe poked her sunny face through a crack in the door. "Did you have a lovely evening? I cannot wait to hear about it."

Then she spotted the bandage and the cringe of discomfort on Sarah's face and stepped into Sarah's bedroom. "Why, Sarah, whatever has happened?"

"I took a tumble in the dark, and I fear I did not adequately clean the wound last night before I went to sleep. My knee is terribly swollen."

"Oh, no! I shall fetch Miss Rose at once."

Sarah did not bother to argue. She knew well enough that Rose—and likely Marit—would be upstairs shortly, bringing with them the "bandage basket" Tabitha had put together for the house's medical emergencies.

Sarah was right; she was still working the old, crusted bandage loose when Rose and Marit appeared in her doorway. Marit carried a basin of warm water; Rose toted the familiar basket.

Rose said, "Let us moisten that bandage, Sarah, lest you tear it loose and cause more bleeding," but it was Marit who took charge.

Pulling up a low seat, Marit lifted Sarah's foot and carefully laid Sarah's leg across her lap. She placed a warm, wet cloth on the bandage to allow the water to soften the dried blood. When she pulled the last strip of the soiled bandage from Sarah's knee, both she and Rose huffed with dismay, and Marit commenced to scold Sarah.

"Vat vere you thinking, Sarah? So much dirt and many bits of gravel left in the vound!"

"Gravel?" Sarah bent forward and peered down at her knee. "I guess I did not notice last night."

"We will have to soak her leg to coax that grit from it, Marit."

"Ja, ve vill." Marit transferred Sarah's foot to the low seat and bustled downstairs to set water on the stove to heat, leaving Sarah and Rose alone.

Sarah could not look Rose in the face when she asked, "What happened, Sarah?"

"I-I fell. On the driveway of the house where we were. I did not realize how hard I had hit my knee."

Rose spotted Sarah's dress hanging on a peg and lifted the hem, finding the jagged hole in the delicate fabric "Oh, Sarah! And your lovely dress is ruined."

Ruth and Pansy appeared, lugging the tin bathtub from the second-floor washroom. They set it on the floor of Sarah's bedroom and disappeared, only to return with clean towels and washcloths.

Blythe materialized behind them, wringing her thin little hands. Rose thanked all three girls and shooed them away, leaving with them. She had not asked Sarah any further questions.

Soon Ruth and Pansy returned to pour the contents of two steaming kettles into the tub. They did so several times until Marit had heated enough hot water for the tub. She and Rose eased Sarah down into eight inches of steaming water. Sarah flinched when the water touched her skinned palms—and she hissed as the warmth penetrated the torn flesh in her knee. She made no further sounds, but tears trickled down her face and dribbled into the tub.

"Let me see your hands, Sarah." Rose washed Sarah's grazed palms with soap and clean water, then dabbed them with ointment. "Your hands will heal in a few days, but I do not like the look of your knee, Sarah. It is quite bruised and inflamed."

"Ja, so svollen." Marit worked a warm cloth across Sarah's knee, sponging bits of debris from the flaps of torn skin. "Ach. This tear is too vide and deep. It vill not stop bleeding."

Rose leaned closer. "I think it may require stitching. We must call the doctor; I shall ring him now." At the door she added, "Later, when you are feeling better, we shall talk further."

Sarah slumped back in the tub, defeated.

~*~

"WELL, MISS ELLINGER, YOU have suffered quite a nasty gouge to your knee, but that may not be the worst of it. You say your knee twisted when you fell on it?"

"Yes."

Sarah gritted her teeth as Dr. Croft pressed gently on and around her knee and bent and moved her leg this way and that. Every manipulation of the swollen joint stung her, but not as much as the indignity of a man touching her bare leg—in particular, *this* man.

"We shall not know the extent of the damage to your knee until the swelling has gone down. I shall stitch the worst of your wounds and paint them all with merbromin. Then I shall show someone the correct way to pack your knee in ice and leave instructions on the duration of the ice compresses, so we do not burn your skin."

He glanced up at her. "You are not to place any weight on this knee for a week. I shall return next Saturday to remove the stitches and appraise your progress. The injury could be only a severe sprain, but you are as likely to have torn or damaged the ligaments or tendons. We shall know more when the swelling abates."

"Next Saturday? But, my work at the shop. I—"

Croft waylaid her objection. "You are excused from work at present, Miss Ellinger. We shall see how you fare in a week's time."

Preparing to stitch Sarah's knee, he laid out the necessary instruments on a clean cloth, poured alcohol into a dish and placed the thread and a curved needle into the disinfectant. "I must warn you that this will sting, Miss Ellinger."

Rose gripped Sarah's hand as he took up the threaded needle with an instrument like a pair of pincers. He drove the needle into her skin and wove the torn edges together. Sarah was determined not to make a sound, and she ground her teeth to make good on her vow—but tears forced their way out and down her cheeks with each tug of the needle and pull of thread through her skin.

When Croft had finished stitching her knee, he painted the skin with a liberal quantity of a carmine-red solution that stung far worse than the needle or alcohol-soaked thread had. Sarah tried so very hard, but she could not hold back a prolonged whimper.

Rose squeezed her hand. "There, there. Almost done."

As Croft bandaged her wound, he smiled in Sarah's direction—a detached, professional smile—and admitted, "You did well, Miss Ellinger. I admire your fortitude."

To Sarah's ears, he was talking down to her, and she itched to retort, "I do not require your approbation, Dr. Croft, nor did I ask for it."

She gnawed a hole in her bottom lip instead.

Croft then produced a brown bottle which he handed to Rose. "Shake this well before each use and see that Miss Ellinger takes one teaspoon every six hours for the pain. Follow this dosage for three days. After three days, you may give her the same dosage as she needs it, but never to exceed one teaspoon every six hours."

He spoke as if Sarah were not in the room—or, worse, as if she were a child in need of adult supervision.

Sarah stuffed her mouth with a fisted hand, fearing what words might jump out should she remove it.

~*~

IN ANSWER TO THE DISRUPTION of their Sunday morning routine, Rose had sent the girls off to church with Billy, Marit, and Mr. Wheatley. She and Olive stayed behind to see to icing Sarah's knee.

"Joy and Mr. O'Dell will fetch us more ice after church this morning," Rose commented. "Perhaps you and Joy can decide how to manage the shop without you this week."

Rose still had not broached the subject of the previous evening, nor had she delved deeper into how Sarah had injured her knee.

All Sarah could think was, *Perhaps Miss Rose has given some thought to my objections over being treated as one of the "girls."*

That afternoon, Joy and O'Dell purchased the required ice and brought it to Marit to store in the house's ice box. Joy came upstairs and sat with Sarah. Blythe was already keeping Sarah company. While they talked, Blythe held baby Jacob in her arms and marveled at his soft skin and minuscule perfection.

"I have decided to work Corrine's hours while you are laid up, Sarah, and Corrine will take your hours. I shall keep Jacob with me, and Tabitha has agreed to have Matty visit Liam while I am at the shop."

"I would keep him for you, if I could," Sarah murmured, drowsy from Dr. Croft's medication. "I am so very, very sorry to subject you to this inconvenience. Very, very, very sorry."

Sarah's tongue felt furry and slow, but not as sluggish as her thinking, nor did she realize her last (and redundant) words came out as, "Verrrrr, verrrrr, verrrrr sorrrrrr." She also did not notice when Joy and Blythe traded amused winks.

Joy cleared her throat to keep from chuckling aloud. "Do not fret, Sarah. We shall manage, and we shall pray for you to recover and suffer no permanent damage to your knee."

~*~

THE ICE APPLIED TO her knee and the medicine Dr. Croft had prescribed managed much of Sarah's pain. However, Sarah began to understand that the medicine—a nasty, bitter concoction—also put her into a dreadful, fog-like state. She spent the rest of Sunday sleeping off the medicine's effects. On Monday morning, she begged Rose to cut the dosage in half.

"I cannot talk or think straight. I have horrid dreams," she told Rose—although her words were slurred and came out sounding as, "Can' talk . . . rrriii . . . think . . . straigh' . . . horrrrd dreamsssss."

"We must follow Dr. Croft's instructions, Sarah. Three days, he said."

The spoon hovered near Sarah's mouth; she shuddered and turned her face away. "Sooo bitt—ugh!"

Rose had taken the opportunity to insert the spoon and dump its contents into Sarah's open mouth. She gagged, then swallowed it.

"Rest now, Sarah."

Rose placed the bottle on Sarah's dresser and closed the door behind her.

~*~

SARAH WAS DOZING AGAIN when Rose stooped over her. "Sarah, dear. You have a visitor."

"Whaaa?"

You have a visitor."

"Uhhh?"

Rose lifted Sarah and tucked two pillows behind her. A moment later, she murmured, "This way, please." Someone entered Sarah's room and Rose closed the door behind her.

"Hello, Sarah."

Sarah cracked her eyelids and tried to focus. "Lo . . . la?"

"Yes, I am here. I heard about your accident. I-I brought you flowers."

"Kind . . . of you."

"Your Miss Rose helped me arrange them in a vase. Would you like me to set them here where you can see them?"

Sarah flopped her head in the affirmative. "Howww?"

"How did I hear of your accident? I stopped into the shop to see you. Mrs. O'Dell and Corrine told me. I already had your address, so I came 'round to look in on you."

"Ohhh." Sarah thought Lola's explanation sounded a little choked and watery, but she was in no fit state to be certain.

Lola leaned over Sarah, took her hand, and stroked it. "Tell me, did you injure yourself at Jason's party, Sarah? Was that where you fell?"

"Mm hmm."

Lola sniffled and wiped her eyes. "Then it is my fault you hurt yourself. I am terribly sorry. Everything about that evening—all of it—was my fault. It was entirely cavalier on my part and unfair to you to thrust you into such unfamiliar surroundings." She caressed Sarah's forehead. "I promise I shall make it up to you, sweet Sarah."

Her touch was soothing, and Sarah nodded off. She did not later recall when Lola departed. To be precise, she was left with only fuzzy fragments of Lola's visit.

Hours later, when Rose reappeared to administer Sarah's next dose, Rose commented in a subdued voice, "It was kind of your friend to visit and bring flowers."

"Mmm."

Sarah did not know that when Rose left her room, she went to her own. She did not know that Rose locked her door or that she dropped to her knees beside her bed to pray.

"O Lord, please help us to win this new friend of Sarah's to Jesus. Help us, Lord, for I am concerned for the influence Lola is having on Sarah."

❧ ✿ ❧

# CHAPTER 11

On Wednesday Sarah refused Rose's first offer of the medicine. "I cannot bear being out of my mind any longer," she declared. "And I really must get shut of this bed and this room! All my bones ache from inactivity."

Shortly after breakfast, Rose enlisted Billy to carry Sarah downstairs to the great room, where Olive appeared with a pair of borrowed crutches. Blythe hovered nearby; she carried a lightweight afghan.

"Dr. Croft said that you are to place no weight upon your leg, Sarah," Rose reminded her, "therefore, I must insist that one of us be with you whenever you move about with these aids. We do not want you to take another fall. So, then. Let us see now how you get on with them."

With Billy on one side and Olive on the other, Sarah stood upright, balancing on her left leg, the crutches under her arms. She swayed—and Billy steadied her.

"Only three days in bed and I am as dizzy and weak as a kitten," Sarah moaned.

"It will pass. As soon as you are steady, try to take a few steps."

Sarah had to learn how to plant the crutches ahead of her and swing her good leg to follow them. After she had mastered the movement, she made two full turns up and down the great room. She was perspiring from the effort.

"That is sufficient for a first attempt," Rose declared. She and Olive had prepared a comfortable chair for Sarah to sit in and an ottoman to support her leg. They helped Sarah into the chair and elevated her leg with a pillow placed upon the ottoman. Blythe spread the afghan over her feet.

Sarah sighed. "Thank you, Billy and Olive. Thank you, Blythe, dear. Thank you, Miss Rose. I shall do much better here."

"How is your pain?"

"I can bear it," Sarah declared. She wanted no more of Dr. Croft's vile concoction!

She laid back with a new book supplied by Rose, Billy left for his job, and Rose and Olive joined Marit in the kitchen to plan the day's household tasks.

That left Blythe, still hovering nearby. "May I do anything for you, Miss Sarah?"

"No, dear heart. Unless you wish to read to me?"

"Oh! I-I do not know how to read very well. I am sorry, Miss Sarah."

"You do not need to be sorry, Blythe. Perhaps I could read to you?"

"I would like that."

So, with Blythe sharing her ottoman, Sarah read aloud.

Later, Rose sat down at her little desk in the corner of the great room and began to answer some correspondence. Olive appeared every hour to help Sarah stand and walk about with the crutches, and Mr. Wheatley, having finished his work in the yard, played three games of checkers with her.

But Sarah was not a person content to sit idle all day.

"You must have something I can do, Miss Rose!"

"Hmm." She thought a bit. "I shall ask Olive to supply you with handwork."

Rose's request resulted in Olive appearing with silver polish and the house's rather sad collection of silver—a dinged and dented tea service and two candelabras that had seen finer days, indeed.

"Yes!" Sarah rejoiced.

"I shall help you, Sarah," Blythe offered. She had not left Sarah's side for more than fifteen minutes during the long morning.

~*~

SARAH HEARD THE BRASS knocker fall upon the house's front door; however, the caller did not wait to be let in. The door opened, and little feet pattered down the foyer toward the great room with a young voice babbling, "Gramma Rose! Gramma Rose! I here!"

Matthew ran into the room and flew into Rose's arms.

"Oh, Matthew! Have you come to see me?"

"Yis, Gramma. I here."

Joy followed on Matthew's heels, carrying Jacob swaddled in thick blankets. "Hello, Mama."

"So lovely of you to come visit. Do you have time for tea?"

"Oh, yes, please, Mama."

Rose bent down to Matthew. "Shall we take your coat and hat off?" Rose helped Matthew shed his coat, mittens, hat, and scarf.

"Goodness, Matthew O'Dell! Have you grown since I saw you last?"

He nodded and jumped up and down. "I big now."

Rose excused herself. "I shall go start the water for our tea. Sarah and Blythe, would you like a cup?"

"Yes, please," Sarah and her shadow answered.

At Sarah's voice, Matthew raced over to her—but hesitated when he saw her leg swathed in bandages. His finger slipped into his mouth. "Owie?"

"Yes, Matty. I hurt my leg. Will you give me a gentle hug?"

He came near and offered her quite a credible one—credible in that he never took his eyes off her bandage. But, as soon as he had completed his task, he ran off to the kitchen, no doubt hoping Marit would have cookies.

Joy sat down across from Sarah, cradling Jacob on her knees. "How are you feeling today, Sarah?"

"Poorly, Miss Joy, poorly, indeed. I am in sore need of a special medicine and, alas! We have none at Palmer House."

"What? A special medicine? Can we not get it for you?"

Sarah snorted a giggle. "I should specify that the medicine is known as baby cuddling. And, if a certain infant were to rest in my lap—why, I am convinced that I would improve directly."

Blythe laughed out loud. Joy, too, chuckled and handed Jacob to Sarah. "You are quite awful, Sarah, giving me pause like that."

"Well, I *know* what I need," Sarah replied. "I shall benefit, indeed, with the application of this soothing balm."

"He is not a soothing balm in the middle of the night, I can promise you. Little screaming banshee!"

Sarah laughed and smoothed Jacob's forelock. "Well, I shall use up every bit of soothing balm while you are here, and then you may take him away home, where he can scream to his heart's content."

"Incorrigible brat! You are as bad as Matty, who thinks Jacob should not take naps."

Rose returned with a tray. "Shall we have our tea now?"

"Oh, yes, please. I have something to say, and I should like Sarah to hear. Blythe, you, too, of course."

When they had settled their cups and saucers on their knees, and Matty had gone outside with Will and Charley, Joy began.

"Yesterday, a young couple, the Simmons, came to the Denver Pinkerton office. They live on their own land fifteen miles outside Denver. Five days ago, their little boy, Jim, who is Matty's age, disappeared from their home. The couple, Bill and Nora, believe their former housekeeper has taken him."

Rose, Sarah, and Blythe listened in dismay. "Oh, no," Rose breathed.

Joy nodded. "Edmund said that the Pinkertons would take their case. Right away, though, he called me and asked if he might bring the Simmons to our home for lunch. He suggested that we had an opportunity to minister to this aching couple. I agreed. Over lunch and afterward, Mr. O'Dell and I told them about my son—*our* son—Edmund. We shared with them our hope for finding Edmund, even after his absence of eight long years, and we talked to them about the Savior and the blessed comfort we have in Jesus.

"Our visit with Mr. and Mrs. Simmons was timely and holy. They were willing, so we led them to pray to receive Jesus as their Lord and Savior, and we prayed with them about their little Jimmy. One of the things I shared with them was Papa's saying, that in God, the lost are found, that he, the Lord, has his eyes and his hand upon our lost children, that they are not lost to *him*, and how all of our good friends pray daily for Edmund's safe return."

Joy had to pause to wipe her eyes and clear her throat. "After Bill and Nora left for home, I felt the Lord's presence upon me. His hand remained so heavy upon me that, later that evening, I could not sleep. I stayed up, praying, asking what he wished to speak to me. I kept hearing Papa's voice, saying again and again, *in God, the lost are found*. I implored the Lord to tell me what he wished me to do, but I could discern nothing.

"I fell asleep on the sofa in our living room and slept the whole night there. When Jacob awakened me early in the morning, I sat there, nursing him . . . and then it all came clear."

The hairs on Sarah's arm prickled. "What came clear?"

"Just this: a ministry to families whose children have gone missing. A means of sharing the hope and comfort of Jesus, and an association of like-minded parents to spread word regarding missing children. I would call it, Lost Are Found."

"An ambitious undertaking," Rose breathed. "How would you begin?"

"Through the Pinkerton Agency. Reaching out to other parents whose children are missing and beginning a correspondence with them. Praying for them and their children. Sharing Jesus with them. Particularly in the larger cities, encouraging them to meet with other families in similar circumstances. I do not know where we might go from there; however, it would be a start."

"How can we help?" Rose asked.

"Thank you, Mama. I knew I could count on you! I wish to gather our friends here some evening soon to present this idea to them, and to pray for the Lord's leading."

"Breona and Pastor Isaac? Mei-Xing and Minister Liáng?"

Sarah added, "Tabitha and Mason? Billy and Marit?"

"Yes. Everyone living nearby who stood with us when Edmund was taken and stands with us now."

"Shall we approach them this Sunday?" Rose asked.

"Yes, Mama."

Sarah nodded. "I hope I can be included?"

"And I?" Blythe asked.

"Certainly. Corrine and Albert, also, and any of the girls living here who wish to attend."

~*~

THURSDAY, SARAH HAD ENDURED enough leisure and again demanded work. "If I am to be an immobile fixture in the great room for the remainder of the week, I really *must* have something worthwhile to do; I cannot abide sitting idle."

In response, Olive had Blythe bring Sarah the house's laundered linens to fold—tea towels, dish cloths, napkins, aprons, sheets, pillow slips, even cleaning rags.

"Thank you; this is a perfect task for me," Sarah declared. When she had finished folding the items Blythe gave her, she declared she wished to fold Marit's family laundry, too.

"Dear Marit! You cook and manage our kitchen all while keeping your own little cottage tidy and looking after Billy, Will, and Charley's washing—not to mention Toby's diapers. Bring me your clean laundry, and I shall fold it."

"I shall help you, Sarah," Blythe declared.

"No, darling; I am greedy for the work, and these are all mine. You keep with Olive and come read with me later."

Sarah went after the baskets of clean linens with zeal and was halfway through the first basket when the knocker fell upon the front door. Rose got up to answer the door and returned soon after.

"You have a visitor, Sarah." Behind Rose's back, Sarah saw Lola's short, curly hair.

"Oh!"

"Hello!" Lola bounced into the great room, her arms filled with a paper-wrapped bundle, and plopped down on the arm of Sarah's overstuffed chair.

"I figured the flowers I brought on Monday must be fading, so I brought fresh ones."

Sarah sniffed. "Mmm. I can smell them. Carnations?"

Lola peeled back the paper to display the riot of colors—deep pink, soft pink, crimson, white, and purple carnations—nestled in a bed of ferns and baby's breath.

"Oh, they are beautiful!"

Lola grinned. "Not as beautiful as you are, Sarah—and I did say I would try to make up for our disastrous evening."

Sarah flinched and glanced over to see if Rose had reacted to Lola's statement, but Rose had returned to her desk and busied herself with her work. Her expression was unreadable.

Lola did not notice Sarah's hesitation. "Shall we get these in water for you?"

"Um, yes, but I am fairly stuck here, not allowed to put any weight on my injured leg at all."

Lola shrugged. "I know the way to the kitchen from last time." She picked up the flowers and moved toward the dining room.

"Oh, um, you may encounter Marit, our cook." Sarah looked again at Rose. She was writing in a ledger.

Lola was halfway through the dining room. "I believe I met her before."

When she returned, the carnations, ferns, and baby's breath were arranged in a large vase. Lola set them on the coffee table to Sarah's side. Then she sat again on the arm of Sarah's chair. She picked up Sarah's hand and entwined her fingers with Sarah's.

"Are you still in pain, dear?"

"Only occasionally, such as when I need to shift my weight a little. Turning over at night is an ordeal."

"You must not be taking as much pain medication. The last time I was here, you were quite off your nut." Lola's giggle was naughty and ended on another cough.

"I-I do not remember much about your visit."

"I wager you do not! But our conversation was entertaining, I can assure you." Lola's fingers stroked Sarah's. "I am sorry. I should not tease you. Now, what can I do to help you pass the time?"

Sarah, growing more uncomfortable, withdrew her hand. "I was folding laundry when you came in."

"Oh, dear—how pedestrian. And while you are recovering? Surely you can just rest and enjoy some idle leisure?"

"Idle leisure? *Ugh.* I begged for the work, to be frank. I rather detest being unproductive."

"My! I had no idea you were so industrious. Compared to you, I am certain to be labeled positively indolent. Well, if you must work, I should help."

"Only if you wish to, Lola."

"I wish," Lola leaned closer, "to be near you, Sarah. If I must fold napkins to enjoy your company, then I shall fold an ocean of them—or, at the least, a basket of them."

Sarah blushed, secretly a tiny bit pleased at Lola's compliment.

When they had finished the laundry, the clock struck two o'clock.

"It has been just oodles of fun, but I must go now, Sarah. The Pythia has a performance this evening. We are playing for an engagement party— cocktails and *hors d'oeuvres* at a private residence. Such parties are The Pythia's bread and butter, but as the hosts tend to open the bar to the band, I declare I spend the bulk of my time urging Meg to keep Dannie from enjoying herself too much—no small feat since I am generally half sloshed myself."

Lola's voice carried, and Sarah could not imagine that Rose had not heard. Her concern was interrupted as Lola turned aside to cough into her hankie.

"Are you all right, Lola?"

"Yes. I often have a tickle in my throat, but it is nothing of matter. I do smoke, and I imagine it cannot be helpful."

"No, I would imagine not."

Lola just laughed. "I really must be on my way."

"Well, thank you for coming to see me, Lola. And thank you for the flowers. They are quite lovely."

Lola dropped a kiss on Sarah's head and whispered, "You are twice as lovely, Sarah."

Speaking at her normal level, she said, "I shall see myself out."

"Goodbye, Lola."

Rose came out from behind her desk. "It was kind of you to come, Lola."

Lola waved to Sarah, then tipped her head toward Rose. "But of course. Christians do not possess a monopoly on kindness, you know."

It was a small but acerbic barb, deftly inserted, and after Lola left, Sarah halfway expected Rose to approach her. She did not.

Instead Rose climbed the long staircase to her room. Closing and locking her door, she knelt at her bed. "O Lord, my God, how my spirit is troubled for my daughter Sarah! I sense darkness crouching in wait for her; I feel the enemy of our souls stalking her, sifting her, seeking to ensnare her.

"Lord Jesus, I plead your precious blood over Sarah's heart: Deliver her from evil, I am begging you, my God."

~*~

BY SATURDAY, ALL THE Palmer House girls were taking glad advantage of Sarah's willing hands. She folded clean clothes, stitched falling hems, mended burst seams, reattached errant buttons, and turned Mr. Wheatley's frayed shirt collars. She took Blythe under her wing and showed her how to embroider her initials on her handkerchiefs. The girls, in turn, fetched Sarah tea and, hourly, helped her out of her chair, handed her the crutches, and kept close by as she limped about the house.

Dr. Croft arrived late that afternoon to remove Sarah's stitches and assess the condition of her knee. Rose saw him into the great room.

"Good day, Miss Ellinger. How are you feeling?"

Sarah did not answer him—not that he, apparently, expected her to: He had turned his back to her, opened his bag, and was laying out his instruments. While he was facing away, she scowled at him—then rearranged her countenance when Rose looked askance in her direction.

Never making eye contact with Sarah, the doctor examined her knee. "The wounds appear clean and healthy, Miss Ellinger." He nodded at Rose. "You have had excellent care."

A few sharp snips of his scissors and tugs on the thread and the stitches were out. Then he carefully palpated her knee on both sides.

"Not surprising to me, your knee presents with continued distension. You may find that your leg swells intermittently as you begin to use it or if you stand upon it too long. However, the swelling should be manageable if you do not overuse the joint. I am going to bend your leg now. Please tell me how it feels."

Quite gently, he took hold of her ankle, put one hand under her knee to support it, and moved her foot toward her, causing the knee to bend. "Does that hurt?"

Sarah ground her teeth. "Some."

He sniffed. "More than some, I should say. What about this?"

He manipulated her knee several ways. Sarah felt no sharp pain, only the continual ache, but stronger, as he moved her knee.

"I believe you have escaped a tearing damage to your knee, Miss Ellinger, but you did strain it badly. This type of injury—and a lingering tendonitis—may pain you for some time to come. The trick is to avoid inflaming the tendons anew—by recognizing and minding your limits.

"Continue with the crutches another week, but you may begin to put a little weight on your leg. As I indicated, you will learn your limits by the swelling and pain your activities produce. I caution you to mind those limits, to rest, elevate, and ice your leg as needed, to walk short but frequent distances, and to avoid stairs and prolonged standing."

"What of my position at the shop?"

"How do you come and go from your work, Miss Ellinger?"

"I take the trolley."

"And you walk several blocks to and from the trolley?"

"Y-yes."

"I see. Well, unless you can be delivered to and from the shop's door and can wait on customers from a chair behind the counter with your leg elevated as needed, I cannot release you to work for another week. I shall come again next Saturday." He began packing his bag.

Sarah flounced against the back of her chair, folded her arms, and glared at his back, aggravated and frustrated.

Dr. Croft should not have been able to witness her sulk—how could he, facing away as he was? Regardless, while he tidied his bag and latched it, he murmured, "As I am not the cause of your indisposition, Miss Ellinger, I should think you aware that it really does no good to fault *me* for it."

Sarah huffed. "I am casting no blame on you, Dr. Croft."

Never looking at her, he replied, "Are you not?"

Finished, he bowed to Rose—and ignored Sarah. "Good day, ladies."

Sarah snarled under her breath at his retreating figure—until she realized Rose was observing her, brows arched.

Rose coughed. "Pardon me," she murmured. She slipped her hand over her mouth as she walked away, but left Sarah wondering . . .

*What? Was Miss Rose . . . laughing?*

# $\mathcal{C}$HAPTER 12

Sarah counted herself blessed when the O'Dells arrived Sunday morning to drive her to church. She had missed the previous Sunday's service, as had Rose and Olive, and she was hungry for this morning's worship and teaching.

O'Dell helped her into the Bergdoll's back seat and placed her crutches on the floor. She sat against the far door with her leg lying across the seat. Joy then handed baby Jacob to Sarah. They had deemed Matty too likely to climb upon or inadvertently kick Sarah's injured knee, so O'Dell lifted the boy into the front seat for Joy to hold upon her lap. Matty, however, was unhappy with the arrangement and pouted all the way to church.

"Want Sar'!" he complained.

When they arrived at Calvary Temple, O'Dell helped Sarah from the car. Then, while he held Matty's hand and walked close to Sarah's elbow, he saw her and his family to seats in the far back where Sarah (keeping two empty spots on the bench between her and Joy) could unobtrusively and safely rest her leg upon the pew.

Sarah closed her eyes during the singing and listened to the swell of voices lifting praises to God. *O Lord! How I love the worship of your people.* She shuddered, thinking of where she had been and what she had witnessed at Lola's "musicale" only eight evenings gone by.

Soon Pastor Carmichael began his message. "This is our fifth week on the study of 'The Overcoming Christian Life.' To recount our previous studies, we began by asking the question, 'Why do some believers overcome sin in their lives while other believers are defeated?'

"Today, our ongoing study looks at the Lordship of Christ—for all victory over sin hinges upon the depth and extent of our surrender to Christ's Lordship over our lives. The Lordship of Christ can be defined by two questions:

"The first question is, do we accept the premise that God the Father has placed his resurrected Son, Jesus, *over all things*—all things being inclusive of us?

"Ephesians 1:20-22 tells us that God, the Father of glory, has raised Jesus from the dead, and has:

"*Set him at his own right hand*
*in the heavenly places,*
*Far above all principality, and power,*
*and might, and dominion,*
*and every name that is named,*
*not only in this world,*
*but also in that which is to come:*
**And hath put all things under his feet,**
*and gave him to be the head over all things*
*to the church which is his body.*

"God the Father has put all things *under* the feet of his Son Jesus and has given Jesus to the church to be the head *over* all things concerning the church. The word 'head' signifies a body's source of leadership or governance. If you are a Christian, God has joined you to the church, the body of Christ; therefore, Jesus, as the head of the church, is your source of leadership and governance.

"It is, today, an unpopular sentiment to proclaim that God requires obedience. Nonetheless, Jesus told his disciples in John 14:15, *If ye love me, keep my commandments*, and in John 15:14, *Ye are my friends, if ye do whatsoever I command you*. Moreover, in 2 Corinthians 10, the Apostle Paul declares that we are to be actively, *Bringing into captivity every thought to the obedience of Christ*.

"When we surrender to the Lordship of Christ, we acknowledge that Jesus is Lord over all things, Lord over the church, and Lord over us. Jesus is not loosely or vaguely 'the' Lord and Master; no, he is, explicitly and expressly, *our* Lord and Master. We are to commit ourselves to obey him and follow his leadership."

Pastor Carmichael paused to let his words sink in. Around Sarah, many congregants were nodding and scribbling furious notes; others were thoughtful. Sarah, too, pondered Carmichael's words.

*I do not think I had realized before—at least not as precisely—that God has placed Jesus over me, and that Jesus is to be my Lord and Master as well as my Savior.*

Carmichael gentled his voice and continued. "The second question that helps us define the Lordship of Christ is, do we accept the premise that God has given us his unchanging, infallible word to speak truth into every area of our lives?

"The second question is not unrelated to the first, for Scripture tells us that Jesus, God's Son, *is* the word of God. The opening verse of the Gospel of John reads:

*"In the beginning was the Word,*
*and the Word was with God,*
*and the Word was God.*

"The following two verses tell us that it was Jesus, the living, uttered Word, the very *logos* of God, who spoke the universe into existence:

*"The same was in the beginning with God.*
*All things were made by him;*
*and without him was not anything*
*made that was made.*

"Farther along in the same chapter, verse 14, to be exact, we are told that the Word is Jesus, God made flesh, sent to live among us.

*"And the Word was made flesh,*
*and dwelt among us,*
*(and we beheld his glory, the glory as of*
*the only begotten of the Father,)*
*full of grace and truth.*

"How essential, then, is God's word to our Christian walk? Let us first consider the weight Jesus himself gave to the written word.

"Jesus is recorded in the Gospels as quoting written Scripture seventy-eight times. His use of Scripture to teach and correct testifies to the eternal credibility of the written word. He furthermore declared in Matthew 5:17 and 18:

*"Think not that I am come to destroy*
*the law, or the prophets:*
*I am not come to destroy, but to fulfil.*
*For verily I say unto you,*
*Till heaven and earth pass,*
*one jot or one tittle shall in no wise*
*pass from the law, till all be fulfilled.*

"Most important of all, when Jesus was led by the Holy Spirit into the wilderness, the tempter came to Jesus three times. Each time Jesus answered him, he prefaced his response with three words: *It is written.*

"*It is written,* Jesus said, *Man shall not live by bread alone, but by every word that proceedeth out of the mouth of God.*

"Listen carefully! By the phrase, *It is written,* Jesus proclaims that we are to live by God's *written word.* Furthermore, 'word' within this quote, 'man shall live by every *word* that proceeds from the mouth of God,' is, again, the *logos* of God."

His voice rising in passionate appeal, Pastor Carmichael shouted, "So, I ask you, the people who name the name of Jesus, you who have confessed your faith in Christ: Is Jesus the Lord of your life? And if Jesus *is* the Lord of your life, does his word have authority over you?

"If his word does not have authority over you, has the preaching of Scripture today convicted you? Has it illuminated what you have withheld from Jesus? Do you wish this morning to acquiesce fully to his Lordship? I implore you, I beg you—surrender this day! Come! Come and relinquish *all* to Jesus!"

A low murmur flowed over the congregation and grew into a deep roar. Chairs scraped, and feet shuffled as individuals and couples—then fives, tens, and twenties—poured from their rows and rushed for the altar, weeping and calling upon the name of Jesus.

Sarah slid her leg to the floor and used the chair in the row in front of her to pull herself up. She stared in holy awe at the Spirit of God moving across the warehouse floor. Her own heart yearned to follow them to the altar, but she knew she risked reinjuring her knee should she join the pressing throng.

So, she watched.

Minutes passed before Pastor Carmichael spoke again, saying, "At this altar and across this building, let us pray to commit ourselves fully to Jesus. All across this building, let us pray together:

"O Jesus! I submit myself to your Lordship, your leadership, your mastery over my life. I declare that you, whom God the Father has placed over *all things,* he has also placed over *me.* I declare that you are the living Word of God, and that every word God has spoken is unchanging and infallible. I commit myself to live by your word, and I allow your word permission to speak truth into every corner of my heart and mind."

*Yes, Lord Jesus,* Sarah prayed. *Every corner of my heart and mind. I surrender everything to you.*

She meant what she prayed; she longed to fully yield herself to the Lord . . . so why did that clear, sweet voice she knew well whisper, *Sarah, my daughter . . . why do you regard sin in your heart?*

Sarah sat down hard. "W-what do you mean, Lord?"

*My word is clear: Forgive.*

She frowned.

*What? Forgive? Forgive who?*

Even as she pondered those words, she avoided looking too closely into the shadowy recesses of her heart.

~*~

THE SUCCEEDING WEEK WAS a trial for Sarah. She was bored and far too inactive for her taste. Stuck downstairs in Palmer House's great room with her leg supported on an ottoman or walking about on stiff crutches, she grew irritable. Additionally, since the Lord had spoken such a cryptic word to her on Sunday, nothing within her seemed entirely "right" or at peace.

In an odd twist, her thoughts returned again and again to the Saturday night party at the Stafford-Polk estate, not yet two weeks past. She recalled the vibrant scene, the music, excitement, wild dancing, and unrestrained passions pulsing all around her; she revisited her conversation with Lola.

And she felt a tiny, unlooked-for itch to see it all again, to taste—merely *taste*—the forbidden fruits that had been dangling before her eyes.

*Lord,* she prayed with fervor, *please help me. I do not understand why I am drawn to these evil doings. Cleanse me of these desires, my God!*

At least Lola was not likely to visit her at Palmer House any time soon. Not after the snide note on which she had departed at the end of her last visit.

*Then again, this is Lola,* Sarah laughed within herself. *I doubt butter would melt in that woman's mouth.*

Lola did not visit; she did, however, have a tin of creamy peppermints delivered to Sarah. Sarah shared them equally with everyone; even Mr. Wheatley was delighted.

Sarah sighed and leaned back in her chair. *I wonder what Lola is doing today?*

~*~

FOR THE THIRD TIME THAT Friday morning, Blythe and Pansy helped Sarah stand with her crutches and take her required walk about the great room, dining room, and foyer. When Sarah returned to her chair, she stared at it with disgust.

"I must have a change. I cannot abide sitting in the same place another hour."

"Sit on the couch, then, Sarah," Pansy suggested.

Sarah plopped into a corner of the couch and lifted her injured leg onto the ottoman Blythe supplied.

"Does this feel better, Sarah?" Blythe asked.

"Yes, thank you. A welcome improvement. Come sit with me, dear?"

Blythe curled herself up next to Sarah. Pansy sat across from them.

"Sarah?" Blythe asked

"Mmmhmm?"

"Tell us about Lola?"

Inwardly, Sarah cringed. "What do you wish to know?"

"She is a very different sort of girl, I think."

"I think you may be right."

"She must be a good friend. She brings you lovely flowers and sends you candy."

Pansy's narrowed eyes regarded first Blythe, then Sarah. "Much like a gentleman caller might."

Sarah frowned. "What are you suggesting?"

"Well . . ."

"For shame, Pansy."

"I am sorry, Sarah. I thought—"

Sarah shook her head in warning, and Pansy stopped. She blinked back a shimmer of wetness at Sarah's chastisement.

Blythe did not seem to notice. "Is Lola a Christian, Sarah?"

Sarah visualized Lola belting out a sultry tune from the piano while piercing her with that alluring yet enigmatic gaze.

"Noooo, I suppose that she is not."

"Then, you will tell her, will you not, Sarah? About Jesus and how he wants to find her? So she will not stay lost. I should not like Lola to remain lost as I was. You will tell her, Sarah, will you not? Tell her like you told me?"

Sarah did not answer, and Pansy, hurt by Sarah's open rebuke, sniffled and stared daggers at her.

~*~

DR. CROFT RETURNED ON Saturday and had Sarah walk about the great room without her crutches.

"How is the discomfort, Miss Ellinger?"

"Bearable."

"Please sit and allow me to check the swelling." He gently palpated her knee and nodded. "Not bad. Coming along nicely."

"May I return to work?"

"If you—with proper precautions—can walk about the house without your crutches the next few days and are able to do so without much pain or increased swelling, I shall give my conditional permission for you to return to work, say, next Wednesday."

Blythe clapped her hands and grinned. "Bravo!"

"Yes, *bravo*, little one," Croft smiled back. "You have taken excellent care of Miss Ellinger."

"Oh, but it was not all me," Blythe said. "Sarah's friend Lola also helped—as did Miss Rose, Olive, Pansy, Marit—oh, everyone here, I should think!"

"It seems that Miss Ellinger is well loved by her friends." Croft murmured.

"Oh, yes. Everyone loves our Sarah," Blythe gushed.

Croft packed his bag. As he walked away, he tossed over his shoulder, "I suppose some individuals might count themselves fortunate *not* to be her friend."

A wide-eyed Blythe asked, "Why, what do you suppose Dr. Croft could mean by that, Sarah?"

"I really cannot say, dear one." But Sarah glared after him, seething inside.

AT LAST, IT WAS THE ENSUING Wednesday, the last Wednesday of October. Sarah's heart sang when she unlocked the shop door. The moment she set foot inside, she felt liberated. Free.

"I shall never take my mobility for granted again, Lord!"

At noon, the bell on the door jingled. Sarah was in the office, adding the previous day's receipts to the ledger. Corrine was with a young couple going over china patterns.

"Good afternoon," Corrine called to their new customer. "I shall be with you directly."

"Thank you, but I am looking for Miss Ellinger."

Sarah recognized Lola's voice instantly, and her heart stuttered in response. She wiped her hands and went to greet her.

"Hello! I was not expecting to see you today."

Lola grinned and held up a brown paper sack. "A little bird told me you were returning to work today. When do you take your lunch, Sarah? It is too cool out-of-doors for a picnic, but perhaps we could share behind the counter? I stopped at Baleks' for kebabs."

"Baleks'? Kebabs?"

"A Turkish café. The kebabs are seasoned chunks of lamb, onion, and eggplant on skewers, slow roasted over an open fire."

"Oh!" Sarah had never tasted kebabs, but the description made her mouth water. She found Corinne watching her. "I shall take my lunch now, Corinne."

She motioned to Lola. "Come into the office with me."

Sarah put the ledger into a drawer, cleared off the desk, and pulled up a second chair. "How is this?"

"Delightful. Quite cozy."

Sarah sampled a kebab and sighed. "These are so good. Mmmm."

When they had polished off the kebabs, Lola asked, "Shall I come again tomorrow?"

"I usually eat lunch with Corrine, and I would hate to make a habit of her eating alone." Sarah hesitated. "Corrine's shift ends at four each day, but I do not close the shop until five. This time of year, we do not have many customers near dusk."

Lola leaned near Sarah's ear. "I shall come tomorrow after four then. When we shall be alone."

Sarah shivered. "All right. I shall see you then."

After Lola left, Corrine was quieter than usual. Toward the time she left the shop for the day, she approached Sarah.

"Sarah? May I . . . may I say something to you? As a friend?"

Inside, Sarah bristled. Outside, what could she do but reply, "Certainly, Corrine," but she was on her guard.

"This new friend of yours, Lola? I-I am concerned."

"About?"

"I suppose I am concerned for her influence over you and . . ."

Sarah had never snapped at Corrine. She did now.

"And?"

"She is not a Christian, is she? And . . ." Corrine blushed. "We knew girls like her . . . in Corinth."

"I am not one of those girls, Corrine, as you well know." Sarah's every syllable dared Corrine to contradict her.

Corrine nodded. "No, you are not. Thank you, Sarah. Good night."

"Good night."

~*~

AS SHE HAD PROMISED, Lola arrived the following afternoon after Corrine had gone home for the day. Lola spent the last hour the store was open observing while Sarah waited on the occasional customer or chatting with Sarah as she readied the shop for closing.

She came Friday and Saturday, too, and Sarah began to anticipate her visits. They lingered in the office after Sarah flipped the sign from "Welcome" to "Closed" and locked the front door.

Lola regaled Sarah with humorous tales of her life as a musician. She read poetry aloud to them. She confided in Sarah, detailing her childhood and the father who had first beaten and abused her mother and then abandoned them.

"My mother died not many years later, and her sister took me in. My aunt and her husband already had six children—what was one more? It was not much of a loving home, but at least they fed and clothed me. The best part was that my uncle owned a bar and a piano. I learned to play by ear in that bar and earned my keep playing for customers until I ran away when I was sixteen."

*Both of us lost our mothers; we have that in common,* Sarah thought, but she did not reciprocate Lola's confidences; she did not share her secrets with Lola.

In the back office of Michaels' Fine Furnishings, hidden from public view, Sarah allowed Lola to touch her—touches that lingered and became more intimate, more demanding, a slow seduction that thrilled Sarah and to which she responded—even as she warned herself of the dangerous path she was treading.

# ℭHAPTER 13

The first Sunday in November arrived, and Sarah dressed and prepared for church with diffidence, even reluctance. She was deeply preoccupied, giving rise to conjecture among the other girls as to why Sarah was holding herself aloof. Blythe, in particular, took hard Sarah's distance, for her indifferent behavior made the girl question whether she had done something to offend her champion.

That morning, following worship, it was Minister Liáng who addressed the congregation. The depth of maturity in Calvary Temple's congregation could easily be attributed to the fact that the church had two pastors, both steeped in Scripture, and whose teaching complemented each other's so well.

"We are in our sixth week on the study of 'The Overcoming Christian Life.' To pick up the threads of our previous studies, we began by asking the question, 'Why do some believers overcome sin in their lives while other believers are defeated?' Last week, Pastor Carmichael taught on the Lordship of Christ. He made the bold statement that all victory over sin hinges upon the depth and extent of our surrender to Christ's Lordship over our lives. To that statement, I say, yes and amen!

"Pastor Carmichael furthermore stated that the Lordship of Christ can be defined by two questions: Do we accept the premise that God the Father has placed his resurrected Son, Jesus, over all things, including us? And, do we accept the premise that God has given us his unchanging, infallible word to speak truth into every area of our lives?

"This morning we shall revisit the question, 'Do we accept the premise that God has given us his unchanging, infallible word to speak truth into every area of our lives?' Our text today is from the second half of James 1:21. It reads:

*"Receive with meekness the engrafted word,*
*which is able to save your souls.*

"Let us divide and examine these lines with care and precision. First, James gives us instruction in the imperative voice: *Receive*. He makes no distinction as to whom he is speaking; it is a command directed at whomever is reading his epistle: You! You there! *You* receive.

ly each insert our own name into the verse to experience how he command: *You! Yaochuan Min Liáng!* You *receive!* And if we accept James' injunction as a personal command to us to receive, we may move on to *how* we are to receive—that is, receive with meekness.

"Meekness should not be confused with weakness, a deficiency of either physical or moral strength. Numbers 12:3 tells us that Moses was the meekest man upon the face of the earth, and yet we know he was, by no means, a weak man. Rather, he was humble before God, deferring to his ways, knowing his place in God's plans, while not displaying a sense of self-importance.

"Meekness is both humility and deference. It is knowing who we are— and who we are not. We begin by saying, 'Lord, you are God Almighty— and I am not.' This exalts God to his proper place while we acknowledge that our place is in submission to him. This is meekness.

"What, then, are we commanded to receive with meekness, with humility and deference? We are to receive with meekness *the engrafted word*. God's word must not merely cross our minds and touch our understanding. It must be grafted onto our hearts, the very seat of our understanding and being.

"We are familiar with the grafting of a superior strain of fruit onto the rootstock of a less desirable or lesser quality tree: A slit is made in the trunk or a primary branch of the tree. A fresh shoot of the superior strain is inserted into the slit. The shoot—called the scion—and the slit in the rootstock are then *bound together* until the shoot grows into the rootstock and becomes one with it.

"May I be perfectly plain? God desires for his word—the superior strain—to be engrafted onto our hearts—the less desirable strain. We have an important part in this process: Our hearts must be willing to *receive* the superior strain and bear and support its growth. As a result of this union, our lives produce the fruit of the superior strain, *the scion.*

"It is no coincidence that 'scion' means both 'offspring' and 'heir,' for are we not the offspring of God through Christ Jesus and joint heirs of eternal life with him? Thus, when we receive with meekness the engrafted word of God, Christ is formed *in* us, and his living presence in our lives saves our souls.

"In human terms, the engrafting of God's word cannot be a strictly painless process. The verse begins with an injunction for me to receive the word with meekness, that is, *proper humility, deference, and lack of self-importance.*

"However, like the slice that must be made in the rootstock, the Holy Spirit must slice open my heart to make a place of entrance for the graft of God's word.

"My fleshly heart will resist! It will not like being slit open, nor will it welcome the entrance of a superior strain of thought and opinion that supplants its own. You see, the human heart prefers its own counsel, for it is by our own counsel that we rationalize our sinful ways and justify our evil deeds.

"What does God say regarding our thoughts and ways? How does he contrast and compare his thoughts and opinions with our own? Isaiah 55:8 and 9 declare:

*"For my thoughts are not your thoughts,*
*neither are your ways my ways, saith the Lord.*
*For as the heavens are higher than the earth,*
*so are my ways higher than your ways,*
*and my thoughts than your thoughts.*

"Nothing in my thoughts can ever approach God's thoughts; nothing in my ways can ever approach his ways. His thoughts, his opinions, his standards, his decrees are and shall always be higher—that is, superior—to mine.

"To receive the engrafted word of God, then, is to allow the Holy Spirit to slice open the deepest part of our self-will and implant the living, active, powerful thoughts and ways of the Lord Almighty. To receive the engrafted word of God is to give place and preeminence to it, to acknowledge it as the 'superior strain,' and to allow it to bear its fruit upon the efforts of our rootstock."

Minister Liáng let his message settle with the people, sensing that the Spirit was about his holy work of convincing and convicting.

"If you recall a previous message in this series, Pastor Carmichael spoke on the bondage of self-deception. He stated that of all deception, self-deception is the most insidious—for when we deceive ourselves, we do not even perceive that we are deceived.

"Now, please allow me to connect today's message on the engrafting of God's word with our previous study of self-deception. And I must teach this in personal form, so that no ear listening to me can misunderstand the gravity of this passage, the serious state of hearing God's word *without* allowing it entrance to our hearts. Listen, friends! Listen with open, teachable hearts:

"If I hear God's word and reject its authority over me?

"If I hear God's word and disagree with it?

"If I hear God's word and deny it the prerogative to shape my standards and principles?

"If I hear God's word and do not allow it to correct my opinions?

"If I hear God's word and refuse to acknowledge that God is *right,* and I am *wrong?*

"If I hear God's word but reject its application to *my* life?

"If my response to God's word is a 'but' that provides my behavior an exception to or exemption from God's word?"

Minister Liáng looked out over his congregation, speaking under the power of the Holy Spirit.

"Then, my brothers and sisters, Christ is *not* the Lord of my life, and I have entered into self-deception."

~*~

THAT EVENING, PALMER HOUSE'S great room was filled. Present were Rose, Sarah, Olive, Mr. Wheatley, Billy and Marit Evans, Edmund and Joy O'Dell, Isaac and Breona Carmichael, Minister and Mei-Xing Liáng, Mason and Tabitha Carpenter, and Albert and Corrine Johnston, as well as Emily Van der Pol, Grace Minton, and Viola Lind.

Several of the girls of Palmer House were engaged three flights up in the house's vast attic rooms where they watched over the lively group of children also brought together by the evening's guests.

Sarah and Olive served tea and cookies around the great room amid happy conversation. It was not often that these people—those who had been at the center of Palmer House's beginnings a decade past and who shared so much history—were able to gather at the same time.

Joy had asked them to come together that she might speak of her burden for missing children.

When the group had fellowshipped for the space of half an hour, Joy asked for their attention. "Thank you for coming this evening. I have something upon my heart that I wish to share with you."

Joy gathered herself. "You, our dearest friends, stood by me when Dean Morgan took our baby, Edmund, and when Grant passed shortly after. I realize it has been eight years since Edmund was taken, and it is hard to imagine that he is now eight years old"—here her voice cracked—"but in the years that have passed, you have been faithful to pray with us and believe that the Lord will, someday, bring him back to us."

Minister Liáng spoke up. "Time means nothing to our God, Joy. We and our families will never give up on friends or family members who walk away from Jesus, and we shall never give up on those who have been taken from us. We shall not fail to pray for your son Edmund, Joy."

Joy swallowed. "Thank you. Thank you all. Your pledge to pray and believe that God *will* return Edmund to us has given me great comfort and strength."

Joy drew a deep breath and continued, "As we have experienced many times, a family that is committed to the Lord has tremendous power in prayer. Papa used to say, 'In God, the lost are found.' We made his saying, *Lost Are Found*, our banner with regards to our baby son." She cleared her throat. "And now, I believe the Lord wishes me to reach out to other parents who find themselves in similar dire straits."

Joy described Mr. and Mrs. Simmons, the young couple who had appealed to the Pinkertons to find their missing child, and how her husband had called upon her to speak to them of her own loss.

"No one understands how devastating it is when your child has gone missing or has been taken—no one but another parent who has suffered a similar tragedy. Edmund and I were, by the grace of God, able to lead this bereft mother and father to the Savior, and it was through this encounter that I felt the Lord speak to me about aiding other families of missing children."

Joy outlined her ideas for a loose association to encourage and minister to parents of lost children. "We would employ all avenues open to us— such as newspaper and radio—to spread word to the public to watch for these children. And, in remembrance of Papa and our own motto, we would call the association *Lost Are Found*."

When she had finished speaking, the group engaged in an hour of lively questions and proposals.

Then, Mr. Wheatley's quavering voice spoke up. "I have something I wish to say."

"Certainly, dear Mr. Wheatley," Joy responded.

"I never married, never had children. You who are in this room have been my family—my only family—for more than a decade. You have cared for me when I was sick, you have fed me and seen to my needs, and you have loved me. I do not know where I would be without all of you. And you, Miss Joy? We been through a lot together; you are as dear to me as a daughter. Your babies are like my own grandsons."

His voice shook with more than age. "I have done what I could to keep this grand old lady of a house in working order and her grounds shipshape. Seems, though, to my very great chagrin, that I have neither the stamina nor the strength I once had, and I fear that what I do no longer pays my way here."

Murmurs of denial swept the room, and it was Rose who put into words what the others were thinking. "Mr. Wheatley, your kind, loving, and stabilizing presence in this home is priceless, particularly to the girls who live here. Many of them have never had the friendship of a father or grandfather. Your position in this house is, without question, invaluable and irreplaceable."

Sarah found herself agreeing with Rose. Mr. Wheatley was the only man of her acquaintance she fully trusted—but she did not see how his statement related to Joy's proposed organization. "Mr. Wheatley? Perhaps you have more to say?"

"Yup. I suppose I said all that to say this: I may not be as productive as I once was, but I would very much like to help with Joy's idea by the making of some signs. They would read, simply, *Lost Are Found*. Palmer House, where it all started, would get the first one. It may take me a bit o' time but, as I am able to make more of them, I would give signs to all of you, our faithful friends."

Mason, Tabitha's husband, appeared thoughtful. "What would we do with these signs, Mr. Wheatley?"

"I had thought we would put them beside the doors of our homes . . . to remind us to pray."

Joy immediately grasped Mr. Wheatley's meaning. "I think I understand! The signs would serve as a reminder to us to continue to pray for Edmund's return—but also, as our organization grows, we could offer the signs to other parents of lost children. The signs would then serve a second, broader purpose, a means of uniting and strengthening this association of bereaved parents and of making the public aware of these missing children."

"That's it," Mr. Wheatley wheezed. "That's it in a nutshell."

"I, fer one, am likin' th' idee o' these signs,' Breona declared. "Aye, we bin livin' an' a-prayin' by this motto near on a decade—bu' what aboot our bairn? These signs be a means o' tellin' them Edmund's story an' passin' on our faith t' them."

"Yes, passing on our faith to our children," Tabitha repeated. "We have given birth to a new generation, and our children will not know or care about Edmund unless we tell them, unless we remind them to pray with us for his salvation and his return. These signs will help ensure that our shared history of what God has done for us—and what we believe he *will* do—is rehearsed to the upcoming generation and the generation after that."

She looked from face to face. "Who here can know the importance of passing on this legacy, *in God the lost are found?* Who can know how vital these signs and their message will prove to our grandchildren and great-grandchildren?"

Tabitha's words were potent, filled, perhaps, with prophetic power. The gathering stilled to consider them.

"Well said, Tabitha," Minister Liáng murmured. "Well said, indeed."

Billy spoke up. "I shall help you with the signs, Mr. Wheatley. You and I together can get them done in quick time."

"Thank you, Billy. Knew I could count on you. Started working on the first one when I heard Miss Joy tell Miss Rose 'bout her idea."

Sarah leaned forward when Mr. Wheatley produced a length of finished metal eighteen inches long and possibly four inches high. He held it up. The background of the sign was painted a dark green; the plain, raised lettering was painted white and read: LOST ARE FOUND.

Mr. Wheatley's shaking hands offered the sign to O'Dell, and he and Joy studied it together.

"It is perfect, Mr. Wheatley," Joy whispered. "Perfect."

"May we have the second of these?" O'Dell asked. "As you suggested, we shall mount it next to our front door to remind us of the faithfulness of God's promises and prompt us to pray daily."

"We shall take one and do the same," Mei-Xing and Minister Liáng chimed in together.

"As shall we," Isaac Carmichael and Albert Johnston echoed at the same time.

Emily, Grace, and Viola said the same.

Joy was overcome. "Thank you. Thank you all. I am grateful to you, our family and friends!"

"Mr. Wheatley, how many can you and Billy make?" Rose asked.

"As many as we be needing."

"Mama and I had thought to write to our family and friends in RiverBend and Omaha, explaining our organization," Joy said. "Søren and Meg. Brian and Fiona. Pastor and Vera Medford. David and Uli. Arne and Anna. Karl, Kjell, and their families."

"I am certain they will join us and ask for signs for their homes, too," Rose added.

Mei-Xing, who had been quiet and thoughtful for much of the meeting, asked a question. "Joy? How do you propose to spread the word regarding the association? Through the Pinkertons? Denver is distant and somewhat disconnected from the real population centers of the country."

Joy looked to her husband. He nodded once; Joy then turned her eyes to her lap before saying, "Yes, the Pinkertons will be most helpful. Of course, as you suggest, what might be needed is a more . . . centralized headquarters for the association."

The room quieted again. Mei-Xing stared steadily at Joy, waiting for her to continue, but it was O'Dell who spoke. "Not soon, not next year, but within two to three years, I may be offered a new position: head of the Chicago Pinkerton office."

Sarah could not believe her ears. "You would move? Away?"

"Nothing has been decided, of course, but I have been . . . approached."

"Chicago would provide a more effective hub from which to grow the association," Joy said softly.

Sarah turned. "And you, Miss Rose?"

Rose met Sarah's concerned gaze. "When they move, I shall likely retire and go with them. However, this is still some time in the future, and we wish this possibility to remain between those of us in this room. At the same time, we covet your prayers for the Lord's guidance."

Sarah's thoughts churned. *Two or three years? In three years, Rose will be seventy-four.*

*I wanted to come alongside her and help her manage Palmer House, take some of the burden from her shoulders. But if Joy sells her shop and moves? If Rose retires and goes with them?*

Sarah knew she could never fill Rose's shoes. Not in a million years.

*What would become of Palmer House? What would become of me?*

She felt the sure footing of her world crack and fall out from under her.

EARLY MONDAY MORNING, Sarah closed the front door of Palmer House behind her and spotted the sign Mr. Wheatley had displayed last evening. It was freshly mounted to the wall beside the door jamb. Her fingertips traced the even, white letters: LOST ARE FOUND.

While her fingers remained on the sign, Sarah prayed for the return of Joy's son, but in her heart, she was consumed with her own situation—with Rose's possible departure and, worse, the failing state of her heart.

It was the first time she had acknowledged her precarious spiritual condition.

*Without Joy's shop and Palmer House, who would I be? No one. I would be jobless and alone in the world.*

Her breath caught as a dark voice whispered, *You would not be alone. You would have Lola.*

Desire stirred within her as she recalled their entwined fingers and Lola's seductive touch. Sarah shivered. She hurried down the walk toward the gate, praying as she went—or was she pleading?

*Lord, you are the God of the impossible!*

*But can you save me from myself?*

*Can you, Lord?*

*For I fear you cannot.*

# $\mathcal{C}$HAPTER 14

A nother week passed. Another Sunday dawned.
The contingent from Palmer House, including Sarah, walked to
church and occupied two rows in the congregation. Blythe planted
herself by Sarah's side, between Sarah and Rose.
She leaned on Sarah a little, looked up, and smiled; Sarah kissed the top of
Blythe's golden curls.

*How I love this girl.*

Pastor Carmichael stepped onto the platform and surveyed the
congregation of Calvary Temple with affection. "My dear brothers and
sisters, let us continue our study of 'The Overcoming Christian Life.' In a
previous message from this series, we looked at the connection between
bondage and deception.

"In that message, I differentiated between overt, external bondages and
covert, internal bondages—those sins we may be able to hide from the
view of others and that we attempt to hide from God himself."

Heads nodded in remembrance.

"Scripture tells us that nothing in all creation is hidden from God, so I
then asked the question: When we think to 'hide' what is in our hearts from
God, are we not deceiving ourselves?"

Some in the congregation murmured, "Yes"; others said, "Amen."

"To refresh what I taught in that lesson, when we deceive ourselves, it
is called 'self-deception.' Anything that contradicts God's word is
deception—a lie. Self-deception, then, is a lie we embrace, a falsehood we
justify and exalt above God's word."

"Self-deception is a form of idolatry—for we have lifted our own
opinions above the Lord's righteous decrees. And, just as every idol must
be torn down, self-deception must also be torn down.

"So, in today's message, I begin with this question: What is the
antidote for self-deception? What empowers the disciple of Christ to tear
down a stronghold of self-deception? The only antidote to self-deception
is truth, truth applied directly to the deception.

"Many people are walking through life asking, not unlike Pontius Pilate, 'What is truth?' Pilate was looking for truth in an ideal or a code of conduct, but truth cannot be relegated to mere knowledge nor can truth be right for one man and wrong for another.

"Scripture tells us that we serve *the God of truth*. Truth is not an idea or a code of conduct; truth is defined by the nature and character of God Almighty.

*"He is the Rock, his work is perfect;*
*for all his ways are judgment:*
*a God of truth and without iniquity,*
*just and right is he*
*(Deuteronomy 32:4),*

"and the Psalmist tell us:

*"Into thine hand I commit my spirit:*
*thou hast redeemed me, O Lord God of truth*
*(Psalm 31:5).*

"When God the Father sent his Son into the world, Jesus embodied and demonstrated all that his Father is. Jesus said, *Anyone who has seen me has seen the Father*. It should be no surprise, then, that Jesus also said, *I am the way, **the truth**, and the life: no man cometh unto the Father, but by me.*

"God's word is infused with his nature and character: His word cannot lie any more than God himself can! 2 Corinthians 6:7 declares Scripture to be *the word of truth*. And truth is of vital importance to the Christian—in fact, we cannot come to God without truth. 1 Timothy 2:3-4 tells us:

*"For this is good and acceptable*
*in the sight of God our Saviour;*
*Who will have all men to be saved,*
*and to come unto the knowledge of the truth.*

"What more had Jesus to say about truth? As he prayed to his Father he said, *Sanctify them through thy truth: thy word is truth*. To us he said, *If ye continue in my word, then are ye my disciples indeed; And ye shall know the truth, and the truth shall make you free.*

"Christian theologians tell us that truth is *ontological*. This large word means that truth is reality—it is the way the world surely is, the way things actually are. God, as the author and creator of life, is likewise the sole author and creator of all truth—what he says is truth, *is truth*.

"To recap, truth is the very nature of God; Jesus is God made flesh and he embodies truth. God has given us his word, and his word is truth! We cannot escape the truth—for God has made it known to us through his Son and through his word. Truth, like God himself, is unchanging and eternal.

"What God says, he will do; what he declares, will never change. God alone determines truth."

Sarah shivered and stared at her hands: They were clenched so tightly that her fingertips were white.

~*~

FOR A SECOND WEEK, SARAH did not return to Palmer House after work until just prior to dinner, having spent the last hour the shop was open—and another half hour after locking the doors—with Lola. Sarah had no doubts that Rose would, at some point, notice her late returns and make mention of them.

Sarah had no intention of lying to Rose; rather, she had practiced a perfectly accurate response: "Lola comes by the shop near closing, and we visit for a bit."

There was nothing false about the statement on its surface—Sarah had worded it with care and was ready to offer it the moment Rose questioned her. Nonetheless, that did not prevent Sarah's conscience from pricking her for what her "clever statement" omitted.

*But what if Miss Rose knew . . .*

"If she knew what? That Lola is my friend? That we spend time together? For pity's sake—am I not permitted to choose my own friends?" Sarah would not allow herself to put into words her emerging sentiments regarding Lola and their escalating physical involvement.

She refused to acknowledge the dark path down which those affections were taking her, so she overruled her conscience with whatever justification came to mind. She even, as she climbed the porch steps to Palmer House that evening, averted her gaze from the sign hanging beside the door.

It did not matter: The image of the white letters on a green field stood before the eyes of her imagination, proclaiming, in God the LOST ARE FOUND.

The lost? Sarah wondered briefly if *she* were lost—not misplaced or absent, but rudderless, without moorings, adrift in a vast sea, drifting farther and farther from shore each day.

*Dear God! Have I lost my way? Am I now the lost one? O Jesus, my Lord! Do you hear me? Do you see me? Can you find me?*

Stiffening her back, Sarah suppressed her cry for help. What mattered at the moment was that she was in time for dinner and had given no cause to pique anyone's curiosity. She entered the house, hung her coat, scarf, and hat on the hall tree, and joined the others gathering in the dining room.

Blythe, who was helping serve the meal, patted the seat she had saved for Sarah next to hers. "Sit with me, Sarah?"

"Of course, sweetheart."

Dinner then proceeded in its normal fashion.

Normal? Amidst the happy chatter around the table, Sarah was mainly silent—as she had been for some days. Sarah spoke when spoken to but said little else.

When the girls began to serve dessert, Blythe whispered in Sarah's ear, "Frances cut the pie a little crooked, and I managed to put by one of the bigger slices for you, Sarah. I know how you love pecan pie."

Sarah looked down at the plate Blythe set before her. "Um, thank you, dear."

Meals were adequate at Palmer House but, with the exception of Sundays, desserts were considered a luxury. Nevertheless, Marit managed to make sure most dinners included a sweet, albeit diminutive, ending. That often meant she baked a single cake or pie and that dessert was cut not six or eight ways, but in sixteen portions, meaning a "slice" was hardly more than a sliver. Since Toby was not old enough for his slice, Marit always gave Billy, whose work was so physically demanding, the leftover piece.

This evening, Sarah was not hungry and could not do justice to the marginally "bigger" sliver of pie Blythe had made special effort to give her. Knowing Blythe had acted out of love, Sarah forced herself to take one bite. When it sat like sand in her mouth, she forced herself to swallow it, then toyed with the rest of the pecan filling.

Unfortunately, Blythe noticed. She noticed everything Sarah did.

"Are you not hungry, Sarah?"

"I suppose I am not, Blythe. Thank you, though, for your thoughtfulness." Sarah set her plate in front of the girl. "Here. You finish it."

Sarah realized that she had injured Blythe's feelings. She reached her arm about Blythe's thin shoulders and hugged her. "Please do not be upset with me, little sister; I merely have a lot on my mind. I would feel much better, though, if you ate my serving. Please? For me?"

Mollified, Blythe smiled. "All right, Sarah. For you."

*I do not believe I have ever met anyone so aptly named*, Sarah thought. *When she smiles, sunshine dances on her sweet face.*

Dinner ended. Everyone stood and began to clear the table and restore the dining room to order. Sarah attempted a quick exit, but Rose waylaid her.

"May I have a moment of your time, Sarah? In the parlor?"

Nothing in Rose's bearing indicated what she wished of Sarah, but still, Sarah's heart pounded in her ears. Over its hammering she heard herself say, "Of course, Miss Rose." She followed Rose through the great room and hallway into the parlor.

Rose sat on the settee and patted the seat next to her. Sarah sank down and waited, her gaze fixed on her hands folded in her lap. She did not want to meet Rose's scrutiny; she was afraid to see disappointment in those sweetly solemn gray eyes.

Rose, too, waited. When Sarah did not look up, Rose said, "You are so very much the daughter of my heart, Sarah, that it grieves me to begin this difficult conversation with you."

"Oh?" was all Sarah could manage.

"Yes, it is very difficult, indeed. However, I cannot imagine that you are surprised that I have asked you to meet with me."

Again, all Sarah could answer was, "Oh?" Her tongue felt glued to the roof of her mouth.

Rose cleared her throat. "Your behavior these past weeks has altered in such a marked manner, that it is apparent to all who know and love you. I have been approached by no less than five of our girls asking, 'Is something amiss with Sarah?'

"For myself, I note this change to have begun around the time you accepted the invitation to Lola's musicale. Although my spirit was disquieted by the invitation, you pointed out—quite rightly—that you are not merely one of the girls here. You are very much a pillar of this house, someone upon whom I increasingly rely.

"And so, since you are not subject to all the rules of the house, I did not ask why you came home later the evening of the musicale than Mr. Williams declared he would have you home. I knew you were late, you see, because I fell asleep on the couch in the great room around half past twelve. I also refrained from questioning you much regarding the fall you took and the injury that resulted from it. Perhaps I was loath to probe too deeply because I was already uneasy. I chose to pray and not to . . . to meddle.

"Conversely, I confess to you now that my heart has not been at peace concerning you since that day, and I have watched this alteration in your mood and behavior with growing distress. I feel that I cannot now allow these changes to continue without comment or understanding."

When Sarah said nothing, Rose reached over and took her hand in hers. "Dearest Sarah, since you returned to work at the shop, you have come home late each day. Can you tell me why?"

The response Sarah had memorized refused to present itself with the polished delivery she had rehearsed; instead, it came out in stiff, disjointed phrases. "Near closing. We visit—that is, Lola and I—she comes by—and then the shop closes. I mean, when the shop is closing, Lola drops by and-and-and we visit for a bit. After."

"You are saying that each afternoon as the shop is closing, Lola comes by and the two of you visit for a spell. Is that right?"

"Um, yes. We are . . . friends."

"I am happy for you to make friends of your own age, Sarah. This is natural and healthy. However, I do wonder, these many weeks now gone by, that you have not brought your *friend* home for dinner as I suggested. Do you not want us to know Lola?"

"I . . ." Sarah's reply trailed off.

"Is it, perhaps, because Lola is not a believer? I think we cannot pretend that she is. She spoke of her and her friends drinking to excess, and you and I both heard her demean those who call themselves by the name of Christ. These are not the actions or words of a disciple of Christ."

Rose waited, but Sarah had no response. At last, Rose said, "I wish to ask you a question, Sarah, and I would ask you to consider it carefully before you answer."

Sarah sighed. "All right."

"Do you not wish for Lola to know Jesus as you do?"

Rose's question confounded Sarah. *Do I not wish Lola to know Jesus? To be saved and set free as I am?* Even worse, Sarah was appalled at the immediate rise of anger Rose's query produced—and the vehement *no* that followed on the heels of her anger. She was horrified, too, because one simple interrogative had sliced open and laid bare the truth—the truth that she did not desire a single thing about Lola to change: not her brash and risqué speech, not her brazen opinions, not her flirtatious, sensual behavior—and certainly not the way Sarah felt herself responding to Lola.

Minutes went by without Sarah replying: She was wrestling with desires she had not, before this moment, admitted to.

Tears shimmering on her lashes, Rose whispered, "You have not spoken, Sarah, but perhaps by not replying, you have given your answer? I can only surmise that you must harbor an affection for Lola. So, I ask you, if you do care for Lola, could you countenance her spending eternity separated from God?"

Annoyed, Sarah shifted. *Well, of course, I do not wish for Lola to spend eternity separated from God.*

But if Sarah believed Rose did not perceive the darker, unspoken issues at stake, her next words rocked Sarah to her core. "Sarah, can you tell me that your affection for Lola is holy before God?"

"W-what?"

"I am asking you plainly: Is your friendship with Lola holy before God? Or has it strayed onto an unholy path?"

Sarah sputtered. "How can you ask such an ugly thing?"

"The matter is simple, Sarah. If you have nothing to hide, you should be able to reply."

Sarah dropped her chin. "I-I do not know how to answer you."

Rose gently persisted. "What can you, as a daughter of God, saved from your sins, have in common with someone whom we have both heard scoff at the name of our Savior? Since Lola is not a believer, have you considered the possibility that she is enticing you away from Jesus? That she is drawing you into temptations that cannot lead to anything other than sin?"

Sarah whispered aloud the phrase that had been haunting her for days. "Is it . . . is it sin?"

"Please look at me, my daughter."

Sarah lifted her head but marginally.

"Sarah, I must answer you directly, in a manner that leaves no room for ambiguity or misunderstanding. Jesus, our Savior, countered the Tempter thusly: *It is written, man shall not live by bread alone, but by every word that proceedeth out of the mouth of God.*

"Jesus is our pattern in all things, and Jesus himself was quoting God's written word. Following his example, then, I shall quote God's written word: It is written,

> *"Be ye not unequally yoked together with unbelievers:*
> *for what fellowship hath righteousness with unrighteousness?*
> *and what communion hath light with darkness?"*

"So . . . you are saying that if Lola were a Christian . . ."

"Oh, Sarah. You are better acquainted with Scripture than that. You know it is also written:

> *"For this cause God gave them up unto vile affections:*
> *for even their women did change the natural use*
> *into that which is against nature"*

Sarah began to tremble, but Rose pressed on. "Sarah, I must be clear: You cannot presume any future in which Lola holds the place only a husband should hold."

Sarah's voice cracked. "But . . . but Lola, she has pursued me; she has drawn me gently to her. No man has ever treated me with such kindness!"

"Shall we not be honest, dear one? You have never allowed a man to woo you."

"Because I do not want *a man* lording it over me, holding my life in his hands, making decisions for me, controlling me, and telling me what to do!"

"Be that as it may, what is evolving between you and Lola is wrong, and it can never be anything *but* wrong. Nothing, including how you feel toward men, my dearest Sarah, can or will ever justify it.

"So, I must ask you: Have you exchanged the love of God Almighty for Lola's affections? If you choose friendship with Lola over communion with God, has she not become an object of worship? An idol? Colossians 3:5 tells us that 'inordinate affection' *is* idolatry.

"What counsel, then, does the Bible provide regarding idolatry? 1 Corinthians 10:14 commands, *Wherefore, my dearly beloved, flee from idolatry.* The hooks of idolatry are insidious and treacherous. We are to flee, Sarah. Flee! Escape! We must run from whatever or whomever we are tempted to place before or beside God himself. *Thou shalt worship the Lord thy God, and him only shalt thou serve.*"

Sarah finally turned to Rose and whispered, "But what . . . what do I do with my heart, Miss Rose? How can I deny how I feel?"

"Oh, my darling girl, I understand that your feelings are real, but do we live only by our feelings? Do you not recall that our uncrucified hearts are flawed? Jeremiah 17:9 tells us, *The heart is deceitful above all things, and desperately wicked.* We cannot rightly judge ourselves with our own flawed hearts, our own standards, or our own eyes. No, we must live by what God tells us is good, right, and true."

Quiet tears slipped from Sarah's eyes, and Rose wept with her, even as she continued, "Sarah. Ephesians 5:5 says that no one *who is an idolater, hath any inheritance in the kingdom of Christ and of God.* I must urge you, then, in the sight of God, to break off your friendship with Lola. You must, Sarah, for your sake and for hers."

"I-I fear it would crush her, Miss Rose, and I could not bear to hurt her so—and is it not wrong to hurt someone?"

Rose considered Sarah. "I must speak truth to you, Sarah, for Jesus told his disciples that the truth and only the truth of his word will make us free. Yes, I must speak truth to the great lie you have voiced."

Sarah's eyes widened. "The lie?"

"You say you cannot bear to hurt Lola, that it is wrong to hurt her so: *That is a lie.*"

"But . . ."

"An enormous gulf lies between 'hurt' and 'harm,' Sarah, and not all that hurts us, harms us: *Faithful are the wounds of a friend.* Judge for yourself—will you speak the truth to Lola so that Jesus has time and opportunity to save her from hell? Or will you deceive her by obscuring the certainty of the coming judgment?

"Which of these choices will actually *harm* Lola? Which is the evidence of *real* love? Painful truth in this lifetime or deception leading to irrevocable judgment in the next?"

"O God!" Sarah cried.

"And it grieves me further to also tell you, Sarah, that not only does your continued relationship with Lola put your walk with the Lord in grave jeopardy, but you also stand to lose everything else good and beloved in your life."

Sarah turned her wet face to Rose. "What do you mean?"

"I am charged with maintaining a godly home within these walls. If you were to choose to continue your relationship with Lola, could I allow you to remain here at Palmer House? No, dear one. I could not allow that."

"What? No!"

"This cannot be news to you, dearest. Do you not recall our first weeks here? Do you not remember that tense morning at breakfast, ten years past now, when I reminded all of us that living at Palmer House was a privilege that came with obligations?"

Sarah had not forgotten. A decade later, Rose's words were still fresh in her memory:

*Each of you knew the expectations before you accepted our offer to become part of this family. Unfortunately, attitudes and behaviors as of late have deteriorated badly. This must change, and it must change today.*

*. . . If you no longer wish to participate, then you are choosing to go elsewhere.*

Sarah whispered, "It was the morning I surrendered my life to Jesus."

"Yes, it was, and you have grown in the truth since then. You know the difference between right and wrong. Therefore, I must ask you, Sarah, have you not considered how damaging your example would be to the young, wounded lives who have only lately begun to trust in Jesus?

"Think, Sarah! *Think of Blythe!* Do you see how your little sister follows your every move with her eyes? How she emulates you and longs to be like you? If I permitted you to remain here and you were to injure her faith . . ."

Rose's throat closed on her words. "I can only quote from Matthew 18:6, where it is written,

*"But whoso shall offend*
*one of these little ones which believe in me,*
*it were better for him that a millstone*
*were hanged about his neck,*
*and that he were drowned in the depth of the sea."*

Sarah buried her face in her hands. "I shall not harm Blythe! No, I shall not! She has suffered far too much already. I could not bear to see her destroyed again."

"Then you will break off your friendship with Lola?"

Through her tears, Sarah slowly nodded.

"I must have your promise on this, Sarah."

Many seconds ticked by before Sarah whispered, "I promise."

~*~

SARAH'S NERVES WERE ON edge Friday morning; she had made a promise to Rose to break off her relationship with Lola, but she was fearful of the confrontation. When the shop's telephone rang around ten, Sarah answered it with trepidation.

"Good morning. Michaels' Fine Furnishings."

"Good morning, dearest Sarah!"

Sarah smiled in spite of her intentions and turned her back to the shop and Corrine's watchful eyes.

"Hello, Lola. How are you?"

"Missing you."

"Um, will I see you this afternoon?" While Sarah admitted that she had to follow through on her promise to Rose, she longed to see Lola once more. She would tell her in person that they must not see each other any longer.

"No, you will not, I am sorry to say. The Pythia has the latest songs to learn and polish before Saturday evening. Also, Meg and Dannie are feuding, and I must play the role of peacemaker or our engagements this weekend will end in disaster."

"So, you will not be coming this afternoon?"

"Not this afternoon nor tomorrow, I fear. I am sorry. I hope you will not be angry?"

"No, not angry. Of course not." Sarah exhaled. On one hand, she was disappointed; on the other, she felt she had been given a reprieve.

"I shall certainly come Monday, my dark-haired beauty, and perhaps I shall bring you chocolate."

"Oh, how lovely! Well, I shall see you then."

When Sarah hung up, she relaxed. *I cannot be blamed for not seeing Lola until Monday*, she thought. *It is not my fault I cannot keep my promise until then.*

The relief she felt was palpable.

# PART 2

*But now thus saith the Lord
that created thee, O Jacob
and he that formed thee, O Israel,
Fear not: for I have redeemed thee,
I have called thee by thy name;
thou art mine.
(Isaiah 43:1, KJV)*

# CHAPTER 15

L ola appeared at the shop Monday afternoon and, as she had intimated, she presented Sarah with a sizable box of assorted chocolates. The box was beautifully wrapped in gilt foil and tied with a wide, red organza ribbon and bow. The scent of newly poured chocolate wafted in the air.

"Sweets for the sweet," Lola murmured as she embraced Sarah, "made fresh this morning by a chocolatier on Grand Street. I selected each piece especially for you."

Sarah was touched. "Thank you, Lola. I-I have never had a whole box of chocolates of my own." She sniffed at the box. "Mmm."

"I shall think of you eating them," Lola said. She caressed Sarah's cheek in a manner that was unmistakably intimate. Sarah blushed and turned away—but she had thrilled under Lola's touch.

*I promised Miss Rose.*
*I promised Miss Rose.*
*I promised Miss Rose.*

"It is all right, Sarah," Lola whispered. "I shall wait for you—as long as I must. Surely you know by now that I love you and long to care for you, Sarah."

Sarah's heart pounded. *I promised Miss Rose I would break off my friendship with Lola, but how can I . . . how can I dash Lola's heart to pieces? I cannot do it . . . today. Perhaps tomorrow would be better.*

Sarah set aside her dissembling arguments; she tugged on the ribbon around the box instead. It fell away, and she lifted the foil-wrapped lid, exposing an exquisite array of candies—pralines, caramels, truffles, bonbons, chocolate-covered cherries, and almond-crusted toffees.

"Go ahead, darling. Try one," Lola urged her.

As Sarah selected her first piece, a convicting thought intruded. *Esau sold his birthright for a mess of porridge; have I done the same for a box of chocolates?*

~*~

SARAH AND LOLA SPENT time together at the shop every afternoon that week. Lola even walked Sarah to her trolley stop each evening, vowing, "It is too dark for you to be walking the streets alone."

Sarah reveled in the care Lola showed for her, in the small gifts she brought, and in her patience. At the same time, Sarah wrestled with her conscience: She had given her word to Miss Rose and had not fulfilled that promise. Not *yet*. She refused to admit the truth to herself: that she had no intention of breaking off with Lola.

Because Sarah was cognizant of Rose's warnings regarding her example before the girls of the house, she was, as a result, guarded around Corrine and withdrawn at Palmer House, even shunning Blythe. Blythe's pained expression did not escape Sarah's notice—but Sarah told herself that she was protecting the girl from the further harm of a bad example.

In reality, Blythe interpreted Sarah's avoidance as rejection, and she suffered the agony of not knowing what she had done to lose Sarah's affection.

~*~

WHEN SARAH STEPPED THROUGH the door Saturday evening, pre-dinner preparations were not ongoing in the normally well-timed routine that Marit demanded. The girls milled about the dining room without direction—and the smell of overdone meat drifted in from the kitchen.

"Goodness! What is happening here?" Sarah demanded.

"Oh, hello, Sarah," Pansy greeted her. "Blythe has a stomach complaint; Miss Rose and Marit are upstairs with her. Dinner will be delayed."

"Why, where is Olive?"

"She is off to visit Gretl for the weekend and will be gone until Monday." Pansy's little mouth tightened. "Really, Sarah, if you were not so distracted lately, you would have remembered."

Sarah shook her head. *I, distracted?*

She addressed the milling girls. "Ladies, I would like half of you to finish dinner the best you can—Frances, please take charge in the kitchen. The rest of you, kindly set the table. I shall find out if Miss Rose wishes us to eat without her."

Sarah ran up the stairs as quickly as her skirts and weak knee allowed her. She gave Pansy and Blythe's door two soft knocks, then entered without waiting for a reply.

Rose and Marit turned at her entrance; Rose spoke. "Ah, Sarah; please keep back. I do not think we need have much concern, but we do not yet know if Blythe is contagious."

"What are her complaints?"

"Fever. Chills, Nausea. Stomach cramps. All indications of stomach influenza."

Sarah relaxed. "Horrible, but short-lived, I hope."

Rose smiled. "We hope so, also. Will you see to dinner and restore order? I can only imagine the chaos downstairs."

Sarah chuckled. "You imagined right! I gave instructions before I came up, but I fear the roast may be beyond rescue."

Marit slapped her forehead. "Ach! I should haf told Frances to take it out from the oven."

At the sound of Sarah's voice, Blythe opened her eyes. She tried to smile but groaned instead.

"Rest, my little sister," Sarah called to her. "You will be fine soon."

Dinner—such as it was—was followed by a peaceful evening without much concern over Blythe's condition. Marit came down and ate from the plate set aside for her. Afterward, she joined her family in their little cottage. Sarah went back upstairs to check on Rose and was relieved that Blythe was sleeping.

"I think she will be fine by tomorrow," Rose said. "The complaint should have run its course by then."

"Come down and have your dinner before it spoils, Miss Rose," Sarah urged her.

"Yes, I suppose I should."

When Rose and Sarah looked in on Blythe near bedtime, Pansy had just settled under her covers on one side of the room; Blythe was still sleeping on the other.

"I am concerned about her fever," Rose murmured.

"Surely, rest is the best thing for her?" Sarah asked.

"Yes, you are right."

Rose nodded at Pansy. "Good night, Pansy. Do wake us if Blythe needs us."

"I shall. Good night, Miss Rose."

Pansy would not look at Sarah, but she muttered, "Good night . . . Sarah."

*She has remained angry with me*, Sarah realized.

"Good night, Pansy." Sarah went to her own bed, confident that Blythe would be better by morning.

~*~

STILL EARLY IN THE NIGHT, Sarah awakened to find Pansy leaning over her, roughly shaking her.

"What is it?"

"Blythe is a-crying something awful. I think she is terrible sick. Shall I wake Miss Rose?"

"I shall get up." Pansy's response was terse. "Well? Should I wake Miss Rose?"

"Not yet. Let me come and check on her first."

Sarah heard Blythe's pitiful wails while she was padding down the hall toward the bedroom. She found the girl thrashing against the covers, her arms wrapped around her middle. Her body was covered in a sheen of perspiration, her bright curls dull and plastered to her head. Blythe moaned and then her moan rose into a shriek.

Sarah placed her hand on the Blythe's forehead. She was burning up. "Blythe! Blythe! Wake up, sweetheart."

"It hurts! Hurts!" Blythe drew her knees up to her stomach until she was bent in two.

"Where does it hurt, child?"

Blythe panted against the pain and tried to answer. "S-stomach. My back. Please . . . make it stop!"

Without warning, Blythe gagged. Sarah reached for a basin and caught the little vomit that came up with a choking cough.

"Pansy. I need cool water and a clean cloth."

"Yes, miss."

Sarah cleaned Blythe's mouth and sponged her face with water, but Blythe's pain only worsened, twisting her groans and squeezing them into screams.

"Wake Miss Rose," Sarah instructed Pansy. "Tell her we need a doctor."

Sarah did not leave Blythe's side until the doctor arrived, half an hour later. By then, most of the house was awake, wincing at Blythe's every cry of pain. Rose sat in a chair near Blythe's head, her hand resting on Blythe's matted hair, her lips moving in prayer.

When Dr. Croft entered the room, he barely nodded in Rose or Sarah's direction; his focus was entirely on Blythe. He stooped over her bed, felt her forehead, then asked her, "Miss, where does it hurt?"

Blythe did not answer. She keened again as the pain took her.

"She said her stomach and her back," Sarah offered.

Croft glanced at Sarah. "I need your help to palpate her abdomen."

He rolled Blythe onto her back. "Hold her hands away from her belly, please."

Sarah did as he asked, but Blythe fought her, grasping at her belly instead.

"Pansy. Help me."

Pansy and Sarah, together, each took one of Blythe's hands and pulled them away. Dr. Croft's examination did not take long.

"The lower right side of her abdomen is distended. I am convinced it is appendicitis. We must get her to St. Luke's as soon as possible—before the appendix bursts."

"What is to be done?" Sarah demanded.

"Surgery to remove the diseased appendix. I shall take her in my motor car." Croft was already gathering Blythe into his arms. He jerked his chin at Sarah. "Bring a blanket for her and follow me. You will keep her still during the drive."

"But I am not dressed!"

"Then go! And do not dawdle. Time is of the essence."

Fuming at his peremptory orders, Sarah, nevertheless, grabbed the blanket off Blythe's bed and raced down the hall to her room. When she had buttoned herself into a clean dress, slipped on her boots and hooked enough buttons to keep the boots on her feet, she ran down the stairs and out the front door.

Croft was waiting for her, still holding Blythe while her wailing cries echoed on the empty street. Sarah slipped into the back seat of the doctor's car. Croft laid Blythe on the seat next to Sarah. She cradled Blythe's head in her lap and spread the blanket over her.

"There, there, darling girl," Sarah crooned. "You will be all right soon."

Blythe writhed and moaned, unable to be still, drawing her knees up and twisting as though attempting to escape the pain clawing at her insides. Then, near the hospital, Blythe suddenly calmed.

"Blythe? Dear? Are you all right?"

Blythe moaned a little. "S-sarah?"

"Yes, dear?"

"I love you so much, Sarah. You were always good to me."

Sarah started to sob. "I am so sorry, Blythe."

"Sorry? Why?"

"I-I have stayed away . . . lately. I have . . . ignored you."

"I know you love me, Sarah. It is—ohhhh!" Blythe cried out in agony.

"Shhhh, little one. Just rest."

"But . . . but I am so glad you t-told me Jesus would f-find me, Sarah. I am not l-lost anymore . . . ohhhh—"

Blythe's groan tore at Sarah's heart.

"Blythe, sweetheart?"

"I . . . it is . . . all right."

Croft turned his head toward them. "How is she?"

"She ceased thrashing just a moment ago. What does that mean?"

"The respite will not last. When the pain returns, it will be worse."

"But what has happened?"

"Her appendix has ruptured."

Croft was right; by the time he drove to a back door in the hospital's main building, the intense pain had reasserted itself with a vengeance. Blythe could no longer speak; she was alternately crying and screaming. Croft lifted the girl from the back seat and commanded Sarah, "Open that door for me and stay close." He gestured at the hospital.

She ran ahead, pulled open the door, then followed behind. She opened a second door, and they came upon a nursing station. Things moved quickly after that as Croft shouted orders; two orderlies appeared to take Blythe away and nurses wrote down Croft's instructions.

A nurse touched Sarah's elbow. "You cannot remain back here, miss. Please wait on the other side of those doors." She pointed at a set of double doors.

Sarah was alone in the waiting room, but she soon realized how disheveled her hair was when she caught sight of her reflection in one of the windows. She finger-combed out her hair and, lacking enough hairpins to pin it across her head, settled for braiding its length down her back.

With nothing more to keep herself occupied, Sarah paced the small room, praying for Blythe, fighting back her fears. When she grew too tired of walking, she sat down on one of the hard benches.

She did not know when she fell into an exhausted sleep.

A HAND JOSTLED SARAH'S arm. "Miss?"

"Mmm?" Sarah came slowly awake. She stretched her stiff neck and shoulders and looked around. Daylight filtered through the windows that last night had been black boxes reflecting her own image.

"Yes?"

The nurse, a young trainee, stared at the floor. "The doctor will be out to see you shortly, miss."

"How is my friend?"

"The doctor will speak to you when he comes." The nurse left as quickly as she had appeared.

Sarah did not like that the girl had evaded her question and avoided her eyes. Her heart thundered in her chest, and when she stood, she cried out, "No, Lord, please! Please let Blythe be all right!"

Only a minute passed before Croft pushed through the double doors. He still wore the gown he had donned in the surgical ward. It was spattered with blood.

Blythe's blood.

"Dr. Croft?" Sarah whispered.

Croft glanced at Sarah, then away. "As I suspected, her appendix ruptured before we got her here. It spewed infection into her abdominal cavity—and back into her intestines. We lavaged her organs with sterile saline to remove as much of the putrefaction as we could. She was young; ordinarily, she might have stood a fighting chance against the sepsis—but the toxins and the shock of the surgery overwhelmed her already impaired system with frightening speed."

He spoke through clenched jaws, still looking away. "I am truly sorry, Miss Ellinger."

Sarah shook in disbelief. "What are you saying? What do you mean? She-she is dead?"

He blew out a deep breath. "I did not leave her side. She was not in much pain . . . at the end."

Sarah could not follow, could not process what he said. Blythe was gone? Was she never to grow into a woman? Have the family she longed for?

*Was her life for nothing?*

"I have called your friends, the O'Dells, so that you will not be alone."

When Croft finally looked at her, his eyes glinted with something angry, even dangerous. Seeing his fury, Sarah took a half step back and swayed. He reached out a hand to steady her, but she swatted it away. "Y-you said, 'ordinarily she might have stood a fighting chance.' What did you mean by 'ordinarily'?"

That dangerous thing flashed again. "What do I mean? What I mean is that this girl, this *child*—what, fourteen or fifteen years old?—has been horribly violated, Miss Ellinger, *horribly*. Someone—no, *a gang* of someones—has raped and tortured this poor girl. Her thighs and belly are covered with the barely healed scars of cigar burns."

"What?"

"Are you saying you did not know? She was used in such a violent and outrageous manner, that she has unhealed tears and ulcerations, inside and out—resulting in what I surmise was a chronic inflammation and infection in her female organs. Her system was already compromised. In short, she had nothing in reserve to combat rampant peritonitis—*nothing!* No wonder she appeared so frail!"

Sarah sucked in a sob. "But we . . . she came to us in late August, perhaps three months ago now? Pastor and Mrs. Carmichael brought her to us. We were caring for her, but we . . . I did not know about—"

"*Someone* should have known. This is outrageous! Monstrous!"

Sarah found herself on the defensive, reacting to his growing indignation. "Y-you are blaming us? But we did not harm her—we took her off the street. We rescued her!"

She growled at Croft. "*We* did not do this terrible thing. *Men* attacked her—men like *you*, men who prey upon innocent children! All Blythe was guilty of was going out after dark to fetch her uncle *his precious drink!*

"So then, you *did* know."

"I knew the little she confided in me—that she was ashamed of what was done to her. She did not go into detail. She said nothing about . . . she did not tell us that she needed a doctor."

"She should have been examined by a physician."

"How were we to know that?" Sarah racked her mind to come up with an instance where Blythe hinted at her condition. "She never complained—not about anything!"

"Excuses."

Sarah's eyes narrowed. "I do not care for what you are suggesting, Dr. Croft."

"Then allow me to remove my indictment from the realm of 'suggestion,' Miss Ellinger: How dare you take a soul as wounded as poor Blythe's off the street without investigating and uncovering what has wounded her so? And to have the gall to fault *me* for what was done to her? I suppose I am also to blame because I could not save her?"

"Yes," Sarah shouted. "Yes, you are to blame! You and every other man who would use a woman in such an abominable way—and I hate you for it!"

A nurse, drawn to the waiting room by their loud exchange, stared at the two of them, her eyes wide.

"You hate *me*? Really, Miss Ellinger—do you feel that you did not make that abundantly and unmistakably evident upon our first encounter? But, I must ask myself, why should you take such an immediate dislike to *me*? What have *I* done to you or yours? What, for that matter, do you even know of me?"

Croft smiled with cynicism, not amusement. "Do you *know*, for example, how my medical studies demanded not only four years of my life but every penny I had and all my attention and efforts? Of course not; you could have no idea what becoming a physician requires.

"Nor could you *know* that I was, immediately, upon graduation, conscripted into the Army—against my will. I spent nearly two years tending an unending line of wounded in Europe before being discharged to the States, before I moved to Denver to partner with Dr. Murphy.

"There I was, newly returned from the war and a stranger to this city. As I had nothing to call my own, my friend George offered to take me out to buy a bed, perhaps a chest of drawers. George is a good friend, you see—but how could you have *known* that George wishes nothing more for me than to be as happily settled as he is?

"*Smile*, George told me. *Say hello to pretty, virtuous girls*, he said. *Find yourself a godly woman to marry and make a life with.* I cannot number the eligible young ladies to whom he introduced me but, fresh from the war, I was in no fit frame of mind to consider any of them.

"That I, myself, would take notice of a lovely, chaste woman on our foray to purchase bedroom furnishings? Why, George was beside himself. Overjoyed, in fact.

"Yet this woman, the first woman to even remotely interest me—*you*, Miss Ellinger—took umbrage over a simple smile and a perfectly innocent attempt to introduce myself. Frankly, I had not seen a tantrum such as the one you threw that morning in your shop since I left home for medical school."

"Tantrum? You accuse me of throwing *a tantrum?*"

"I grew up with three older sisters. I recognize a tantrum when I see one."

Sarah's jaw dropped. "How dare you speak to me with such outrageous familiarity?"

"How dare I? Because it is not *me* you dislike. No, Miss Ellinger, to put it plainly, you do not like *men*. It should have been obvious to me the day I met you, but I see it plainly now: You hate men, and you are trying to make me—and every other man on the planet—pay for the misdeeds for which one or more men are guilty."

The bones in his face and jaw turned to stone. "How does it feel, Miss Ellinger, to have judged, convicted, and condemned half of the human race based on the narrow scope of your own experiences—a sample size that could not even approach the realm of statistical significance—and yet you call yourself *a Christian?*"

Sarah was not educated, not in mathematics or the physical sciences. Everything she had learned after her childhood ended, she learned via the school of hard knocks—a curriculum devised by the lusts and demands of "cultured gentlemen." She had, therefore, no understanding of the term, *statistical significance*, but she could infer the meaning of *sample size* from its context.

"If you, Dr. Croft, had any inkling what I have lived through, what I have endured and survived, then you would believe me when I say that the overwhelming majority of males in my experience—quite a "significant" number, if you must know—have earned my distrust and disdain."

"Miss Ellinger, I can hardly credit your assertion! *The overwhelming majority of males in your experience?* If I were to name and list every male of your acquaintance, could you categorically condemn the overwhelming majority of them for their behavior? What of your friend, Mr. O'Dell? What of kind old Mr. Wheatley and Billy Evans at Palmer House? How can I believe that you, a confessed Christian woman, have had the introduction of, let alone the exposure to, a number of males large enough to support the wild statement of 'what I have endured and survived'?"

Sarah paled. Her expression transformed before him to a picture of such gravity as to cause Croft to lick his lips and stammer.

"I-I must apologize, Miss Ellinger. I blame my very bad behavior this morning upon being brought up with three sisters who could argue the paint off the walls. I should not have gone after you, hammer and tong, as I would with them.

Sarah waved off his regret with icy scorn. "Please do not apologize *yet again*, Dr. Croft. I do not shy away from truth in conversation. In point of fact, while I laud civility, the overreaching restrictions of 'polite' society can stifle honesty and-and-and . . ."

"Yes, Miss Ellinger?"

"I suppose I should simply say that I prefer honesty between us. Without it, you will continue to disbelieve my assertions."

He folded his arms. "You wish honesty? Very well, then. Tell me what 'the overwhelming majority of men' have done to you."

Sarah opened her mouth, only to splutter, "B-but, surely you know?"

"Know what?"

She shook her head. "No. I cannot tell you. You would not believe me."

"Then whom would I believe? Who could I call upon to give credence to your tale?"

Sarah lifted her chin. "You are new to this city. Have you not speculated about Palmer House? Has no one mentioned what it is?"

It was his turn to be perplexed. "I thought . . . I thought a Christian boardinghouse."

Sarah snorted. "Perhaps you should ask Mr. O'Dell about Palmer House. Then you will have your answer."

"You can tell me yourself."

"I shall not. As you are not a Christian, you would not understand; you would judge us."

"You are wrong about me once more, Miss Ellinger. I *am* a Christian. I love the Lord Jesus. I have dedicated my entire life to serving him in the medical profession. It is not God I have a problem with—it is the church, the bigoted, hypocritical, self-righteous church—such as those who denied Christian burial to enemy soldiers who were but boys sent on a fool's mission by the bigger fools in the German Kaiser's cabinet."

Sarah put her head to one side and considered him. For a long, charged pause she said nothing. And then she murmured, "How does it feel, Dr. Croft, to have judged, convicted, and condemned *the entire Body of Christ* based on the behavior of a sample size that . . . that does not, uh, approach the realm . . . that is not big enough to, that does not—"

Bryan Croft put back his head and laughed. "Oh, that is rich indeed. You had it perfectly—if only you had not lost it before you delivered your *coup de grâce*."

His sarcasm baited Sarah yet again, and she readied a retort—but at that moment, Rose and Edmund O'Dell burst into the waiting room, interrupting Sarah and Croft's fractious row.

For those minutes while they argued, Sarah had forgotten why she was in the waiting room. She had forgotten the dreadful news Croft had delivered.

*Blythe was gone.*

Rose drew near. "Sarah?"

Sarah took a step toward her, then sobbed, "Oh, Miss Rose! Blythe is dead!"

Rose gathered Sarah to herself. "I know, I know. Come, dear. Let me take you home."

Sarah allowed Rose to lead her away, out of the hospital, and into O'Dell's Bergdoll. She said nothing as they drove.

When they arrived at Palmer House, Sarah was immediately surrounded by friends who hugged her and wept with her. It was then that Sarah realized that she did not want to be held and comforted—not, that is, by Rose or Olive or Marit.

Not by anyone but Lola.

# CHAPTER 16

The remainder of Sunday passed in a haze of mourning. The following afternoon, Monday of Thanksgiving week, Palmer House's residents and their friends gathered to lay Blythe to rest. Dr. Croft attended, also. Sarah, crushed by grief and a heavy measure of regret, could not be bothered with him, so she ignored his unwelcome presence. She could only stare at Blythe's little coffin and recall the golden-haired child's last hours: Blythe's head lying in her lap, her knees drawn up to her chest; Blythe crying and moaning in pain.

*Oh, Blythe. Oh, my dear girl! How did we not know—why did you not tell us how badly those men had hurt you? If only we had known, if we had taken you to a doctor, we might have saved you . . .*

Pastor Carmichael had located Blythe's uncle, and he had come to the service—likely more sober than he had been in many months. He seemed confused, however, as to where Blythe had been for the past three months.

"Girl went t' get' m' drink an' niver come back," he grumbled. "Don' know what b'came o' her."

Mr. Wheatley stood with the befuddled man, telling him that Blythe had been with friends, that she had been greatly loved, that she had come to faith in Jesus.

Blythe was buried in Riverside Cemetery, the same cemetery where Joy's first husband, Grant, was buried. After the brief graveside service, Sarah observed Joy and O'Dell, with their two boys, wander toward Grant's headstone. Joy carried flowers with her.

Sarah was grateful that the service had been short. The pain she felt was so acute that, as soon as the mourners began to disperse, she strode away from her friends, across the grassy park. Then she ran. She ran and ran and ran, not knowing where she was going—not until she reached a trolley stop some distance from the cemetery. Then she knew: The shop was closed out of respect for Blythe's funeral, but Lola did not know that. She would be waiting for Sarah at the usual time, outside the shop's back door. All Sarah longed to do was to forget. Forget Blythe's death, forget her guilt, forget everything and fall into the solace of Lola's arms.

~*~

THANKSGIVING INTERRUPTED THEIR mourning: The holiday came whether those who lived at Palmer House wished it to or not—whether they were prepared for it or not. Sarah dreaded the holiday, not only because it was supposed to be a time of gratitude and fellowship, but because the shop would be closed Thanksgiving through to Monday, and she would lose those opportunities to see Lola. Instead, she would be stuck in the house, pretending to enjoy the festive dinner, and expected to spend the long weekend with Palmer House's guests.

All without Lola.

Palmer House's telephone rang that morning during the flurry of cleaning and preparations.

Olive answered it. "Palmer House. Olive speaking."

"Miss Ellinger, please," the voice directed.

"Whom shall I say is calling?"

"Miss Pritchard."

Olive climbed the stairs on nimble feet and rapped on Sarah's door. "You have a telephone call, Sarah. A Miss Pritchard."

Sarah had been dawdling in her room since breakfast. With news of the call, she ran down the staircase and into the great room, arriving at the telephone out of breath.

"Hello?"

"Hello, darling. What time is your turkey dinner?"

"Um . . ." Sarah glanced around to see who might be listening. Most of the activity was in the kitchen and dining room. The great room was, to her surprise, empty.

"Dinner is at one o'clock."

"How soon afterward can you get away?"

Sarah realized, suddenly, how simple it would be to leave the house after dinner. Chaos would reign until the meal was on the table and everyone settled down to eat. But afterward, when the dinner was over, the house and its guests would clean up and spend the remainder of the day visiting, playing games, and eating pie.

"Quite soon, I should think."

"Meet me in the park down the street from the house?"

"Oh, yes! I shall plan to be there no later than two o'clock."

"Dress warmly, my dear."

Thanksgiving Day was suddenly much brighter as Sarah hung up. She entered into the festivities with a small smile playing about her mouth, not at all concerned that she was, more and more, hiding her comings and goings from those who loved her.

~*~

AS SOON AS EVERYONE was engaged in clearing the table, Sarah left the dining room. She grabbed her outer clothing from the hall tree in the foyer, took them into the parlor, and bundled up there, putting hat, mittens, and scarf over her long coat and sturdy boots. Then she stepped quietly to the front door and stole outside. She covered the distance to the gate in brisk strides. Once through, she turned right, toward the park, two blocks away.

Lola saw her coming from a distance; she waved and ran to meet her. Although the park had a lovely, wending path through evergreen trees, the center was planted in maples and ash trees. The grass was already strewn in golden-red leaves, but more were falling in the chilly air.

Lola tugged Sarah by the hand, and they ran through the piles of fallen leaves, laughing like children, watching their breath come out in white puffs. Then Lola pulled Sarah behind a particularly wide tree trunk.

"I cannot tell you how glad I am to see you, Sarah. I . . . I cannot bear to be apart from you."

Raw emotions and urges Sarah had thought dead awakened, kindled, and flamed to life. Lola saw Sarah's longing. She leaned toward Sarah and kissed her.

~*~

DR. CROFT SPENT THANKSGIVING with George and his family. It was a pleasant enough day, but he was distracted, his thoughts turned inward, rewinding his argument with Sarah Ellinger.

He took a long, meandering drive that afternoon, replaying the insults of their quarrel. Pieces of what she had shouted made no sense to him.

*You are new to this city. Have you not speculated about Palmer House? Has no one mentioned what it is?*

*Perhaps you should ask Mr. O'Dell about Palmer House. Then you will have your answer.*

On Friday following the holiday, Dr. Murphy had insisted they close the office. Finding himself at loose ends that morning, Croft drove his motor car into downtown Denver and parked. From across the street, he read the lettering upon the windows of a modest set of offices: *Pinkerton Detective Agency.*

At the front desk, he introduced himself. "Bryan Croft. I would like to see Mr. O'Dell, if he is available."

A moment later, O'Dell walked toward him. "Dr. Croft? How can I help you?"

Croft shook his hand. "May I buy you a cup of coffee, Mr. O'Dell?"

~*~

SARAH HAD TO GRIND HER teeth in order to tolerate the remainder of the Thanksgiving weekend as it crawled by at a snail's pace. She was irritable and easily provoked, causing the household at Palmer House—even Rose—to steer clear of her. They attributed her capricious mood to anguish over Blythe's untimely death, and no one protested when Sarah spent as much time as she could in her room, away from the daily life of Palmer House.

Until Sunday came around.

Sarah could not sidestep the trek to church and, once seated in the warehouse, surrounded by followers of Christ, she could not ignore the vibrant worship. Nor could she evade the convicting sermon.

This morning, Minister Liáng brought the message. Compared to Isaac Carmichael, Minister Liáng's teaching and preaching was generally reserved, even bookish—that is, until the Spirit came upon him. When the power of God hit Liáng, he was a changed man, a vessel from which flowed pure, living water.

And nothing Sarah tried could keep out that flow.

"Good morning, my dear friends. In our series, 'The Overcoming Christian Life,' we began by asking the question, 'Why do some believers overcome sin in their lives while other believers are defeated?'

"Last week, Pastor Carmichael taught on truth and deception. This week, we shall continue that theme by comparing the nature of truth to the nature of deception.

"To what end, you ask? A bank teller is trained to know real currency and to recognize the counterfeit. We must be trained to do the same, to know what is of God and what is counterfeit: that which masquerades as the real thing but is a cleverly disguised fake."

Sarah had longed to run away during worship; now she positively itched to flee the building. But if she left, Rose would surely corner her later and ask why—and Sarah wanted to avoid another conversation with Rose at all cost.

Sarah had no choice but to clench her jaw and endure the preaching of the word—the same preaching she had, until recently, embraced as the Bread of Life; the same teaching that had brought her peace and comfort. The same word that, today, stabbed her heart with increasing conviction.

"If you recall, Pastor Carmichael showed us in Scripture that truth is integral to the nature and character of God—truth is part and parcel of who God is. Conversely, Jesus tells us in John 8:44 that deception is integral to the nature and character of . . . someone else.

---

*"Ye are of your father the devil,*
*and the lusts of your father ye will do.*
*He was a murderer from the beginning,*
*and abode not in the truth,*
*because there is no truth in him.*
*When he speaketh a lie, he speaketh of his own:*
*for he is a liar, and the father of it.*

"Who is the father of lies? It is none other than our enemy, the devil, also known as Satan. Jesus bears witness to the nature of the devil: that he is a murderer and always has been, that *no* truth abides in him, that whatever he speaks is *always* a lie—for he is not merely a liar but the progenitor of lies. After the same manner that Satan is the enemy of God and his people, deception is the enemy of the truth.

"Deception, if we allow it entrance into our hearts and minds, is not static or inactive. Deception grows; it progresses. If we allow deception to develop unchallenged, its mature state is delusion. What, you may ask, is delusion?

"Truth is reality—it reflects the genuine condition of the world, the way things actually are. Delusion is the opposite. Delusion is detached from reality, separated from the genuine condition of the world, the way things actually are. Delusion causes men and women to build their lives upon a false foundation, a foundation that dwells in the realm of fantasy."

Despite her best efforts to block out his voice, Sarah heard each word Minister Liáng spoke. When he paused to allow the Spirit to lead him, Sarah had to whisk perspiration from her upper lip.

"We understand, do we not, that the man who insists he is Napoleon Bonaparte is suffering from delusions of grandeur? We all agree that the man has an illness of the mind, so we soothe and placate him and place him in the custody of those who will see that he cannot harm himself or others. This is a picture of delusion."

Minister Liáng walked from one end of the platform to the other. "Let us delve a little deeper. The word 'delusion' in Scripture is translated elsewhere as 'error.' In 1 John 4:6, this word is referred to as the *spirit of error.*

"We accept that a woman who maintains that she is Catherine the Great, Empress of Russia, is in error; this delusion, this *error* is evident to all. However, spiritual delusion—or a *spirit of error*—is not universally understood or accepted. Why is this? Because, as 1 Corinthians 2:14 tells us:

*"The natural man receiveth not the things
of the Spirit of God,
for they are foolishness unto him;
neither can he know them,
because they are spiritually discerned.*

"Those who have been born from above, who put their faith and trust in Jesus and his word, who can discern and identify spiritual delusion, are in the minority. I speak of us, brothers and sisters: We are in the minority. Sadly, when we proclaim the truth regarding delusion, regarding error, we are often labeled as fanatics and zealots—out of touch with 'reality'—because those who do not know Jesus cannot perceive spiritual things.

"We see how the unbeliever can be blind and, therefore, deceived. But can the believer in Christ be deceived? Can the believer fall into error, into delusion? Yes. Jesus warned his followers of deception many times. The Epistles, written to the people of God for their benefit, contain more than thirty similar warnings.

"Listen, my friends: Error and delusion are spiritual strongholds—*and those strongholds must be demolished.* The word 'stronghold' in the Greek means a fortification such as a castle or fortress. In spiritual terms, a stronghold is a garrisoned encampment, a reinforced position where our enemy, Satan, has gained a "strong hold" upon an individual. From the stronghold, the spirit of error wages ongoing war against the Spirit of truth."

The congregation hardly breathed, so commanding were Liáng's words; Sarah trembled and quaked under the Spirit's hand.

"What becomes of a believer who succumbs to error? Jesus taught in Mark 3:25, *And if a house be divided against itself, that house cannot stand.* When a stronghold exists within the believer, he is divided, of two minds—he is a double-minded man, unstable in all his ways! Two voices within the double-minded man battle for supremacy, and I tell you most truly: *only one will win.*"

Sarah shuddered. Two voices? How well she recognized what Liáng preached!

"The root of every stronghold, undergirding it, is the falsehood the believer has received and embraced. This lie, this deception, opposes and rejects God's written word. Where God speaks, the stronghold resists and declares, 'This does not apply here!' The stronghold cries, 'My situation is different; my circumstances are unique. Therefore, I do not need to obey God's word in this area.' When we exempt ourselves from God's word, we negate the living, active power of his word in us."

Liáng's voice thundered across the congregation. "It is now time to reassert the lordship of Christ over our houses and our lives! It is now time to apply the truth of God's word directly to the stronghold. It is time to identify the undergirding lie, tear it down, and root it out!

"If you have embraced delusion and allowed it a dwelling place within you—

"If you have allowed a spirit of error to take up residence in your soul—

"If you have, on a continual basis, rejected the correction of Scripture—

"If you recognize a stronghold of the enemy within you—

"If you are a double-minded man or woman, a house and heart divided—

"And if the preaching of the living, powerful word of God has, today, opened your eyes to the jeopardy of your soul—

"Come *now!* Come now to the altar and repent! Repent of the lies, the deceptions, the divided heart. Be delivered from the stronghold of delusion and error."

When Minister Liáng called to the altar those who desired to break the spiritual strongholds in their lives, the congregation erupted. Many believers streamed to the altar, but Sarah sat rigid and still, fighting desperately against the Spirit's convicting work in her heart.

Separated from Sarah by only two seats, Rose discerned the fierce battle within Sarah—a battle Rose was no longer certain Sarah wished to win.

*I shall fight for you, my daughter—I must!*

Rose stood and made her way to the front and knelt.

"O Lord God!" Rose began, but she could not go on; she broke down and sobbed. When she could continue, she prayed, "O Lord, my God, in the name of Jesus, I contend for Sarah's heart and soul. I know I must confront her yet again. Please guide me and show me how, my Lord!"

With many sorrowful groanings, Rose fought for Sarah, pouring her earnest pleas upon the altar where she knelt.

When she came to the close of her travail, Rose wiped her eyes and whispered, "Be pleased, Lord, to pour your Holy Spirit through your servants that we might overcome the evil one and his devices, that by the power of your Spirit you would bring Sarah's heart to godly sorrow and repentance . . .

"That you would restore her, Lord, to yourself and to us."

❧ ❀ ❧

# $\mathscr{C}$HAPTER 17

I t was Tuesday, the close of yet another workday. Sarah trudged up the walkway to Palmer House—almost, but not quite, late for dinner. She and Lola had eked out every minute of the time they had after Corrine left for the day, staying together until Sarah had to catch the last trolley home to avoid being late.

Sarah's heart was in turmoil as it was continually lately. Every fiber of her heart hungered to be with Lola, to remain with her. Her spirit, however, clanged an unceasing alarm in counterpoint to her desires.

The more Sarah reasoned why she could not be with Lola—in the way Lola begged Sarah to be with her—the more her heart rationalized why she could.

*Lord, I know you **say** that what I am doing is wrong—but is it wrong in every instance? In all circumstances? I am grieving, and Lola listens to me. She comforts me as I weep for Blythe; she consoles me in my sorrow. Is that wrong?*

*And you know that I cannot, I shall not, marry a man. This I have vowed. So, if I cannot marry, am I then to be condemned to be alone the remainder of my life? Without love? Without companionship?*

*Is that fair?*

*Why must I pay such a heavy price for what evil men have done to me? Why must I suffer for what Richard did, for what Willard did, for what Judge Brown did—why must I live in loneliness because of the brutes who beat and raped me and the 'gentlemen' who paid for me to pleasure them?*

*How is that right? How is that just?*

Instead of resolving never to see Lola again, Sarah's mind bent its obdurate efforts upon achieving a means of having what she desired while justifying that means to her conscience.

*Lola loves me . . . and I love her. Does it matter where I find love as long as I do?*

One voice within insisted, *If we were together, we would be so happy . . .*

The Other whispered, *Sarah . . . if you love me, you will obey me and forgive.*

Sarah climbed Palmer House's porch steps and let herself in the front door. Turned inward, focused on her own unrest, she hung her coat and hat and scarf on the hall tree and did not notice the unusual quiet of the house.

Until she entered the great room.

On any ordinary evening, several girls would be helping with the meal, shuttling dishes from the kitchen to the dining room and bustling about the table. The remainder of the house's residents, including Rose, Mr. Wheatley, Billy, and his children, would be gathered in the great room, waiting to be called to dinner.

But the great room was empty when Sarah entered; she heard none of the usual dinner commotion coming from the kitchen. The house was eerily quiet.

"Hello?" she called. She turned when she heard a step behind her.

"Hello, Sarah."

"Hello, Miss Rose. Where is everyone?"

Rose was composed, but her expression was grave. "I have sent everyone away for the evening, Sarah."

Sarah wrapped her arms around herself against a sudden chill. "Away? Where? Why?"

"Please come into the parlor, Sarah."

With dread trickling through her bones, Sarah followed Rose into the parlor. There, Pastor Carmichael stood. Waiting.

"Good evening, Sarah."

"Good evening, Pastor. I . . . what is the meaning of this, Miss Rose?"

"Please sit down, Sarah. We must talk."

Sarah swallowed hard; she found a chair and sat.

"Yes?"

"Sarah, you and I spoke some three weeks past regarding the dangers of your friendship with Lola. Although you listened, wept, prayed, and committed before the Lord to break off your friendship with her, you have not."

Sarah was aghast; she felt faint. "How . . ."

"Someone witnessed you with Lola, down our street, in the park, on the afternoon of Thanksgiving Day. You and Lola were exhibiting what was described as 'an unnatural affection.'"

Sarah choked but managed to ask, "Who? Who has said this?"

"Someone who, I assure you, cares very much for your wellbeing. They came to me and only me, no one else."

"But—"

"You have a right to confront your accuser—although the issue is not, at this moment, who saw you, but whether or not you will declare the accusation to be untrue. If you pronounce this person's testimony to be false, we shall bring you and your accuser together and allow you to refute this lie.

"First, however, I must ask you to respond. Have you kept your commitment to the Lord to sever your friendship with Lola?"

Sarah stared ahead. "No."

Tears trickled down Rose's cheeks. "I am so very sorry, Sarah. As I carefully explained when you and I met one on one, if you persisted in your relationship with Lola, you could not continue to live at Palmer House."

"Have you decided I must leave?"

"Until recently, you have been a wise and caring sister, a loving, encouraging mentor to the girls of Palmer House younger than you, an example of godliness. I could not have been more proud of you."

"But you no longer hold me in high regard?" The loss of Rose's approbation struck Sarah the hardest. She began to crumble under the import of Rose's declarations.

"I must go?" she wept.

"I think your decisions this evening will determine that."

Rose had to speak above Sarah's muffled sobs. "As I said when we met previously, you stand to lose everything good and right in your life—not to mention your walk with the Lord. I assure you, however, that this outcome is *not* what I wish or what anyone who loves you wishes."

"O God, O God!" Sarah mourned.

"In the manner that Scripture instructs us, I met with you a first time to confront you with your sin in private. Since you have not turned from your sin, this second time I have brought a brother, Pastor Carmichael, with me, in hopes of restoring you.

"Sarah, Pastor has been sharing with me while we waited for you to arrive, and I believe the Lord has given him insight into your heart. I hope you will be open to hear him out. Will you?"

Sarah continued to sob, but when she did not respond to Rose, Carmichael said gently, "Miss Ellinger, we are all—every person who has ever lived—broken in some manner or fashion. We enter the world with a sinful nature. As we grow and learn the difference between right and wrong, we may make many right choices, but we also, *inevitably*, choose what is wrong."

Sarah moaned into her hands. "Oh, how I regret ever meeting Lola, ever allowing my heart to consider that she and I could be more than friends."

"Regret is not repentance, Sarah," Carmichael said softly. "Regret is sorrow for an adverse outcome, not sorrow for grieving the heart of God."

"But what can I do? I-I am drawn to Lola, engaged and compelled by my feelings. How can I deny this?"

"You do acknowledge your relationship with her is sin?"

Sarah nodded her head. "I know it is . . . with my mind, but my heart is trapped. How do I escape from this snare?"

"We must, with careful discernment, identify the root of this sin, Sarah. I believe we can guide you in this, but you must allow the Holy Spirit to do his convincing work in you and then follow through."

Sarah sniffled. "I am listening. I want to do what is right."

"I am glad to hear it. Do you recall Minister Liáng's message Sunday on delusion and spiritual strongholds?"

She nodded. "Yes."

"He said in his message that a stronghold is a place in our hearts where our enemy, Satan, has a 'strong hold' upon us, a place that is resistant to the Lordship of Christ and his word.

"He also said that at the core of every stronghold is a lie. This lie, this deception, opposes and rejects God's written word. The stronghold cries, 'My situation is different, and my circumstances are unique. Therefore, I do not need to obey God's word in this area.' Do you see the lie, Sarah?"

"I suppose so . . . in principle."

"Then, let us bring the principle to bear upon your life, shall we? I know something of the time you spent in those houses of evil in Corinth. I know what you were forced to do; however, we are not here to talk about that which the blood of Jesus has washed away and made clean. Rather, let us speak of the men who abused you, and let us begin before you were taken to Corinth."

"Why?"

"Because, in my limited and imperfect experience, I have found that women who struggle with sexual sin were often abused as children. Were you, as a vulnerable child, abused by evil men? Were you unable to escape from the evil things done to you? This is where we must begin, Sarah, with those men.

"To what end?"

Even in her sorrow, a hard edge had crept into Sarah's voice.

"That you may forgive them."

Sarah stilled, and her lips thinned. "Forgive them?"

"Yes. Although Minister Liáng and I have preached many times on forgiveness, I believe this area of your life has escaped the working of God's word. I believe this is where the falsehood resides, where the stronghold draws its strength."

"You do not know what they did to me."

"No, we do not," Rose said. "In the decade I have known you, I do not believe you have shared with anyone about your childhood."

Carmichael asked, "Have you hidden these abuses away rather than bringing them into the light, Sarah?"

"I-I have no wish to exhume what is dead."

"But are these memories truly dead? If they have been dealt with scripturally, then they will have no hold over you. However, what I contend is that these memories are very much alive, and, to this day, you hold these evil men accountable for their trespasses."

"As I should! What they did was—is—monstrous. Unconscionable!"

"You must forgive them, for your own sake."

"Me? I must forgive? I was the one whose stepfather molested and sold her into prostitution! I am the victim—and these men do not deserve my forgiveness!"

Pastor Carmichael exhaled. "There is the lie, Miss Ellinger; that is the stronghold speaking, the stronghold's deception."

Sarah looked at him with suspicion. "What do you mean?"

"You declare these men do not merit forgiveness. Do any of us? No. Not one of us is deserving of forgiveness. Here is the lie: That they must warrant your forgiveness."

"But they-they—"

"Did you hear how you prefaced your objection with 'but?' We cannot use 'but' as justification to disobey God. Miss Ellinger, I believe the Lord has revealed the stronghold in your heart—a judgment against men. All men."

Sarah looked from Carmichael to Rose and back. "A judgment? I do not understand."

"You refused these men forgiveness, not realizing that your unforgiveness gave Satan a foothold in your heart. Your wounds festered over years of abuse, and you became angry, filled with rage—an uncontrollable rage that erupted whenever you were offended."

"No! That is not true, I—"

"Yes, it is true. Those who know you best attest to it. And when your anger fed upon new transgressions—both real and perceived—Satan's hold on you grew stronger. Your anger strengthened to the point that you passed judgment upon an entire class of people, upon all men."

Sarah folded her arms. "I do not believe you."

"You spoke of Lola as a snare. If you did not hate men, if you were able to form a godly attachment to a man, would she have ever tempted you?"

"But these men . . . men, in authority over me. Men like *you*," Sarah spat, "who abused and degraded me!"

Carmichael tried again, gently. "Does not your response support my point, Miss Ellinger? That you have judged all men and found them guilty?"

Sarah's anger, never far from the surface, was close to erupting; she was only able to keep it in check because what Carmichael insisted seemed similar to what another man had said to her not long ago:

*. . . It is not me you dislike. No, Miss Ellinger, to put it plainly, you do not like men. It should have been obvious to me the day I met you, but I see it plainly now: You are trying to make me—and every other man on the planet—pay for the misdeeds for which one or more men are guilty.*

Sarah's lips parted. *Is it true? Do I hold all men guilty?*

"Sarah," Rose whispered, "please allow us to help you. Will you tell us of your childhood?"

"It is too painful to dredge up."

"We shall be with you in that painful place."

"Why? Why is it so important?"

"Because," Pastor Carmichael said, "the Lord requires that you forgive those who abused you. It is the only way you will ever be free of the rage and free to move on with your life. You must call these men out by name and offense and fully forgive them."

Sarah shook her head. "No. I shall not."

Rose dabbed at her eyes. "But if you refuse our counsel . . . if you will not obey God's word in this, I have no other recourse . . ."

Sarah stared at Rose. "Wait. You are saying if I do not bare my secrets, I must go?"

"You know you must, Sarah. I am sorry, but yes."

Still quietly and with gentleness, Pastor Carmichael urged her. "Please, Miss Ellinger. Let us help you. Tell us, and we shall stand with you. We shall neither condemn nor abandon you; we shall help you overcome this stronghold."

Sarah gripped her skirt with both hands. *Is it true? Is this what is wrong in me, what the Lord has been trying to tell me?*

*But I cannot forgive them! They . . . what they did. But if I do not, Rose will cast me out of Palmer House.*

As her eyes darted about the room, finding neither rest nor escape, her hands crushed and wrung the folds of her skirt. She began to moan softly and to rock forward and back.

It was apparent to Rose and Pastor Carmichael that Sarah was in the throes of a great internal battle.

"Sarah, Jesus is waiting to free you. Give way to him," Rose begged her. But Sarah became more agitated; as she swayed, she dug the nails of one hand into the back of the other, gouging the skin and drawing blood.

Rose tried to pull her hands apart. "Sarah! Stop! You are hurting yourself!"

Carmichael helped Rose; they each grasped one of Sarah's hands—but she began to keen and weep in her distress.

Carmichael put one palm to Sarah's cheek. "Miss Ellinger. Look at me, please."

Sarah blinked and stopped moaning. Her eyes fixed on Carmichael.

"Miss Ellinger, perhaps you could begin . . . with your mother and your childhood home?"

"My mother?"

"Yes. Did you love your mother? Was she good to you? And where did you live as a child, Sarah?"

Sarah seemed to take to Carmichael's suggestion. "My mother . . . I loved her very much, but she became sick with consumption. She knew she was dying, and I was only eight years old. She had no one to entrust me to, and it worried her. We . . ."

Without warning, Sarah's body went slack; her eyes became focused far away.

"We . . . lived in upstate New York. Albany. Our home was across the street from a beautiful park—with many trees, a pond, and ducks. We went there every afternoon. I rolled her chair along the edge of the pond, you see, when she became weak, and we would feed the ducks. She dearly loved to feed the ducks, and the tulips in the park were so beautiful that year."

"It sounds lovely, Sarah," Rose murmured.

"It was. I was happy, even though Mama was ill. But . . . one day, in the park, a man approached us. He said his name was Richard. Richard Langston."

~*~

MORE THAN AN HOUR later, Sarah finished, "After Judge Brown purchased me from Willard, he brought me by train to Denver and then to Corinth. You . . . know the rest."

Sarah was exhausted. Rose's hankie was drenched with her tears; Pastor Carmichael's expression was grave.

"You have shown yourself valiant, Miss Ellinger, and I wish you to know that you are no longer alone in your battle against these horrors. Mrs. Thoresen and I are with you."

Sarah nodded once. She stared at nothing; her visage was open and stark.

"What was done to you injured you in ways I, as a man, cannot fathom, for it is so abhorrent, so very wrong. I grieve over what was done to you— what men did to you! Evil men hurt and broke you, Miss Ellinger, but take courage—Jesus came to heal the brokenhearted."

Carmichael hesitated. "Before we go further, I would like to pray." He did not wait on Sarah or Rose's agreement; he simply closed his eyes and spoke aloud.

"O Lord God! I deeply repent; I bare my soul and repent before you, O God."

Sarah's eyes fluttered. She became alert, and her lips parted in confusion. She slid her eyes toward Rose and found her similarly perplexed.

Pastor Carmichael, however, demonstrated no uncertainty. He continued in a strong voice. "I repent, Lord, for myself and for all men everywhere: I repent of the mistreatment of women, the exploitation of sacred trust, and the abuse of authority. O God, you know the sinful hearts of us all. If not for your grace and mercy early in my life, *I* could have committed such unspeakable evil. *I* could have used the female form to satisfy my selfish lusts. *I* could have damaged the fragile hearts and souls of the beautiful female creatures made in your image and likeness. *I* could be guilty—even of the misuse of my pastoral office.

"Therefore, I repent before you, Lord, and before Mrs. Thoresen and Miss Ellinger. I am grateful for your unmerited forgiveness and for the new birth that saved me from my own evil inclinations—for I confess that, in myself, in my flesh, there dwells no good thing. I know and acknowledge this.

"So, Lord God, I repent. I repent for what men like myself did to my sister Sarah. Lord, please give her the grace and the fortitude to forgive me and then to forgive the men who have abused her. I ask this, Lord, in the name of Jesus."

When Pastor Carmichael opened his eyes, he reached for Sarah's hand. "Miss Ellinger? Sarah? Will you forgive me?"

Sarah's breath caught in her throat. "But . . . but you have done nothing to me."

He nodded. "I know—nevertheless, you have a judgment—a stronghold—against all members of my gender for what a number of us have done to you. Today, we shall break the back of that stronghold. Thus, I plead for your forgiveness, Miss Ellinger. Please. Will you forgive me?"

Although Sarah understood that Carmichael was innocent of trespassing against her, when she tried to say the words, they stuck in her throat: She could not bring herself to say, "I forgive you."

"You are sensing the power, the strength of that stronghold, Miss Ellinger. Satan will not give up his fortified position easily. He knows that if he can keep you *here*, he can keep you forever. I remind us all of what Matthew 6:14 and 15 tell us:

> *"For if ye forgive men their trespasses,*
> *your heavenly Father will also forgive you:*
> *But if ye forgive not men their trespasses,*
> *neither will your Father forgive your trespasses.*

"Miss Ellinger, if you do not forgive the trespasses of others, God the Father will not forgive you. For this reason, Satan will fight—and fight dirty—to keep you from obeying God in this. He will fight to maintain his hold over you. If you truly wish to be free—free of this bondage—you must determine to speak forgiveness over every individual who has ever abused you—beginning with me."

"Wh-what if I do not feel forgiveness? What if I harbor hatred and anger in my heart afterward? Am I not merely parroting words? Am I not a hypocrite?"

"Not if you forgive in faith. God has given us free *will*. What we *will* to do, what we *choose* to do, determines our obedience—our feelings do not. When we declare our obedience to the Lord, our emotions must, soon after, fall into line with our will. Speak your forgiveness over me, Miss Ellinger. It is the first step in your deliverance."

Sarah did not move.

"Please," he said again. "Please forgive me."

"I—" She sighed. "I-I do. I forgive you."

"Thank you, Sarah. From the bottom of my heart, thank you. Now . . ." he drew a deep breath, "let us deal with the men who did you such grievous harm. Let us begin with Richard Langston."

Sarah shook her head. "I do not think I can."

"I shall help you, Sarah. I am willing to lead you in prayer, but it must be you who breaks through the stronghold into freedom. Will you pray with me?"

He closed his eyes. "Jesus, because of your cleansing blood on Calvary, I am forgiven."

Sarah bowed her head and repeated, "Jesus, because of your cleansing blood on Calvary, I am forgiven."

"I declare that you, Jesus, that *you* are my Lord. I surrender in obedience to you. I hold Richard Langston before you and declare, 'I forgive you, Richard. In the eyes of God Almighty, I forgive you. I forgive you for misusing the sacred trust my mother placed in you. I forgive you for abusing me, for stealing my childhood and my innocence. I forgive you for selling me. I forgive you for every wrong you committed against me. I now release you from judgment so that the Holy Spirit can seek you, convict you, and bring you to godly sorrow, true repentance, and salvation.'"

Choking and gasping, grappling and fighting against her long-lived habit to spew recrimination, not forgiveness, Sarah slowly repeated the words Pastor Carmichael prayed for her benefit.

"Now this, Miss Ellinger: 'I forgive you, Richard Langston, and I renounce hate, bitterness, accusation, and punishment. Richard, Jesus has taken your punishment, if you will but receive it—but despite what *you* choose, I forgive you so that *I* can be free of the bondage of judgment.'

"Lord God, please be merciful and save Richard Langston. I ask this in Jesus' name. Amen."

Sarah was sweating profusely; with Rose still clutching one hand and Carmichael the other, she shook from head to toe, but she prayed as Carmichael led her.

"Now, Willard Abernathy, Sarah," and Carmichael began to pray.

Her voice quavering, Sarah followed Carmichael's lead . . . until something within her, something holy and righteous, rose up and burst from her.

Sarah's voice rang out of her own accord. "O God! In the name of Jesus, I forgive Willard! I forgive him, Lord, I forgive him! I repent of my bitter hate toward him and toward others. I repent of my accusations against innocent men. I repent of my hostile, judgmental attitude. Lord, please forgive me! Please forgive me! Please forgive me!"

She fell to her knees, praying, begging, pleading for forgiveness and granting it to every man she could recall, even to the nameless 'gentlemen' who had paid for her in Corinth, and to the guards who had beaten and raped her.

Rose and Pastor Carmichael knelt beside her, rejoicing and weeping over her as the power of God swept down upon them in sweet, sweet, healing virtue.

~*~

MUCH LATER, IN THE DARKEST hour of the night, Sarah awoke. She had been drained when she climbed into bed, but she had been through too much to sleep well. She had tossed and turned until now, she had awakened.

She sat up and stared though the deep shadows of her room, reliving those difficult hours. Regardless of her obedience and despite the move of the Holy Spirit earlier that evening, her repentance had left her spent and empty.

Hollow.

Alone.

She was not at all convinced that the sin in her life would release its hold on her just because she had repented. As she sought the Lord, all she could feel within herself was that vast emptiness.

*O God, my God! Have you left me?*

The beats of her heart crashed in her chest, one upon the other, in an agony so great she felt she could not bear it without crying out. It was all she could do to whisper, when she wanted to scream, grieve, mourn, and keen her pain.

"Oh, Jesus!"

Hopelessness so deep she thought she would drown in it swept over her. She clenched her hand and stuffed it into her mouth to keep the low moans within her; she bit down upon her knuckles, bit down and tasted blood.

*O God, please help me! Speak to me! You know I love you—but please! Deliver me from this despair that consumes me!*

Her breath came in great gasps, and she cried aloud, "Oh, Jesus! Oh, Jesus, I am so afraid! Do not leave me, Jesus! I shall die without you! Please!"

Then . . .

A breathy warmth caressed her cheek, and the scent of . . . perfume? wafted nearby, its fragrance sweet, reminiscent of flowers and sunbaked tree sap. She searched in the dark but could see and perceive nothing.

Then she again felt his presence. *His presence!* It swelled and grew until it filled every corner of her room and pressed in on Sarah, until she was surrounded, swaddled, and sheathed by it. And then a Voice cracked like thunder, so loud that it eclipsed the pounding pulse in her head:

*SARAH!* it boomed.

Sarah quailed before the rolling reverberations. She found herself face down on the floor, pressed there by the weight of his Presence.

*Sarah!* the Voice commanded, *Lift up your head, for your redemption draws nigh.*

"Yes, Lord!" she cried.

In obedience, Sarah somehow dragged herself up to her knees; she tipped her face up as though to sunlight. "H-here I am, Lord!"

Like a gentle soaking rain, living water pattered upon her upturned features.

*"But now thus saith the Lord*
*that created thee . . . **Sarah**,*
*and he that formed thee . . . **Sarah**,*
*Fear not: for I have redeemed thee,*
*I have called thee by thy name;*
*thou art mine, **Sarah**!*

*When thou passest through the waters,*
*I will be with thee;*
*and through the rivers,*
*they shall not overflow thee, **Sarah**!*
*When thou walkest through the fire,*
*thou shalt not be burned;*
*neither shall the flame kindle upon thee.*

*Fear not, Sarah, for I have redeemed thee. I have called thee by name. You are mine.*

"Jesus," Sarah gasped. "Yes, my Jesus! I want to be yours, all yours."

*You **are** mine.*
*Fear not, Sarah Redeemed.*
*You are mine.*

# $\mathscr{C}$HAPTER 18

Sarah climbed from her bed early in the morning, sensing that something within her was different. Changed. A cloud of peace enveloped her. She probed and prodded at that peace—tenuously at first, then more rigorously. It did not budge. *You heard me, Jesus! You answered the cry of my heart!*

Strength and hope swelled within her. *Oh, my God, thank you! I surrender myself to your Lordship, and I surrender this day to you. In all things, Lord, I surrender!*

She decided to leave early for the shop, for she could not face her Palmer House family at breakfast—not without first having dealt with her improper relationship with Lola.

Sarah washed and dressed for work. When she was done, she sat on the edge of her bed and opened her Bible. The Scripture she sought was percolating within her spirit before she found it. She read aloud from Galatians 5:

*"Stand fast therefore in the liberty*
*wherewith Christ hath made us free,*
*and be not entangled again*
*with the yoke of bondage."*

Nodding, she declared, "By your grace, Lord, I shall stand."

She left the house that morning while the household was in the dining room having breakfast. As she strode toward the trolley stop, she repeated, "Stand fast. In the liberty. Wherewith Christ has made me free. Be not entangled again. With the yoke of bondage."

On the trolley, she whispered, "My God, I am your willing, obedient daughter. In all things, I am yours. Please help me to stand fast today and fully conform to your will."

When she unlocked the empty shop and stepped inside, her first determination was to make a clean breast of everything with Corrine. She prayed, "I shall not fight these battles alone any longer, Lord. I shall seek wise counsel and support from my family—my brothers and my sisters—and I shall follow the leading of your Holy Spirit."

Corrine arrived for work ten minutes ahead of time.

"Corrine? May I talk to you?"

Sarah's friend drew near her, hesitation in her steps.

Sarah stared at the floor. "I do not deserve your help, but I wish to ask a favor of you."

Corrine sighed. "I would do anything for you, Sarah. Anything that does not displease the Lord."

"I shall not ask you to compromise yourself—you have my word. What I ask is, could you . . . would you stay an extra hour with me today?"

Corrine was wary. "May I know why?"

Sarah wet her lips. "You were right, Corrine, to warn me, and I was wrong to reject your counsel. Lola was not a good influence upon me, nor I on her. I shall not blame her—how can I? My own stubborn choices put me in the way of temptation and sin. However, today I must say goodbye to Lola.

"I realize that I shall grieve and wound Lola's heart, so, I-I would ask that you stay and help me remain true to my resolution and not give in to her entreaties. And . . . I do ask your forgiveness for the cruel, hurtful manner in which I have treated you."

Corrine patted Sarah's arm. "I forgive you, Sarah. And I shall stand by you."

"Thank you, Corrine. I love you so."

~*~

THE DAY CREPT BY AT a snail's pace, and Sarah's newfound confidence began to slip. She was worried and uncertain, fighting the same battle again and again—how (and if) she could break off her relationship with Lola. Each time she began to waver, she returned to Pastor Carmichael's words from the previous evening:

*You refused these men forgiveness, not realizing that your unforgiveness gave Satan a foothold in your heart. Your wounds festered over years of abuse, and you became angry, filled with rage—an uncontrollable of rage that erupted whenever you were offended. And when your anger fed upon new transgressions—both real and perceived—Satan's hold on you grew stronger.*

*Your anger strengthened to the point that you passed judgment upon an entire class of people, upon all men. If you did not hate men, if you were able to form a godly attachment to a man, would Lola have ever tempted you?*

"No," Sarah admitted to herself. She relied, too, upon an additional piece of wisdom Pastor Carmichael had shared last evening.

*You may need to forgive those who have injured you many times, Sarah, each time exercising your will over your feelings. Like the layers of an onion, as you peel off one layer of offense, another will show itself as surely as the enemy returns to tempt us with sin.*

*Concerning Lola? Continue to repent before the Lord; follow through with your decision to break off your friendship with her. Make it quick and final. Be watchful. Be diligent. Guard your heart with great care.*

Sarah bent her head and prayed. "Lord, I repent of my wrong relationship with Lola. I give my broken feelings to you; I declare that, with your help, I shall sever those ties today. I trust you to see me through this ordeal, Lord. Amen.

"And my Lord? I forgive Richard for sinning against me. As you forgive me time and again for sinning against you, I continue to forgive him. I ask that you soften his heart. Send someone to tell him of Jesus and bring him to a place of godly sorrow and repentance. I ask that you save him, Lord, as you saved me. He does not deserve your mercy, my God, but neither did I. I forgive Richard; I shall not allow the devil to divide my heart. I shall not give him portion or place—not a foothold, not a toehold, not the nail of a single one of his claws."

Throughout the day, she forgave and prayed for Willard Abernathy. She forgave Judge Brown for lying to her and taking her to Corinth instead of to his home. She forgave him, although he had gone missing when Dean Morgan assumed ownership of the houses and was, by all accounts, presumed dead.

*It may be of no help to Judge Brown if you forgive him, but it will heal you, Sarah,* Pastor had said. *Forgive every offense and every individual as you recall them.*

Following Pastor Carmichael's advice, Sarah worked with meticulous attention through a list she had drawn up of men she could remember from her time in Corinth. Many of them had been "regulars" at the clubs. Partway down the list she saw the name Armand Schumer and sucked in a breath. Sarah would never forget her encounter with Schumer and his wife soon after *Michaels' Fine Furnishings* opened . . .

~*~

WORD HAD GOTTEN AROUND Denver that the owners of the new shop, Grant and Joy Michaels, employed two women from "up the mountain." Grant, Joy, and the shop's employees had endured a number of protests and other methods of censure—those delivered in person.

"I should like to be shown your selection of lace tablecloths," the customer had declared in a loud voice.

The matron arched a haughty brow and waited for assistance to come to her while her husband, with an air of bored compliance, lifted glasses to his eyes and studied a wall painting hanging near them.

Sarah had stepped to the woman's side, smiled, and gestured toward the rods hung with neatly folded table linens. At that moment the woman's husband turned toward her, and Sarah gasped. She whirled away, her hand to her mouth to cover her shock, but the damage was done. He had recognized her—and she him. A laughing, cruel smile tugged at the corner of his mouth. Standing behind his wife, the wink he threw Sarah went unseen by that woman.

Sarah composed herself and, ignoring the man, continued toward the table linens. As Sarah pointed out the styles and sizes in stock, the woman scrutinized her, and her mouth turned down in derision.

"Tell me, young lady. Are you one of those women come down from that little town up the mountain? One of those women living in Martha Palmer's house?" The question had been intentionally strident, clearly spoken for the benefit of others than Sarah to hear as well.

Sarah had not moved, but she did not know how to answer, and Corrine, who had been ringing up a purchase, froze. Joy, who had also overheard the question, tried to excuse herself from her present customer.

Finally, Sarah had squared her shoulders. "Yes, ma'am, I *am* 'one of those women.' Now," she turned stiffly toward the display of table cloths, "what size cloth would interest you today?"

The woman's nose lifted higher. "Well! I simply did not believe it when I heard it. Employing women of ill repute in what is advertised as a respectable establishment! I wish to see the owner immediately."

Sarah set her lips together as Joy hurried to her aid. Joy composed herself as she reached the matron's side.

"I am Joy Michaels, the owner of this establishment. May I be of assistance, Mrs.—?"

"Mrs. Schumer," Sarah provided.

She had been angry when she answered Joy. Angry and growing angrier.

"Mrs. Schumer, is it? How may I help you today?" Joy asked.

The woman had cast Sarah a wary glance. "I do not believe I introduced myself." She frowned. "I *know* I did not introduce myself." She turned to Joy. "How did this . . . this *woman* know my name?"

Joy was perplexed. "I, well, I am certain I do not—"

But Sarah had answered the question. "I know your name," Sarah replied, "because I know your husband, Mr. Schumer."

"I am sure you are mistaken," Mrs. Schumer had expostulated. "I am aware of all of my husband's acquaintances." The matron raised her finger and wagged it at Sarah. "—and you may well claim to know him, but I am certain he does not know you!"

She had ended on a loud note of triumph.

Sarah had not been cowed. Ignoring Joy's hand squeezing her arm, she had retorted, "Oh, I do assure you, Mrs. Schumer, that I am *well* known to Mr. Schumer. Of course, I refer to the *biblical* manner of knowing. After all, I am one of *those* women. Oh, yes. He 'knows' me all right. *Not that I ever had a choice in the matter!*"

Joy had stepped in then and sent Sarah to the office, and Sarah had not witnessed the dawn of Mrs. Schumer's understanding or her mortification. But it was in that moment, in her confrontation with Armand Schumer, that Sarah's long-simmering resentment had ignited into a full-fledged hatred of men.

She had gone out the shop's back door and fled to Palmer House, convinced that Joy would sack her and that she would be asked to leave Palmer House forthwith. Rather than go into the house, Sarah had stumbled across the front porch and taken shelter in the house's gazebo. There she had collapsed, sobbing her heart out.

That was where Mr. Wheatley, sprier by a decade back then, had found her. He had plopped down on the seat near her and, patting her shoulder over and over, asked, "Now, Sarah girl, whatever is the matter?"

"Nothing!" Sarah had declared.

"Pshaw! Come, now. Tell this old man what has hurt you. You can trust me."

And the startling truth had been, Sarah *had* trusted him. Perhaps, due to his advancing years, she did not count him as a danger or, perhaps, his always kindly manner had won her over. All Sarah knew was that she had found herself weeping into the front of Mr. Wheatley's shirt, and he had held her, gently, until the storm passed . . .

~*~

WHY, MR. WHEATLEY IS *the only man I have ever confided in*, Sarah realized.

Wiping unexpected moisture from her face, she again looked at her list and the name: Armand Schumer. *Pastor Liáng was right—I have been living in self-deception for years. Why, I never actually forgave Mr. Schumer; I only put him out of mind.*

*In truth, I added his name and his sins to the list of trespasses I was hiding in my heart—a list I was storing up in order to justify my anger toward all men.*

"O Lord God! In the name of Jesus, I forgive this man, and I forgive his wife, too. She did not know, Lord, what a despicable, unfaithful husband he was until that day. Please, Lord, help her. Help her to forgive him, for her own sake. I pray that you pour your grace and mercy upon her . . . and upon him. I thank you, my God, for helping me to forgive and let go of these offenses. Thank you for taking this terrible burden of judgment from my heart.

"And please, dear Lord? Give me strength for the battle ahead of me today. How I need you!"

~*~

AS CORRINE'S REGULAR WORK day drew to a close, Sarah grew anxious—and her agitation began to make Corrine nervous.

"Will Lola come to the front or the back door, Sarah?"

"The back," Sarah whispered.

"Do you wish me to answer it for you?"

"No, but do remain with me, please."

"Of course."

"I think it wise, too, that we close the shop at four, so we do not run the risk of a customer happening upon . . ."

"I agree, Sarah. That would be best."

"Oh, Corrine! How? How did I fall so far?" Sarah sank down upon a chair and wept bitterly.

"Be strong, Sarah. The Lord is your Rock. He will be your Courage."

~*~

LOLA'S LIVELY RAP ON the back door came at ten past four.

Sarah swallowed hard. *Jesus, please help me!*

She unlocked the door, and Lola bounced inside, her smile bright. "Hello, sweetheart!"

Aware that Corrine was watching, Sarah cast her eyes to the floor. That was when Lola became conscious of Corrine's presence.

"Oh. Hello . . . Corrine." Lola glanced from Corrine back to Sarah and realized, too, that Sarah had not greeted her. "What is wrong, Sarah?"

Sarah clasped her fingers together and looked into Lola's wary face. "Lola, I must tell you something, something difficult."

Lola frowned, and her breath quickened. "What?"

"Our friendship has . . . strayed onto a wrong path, and I-I must end it. I am sorry to have led you on, Lola, but I-I cannot see you any longer."

Every syllable strangled Sarah—and she saw that her every word was a dagger in Lola's heart.

"You are joking. You must be—I know you love me."

"I do love you, Lola, but this kind of love is wrong. I have repented of it before God, and he has forgiven me, but now I must say goodbye to you. Please. Do not call me or come here again."

Lola's features crumpled. "Sarah? No. No, you cannot be serious! I love you!"

"I am so very sorry, Lola."

Covering her mouth to hold back a sob, Sarah ran through the office door into the shop, leaving Corrine and Lola together. Lola made to follow Sarah, but Corrine carefully closed the door after Sarah and stood against it.

"Sarah is grieved to her core that she has hurt you, Lola; she did not want to."

"Did not want to hurt me? You know nothing! *She has killed me!* Move aside—she will change her mind. She must. I know she loves me as I love her."

Lola put her hand on Corrine's arm to push her aside—but Corrine covered it with her own.

"Lola. Please look at me."

Lola turned an anguished face to Corrine.

Corrine, shedding tears of her own, whispered, "Sarah has made her choice. Please honor her decision."

Lola's empty gaze regarded Corrine for many agonizing seconds before she shook off Corrine's gentle hold. She said nothing further, but stumbled through the back door, closing it quietly behind her.

# CHAPTER 19

Sarah went directly to her room following dinner and locked herself in. No one at the table had asked her about the previous evening during the meal or mentioned where they had gone or what they had done while Rose and Pastor Carmichael waited for Sarah to come home. Few of the household had spoken to her at all other than to say "hello" or "pass the potatoes, please." But they had watched her when they thought she was not aware and had averted their eyes when she glanced their way.

Sensing that Rose may have already filled them in, Sarah blushed in hot shame.

Mr. Wheatley had not looked away; he had nodded encouragement in her direction. At the same time, he could not hide his sadness at the situation.

*I have let them down, all of them. Me, who had the prideful audacity to think myself an example to the younger girls, a helper Miss Rose could lean on. Nothing could be further from the truth.*

And Sarah's difficulties were not at an end. Yes, she had obeyed the Lord and severed her association with Lola. She had seen that heartrending decision through—but this time tomorrow, following dinner, Rose would convene the house.

Sarah had agreed to confess her sins to her sisters and brothers in Christ and ask their forgiveness.

Sarah shuddered. *How can I face them? How will I be able to tell them the truth? How will they react when I lay bare the vile state of my heart, the ugliness of my sins?*

*I said I would do it.*

*But I cannot.*

Sarah wrestled all night with what was before her. Sleep was out of the question, so she paced, walking up and down her room, struggling with what was ahead, what she could neither elude nor circumvent.

In the earliest hours of morning, she stood at her window and, not unlike another night long ago, Sarah looked out into the shadows. Only a skiff of snow lay upon the ground here in Denver, this first week of December.

No icicles hung from the eaves. Out beyond the gate to Palmer House, the streets were not heaped with ice and frozen, filthy slush—not as they had been on that night from her childhood.

Still, like that night so many years past, she thought, *I shall run away. I shall leave—now, this morning, before the house awakes. I have a little money set by. I shall go some place where no one knows me.*

Sarah packed quickly, taking only what she absolutely needed and what her bag would hold. Then she dressed herself for the cold, adding a woolen petticoat for warmth and putting extra socks on before she donned her boots.

She tiptoed down the wide staircase to the black, echoing foyer. By touch, she found her coat, hat, and scarf hanging on the hall tree. Making barely a sound, she put them on.

When she was ready, she took up her bag and approached the front door. She knew it well, even in the dark: It might stick a little, but it was not likely to make much of a noise. In any event, Mr. Wheatley was the only occupant of the first floor, and his hearing was not as keen as it once was.

Sarah turned the lock. She grasped the door's handle and twisted it, pulling the heavy door toward her. As the door opened halfway, it encountered an object in the corner behind it, unseen in the darkness of the wide foyer.

Something startled and awoke, mumbling, "Huh? What? What's that?"

When a quivering hand reached out and grasped her wrist, Sarah shrieked and dropped her bag.

"And where do you think you be going, this time of the night, Miss Sarah, hey?"

Holding on to Sarah's wrist more to keep himself from falling over than to detain her, Mr. Wheatley slowly pulled himself up from the kitchen chair behind the door upon which he had been dozing. When he had his balance, he released her and fumbled on the wall until he found the switch and the foyer's light bloomed.

He closed the front door and, tottering in front of Sarah, he said, "Figured when I saw that look in your eye at supper you might try a runner. So, I set myself up to sleep right here to find you out and talk some sense into you."

Sarah's heart was racing; she could not catch her breath to respond.

"Asked you a question, Miss Sarah. Where do you think you be going, sneaking off like this in the night, it being nearly winter and all? Out for a brisk pre-dawn constitutional, are you? Or something a tad more exotic, say, like running away?"

Sarah's teeth chattered. "R-running away."

"Don' sound like the Sarah Ellinger I know."

"Th-that is the problem. I am not who anyone here thinks I am."

"Oh, psht! God himself knows you through and through. Knows your end from the beginning, he does. No, you told Miss Rose you were going to face us all t'night, and now you are scared and ashamed and want to run off instead. You are better than that, girlie, stronger than that. You need to 'fess up and put this thing behind you for good—but if you do not, you will run from it the rest of your days."

"I-I cannot do it. Everyone will despise me."

"If you think that, then you know less about God's grace than I thought you did, Miss Sarah."

"Please let me pass, Mr. Wheatley—just let me go!"

"Let you go? I love you, missy, and I hang on t' those I love. No, now you listen to me: This is your home, and we are your family. You do not turn your back on the people who love you. So, you are a-going back up those stairs to your room. You should pray your way through your mess, not run from it."

Sarah fidgeted; she flicked her eyes toward the kitchen, thinking to grab her bag and sprint for the back door.

Mr. Wheatley straightened his bowed back and shoulders as tall as he could and addressed her with a sternness she did not know her kindly old friend possessed. "I know what you are thinking. Sure enow, you can outrun these stiff old legs. But hear me first: If you run off alone, into the cold, you will break this old man's heart."

With a tear in his eye, he whispered, "Do you want to break my heart?"

Sarah's mouth opened a little—and then she hung her head. "No. Never."

~*~

SARAH DID NOT GO INTO work that morning.

She had prostrated herself before the Lord, face down on the floor of her room, for an hour after Mr. Wheatley convinced her not to leave. Then, while still praying, she had fallen into an exhausted sleep where she was.

When she did not appear at the breakfast table, Mr. Wheatley— looking rather worse for wear himself—drew Rose aside and conveyed what had taken place only hours before.

"We should let her sleep," Rose decided. "I shall call Joy and let her determine how to handle Sarah's hours at the shop today."

It was near noon when Sarah, clad in her robe and nightgown, her hair a mess, raced downstairs. She was frantic.

"I overslept! I must call Joy."

"It has been done already, Sarah. Joy opened the shop herself today and is working with Corrine."

"But . . ."

"You required sleep, Sarah. And, perhaps, you need this afternoon to prepare yourself for this evening."

Mute and resigned to her fate, Sarah climbed the stairs to her room to wash, dress, and prepare for what lay before her.

~*~

THAT EVENING, AT DINNER, Rose spoke to those gathered at the table. "Immediately following our meal, we shall hold a family meeting. I would ask that all of us pitch in to clear the table and clean the kitchen. As soon as those chores are finished, please assemble in the great room."

While the girls glanced silent questions at each other, Sarah fixed her eyes on her plate. After much prayer and soul-baring before the Lord, she had found a small measure of strength. She prayed it would be enough for what was ahead. She held little hope for the outcome, but she was committed to making her confession.

*Come what may, Lord, I shall be obedient to you in this.*

Near seven o'clock, the after-dinner chores were complete. Rose, Sarah, Olive, the girls—Ruth, Pansy, Frances, Tilda, Naomi, and Dinah—Mr. Wheatley, and Billy were seated and waiting in the great room. Marit and Billy had agreed that the meeting would not be appropriate for their children, so Marit had taken them to their cottage.

Rose seated Sarah next to her. When the household quieted, Rose folded her hands in her lap and addressed them.

"This evening's assembly is a solemn, serious affair. One of our own will speak to us directly. While she is speaking, please give her your complete attention. And I am asking that all of us listen well and heed what Scripture instructs us in Galatians 6:1:

*"Brethren,*
*if a man be overtaken in a fault,*
*ye which are spiritual,*
*restore such an one in the spirit of meekness;*
*considering thyself, lest thou also be tempted."*

Rose tipped her head toward Sarah. "Sarah, will you speak to us?"
Sarah swallowed. "Yes, Miss Rose. Thank you."

For several minutes, in a calm, dispassionate tone, Sarah spoke of her relationship with Lola. Then the volume of her voice dropped and those listening had to strain to hear her.

"I transgressed, not only against God by this unholy intimacy," Sarah whispered, "but against all of you. I . . . I lied. I deceived. I hid what I was doing while pretending I was right with the Lord. My behavior was terribly wrong, and I am sorry. I have asked the Lord for his forgiveness . . . and I humbly ask you for yours."

Olive and a few of the older girls nodded, indicating to Sarah that they had suspected: for Sarah's uncharacteristic behavior and the strain it placed on the house had given rise to speculation and concern. Then, the removal of everyone from the house Monday evening—with only the request that they pray for Sarah as explanation—had been unprecedented.

However, as Sarah disclosed her sins, the shock of the house's two newest girls—Ruth and Pansy—showed Sarah the extent of the damage she had caused. Pansy, in particular, shed hot, angry tears of betrayal that tore at Sarah's heart.

She had to look away. *O God! Please do not allow my hypocrisy to cause any of these little ones to stumble!*

With quaking voice, she continued, "My stepfather molested me as a child. When I was thirteen, he sold me to another man. That man sold me to the owner of the houses in Corinth. I spent nearly two years servicing every man who paid for me before Joy and Rose rescued us.

"I tell you these things only to say this: Although I surrendered to Jesus soon after arriving at Palmer House, my surrender to Christ was incomplete. You see, I never forgave any of those men—beginning with my stepfather. For ten years, I told myself a lie, that I had good reason not to forgive them, that what they had done was unforgiveable.

"What I did not understand is that, because I refused to forgive them, I began to hate them—and not only them but, eventually, all men. Recently, someone told me that I was attempting to make all men pay for the sins of a few. I think this is true.

"Rather than casting down those vain imaginations, those memories that opposed the knowledge of Christ, I rehearsed every abuse again and again, and my hatred grew. I was not only filled with hate, but with anger as well, so much anger! With little provocation, I-I often took my anger out on those I love. On you. I beg your pardon for this offense, too."

Some of Sarah's listeners looked up, acknowledging that they had seen—and even tasted—the lash of her anger. Pansy's expression darkened further, and Sarah licked her dry lips.

"Pastor Carmichael and Minister Liáng have been preaching for months on 'The Overcoming Christian Life.' They have taught deep Scriptural lessons on the lordship of Jesus and the preeminence of his word and how, when we allow anything that opposes his word to remain in our lives, it is idolatry. On the heels of idolatry, we fall into self-deception and then delusion or error.

"I did that—all of it. I resisted the Lord. I excused my disobedience to God's word. I created a snare of self-deception for myself and fell into it.

"My unforgiveness gave Satan a foothold in my life. My hatred—my *judgments* against men—became his stronghold. I was eaten up with the hatred of men, and yet my heart was lonely. I longed for love and affection—but not from any man. That was when Satan presented me with a different kind of snare: Lola."

Sarah's throat was so tight that she had to stop and drink some water before she could speak again. "Nothing that happened to me in my past excuses what *I* did, for Scripture in Matthew 6:14 and 15 is clear:

*"For if ye forgive men their trespasses,*
*your heavenly Father will also forgive you:*
*But if ye forgive not men their trespasses,*
*neither will your Father forgive your trespasses.*

"Only by forgiving every man who had abused and trespassed against me have I been able to see clearly, to perceive the self-deception in my life. I have repented of my sin and received the Lord's forgiveness. He gave me the strength to break free from my attachment to Lola. He gave me the strength, also, to confess my sins to you, my family. I am asking now if you will pardon my sins against you."

Sarah waited, eyes downcast, but Palmer House's great room was silent except for the sniffles of those who were crying. Sarah stared at the carpet, afraid to look into the faces of those she loved so dearly. She knew, in her head, that they would feel obligated to forgive her but, in her heart, she did not see how she could remain at Palmer House.

*I was supposed to be an example to my little sisters, but my continued presence here may be a stumbling block that cannot be overcome.*

The silence lingered until Rose stood and spoke. "If you forgive Sarah, fully and freely from your heart, and you release her from your debt, please come forward and tell her to her face."

Rose turned to Sarah. "Sarah, will you stand?"

Sarah's body was exhausted and weak. Somehow, she got to her feet.

"Sarah?" Rose asked.

Sarah looked into Rose's solemn gray eyes. "Yes, Miss Rose?"

"I forgive you in Christ, my daughter. I forgive you fully and freely from my heart."

Sarah's eyes, brimming with tears, overflowed. "Thank you."

Rose moved aside as Olive approached.

"Sarah?"

Sarah stared again at the carpet. "Yes, Olive?"

"I have been praying for you for months, and my heart is glad that you have repented. I rejoice that the Lord has freed you."

Olive hesitated. "Do you recall months ago when I broke your confidence and shared a secret you had asked me to keep?"

Sarah nodded. "Yes."

"You could have held my breach of trust against me, but you chose not to. You reminded me that mistakes and misunderstandings—even sins—are how our enemy divides and separates brothers and sisters."

Sarah nodded a second time and cut a fleeting glance toward Pansy. The girl's expression was unchanged, but she was listening.

"Sarah, you said that the fear of rejection after such a blunder can cause us to run away rather than face and confess our faults. You were very wise in that moment, Sarah, and I have often pondered your words. Do you remember telling me that?"

Sarah's throat was too tight to speak; she could only, again, nod.

"I do not wish to lose you, Sarah. You are my beloved sister—and you always will be. I forgive you, just as you forgave me. With the Lord's help, we *shall* work this out."

As Olive embraced Sarah, the dam of guilt and hopelessness in Sarah's heart gave way, and she wept. When Sarah at last lifted her head from Olive's shoulder, Pansy stood close by. She stared into Sarah's face, searching.

Fresh tears ran from Sarah's eyes. "Oh, Pansy! I treated you with such contemptible disdain. I was horrid to you. Please, please forgive me."

Pansy blinked and looked away, but she did not hide her own tears. "I do. I forgive you, Sarah."

The remainder of the household followed Pansy's example. No one withheld their forgiveness and restoring love.

~*~

FOLLOWING THE EVENING OF Sarah's confession to the household, Rose and Sarah began to meet daily to continue the cleansing work of the Holy Spirit in Sarah's heart. They prayed together, Rose counseled and encouraged her, and she often held Sarah as she wept over her many regrets and her aching heart.

Rose also gently warned Sarah against complacency. "Be on your guard, dear one: You have broken Satan's hold over your life, but that does not mean he will simply give up and leave you in peace. That is not his way. Jesus admonished Peter with these words, *Watch and pray, that ye enter not into temptation: the spirit indeed is willing, but the flesh is weak.*

"Because our enemy is crafty, you may find yourself waylaid or 'ambushed' in modes you did not foresee and by individuals you were unprepared to encounter—even, perhaps, by Lola herself. Because she has such strong feelings for you, our enemy may provoke her to attempt to renew her relationship with you. She may fight to convince you to return to her.

"Be forewarned, Sarah: Watch and pray that you do not enter into temptation."

~*~

TWO WEEKS PASSED, AND the shortest day of the year was not far off. Evening was already darkening into night when the trolley dropped Sarah several blocks from Palmer House.

All was right in Sarah's heart. The blessed season of Christmas was before them and she looked forward to those happy, hallowed days. Nonetheless, the past weeks had taken their toll on her. She was worn and, as she approached the house's gate in the last of twilight, she was not as vigilant as she might normally have been.

The hand that shot out of the dark and gripped her shoulder shattered her inner reflections. She cried out and stumbled backward.

"Don' be 'fraid, Miss Ellinger. It is only I, Blake Williams. I figured you had t' come home sooner or later, an' I would accost you when you did."

Sarah heard a slur in his words. "Blake! You scared me! Wh-why are you here? What do you want with me?"

"What do I wan' wi' you? Should you not ask wha' Lola wan's? I heard wha' happened: You ditched her, Miss Ellinger. Destroyed her. Should see wha' you've done t' her. I warned her, tol' her she was foolish the nigh' I met you, that you would break 'er t' pieces. Congrachalations. You ha' done quite th' job."

Sarah sent up a silent plea for help. *O Lord, grant me your wisdom and counsel. Give me courage, my God!*

"You have been drinking, Mr. Williams."

"Tha's right. I have. Does't bother you? Li'l virginal Sarah—too good for Lola. Too good for us *sinners*. Pure as th' driven snow."

"Me? Pure? You mistake me for someone else, Mr. Williams."

"Pretty certain Lola thin's you an innocent."

"Well, she is mistaken—as are you, Mr. Williams. I am as sinful as anyone at that party you escorted me to. By the way, where is your friend? Juan, I believe you called him?"

Blake's mouth twisted in the deep twilight. "On t' greener pastures—greener referring t' th' color an' quantity of money. 'Parently, my money wasn' green enough."

He sneered. "Inconstancy in our circles is common, an' heartbreak frequent."

"But you thought to come all this way to chide me for discontinuing my friendship with Lola?"

Blake laughed under his breath. "Well, you ha' me there, m' dear. I salute you. Few in our circles stay togeth'. Always on th' hunt, lookin' for somethin' better."

"May I say something to you, Blake? Something personal?"

He slouched against the gate. "S'pose so.

"If you are longing for fidelity, for faithfulness, I have found such a one."

"Yeah?"

"God, the Lord of all, is faithful. What he says he will do, he will not fail to do."

"Shoulda known you'd throw religion a' me."

"Not religion, but intimate communion with the Lord God Almighty. He loves you, Blake. His love is finer and more constant than any man's."

"Don' preach constancy t' me, Sarah. Not after what you did t' Lola."

"You do not under—"

He held up a shaky hand. "Stop. Said m' piece. You're dead t' me now. Like Juan."

He staggered across the street where Sarah realized he had parked a motor car. She watched him drive away, weaving down the road, this way and that.

"Lord, he should not operate a motor car in his condition! Please do not allow him to harm himself or anyone else in his drunken state. And Lord? Will you quicken to his spirit the few words I was able to share with him? Burn them upon his heart, O God, so that he must ponder them."

Sarah went through the gate and walked toward Palmer House's front porch. Blake's last words cut her deeply.

*Don' preach constancy t' me, Sarah. Not after what you did t' Lola.*

"Please help me, Lord! Help me to not allow the whispers of the enemy's condemnation to find soil in my heart in which to grow. My first duty is to obey you in all things. I am so sorrowful for the pain I caused Lola, but I must trust her to you."

&#x223f; &#x2739; &#x223e;

# CHAPTER 20

I It was Sunday afternoon. Sarah was thinking on Pastor Carmichael's message and reading the Scriptures he had taught on. Church was once more a blessed place of worship and communion for her—now that her heart was again right before the Lord. Olive put her head into Sarah's open doorway.

"Sarah? Someone is here to see you."

Close to three weeks had passed since Sarah last saw Lola, since she had broken off their friendship. The Lord had done a cleansing work in Sarah's heart in those weeks—but now she had an unexpected visitor.

Sarah heard the reticence in Olive's voice and knew at once that the visitor was Lola.

Rose had warned her this might happen. *Be careful, Sarah: Lola may fight to convince you to return to her. Be forewarned, Sarah.*

Sarah had known that Rose was right: Lola would not give up without a fight. Sarah had prayed and prepared for this moment.

*Please help me to be kind but firm, Lord God. I know it is not Lola I am fighting, but my own sinful desires and the snare the enemy so cunningly crafted from my earliest youth. Help me to fight him and win, my Lord.*

*If only the ache of this loss would leave. Please, Lord, heal my heart!*

"Thank you, Olive." She began to pass by Olive in the hallway, when Olive put her hand on Sarah's arm.

"Sarah?"

She found it hard to meet Olive's earnest gaze. "Yes?"

"We are praying for you, Sarah; all of us are. You shall *not* fail, Sarah. Jesus has you, and he is holding you—like this." Olive wrapped her arms around Sarah's unresponsive frame, and strained Sarah to her. "He shall never let you go, nor shall we. Never!"

Sarah leaned into Olive's embrace and wept. "Oh, Olive, my heart hurts so! I have never felt such pain. I-I cannot bear it."

"You can bear it, because the Lord will bear it with you, sweet Sarah."

*Sweet Sarah. That is what Lola used to call me. O God!*

Olive handed her a handkerchief, and Sarah mopped her eyes.

"Thank you, Olive. You cannot know how much you mean to me."

Sarah composed herself and went down the staircase. She found Rose watching for her. "Lola is waiting for you in the parlor. I have sent most of the girls to the park, and they understand why. They will be praying for you, Sarah, as shall we all. If . . . if you should need to run away, go to the kitchen. Marit, Billy, and Mr. Wheatley will be there."

"Thank you, Miss Rose."

Sarah opened the parlor door and walked inside, closing the door behind her. "Hello, Lola."

Lola was standing, pacing; her face was ashen with grief. "Sarah. Please. Can we talk?"

"Yes—this one time." Sarah indicated a chair. "Please sit down."

"No. You have been swayed—indoctrinated—into some wretched cult. I want you to come with me, Sarah. This instant. We shall talk when we are far removed and you are safe. Come away with me from this horrid place and your *precious* Miss Rose!"

"There is nothing horrid about Palmer House or about Miss Rose, Lola. She rescued me."

"Rescued you? From what? From doing as you wish with your life? From making your own choices?"

"No." Sarah hesitated before she added, "She rescued me from a brothel."

Lola's countenance shriveled in dazed disbelief.

"Please sit down, Lola."

Lola did as Sarah asked, but slow tears trailed down her cheeks.

Sarah sat opposite Lola. "Do you recall our conversation at Justin Stafford's party? Do you remember when you asked me, 'Tell me, Sarah, are you as innocent as you seem?'"

Lola nodded. "Y-you said, 'No.' I did not believe you."

"You should have."

"But why did you never tell me?"

"Tell you that I was a whore?"

Lola's chin trembled as she shook her head. "Do not call yourself that. Please. Do not."

"I *was* a whore, Lola—and a high-dollar one at that—although I did not choose such a life. My stepfather was what I believe is now being called a pedophile. He liked little girls and, when I was nine years old, as soon as my mother died, he molested me. For four long years, he preyed upon me. But when I turned thirteen and began to mature, his feelings toward me changed. He no longer desired me. In fact, he hated me because I was becoming a woman. So, he sold me."

"Stop! I cannot listen to this—"

"I am sorry, but you need to hear what I have to say. All of it. When I was thirteen, Richard sent me to live with a man named Willard. Willard told everyone that he was my guardian, but he, too, was a pedophile; he just preferred girls my age—still quite young, but not little children."

"Oh, Sarah!"

Sarah ignored Lola's remonstrations. "While I was with Willard, we lived something of a make-believe existence. He treated me like a princess. He clothed me in exquisite gowns, taught me to pour tea and converse like a debutante, and showed me off to his wealthy friends. It was rather like playing dress-up in my mother's clothes—that is, until night fell. Then he would come to my bed, and it was no longer make-believe.

"I had been with him a while, when the servants warned me. They told me he only kept a girl until she was sixteen; then, he would pass her on to a friend. I was with Willard for two years when I caught the eye of a certain Judge Brown. He was visiting Albany from Denver, and he told Willard I was just what he was looking for. He convinced Willard to sell me to him, and he promised me I would be the toast of his townhouse in the 'Mile-High City.'

"I believed I was being passed to him as Richard had passed me to Willard, that Judge Brown would keep me for his personal use much as Willard had. I did not know the judge owned two brothels in a mountain village above Denver—two *special* brothels. 'Special' in that they 'specialized' in every sort of perversion imaginable.

"Judge Brown and I took the train from Albany to Denver. When we arrived in Denver, instead of leaving the station, we transferred to another train, and the judge took me on to Corinth. It is not far from here, actually, only a short train ride up the mountain from the city. Once we reached Corinth, he installed me in his 'Corinth Gentleman's Club'—one of two exclusive whorehouses he operated for the pleasure of the wealthy men of Denver, men who wished to practice their vices and perversions in a cultured environment and at a distance from polite society and their 'prudish' spouses."

Lola's hands covered her face, and she wept in incredulity and revulsion. Her sobs ended on a spate of coughing brought on by her distress.

Sarah pushed down the urge to help or comfort Lola. Instead, when Lola's coughing subsided, Sarah pressed ahead.

"Many of the girls I met in the club had been lured to Denver by false employment advertisements. Some were unsuspecting innocents—and virgins were in particular demand by men who wished the experience of deflowering them.

"Once a girl was deflowered and healed, she was put into 'circulation,' but the adjustment was horrifying for her. As a means of overcoming a girl's natural reticence, 'discipline' in the houses was swift and severe. Any girl who refused to cooperate, to be charming and accommodating to the clients, was brutalized. She was starved, beaten, and raped—repeatedly—until she submitted.

"I did not suffer as much as those girls who defied the house's madam. My spirit had been broken years before. Moreover, I saw what they did to the girls who refused to work."

Sarah shrugged. "I chose not to resist."

"Oh, my sweet Sarah!"

Lola tried to reach for her, but Sarah held her off. "No. Please do not touch me. Just . . . just allow me to finish.

"I learned that girls in the clubs stayed a year, perhaps a year and a half, before they were replaced by 'fresh stock.' The 'old' girls were shipped down the mountain to less discriminating brothels. Then, six months after I arrived, something odd occurred: Judge Brown disappeared. Rumors flew among us girls, but no one saw him ever again.

"A new owner took over, and conditions for us worsened. The men working for the owner used their fists and their guns to intimidate and cow not only us, but the entire village. No one—not even the sheriff—would stand up to them. Those who did were beaten, or they simply disappeared."

Sarah looked back to that moment when the last of her hope flickered and went out. "I had been in Corinth just over a year when I lost all confidence in any future but more of—and worse than—what I had. My fate would be like every girl whose "freshness" diminished with time. I think I had just turned seventeen."

Lola cursed then, using words Sarah had not heard since she left Corinth.

Sarah's mouth twisted. "I do not wish to belabor or glorify my suffering in that place. It is behind me. What *is* important happened not many months after. A new girl arrived at the club, a very brave little Chinese girl—only fourteen years old!—but made of tougher stuff than I was. Mei-Xing was determined to escape or die trying. She was caught trying to run twice and paid dearly for her rebellion."

Sarah shuddered. "I can still hear her screams as they took turns using their fists on her."

Lola seemed caught up in Sarah's tale.

"But, you see, Miss Rose's daughter, Joy, had moved to the village in the early fall and opened a guest lodge. Joy became little Mei-Xing's hope for refuge.

"Bloody and bruised from her most recent escape attempt, her face ruined, Mei-Xing climbed down a rope of sheets from the window of her third-story room. She dropped to the ground in the dead of winter, and walked, barefoot, through the snow and ice to Joy Thoresen's guest lodge—and Joy took her in."

Lola's expression turned incredulous. "You are speaking of Joy O'Dell? Your employer? *That* Joy? But-but what of the all the men you spoke of? Their fists and guns? How they had the whole village cowed?"

"Lola, you believe Joy to be just another weak-willed woman, dependent upon a husband simply because she is married. You have no idea how courageous she is. She hid Mei-Xing at great personal risk, and those men could neither find Mei-Xing nor could they prove that Joy had taken her in.

"Some weeks later, emboldened by Mei-Xing's flight, a few other girls also escaped. They, too, went to Joy. She hid them and got them safely off the mountain—but at a terrible cost to her. Once the owner of the club decided that Joy had to have helped those women? He ordered his men to burn her out."

"And then?"

"The Pinkertons and the U.S. Marshals arrived in time to save Joy, her mother, and her friends, but it was too late to save her lodge. Happily, the marshals *did* arrest the club's owner, his men, and the club's madam. I shall never, as long as I live, forget Joy's mother—yes, my precious Miss Rose—coming to the club in the early hours of that morning, waking us up, and telling us we were free.

"It was the first time I saw Miss Rose; it was my first experience with a true woman of God. And it was the first breath of freedom I had dared to draw since my mother died."

When Sarah stopped, she and Lola sat, each silent and solemn in her own thoughts, until Sarah picked up her tale.

"Several weeks went by. Rose and Joy left Corinth to visit Denver, to look for a house for them and us. They met a woman named Martha Palmer. You may have heard me speak of her; she passed away recently. Well, Martha gave Rose and Joy this house—Palmer House.

"When Rose and Joy returned to Corinth, they shared their vision with us whores, for the family we could be part of if we came with them to Denver. I was alone in the world. I had nowhere else to go—nowhere. Rose and Joy took me in. They loved me and held me when I wept and shook with agony and shame. They told me about Jesus, how he would save my wretched, wounded soul—and he did."

VIKKI KESTELL

Sarah glanced at Lola. "So, you see, there is nothing horrid about Palmer House."

"But all the rules? The restrictions? The lack of freedom?"

"Rules are necessary for peace and harmony when so many live together under one roof. However, no one forces us to stay. Each of us chooses to live here or not. If we choose to stay, we agree to live in unity of heart and purpose. You may believe me or not, but I *am* free. I am free from my past, from guilt, and from sin."

"And us? What about us?"

Sarah sighed. "I think you might understand, if you will hear me out. My stepfather, then Willard, abused me. Willard sold me to Judge Brown, who forced me into prostitution, after which I endured an endless line of men who used me to satisfy their evil lusts. These were the only men I had ever known, and I hated them."

"As well you should," Lola murmured.

"Yes, I had reason to hate them—and I thus did. But my hate did not end with them. I grew to hate *all* men."

Lola laughed without mirth. "Men are pigs."

"I know your life has not been a bed of roses, Lola. Your father beat your mother and abandoned you."

"So?"

"So, you hate men, too, but hatred is a poison that warps and disfigures the soul. In my hatred, I vowed I would never allow another man to abuse me. I judged all men alike: guilty. As a result of this judgment, I do not desire a man's affection or regard. I cannot bear the thought of a man touching me; I cannot even consider intimacy with a man without great revulsion and abhorrence. My soul is broken in this area, Lola."

Lola shifted uneasily. "Are you saying that you only love me because you are *broken?*"

"I suppose that is what I am saying."

Sarah's reply angered Lola. "What nonsense! Love is love—I know you love me as I love you."

"Yes, I admit to having deep feelings for you, but those feelings are wrong. They are broken. Perverse."

Lola's anger increased. "How dare you spit on what is most precious to me!"

Sarah shook her head. "I am sorry. It is not my intention to disrespect you, Lola. I had hoped you would understand.

"Understand? I understand this: I want you, Sarah! More than life, more than breath! Come away with me. I can make you happy."

"No, I shall not, and this is the last time I shall consent to seeing you." Sarah could not contain her tears. "Please, Lola. If you care for me as you say you do, then leave me alone."

"How can I leave you alone? I love you, Sarah!"

"No, you *want* me, but you do not want what is *best* for me—such a vast difference! And if I were to choose you, I would be doing the same thing: choosing what I *want*, not what is *best* for you, not what is good or holy or eternal."

"No man can offer you the love I can!"

Sarah exhaled and calmed; she gazed into Lola's anguished face. "As much as I care for you, I already love a man more than I love you. I choose him."

"You are choosing *a man* over me?"

Sarah nodded.

"Who? Who is he? What is this man's name?"

"His name is Jesus, Lola. I choose him."

The laughter that burst from Lola was loud and frightening, tinged with hysteria. "Jesus is not real! He is not a *real* person—he is only a myth, a story. These people have deceived you!"

"They have not deceived me. I know him: I know Jesus for myself."

Sarah stood. "You must go now, Lola. Again, I am sorry to have wounded you. Please forgive me."

Gasping in rage and frustration, Lola grabbed for Sarah's hand, but Sarah pulled away. Lola released her anguish in a high wail. "Sarah, no! Please!"

Not waiting for Lola to leave as she had asked, Sarah fled the parlor. She ran down the long hallway to the kitchen—where she knew Marit, Billy, and Mr. Wheatley were waiting, where they would open their arms to her, and where they would step between her and temptation, if necessary, should Lola try to follow her or should Sarah's resolve fail her.

~*~

ONCE LOLA HAD SHAKEN off her initial despair, she had, as Sarah feared she would, attempted to follow after Sarah. Lola flung wide the parlor door—and encountered Sarah's "precious Miss Rose" standing outside the doorway, her hands folded before her. Rose did not move— and she blocked Lola's egress.

Lola sized up the woman and considered how she might fare if she were to shove Rose aside. Rose was slender and smaller than Lola, and she was twice Lola's age—but it was the calm stillness reposing within the depths of those wise, gray eyes that gave Lola pause, that made her hesitate.

However, this was no "dead" calm, for Lola glimpsed a well of vigor and resolution in Rose's serene expression. No, nothing "dead" filled this woman's soul.

Lola licked her lips. "I suppose you despise me for trying to take Sarah away from here. From you."

"Despise you?" Rose shook her head. "No, quite the opposite, Lola. I wish only God's best for you."

"If you want what is best for me, then let Sarah go!"

"But we are not holding Sarah. She has chosen what is best for her of her own free will. God's best for you lies elsewhere."

"But I love her. I need her. I hunger for her."

Rose nodded once. "I am sorry for your pain, but not every hunger comes from God. The Bible tells us that love does not seek its own way; rather, it seeks what is good and right. Love rejoices in the truth."

"The truth? The truth is that I want Sarah. I long for her!"

"You are, perhaps, describing obsession."

"Is that not what love is? A magnificent obsession? Complete and utter abandon? Surrendering oneself to a passion that demands all? Sarah compels my heart and mind; she inspires me to be nobler, kinder than I am."

Rose's slight smile was tinged with sadness. "What you describe sounds more like worship than love, and worship of something or someone other than the Lord is idolatry."

"Idolatry! What nonsense."

"Idolatry can take many forms, Lola. Anything or anyone we place beside or before the God who made the heavens and the earth—and who made us—is idolatry."

"Then that is something we can agree on, for I do worship Sarah. What can be wrong with that? If I choose to make Sarah the center of my miserable life; if I choose to devote myself to her and her happiness, what is that to you?"

"But Sarah is not worthy of your worship. She is flawed, just as you and I are. She would be the first to tell you so."

Lola spat a curse filled with mockery. "Sarah is lovely, pure, and good."

"I think not. Jesus said that no one is good but God. I, too, love Sarah, but I know she is a sinner—just as I am. Just as you are."

"God and Jesus! God and Jesus! Is everything about them? What about me? What about Sarah? Do our feelings count for nothing?"

"I do not doubt your feelings, Lola. I know they are real; I even know that you are suffering in this moment, and I am so very sorry. But our feelings are not the arbiter of what is right or what is wrong in this life—nor can we trust our feelings not to lead us astray.

"Untaught and unrestrained by truth, our feelings are quite deceptive."

"You are saying my *feelings* are lying to me?"

"I could not have put it better. You believe that a life spent with Sarah would be good—but this life is only temporary, a precursor to eternity. Would you trade the good of eternity for what is but a passing mist?

"More importantly, if you love Sarah, would you wish to condemn her to an eternity of torment? For that is the destination of all who deny the Lordship of Christ. Is it love to cause her to stumble and fall away from God's grace, the grace that delivered her from her past?"

"I do not believe in such malarkey—neither a blissful heaven nor the fires of an eternal hell."

"What *we* believe cannot alter truth, can it? If you believed you could live without water, and you refused to drink, would you not die? If you believed you could fly, and you jumped from a building, would you not perish? If you believed yourself to be a man, would that make you one? God himself has determined what is truth, what is right, what is wrong, what is *real*. He does not ask for our opinions, nor do they affect what he has already defined as truth."

"I *will* talk to Sarah again. She will listen to reason—she will listen to me."

"Lola, are you saying that you are determined to override Sarah's choice? You decry the state of society and, in particular, you disparage men who take choice from their wives. Are you not purposing to do the same thing? Are you not guilty of that for which you condemn so many men?"

"Let me pass."

"No."

It was a simple, one-syllable reply, neither harsh nor cruel. Then Lola saw the figure of a muscled young man step from the great room into the foyer. He, too, stood with hands folded before him, kindly, but unyielding.

Lola stood still, weighing her options, knowing she had none for the present situation.

Her voice broke on a sob. "Very well. I shall go."

That was when Rose opened her arms. "Come to me first, Lola, and let me comfort you."

"What? No! You are my enemy!"

Rose shook her head, her arms still extended. "No, child. I am the mother you never had."

Rose took two steps toward Lola and pulled her into her embrace. Lola collapsed within Rose's arms and wept bitterly; Rose simply twined her arms more tightly about the younger woman, and Lola sobbed against her shoulder.

"Oh, Lola! I love you, my dear child, with the love of a mother. I love you with the love of a sister. And I love you with all the love and forgiveness God has poured upon me."

Lola seemed to come to herself. She jerked and pulled away; she pushed Rose back from her and swiped at her wet eyes. "God? No. I hate God. I hate him!"

Rose's hands dropped to her sides. "Your hate does not change his great love for you. The Lord made you, Lola, and because he made you, he knows you better than you know yourself. I promise you, he will continue to seek after you."

Lola stumbled toward the front door.

Rose called after her, "I shall pray for you, Lola."

Lola stopped. Turned around. Her words were icy. "Please do not."

"Nevertheless, I *shall* pray for you, Lola. I shall pray that you find the peace that passes all understanding that can only be found in Jesus."

Lola slammed the door behind her.

# ℭHAPTER 21

Sarah slogged through the ensuing days, determined to work hard and perform her duties well. She unburdened herself to Corrine, who simply listened and nodded.

"You shall always be my closest friend, Sarah. We shall get through this . . . together. The Lord will help you to heal."

Pastor Carmichael, too, was a listening friend Sarah had not expected. He had suggested that Sarah meet with him weekly for prayer and counseling. "Breona and I would like to support you, Miss Ellinger, as you find your footing in the Lord again."

Sarah had to confess to the Lord, to herself, and to Isaac Carmichael himself, that Carmichael was not the domineering ogre she had painted him—and all men—to be. Once she had forgiven Carmichael and repented of the judgments she held toward men, she was able to see his humility and the authentic care and concern that he had for her.

*I have been so very blind! My judgments against men were like the scales upon the Apostle Paul's eyes—making me utterly insensate to reality. I was deluded for so long that I scarcely recognize the world around me.*

Sarah left work two hours early on Friday to keep her appointment; Corrine stayed late to take the shop's last hours. Sarah rode a streetcar to within a few blocks of the Carmichael's home, a modest little rental. Sarah looked forward to her visit with Isaac Carmichael with equal parts trepidation and earnest inquiry: She had questions and hoped he could advise her.

She walked from the trolley stop to the parsonage. Breona let her in, hugged her, and showed her to their living room. Sarah heard the sounds of children playing not far away.

"I be makin' a pot o' tea for ye an' keepin' our Sean an' wee Rowen busy in th' kitchen whilst ye talk," Breona murmured as she left Sarah.

"Will you make yourself at home, Miss Ellinger?" Isaac Carmichael asked.

"Thank you, Pastor." Sarah took the chair he indicated across the low table between them.

"Have you had a good week?"

"Yes, I would say so. I continue to declare forgiveness over men as the Holy Spirit brings various offenses to my mind." Sarah placed her hand upon the journal in her lap. "I have listed them, beginning again with my mother's husband, Richard Langston, since that was the birthplace of my fear and hatred. I asked the Lord to help me recall each painful occasion of his abuse. Some of the instances are veiled in the mist of childhood, but whenever a memory emerges from that fog, I pray over it and make the deliberate choice to forgive the perpetrator.

"I speak my forgiveness aloud—and you were quite right. It is difficult to release the pain and anger, but when I choose to do so regardless of how I feel, I find that my feelings begin to give way to my will.

"Then, as you recommended, I pray daily for my stepfather. I do not know if he is alive or dead. Nevertheless, I try to see him as the Lord sees him: destined for eternal destruction if he does not repent and turn to Jesus. I know it grieves the Lord when anyone rejects him. For that reason, I pray for Mr. Langston's salvation. I ask the Lord to be merciful to him, to soften his heart and cause him to seek God."

"How difficult is it for you to pray for his salvation?"

"More than I can say! I could not do it at first, for my flesh craves to see him suffer and insists he does not deserve God's mercy."

"How do you get past this sticking point?"

Sarah tucked her chin to her chest. "I-I think on how close I came to rejecting the Lord, how near I was to choosing Lola over him. If Miss Rose had not acted, if she had not called on you to help her confront me?"

A sob caught in Sarah's throat. "Such a near thing! When I think of how I could be lost right now but for the Lord's compassion and the love of faithful friends, I am able to see Mr. Langston as the Lord sees him— rather than through the lens of my hatred."

Sarah sighed. "Each day, I make a little headway, but I declare it is slow progress."

"I daresay you must go over the same ground more than once?"

Sarah gave a wry chuckle. "How did you know?"

"You have a long-standing habit of hate, Miss Ellinger. Moreover, you are practiced at hiding that hate from yourself. That twofold stronghold of hate and of self-deception must be dismantled—brick by brick—until not one brick remains upon another and until every brick has been crushed to dust."

"Oh, my. That is a powerful and apt analogy." She nodded to herself. "Dismantled, brick by brick. Every brick crushed to dust."

Just then, Breona brought the tea tray. When she had placed the tray between them, she excused herself.

"Shall I serve?" Sarah asked.

"If you please."

When she had handed him his cup and poured one for herself, she grew still.

"What is troubling you, Miss Ellinger?"

"I must tell you something," Sarah whispered.

"I am listening. We are safe here in the presence of the Lord—you can speak of anything to me and before him."

"Thank you; you give me courage to bare my soul. It is just . . . that Lola continues to call the shop."

His response was grave. "I see."

"No—you misunderstand. When she calls, I do not speak to her. I did, once, answer the telephone when I did not know it was her calling. However, now, because she calls more than once a day, Corrine takes all calls. She is kind but adamant when she tells Lola that I shall not speak to her."

Isaac nodded, his eyes sad. "That is wise. Are you praying for Lola?"

"I am, Pastor, but it is painful work. The thing is . . . I know she is suffering terribly, and it grieves me so much. When she called and I, unknowingly, answered, she begged me to see her, begged me to-to-to take her back. When I refused and asked her not to call anymore, she wept and pleaded with me."

"But you were resolute?"

"Yes." Sarah's voice caught. "But she is suffering so—and it breaks my heart. I understand what she is suffering, for I am suffering in the same manner. I-I do not know how to stop this aching in my heart, this longing for her. And this longing leaves me confused."

"Confused about?"

"I suppose I am confused about my feelings. *Why* do I long for her? When I was with her, I was not satisfied, yet apart from her, I ache and grieve."

Carmichael put his cup on the table in front of him and took up his Bible. "Since I became aware of your struggle, Miss Ellinger, I have felt led to study more on this topic, searching the Scriptures to better understand. I wish to share something with you. Although it may distress you initially, I also hope the Lord will grant you insight into the pain you describe—and help you to heal."

Sarah, too, set down her cup. She folded her hands in her lap. "Very well, Pastor. I am listening."

"I am reading from Romans 1, verse 26.

*"For this cause God gave them up unto vile affections:*
*for even their women did change the natural use*
*into that which is against nature."*

Sarah cringed. "I have committed this passage to memory."

"As I said, I did not read it to distress you further. Rather, as I studied out this verse in the original text, I believe that I came upon an answer to your question."

"Oh?"

"Yes. The word for 'affections' in this verse is, in the original Greek, the word, *pathos*. It indicates deep feeling, a passion, from which the mind suffers. Perhaps a 'suffering passion' best describes it. Of course, it is the same word from which the English language derives our word, pathos. In our current language, pathos means to evoke pity or compassion."

"Pathos. That describes what I feel for Lola. I am sorry to have hurt her; I truly understand what she is suffering, and I have compassion for her, for I am suffering the same."

Carmichael slowly nodded. "I believe it would be helpful, too, for us to look at the Greek word from which *pathos* descends, for it means to experience a painful sensation, to suffer and to be vexed by passion. Unfortunately, such a passion can have no godly conclusion, satisfaction, or fulfillment—which only increases the insatiable longing, a longing that has no hope, a suffering with no healing salve."

Sarah stared ahead, turning his words over in her mind. "Insatiable longing. Suffering. That was my own word, was it not? I said Lola was suffering . . . as am I."

"I recognized the emotion as you described it."

Sarah exhaled. "I am glad, at the least, to put a name to this sadness, Pastor." She swallowed. "And you say there is no remedy for this suffering?"

"I believe that daily surrender to the Lordship of Christ makes all suffering bearable. I am not saying change will be easy or quick. However, in time, when the work of demolishing the underlying spiritual strongholds in your heart is complete—if you earnestly and persistently disallow any taint of the former judgments to regain even a fingerhold in your heart—then, I believe that what was once an 'inordinate' or 'vile' affection can be replaced and overcome by a godly one."

"Replaced and overcome by a godly affection? You believe I could ever care for a man as I do for Lola? I confess, my heart resists such an idea." Sarah shuddered. "I cannot abide the idea of a man's intimate touch."

"I should have been clearer, Miss Ellinger: I believe you shall find *relief* from the painful affections you feel at present.

"If you allow the work of God to continue in your heart, he will give you rest from this pain. After all, your objective is not to find a husband; your objective is to follow hard after the Lord. Let the Holy Spirit lead you to utterly destroy the strongholds and bring you into perfect peace and liberty in Christ."

Sarah laughed a little. "I am glad my goal is not to get a husband, for I have vowed not to marry."

Carmichael said nothing for a moment. Then, with a gentle smile, he said, "Perhaps that is a vow you need to break, Miss Ellinger."

She frowned. "What do you mean?"

"If your goal is to follow hard after the Lord, should you have anything in your heart you have vowed you will not do? I am not referring to sin, of course."

Sarah blew out a breath. "But the Lord would not force me to marry, would he?"

"No, he would not—and yet does not a vow such as yours say to the Lord, 'You are unable to heal my heart, unable to work a miracle'? Does it not also say, 'Lord, even if you did change my heart, I would not accept your gift of a husband's love'? Is not this vow simply another piece of your heart you have not surrendered to the Father?"

Chagrin swept across Sarah's face. "Oh, *bother*," she said under her breath.

Carmichael laughed aloud.

Sarah smiled at his laughter, and she realized how comfortable she was with her pastor, what a blessing he was to their church. To her.

"Bother? Indeed!" he chuckled. "I quite agree."

Carmichael then added, "I hope you will pray on it. I am certain the Holy Spirit will lead you aright."

He paged through his Bible. "We are all tempted, Miss Ellinger, and each of us has particular sins we struggle with to the point of suffering— and 'bother.' I find great comfort in knowing that Jesus himself suffered when he was tempted—and that he *understands* and is able to strengthen us when we, too, are tempted. Hebrews 2:18 tells us:

"*For in that he himself hath suffered being tempted,*
*he is able to succour them that are tempted.*

"With his help, I am confident that you will prevail."

Sarah replenished their cups and they sipped their tea for a period of quiet camaraderie until they had finished.

Sarah stood. "Thank you, Pastor. I shall pray over your counsel and insights."

"Shall we meet again next Friday, Miss Ellinger?"

"Yes, thank you, Pastor."

~*~

LATER THAT EVENING, Sarah approached Rose. "Miss Rose? May I have a moment?"

They again used the parlor to speak privately.

"Yes, Sarah?"

"As you may recall, I had an appointment with Pastor Carmichael today. Our time together was valuable. He helped me to understand the sorrow and pain I have been feeling—and I came away with hope that I might, someday, be free of it.

"Miss Rose, you know that I have recommitted my life to Jesus, and you see that I have begun the arduous work of forgiving every man who has ever harmed me. You have seen how this work has begun to bear fruit: The Lord has enabled me to sever my relationship with Lola and, more importantly, is helping me to sever my emotional ties to her.

"However, I admit that the passage of time is essential to demonstrating the depth and completeness of my restoration. I hope, though, as the Lord leads, to make good on my promise to come alongside you to help in the leadership of Palmer House—at least, until you retire."

Sarah shook her head. She knew Rose could not continue to manage the house many years more, particularly if O'Dell accepted the offer of promotion to the Chicago Pinkerton office. Still, the thought of Palmer House without her was bleak indeed.

She looked up into Rose's face. "I just wanted to let you know that my intention is still to help you. Someday. Again, I know it will take time before your confidence in me is repaired."

Rose smiled. "My confidence is not in you, but in the redeeming power of Jesus, Sarah, my daughter. And may I also say? No faith is made stronger or purer without the Lord's refining fire. Isaiah 48:10 and 11 tell us:

*"Behold, I have refined thee, but not with silver;*
*I have chosen thee in the furnace of affliction.*
*For mine own sake, even for mine own sake, will I do it . . .*
*I will not give my glory unto another.*

"It is within the furnace of affliction that the Lord chooses us—not for our own sake, but for his sake, so that, ultimately, our lives give glory to the Lord and him alone. I shall look forward to having you join me, Sarah, when the time is right. Shall we wait together upon the Lord to lead and guide us?"

Sarah sighed in relief. "Thank you, Miss Rose. Yes, and amen."

# PART 3

*O the depth of the riches*
*both of the wisdom and knowledge of God!*
*how unsearchable are his judgments,*
*and his ways past finding out!*
*For who hath known the mind of the Lord?*
*or who hath been his counsellor?*
*Or who hath first given to him,*
*and it shall be recompensed unto him again?*
*For of him, and through him, and to him,*
***are all things:***
*to whom be glory forever.*
*Amen.*
*(Romans 11:33-36, KJV)*

# ℰHAPTER 22

## *Denver, 1921*

I t was early in the day for the telephone to ring. Sarah left her seat to answer the telephone hanging on the wall not far from her desk in Palmer House's great room. She no longer worked for Joy in her shop. Four months past, Sarah had resigned her position and taken over many of Rose's responsibilities.

Rose was seventy-three now, vibrant in her faith and still guiding the spiritual needs of the house, but less able to stand up to the rigors of managing the house alone. She also wished to spend more time with her three grandsons, Matthew, Jacob, and newborn Luke.

Palmer House's board of directors, as established in Martha Palmer's will, had approved Sarah coming alongside Rose to take the strain from her shoulders. Next year, when Rose retired from her duties and moved to Chicago with Joy and her family, Sarah, with Olive's help, would be ready to assume them.

Sarah picked up the telephone's receiver. "Good morning; you have reached Palmer House."

A male voice inquired, "Am I speaking with Miss Ellinger?"

Sarah identified the voice although she had not had opportunity or reason to see the man behind it in more than a year. "Yes, you are."

"Bryan Croft here, Miss Ellinger."

Sarah closed her eyes and mouthed a familiar prayer of thanksgiving. *Lord, I thank you for delivering me from bitter hate and judgment against men. From the bottom of my heart, I rejoice that old things have passed away; you have made all things concerning me new. I walk in forgiveness. I refuse to entertain offense or allow it a place in my thoughts or heart. I sow mercy wherever I go. Lord, I sow grace.*

Sarah had schooled herself to be open and courteous, and graciousness came naturally now. "Yes, Dr. Croft? How can I help you today?"

The man hesitated. "I . . . I have taken a patient into my clinic, Miss Ellinger. She is suffering through the final stages of tuberculosis.

"The hospital wished to send her directly to a sanatorium in Colorado Springs, but the woman has no money. Moreover, she objected to leaving Denver.

"I do not, ordinarily, provide hospice care at my clinic nor is the clinic set up for twenty-four-hour nursing, but this woman had no place to go, and I felt . . . led to make an exception in this case."

"I see." A sliver of concern shivered along Sarah's arms. "May I ask why you are telling me of this, Dr. Croft?"

"My patient is asking for you, Miss Ellinger."

"Oh? And w-what is her name?"

"She calls herself Lorraine Pritchard."

*Lola.*

Sarah leaned against the wall, and a great weight settled upon her. Tuberculosis. It was—until recently—known as consumption.

It had no cure.

*Mama died of consumption. It is a miracle that I did not contract the contagion from her.* Recalling Lola's frequent bouts of coughing—to which Sarah had attached no concern or alarm—Sarah added, *It is, perhaps, a greater miracle that I did not contract it from Lola.*

Sarah knew from experience what Lola was facing: a horrible death from the coughing, choking, wasting disease that would sap the breath from her lungs and strip the flesh from her bones—just as it had done to Edwina Ellinger.

And Croft said Lola was in the final stages of the sickness.

*O Lord, I accept that I cannot go to Lola. I acknowledge your will in this . . . but how I wish Lola knew you! I care for her soul, Lord, for where she will spend eternity. You know how faithfully I have prayed for her salvation.*

*And I must inquire of you, Lord—why did you have this man bring me news of Lola? I do not wish to resurrect what is and must remain dead in my heart. So, what can his call possibly mean?*

While those thoughts were flitting through her mind, a comforting presence crept over her.

*Fear not, for I have redeemed thee. I have called thee by name . . . Sarah, my redeemed one. You are mine.*

The familiar words calmed her. "Oh, yes, Jesus," she breathed, "Thank you for your loving presence. I need not be afraid if I am wise and obedient. You will never leave me nor forsake me."

"I beg your pardon, Miss Ellinger?"

"No, it is I who should apologize, Dr. Croft. I was speaking aside."

He cleared his throat. "I see."

*Do not be afraid, Sarah, my redeemed one. I shall lead you in paths of righteousness for my Name's sake.*

"What are you asking of me, Dr. Croft?"

Her question troubled him. "I suppose . . . I suppose I am asking if you will come. I believe the woman wishes to clear her conscience before she dies. She seems tormented by regret."

As long as she lived, Sarah would never be able to hear the word "regret" without Isaac Carmichael's voice ringing in her ears: *Regret is not repentance, Sarah; it is sorrow for the outcome, not sorrow for grieving the heart of God.*

Did Lola have more than regret in her heart? Would she be open to the Gospel?

"I need time to think. To pray. May I call you back, Dr. Croft?"

"Yes, of course; however, it is Monday morning, and I shall be seeing patients soon. Mondays are usually hectic; if you can come, please do so."

Sarah returned the receiver to its hook upon the telephone. She sat down at her desk and put away the ledgers, correspondence, and pens. With the desk clear, she laid her forearms on its surface and buried her face in her hands.

"Lord God, I am yours. You know my heart; I do not desire to see Lola—but I do desire to see her in heaven with you. O God, what would you have me do? I would not knowingly walk into temptation, so please, Lord: Speak to me."

She prayed the remainder of the morning. She was still praying when Rose found her at lunchtime.

"Sarah? Are you all right?"

She sat up. Her eyes were dry, her heart at peace. "I am glad to see you, Miss Rose. I must ask your counsel."

They sat together in the great room, and Sarah repeated Dr. Croft's telephone call and his request. Rose considered what Dr. Croft had asked.

"You have been praying for guidance?"

"Yes."

"What has the Holy Spirit spoken to you?"

"That I need not be afraid to see Lola; that she will listen when I present the Good News to her."

"Then you must go and win her to Christ."

"Thank you for confirming the Lord's guidance to me."

Sarah sighed. "I know from watching my mother die, that Lola will be weak and growing weaker by the day. She will have moments of lucid thought with horrible coughing and gasping for air interspersed with restless sleep."

"You should be prepared to stay as long as it takes to see her through to the kingdom of heaven."

"That is what I thought, also."

Sarah called Croft's office. A nurse answered; Croft was, as she expected, unavailable. Sarah asked for and received the address of his clinic. "Please tell Dr. Croft that I plan to arrive near five o'clock."

Sarah then bent to her work, finished it, tidied up her desk, and packed a carpetbag with necessities. She called a cab to pick her up.

When the cab arrived, Rose joined Sarah at the door. "I shall share this need with the house at dinner, Sarah. We shall pray and believe God for Lola's salvation, and we shall hold you up to the Lord until you return to us."

Sarah embraced Rose, reluctant to let her go. "How I thank God for you, Miss Rose. And I am so grateful for the love and prayers of my family here."

~*~

THE CAB PULLED OVER to the curb, and Sarah stepped out into an unfamiliar neighborhood. She was somewhat surprised by what she saw.

Dr. Murphy's offices had been on the second floor of a fine, four-story stone building in downtown Denver—a quiet, tasteful location suited to the class of patients he saw. When Dr. Murphy had retired last year, he had given over his practice to his partner. Sarah had heard that Dr. Croft had relocated the practice, but she had not had cause to visit him in his new situation.

In contrast to Dr. Murphy's offices, Dr. Croft's practice comprised the first floor of a corner building in a somewhat less discriminating area of the downtown—and it had two entrances: The plain lettering on a side door proclaimed that the clinic was open to walk-in patients from eight o'clock to noon, Monday through Saturday; the ornate lettering on the door fronting the main avenue stated that appointments were available from one o'clock to five o'clock, Monday through Friday.

The two entrances puzzled Sarah, but since the clinic was closed for the day, she entered through the door facing the main avenue into a tastefully arranged waiting room. A nurse greeted her.

"Ah, good afternoon. You are Miss Ellinger?"

"Yes, I am."

"We spoke earlier. This way, please."

The nurse walked through a doorway, turned right, and led Sarah down a hall, past two examination rooms and a surgery, to the door of a fourth room, where she knocked softly.

"Stand just there, please," the nurse directed. She moved away from the door, and Sarah followed.

Dr. Croft came out and closed the door behind him. He was garbed in gown, gloves, and mask. As he stripped them off and placed them in a bin near the door, Sarah noticed deep lines about his mouth that had not been there when she last saw him; dark half-circles hung below his eyes.

"Thank you, Miss Taylor. If the charts are up to date, you may leave for the day."

"They are, doctor. Good night."

"Good night, Miss Taylor." He nodded to the nurse, then turned to Sarah. "Thank you for coming, Miss Ellinger. Shall we talk in my office?" He gestured to the last room at the end of the hallway.

Croft's office was nicely appointed: Oak bookshelves for his medical library lined one wall, degrees and medical license hung behind a fine desk, and two plush chairs faced the desk. It was a suitable setting for Croft to meet and consult with his clientele.

The cot against the wall behind the two chairs, however, was out of place.

*He has been sleeping here.*

"Would you care to sit down?" Croft took the rolling chair behind the desk after Sarah sat in one of the chairs facing him.

"I suppose you have questions about the unusual arrangement of my offices? Most of my patients do. A downtown location near the edge of what my respectable patients will tolerate. Separate doors and hours split between the clinic and my private practice."

"I presume you have your reasons."

He nodded and rubbed at bloodshot eyes. "I wanted to offer good medical care to Denver families who could not always afford my normal fees, but a doctor can hardly pay his bills and provide excellent care to anyone without a steady form of income, can he? My friend George and I pondered how I might accomplish both objectives. We hit upon this arrangement."

*Poorer patients in one door; well-to-do patients in the other,* Sarah surmised, *the wealthier patients' fees allowing Dr. Croft to care for those who can afford to pay less.*

"I believe I follow you." She felt a measure of respect for the doctor's clever plan.

"Well, enough about me, Miss Ellinger. I am glad you have come—" his gaze lit upon her carpet bag "—and it appears you have come prepared to stay. Excellent. I do not know how long Miss Pritchard will linger, but

I have already spent four nights here, getting up when Miss Pritchard needed care. Frankly, I was not sure how I would be able to manage much longer without help."

Sarah had not understood that Croft meant for her to help nurse Lola, but she was suddenly relieved that she had packed her valise. "You may count on my assistance, doctor."

"Good, good. Shall we discuss Miss Pritchard's condition and care, then?"

When Sarah nodded, he said, "As I mentioned over the telephone, she is weak, unable to rise from her bed. This means she requires care for all her needs. Are you squeamish?"

"Not particularly so. My mother died of consumption when I was a child. I stayed by her bed and helped the nurse care for her through the last weeks of her life. I know what is required."

Her mind wandered to another place and time and to very different circumstances: *I also cared for my sister prostitutes after they were raped and beaten into submission.*

A shadow of her introspection must have crossed her face, for Croft frowned. "Are you quite all right, Miss Ellinger?"

Sarah automatically smiled. "Yes. Only memories."

He studied her with probing regard before saying, "Very well. Let us, then, discuss precautions. We must consider *everything* within the patient's room to bear the tuberculosis bacterium: the air, the patient's bed, linens, clothing, body, and bodily fluids—in particular, her sputum. You are never to enter the patient's room or assist her without proper protection against the contagion at all times. Is that understood?"

"Yes. I understand."

He again searched her face before saying, "Good. Shall we look in on our patient?"

"Yes."

"You are prepared for what you will encounter?"

Sarah thought his question implied something further, something oblique, but she was preoccupied. *O Lord God! Please help me to be strong. Help me to acquit you well.*

"I am ready."

# $\mathscr{C}$HAPTER 23

Sarah followed Croft from his office into the surgery two doors down. A gleaming metal table occupied the center of the room, and a powerful light hung above the table. The remainder of the room's contents were hidden away in a wall of cupboards and drawers.

"I perform minor procedures and surgeries in this room; therefore, I require a sterile environment," Croft said. He pulled open a drawer and offered Sarah a surgical mask. "Place this over your mouth and nose and turn your back to me. I shall tie the strings for you."

When the mask was in place and secured, Croft held out a white gown. "Slip this on; again, I shall tie the back closures for you." When Sarah was gowned, he retrieved a pair of rubber gloves. "Slip these on and pull them up, over your sleeves."

While Sarah struggled into the clumsy gloves, Dr. Croft gowned himself, then rechecked Sarah's preparations.

"Clean items come out of this room, Miss Ellinger. Once you leave this room, do not return to it without first removing your mask, gown, and gloves and disposing of them. They are to be placed in the bin just outside the patient's room. Nurse Taylor sees they are washed and re-sterilized."

"Yes, Dr. Croft."

He led her out into the hallway and into the room between the surgery and his office. Her quick perusal told her that they were in a formulary. Like the surgery, an entire wall was given to glass-fronted cupboards built above sink, countertop, cabinets, and drawers. Through the cupboard windows, Sarah saw rows of neatly labeled boxes, bottles, vials, and flasks.

"I have removed an ample supply of medicines from here to the surgery for the duration," Croft murmured. "This room will be re-sterilized . . . later."

Against an adjacent wall Sarah spied a simple cot like the one in Croft's office. The formulary had no window, and the air was stuffy and stale. Ragged breathing came from the form lying on the cot.

Dr. Croft approached the cot. "Miss Pritchard?"

The patient's head turned a little toward him. "Y-yes, doctor?"

"I have brought Miss Ellinger as you requested. Miss Ellinger, stand at the foot of the cot, please."

Sarah moved toward the bottom of the cot as Croft had directed her. From there she could observe the patient from a distance of several feet. Neither she nor the woman spoke as they regarded each other, but Sarah clenched her hands in front of her.

The patient *was* Lola—but not the Lola Sarah had known.

"S-Sarah?"

"Yes, Lola. I have come."

Sarah had to blink continually to keep her tears at bay. Lola's curly auburn hair was matted against a skeletal head with sunken eyes and protruding cheekbones. Her body, beneath the sheet and blankets, appeared nearly flat.

Lola tried to lift her hand toward Sarah, but she was immediately overcome by a fit of coughing. Dr. Croft reached for a nearby basin and a cloth. Lola coughed and retched into the basin. Sarah saw the bright blood in the basin and the darker streaks that Croft wiped from Lola's mouth and chin.

When Lola fell back, exhausted, Croft set the basin and cloth aside. "Rinse the basin in the sink just there as needed. Now, if you do not mind, I have eaten nothing all day. I should like to step out and get dinner. I shall return in an hour, and we can discuss a care schedule."

Croft departed. Sarah and Lola stared at each other until Lola's eyes closed in exhaustion and Sarah came to herself.

"Would you like a sip of water, Lola?"

"Yes, please."

Sarah knelt beside the cot and lifted a glass with a straw to Lola's mouth. "Slowly, so you do not choke." The words the nurse had often directed at Sarah's mother came to her effortlessly.

Lola sipped twice. "Thank you."

She looked at Sarah again. "I had hoped you would come . . . but I did not believe you would."

Sarah dropped her eyes. "I-I think we have things to say."

"And not much time to say them. I—" Lola choked, and a fit of coughing took hold.

Sarah reached for the basin and the stained cloth; she supported Lola as she coughed up phlegm and blood into the basin. When Lola finished, Sarah wiped her mouth, pulling strings of bloody mucus from between her lips, then offered her more water.

"I did this for my mother," Sarah whispered. "She . . . had the same disease."

"You never told me."

"I did not tell you many things, Lola. Until our last meeting."

Lola lifted claw-like fingers and placed them on Sarah's gowned arm. "I have thought often about that afternoon when you told me about . . . about . . ."

"About being a prostitute?"

Lola's eyes filled with tears. "I cannot bear to think of you that way, to think of you beaten. Violated. Suffering."

Sarah nodded. "The abuse, from childhood on, warped my soul. It has been a long, difficult journey to healing, to freedom. If not for Jesus? I do not know where I would be."

"You would be with me."

Sarah sighed and shook her head. "No, I think I would be dead, Lola. I often considered killing myself when I lived in Corinth."

Lola hissed. "No! I would never have let you do that!"

"You do not understand, Lola. You and I? We would not have met before I ended my life. You see, in my own eyes, I was vile and dirty, good only for the most abhorrent uses. Even when Rose and Joy opened Palmer House and I moved there with them? I was filled with rage and hate—hate for most everyone, but I reserved the greatest of it for myself."

Lola again tried to protest but her agitation only set off more violent coughing. Sarah lifted her up and helped her as before, but Lola had difficulty catching her breath. She gasped and panted but seemed unable to draw air.

Before Sarah's eyes, Lola's face reddened as she tried, desperately, to inhale. She reddened further as she whooped in dire need—and then her complexion darkened and turned blue.

"O God!" Sarah cried. "Please help Lola! Please!"

Lola's frail, convulsing body went slack in Sarah's arms. Terrified that Lola had died, Sarah shook her.

"Lola! Lola! No, Lord Jesus! She is not ready to meet you—please! Please help her!"

Lola jerked, stiffened . . . and eventually breathed.

Sarah laid Lola's unconscious body on the cot and sobbed.

~*~

LATER, THROUGH THE DOOR, she heard Croft ask, "Is she resting?"

Resting? Sarah watched the slight rise and fall of Lola's chest.

*Thank you, Lord. I know you sent me here to bring Lola to you. Please grant me the time and opportunity I need!*

"Yes, she is resting."

"Come out and eat something."

Sarah slipped through the door and, under Croft's watchful eye, stripped off her gloves, gown, and mask. She stuffed them into the bin near the door as he indicated.

"As an added precaution, please go into an exam room and wash your hands and your face, Miss Ellinger, then join me in my office. I have brought you some dinner."

Sarah did as he ordered. After she had washed, she wandered to his office and sank into a chair.

He had prepared a tray for her and placed it in her lap. When he saw her white face and stillness, he said, "Eat, Miss Ellinger. I can tell you need nourishment."

Sarah stared at the food. She was not hungry; what she felt was a burning in her throat.

"I-I am thirsty."

Croft leapt to his feet and filled a tumbler from a pitcher. "Here. Drink."

Sarah downed the glass. He set another before her and she drank it, too.

"You are in shock. What happened while I was gone?"

"I thought she had died. She could not catch her breath—she convulsed, and her color turned."

He resumed his seat. "It sometimes happens that they pass suddenly like that. More times, they lose consciousness and pass gently."

"She *was* dying. It is possible that she did die for a moment, but I-I prayed over her. I begged the Lord to give me more time to win her to Jesus. I believe the Lord heard me and brought breath back to her body."

"That is your purpose? That is why you came?" Again, he seemed to be looking for something deeper than his question asked.

"It is."

He nodded, more to himself than in response to her. "I am glad of it, and I shall pray with you for Miss Pritchard's soul." He put his elbows on his desk, folded his hands, and dropped his forehead onto his hands.

Sarah blinked. The shock was wearing away; the water had restored her. She glanced at Croft—and saw he had not muttered mere platitudes—he had straightway gone to prayer for Lola.

*Thank you, Lord, for hearing my cry! Thank you for the opportunity to share Jesus with Lola.*

While Croft prayed, Sarah picked up a fork and tasted the food before her. Before she knew it, she had wolfed down everything on the plate.

"You have eaten. Good."

"I appreciate you for bringing it to me. I did not realize I was hungry. Thank you, too, for praying for Lola."

"Lola?"

"Short for Lorraine."

"You knew her well?"

He seemed to be hedging, which Sarah found curious. "She and I were once . . . acquainted. I was a believer in Christ, but she was not, and our friendship became a snare to me. I had to sever our relationship. I have not seen her in two years."

Sarah had been intentionally vague, but he did not appear scandalized or affronted at her explanation as she had anticipated. Rather, something akin to relief smoothed his expression.

"This fallen world overwhelms and defeats all of us in some way, Miss Ellinger. Few of us escape unscathed. I did not."

"Pastor Carmichael said something very similar to me. He said, 'We are all—every person who has ever lived—broken in some manner or fashion.'"

"Then he is wiser than many men of the cloth I have met."

Sarah licked her lips and dared to ask the question for which she wanted an answer. "In what way . . . did the world break you, Dr. Croft?"

He sighed. "The war, Miss Ellinger."

"Ah. I remember now that you served in the war."

"Nearly eighteen months of the closest thing to hell possible on this earth."

"I am sorry."

As if he had not heard her, he whispered, "So many soldiers I could not save on the battlefield. My arms soaked in their lifeblood, standing in pools of it, and yet I could not save many of those young men. I saw things I cannot forget—such things as haunt my nights. I tended boys whose deaths were, in the end, a blessing."

The depth of his pain struck Sarah forcibly. She could only repeat, "I-I am so sorry, Dr. Croft."

"No, it is I who should apologize. It was ungentlemanly to raise such an unpleasant specter to you, Miss Ellinger. I apologize."

They were quiet for a time, listening together to the ticking of the clock on his wall, before Sarah said, "I have come to understand that we cannot escape some measure of hurt in this fallen world. Our dear friend, Tabitha Carpenter, was a nurse in the war. She left in July 1915 to volunteer with the British Nursing Service. She served three and a half years, the last year in France during the influenza."

Croft grew agitated. "Dear God! What she must have seen! What she had to have witnessed and endured!"

"She does not talk of it often, but she and her husband brought home two orphans when they returned."

"The Lord bless her and her husband for that. I saw far too many children without parents . . . parents without children . . . and children without hands, arms, or legs. And the burns! Some so fearfully disfigured that . . ."

He could not go on, and Sarah had to look away from the horror she glimpsed behind his eyes—horror, she realized, he lived with daily, even though he was many miles and days removed from what he had experienced.

Croft stared into the distance. "All the blood and agony and loss of the war? I was not prepared for it, and we were continually short-staffed and overworked. We lost so many boys and young men simply because we could not help them all in a timely manner."

His mouth twisted into a grimace. "I allowed what I saw and experienced in the war to grieve me too deeply. I suppose you could say that I had something of a breakdown."

Sarah stilled, wondering why he was baring his soul to her.

"While I was recovering, instead of giving my anguish to the Lord, I looked to blame—to castigate—someone. Anyone! I fed upon that blame until my soul became a dark, angry pit. When I returned to the States, George came alongside me. I stayed with him for months before joining Dr. Murphy's practice.

"George is a faithful friend; he helped me surrender my anger to the Lord. He also seemed to understand that I had a need to be of use to those in real need. He provided some of the funds to move my practice here. With this work, I have begun to heal."

Sarah blinked, at first troubled—and then oddly touched—that he would share such details of his life. "May I offer an observation, Dr. Croft? A personal one?"

He nodded, but he remained pensive, distracted by his reflections on the war.

"It is only that I find that most men . . . the men I have known, do not readily admit to having struggles. They seem bent on preserving an outward appearance of strength and of competence, of self-sufficiency. However, you . . . have confided your turmoil to me, and I confess, I do not understand why."

He stared at the floor, fatigue written on the sharp planes of his face.

"I suppose it must seem peculiar to you. When we met, you and I were instantly at odds. We quarreled and argued—and quite vociferously at that. I cannot explain why, then, I am now comfortable in your presence, comfortable revealing my inmost struggles."

A moment later, he added, "Perhaps it is because I have come to understand that you were as broken as I was."

Sarah looked away. "You must have asked Mr. O'Dell about Palmer House as I . . . suggested."

"I did. When he told me? I could not but think what a fool I was to have patronized you as I did. I am so very sorry."

Sarah whispered, "I . . . forgive you, Dr. Croft. Actually, I forgave you some time ago. It is of no matter now."

He did not respond for so long, that Sarah decided he had not heard her. But he had.

"I have something else to confess to you, Miss Ellinger."

"You-you do? I do not understand."

"I have determined to make a clean breast of it and ask your forgiveness. Yes," he mused, "it is the only way forward."

Sarah's confusion only grew.

He took a deep breath. "I know of your . . . former relationship with Miss Pritchard. What it was."

Sarah was speechless. She pulled her top lip between her teeth as shame washed her neck and face.

"Please do not be dismayed. It is the reason I took Miss Pritchard into my clinic."

Sarah shook her head. "I-I do not take your meaning."

Croft faced her. "I must ask *your* forgiveness, Miss Ellinger. It was I— *I* was the one who saw you in the park on Thanksgiving afternoon, two years past. I saw you in a . . . compromising state with Miss Pritchard. I was the one who spoke to Mrs. Thoresen of what I had seen."

Sarah's breath hitched as his words sank in.

*Someone witnessed you with Lola, exhibiting what was described as 'an unnatural affection. Someone who, I assure you, cares very much for your wellbeing. They came to me and only me, no one else.*

"At the time, Miss Ellinger, I felt it was the right thing to do. I promise you that I meant it for your good, not your ill, but I know I caused you great pain. I-I am asking if you could find it in your heart to forgive me?"

Sarah lifted her chin. She studied Croft's weary, pain-filled eyes; she delved into what she saw there. "You meant it for my good?"

"Yes. Truly, I did."

Sarah nodded. "I choose to believe you, Dr. Croft, and I forgive you."

"I am sorry that I wounded you."

"No, you should not be. You obeyed God, and the Lord used your obedience to bring about my repentance and, eventually, my freedom. Breaking free of this bondage was by far the most painful ordeal of my life; however, it was necessary. I am free of it now. Jesus has made me free."

"Thank you for forgiving me, Miss Ellinger."

"Of course."

They were again quiet, lost in their own reflections, until Croft mused. "It is ironic, is it not? When we met, we began badly, at cross-purposes. It would seem that we were both in need of healing and freedom."

Sarah nodded. "So it would seem."

~*~

DR. CROFT GESTURED TO the cot in his office. "I have spread clean sheets atop my own. As I am accustomed to staying up late, will you sleep for a while? I shall wake you when I need you to take over for me."

It was an odd, unconventional arrangement, but Sarah was fatigued, so she laid down on the cot and fell asleep straightaway. She had slept four or five hours when someone shook her gently.

"Miss Ellinger?"

Sarah opened her eyes to lamplight. "Yes? What time is it? Is it my turn to watch?"

"Half past midnight. Miss Pritchard is alert at present; it seemed the opportune time for you to speak with her."

Sarah got up; Croft removed her sheets, folded them, and laid them aside.

"Our doctors often shared cots while working shifts around the clock in the war—and with considerably less concern for hygiene, I can tell you. Can you gown yourself without my assistance?"

"I believe so."

With no further instructions, he stretched himself out on the cot and became still. Sarah watched his recumbent form and listened, amazed at how quickly his breath slowed into the rhythm of slumber.

Remembering that Lola was awake and aware, Sarah wiped the last traces of sleep from her face and sped to the surgery to gown herself. She had some difficulties with the ties, but finally managed. When she was ready, she entered the sick room.

Lola was waiting for her.

"Sarah."

"I am here, Lola."

Lola labored to breathe and speak at the same time, staggering her words between shallow, inadequate breaths. "I have missed you so, but it grieves me to have you see me like this."

Sarah nodded. "It grieves me also."

"You have been well?"

"Yes. Thank you for asking."

Sarah did not know what to say next, but Lola filled in the awkward silence.

"We took The Pythia to Europe for a few months."

"Did you? It must have been sad to see all the destruction from the war."

"It was. Still, it was a good trip until I realized I was suffering from more than a chronic cough. But we had to come home early anyway."

"Oh? How are . . . Meg and Dannie?"

Lola did not answer immediately. When she did, Sarah glimpsed sorrow behind her words. "Dannie always drank too much, could not control herself. Meg had enough at last. It was the end of them and the end of our band, too."

"I-I am sorry, Lola."

"Dannie . . . when Meg left her, she killed herself."

Sarah's face twisted. "Oh, no!"

"I know how Dannie felt, Sarah. When you left me, I tried to find someone else. I tried so hard, but nothing worked. What I saw in you, I could not find in another woman."

Sarah closed her eyes against the onslaught of emotions she anticipated—but instead found . . . the Lord comforting her, surrounding her, protecting her. Keeping her safe.

Separate.

Unbidden, the lines of Psalm 125 rose within her.

*They that trust in the Lord shall be as mount Zion,*
*which cannot be removed, but abideth forever.*
*As the mountains are round about Jerusalem,*
*so the Lord is round about his people*
*from henceforth even forever.*

*Ah, my Jesus! How I love you.*

Lola's ragged words pulled her back. "It broke my heart when you told me you had been a-a prostitute, Sarah. To me you were so good, so pure and unsullied."

"Could it be that it was not me that drew you, Lola? That it was not me you saw, but the One who lives in me?"

"Do you mean God?"

"I do. You know now that I am not the pure and unsullied woman you thought me to be, but something did draw you . . . to me."

Lola shifted with discomfort, then asked, her voice rough, "Could it not have been that we were fated to meet? That ours was a love destined to be?"

"I cannot believe so, Lola. I trust in and credit neither 'fate' nor 'destiny,' for my Lord is the creator of all things—and it is his purposes that will prevail. I believe you saw *him* in me—and you longed for him without knowing it was him you craved and needed."

"You think I longed for God? That I craved him—and not you?"

"In your deepest being, yes; I believe that."

Lola closed her eyes, exhausted by their conversation. Nonetheless, Sarah hoped Lola was thinking on their exchange. Soon, Lola drifted off to sleep, leaving Sarah sitting quietly, patient and waiting, for Lola's next lucid moments.

~*~

WHEN MORNING CAME, Croft went out and brought back coffee and pastries for breakfast. Before the clinic opened, he moved the cot and one of his office chairs into the sick room.

"I shall be about the business of the clinic until lunchtime, Miss Ellinger. If you need to rest, do not use the cot. Instead, sleep sitting up in the chair. I would not have you inadvertently rub a contaminated gloved hand over your mouth or nose; you would be more inclined to do so if you are lying down."

He checked Lola's condition and reviewed Sarah's ministrations to the patient through the night.

"You are doing well, Miss Ellinger, but she requires less care now. Her bodily functions are shutting down."

"I-I understand."

~*~

THE HOURS PASSED SLOWLY. Sarah read from her Bible. She paced and prayed; she stood over Lola's unmoving form, pleading with God for Lola's soul.

"Sarah?"

"Here I am."

"You . . . you have changed. I realized so as we talked."

"Have I?"

"You used to be . . . more vulnerable . . . but you kept that hidden. Except, maybe, from me."

Sarah thought about what Lola said. "I carried a great deal of pain in my heart—the wounds of what was done to me. I also carried considerable anger toward those who hurt me."

"Is that what is different? How . . . did you change?"

"I repented. I forgave those who had sinned against me. When I did, the Lord took away my anger and gave me peace in place of my pain and anger."

Lola's examination of Sarah's face seemed to drill deep into Sarah's psyche.

"Why?"

"Why what?"

"You said the Lord took away your anger and gave you peace. Why? Why did he do that?"

Sarah was surprised. "Because he cares."

Lola turned her face aside, and Sarah could see that she was upset. Disturbed. Perhaps angry herself. Sarah waited a long time before Lola looked at her again.

"Why do you believe God cares for people? I mean, why would he?"

Lola's question was so pointed and unexpected, that Sarah fumbled for an answer. Unwilling to respond in a trite or pat manner, Sarah paused— and asked for the Holy Spirit to speak through her.

"I do not understand why he cares, Lola. Obviously, we do not deserve his care and concern. Nonetheless, he tells us that he loves us in spite of our wicked ways."

"Where?"

"Where what?"

Where does it . . . tell us?"

The last bit of Romans 5:5 dropped from Sarah's lips without effort.

*"The love of God is shed abroad in our hearts*
*by the Holy Ghost which is given unto us.*
*For when we were yet without strength,*
*in due time Christ died for the ungodly."*

"Is . . . that all?"

"No. Here is more from the same passage."

*"For scarcely for a righteous man will one die:*
*yet peradventure for a good man*
*some would even dare to die.*
*But God commendeth his love toward us, in that,*
*while we were yet sinners, Christ died for us."*

Lola stared far away. "While we were . . ."

"While we were yet sinners, Christ died for us."

Lola shook her head slowly. "I do not believe I can be forgiven, Sarah. I have done horrible, detestable things."

"God's written word disagrees with you."

"What about every commandment and every 'thou shalt not?'"

"They are sin, certainly."

"Then how . . ."

"God's plan of salvation works like this: *If we say that we have not sinned, we make him a liar, and his word is not in us.*"

"I do not dispute that I am a sinner."

"No, but you say you cannot be forgiven. This is what Scripture says about God's forgiveness:

> *"If we confess our sins,*
> *he is faithful and just to forgive us our sins,*
> *and to cleanse us from all unrighteousness.*

"The Lord requires that we confess our sins, Lola."

"Is what I feel for you a sin?"

Sarah hesitated before answering. "Our feelings alone are not necessarily sin; they become sin if we hold them in higher esteem than we hold the Lord, if we refuse to surrender them to him, if we act upon them."

"I must surrender what I feel for you to the Lord?"

"Yes."

"I cannot."

"I understand your struggle but . . . if I could do it, you can, too."

"It is too much. Too much."

"He will help you, Lola."

Lola turned her face away. "Do not . . . vex me so, Sarah. I am . . . too weary."

# CHAPTER 24

"**I** cannot imagine Lola lasting more than another day or so," Croft murmured. "She is fading quickly."

It was Friday evening. Sarah had been at the clinic helping to care for Lola for four days; she was fatigued and at her wits' end. Lola was slipping away, hour by hour, minute by minute, and still she resisted receiving Jesus.

Sarah ran to an exam room, slammed the door behind her, and leaned against the wall, sobbing, begging God for his help.

"O Lord! What am I to do? Did you bring Lola back into my life for me to see her go into eternity without you? No, I cannot believe that, my God. Please, Jesus. Please show me what I must do to break down Lola's walls, to show her you, Jesus!"

Sarah wept and cried out to the Lord into the wallpaper, her bitter tears burning their way down her face. She was exhausted and faint, near to falling down, at the ragged edge of her own capacity. She did not notice when the door behind her opened, not until a gentle hand rested upon her arm.

"Sarah. You have been strong by yourself a long time. Will you not lean on me a moment? I am your brother in Christ; borrow from my poor strength a while—for just a little while."

When Sarah's legs collapsed from under her, Croft did not let her slip to the floor; his arm caught and turned her and held her to his chest. Sarah sank against him, crying and disconsolate.

Croft rested his chin upon her hair. "There, there," he whispered. "Rest on me. I can be strong for both of us."

There was nothing grasping in how he supported her, nothing selfish, nothing licentious. He asked for nothing but the opportunity to grant her temporary respite. Sarah had only once before felt safe in a man's arms—those of her friend, old Mr. Wheatley.

As her consciousness seeped away, she felt safe again. More than safe. She felt protected.

And she slept.

~*~

*SARAH.*
Sarah stirred in her sleep. "Blythe . . ."
*I love you so much, Sarah. You were always good to me.*
"Blythe . . ."
*I am so glad you told me Jesus would find me, Sarah.*
Sarah blinked her eyes, coming slowly awake. She had been dreaming . . . of Blythe. She could clearly hear the girl's voice.
*Sarah! I am not lost anymore, Sarah.*
"Oh, Blythe. I shall see you again, little sister."


Still rubbing sleep from her eyes, Sarah rose from the cot in Croft's office. She was confused for a brief moment. "How . . ."

She remembered then, the rub of her face against Croft's rough shirt and his arms supporting her, holding her up.

And she remembered his whisper. *There, there. Rest on me. I can be strong for both of us.*

She recalled those details without acrimony. Without anger or agitation. "Lord?"

Then she knew: Something had changed. *In her.*

She struggled to her feet. She had not eaten for a day and a half, and she was shaking, but her pressing concern for Lola reignited. "I have, perhaps, only hours to persuade Lola to turn to Jesus. O God! What can I say to her that will move her heart to repent?"

*I am so glad you told me Jesus would find me, Sarah.*

Sarah sat on the cot again and dropped her face into her hands—and she heard Blythe's words again: *I should not like Lola to remain lost as I was. You will tell her, Sarah, will you not? Tell her like you told me?*

Sarah recalled the hospital waiting room and the morning Croft came to tell her Blythe had died. *I could not believe him. I could not follow his words. Blythe gone?*

*Was she never to grow into a woman? Have the family she longed for? Was her life for nothing?*

"My Lord?"

She again heard Blythe's last words to her: *I am not lost anymore, Sarah.*

Sarah rose from the cot. "No, you are no longer lost, sweetheart. And your life was not for nothing."

~*~

THE FORMULARY WAS DIM, lit only by the lamp placed near Lola's cot. Sarah could hear the rasp of Lola's labored breathing—but she rejoiced that Lola was breathing.

Disregarding Croft's fierce injunctions, Sarah did not don gown, or gloves, or mask. Sarah knew this would be the last time she could share the Gospel with Lola. She wanted—she needed—to speak to her face to face and heart to heart.

Lola's face had sunk in on itself. Her eyes, especially, seemed deep and hollowed, covered by skin so tissue-paper thin and translucent that Sarah could see through it.

She took Lola's fragile hand and pressed it between hers. "Lola? Are you awake?"

Although Lola did not open her eyes, Sarah felt the slight pressure of Lola's fingers in response.

"Lola, I wish to tell you about Blythe. Do you remember her? She lived at Palmer House perhaps only six weeks. I think—no, I am certain—that you met her while I was recovering from hurting my knee?"

Lola's mouth worked. Sarah released her hand and brought the glass of water with a straw in it to her lips. Lola struggled to pull even a sip up the straw and into her mouth. When at last she had, she held it in her mouth for a moment before swallowing.

"Y-your little sh-shadow?"

"What?"

"B-Blythe."

"Yes, Blythe, my little golden-haired angel. I wanted to tell you about her. She came to us very damaged. We did not know how damaged."

"H-how?"

Sarah took Lola's hand again. "She confided in me that she went out after dark to-to fetch something. It does not matter what, but while she was out, a gang of street thugs . . . they found her. Cornered her."

Lola's eyelids fluttered, and she raised them a little. Asking the question.

Sarah's chin bobbed up and down. She could not stop it. "Yes, they violated her."

Lola's eyes closed, and she turned her head away.

Feeling that she was losing Lola, Sarah rushed on. "Breona and Mei-Xing's street ministry found her, you see, wandering the alleys, dirty, disheveled, and half-catatonic. They had no idea what had happened and could get no answers from her; they saw only that she was alone and incapable of caring for herself.

"Breona took her home. She and Pastor Carmichael tried to feed her, but Blythe would take no food, only water. Since she was falling asleep while they spoke to her, they put her directly to bed. Blythe slept for two days. When she awoke, she was able to tell them her name, but would say little more. And she was frightened of being put back out on the street.

"Breona and Pastor Carmichael told Blythe about Palmer House. 'A family,' they told her. 'A safe place. A home with a mother and sisters who will love you. Where you will not have to be afraid.' So, she came to us, still filthy and half starving."

Sarah had been staring at Lola's fingers, twined in hers; when she glanced up, she found Lola's gaunt eyes fixed upon her.

"Do you wish me to continue, Lola?"

"Y-yes."

"Blythe had lived with an uncle, and I believe that she had never had more than him, never had a real family. Living at Palmer House was a dream come true for her—and she was so easy to love. She followed me everywhere—my little shadow as you called her. She loved me as an older sister."

Sarah smiled, even as the tears drained down her face onto Lola's sheets. And she saw when a look of dread crossed Lola's expression.

"Yes, Blythe passed away two years ago, a few weeks before we last spoke. Do you remember?"

Lola nodded and seemed more awake, more attentive now.

"Of course, when she came to live at Palmer House, we began to tell her about Jesus. She was curious, but not overly interested. You see, we had not yet met her at the point of her need, the place where she hungered for healing.

"Then Martha Palmer died. And did you know? She left every girl who lived or had lived at Palmer House five hundred dollars?"

Lola moved her head marginally.

"Yes, five hundred dollars—as a bridal gift to every unmarried girl and a payment to every married girl."

Sarah could tell Lola was thinking on what she had said. Again, she moved her head in the negative.

"I know. I was unhappy about it also. That was why I never mentioned it to you. I shall not receive my gift from Martha until I turn thirty-nine—another nine years—because, as you well know, I had chosen not to marry."

She was quiet for a moment, thinking back to the reading of Martha's will. "I was upset at the time, but again, I was angry about everything back then. Since that time, I have come to accept Martha's wisdom. Her gift will mean a great deal to me when I am on the cusp of forty. It will be a blessing indeed."

Lola squeezed Sarah's fingers and Sarah laughed a little. "Yes. Back to Blythe. What she wanted above all things was a family. Husband, children, home. But she was so ashamed that she had been raped. She considered herself damaged goods and thought that no decent man would ever love her.

"Then I told her that Jesus came to take not only our sin, but also our shame, because God gave what was his most precious gift—his Son, Jesus—to pay for our sins, to buy us back. I told her that after we are born from above, we no longer feel guilty, dirty, or worthless."

Lola frowned a little.

"You did not know that either? Hmm. Well, I shall tell you just as I told her: God made every individual in his likeness, and he loves us very much. We are so special to him! Like his children. Inevitably, though, each of us goes our own way. We sin against God. We sin against others. We stray far away from God until we are lost, so very lost, and cannot find our way to him.

"I asked Blythe, 'Do you know what it feels like to be lost, dear one?'

"Blythe said, 'Oh, yes. I think I have been lost forever.' It nearly broke my heart, the way she said it. Do you know what she said after that?"

Lola's attention was focused wholly on Sarah's tale; she pressed Sarah's fingers, urgently.

"Well, Blythe said, 'I do not want to be lost anymore, Sarah.'"

Sarah was weeping again. "So, I told her, 'That is why Jesus came. He came to seek and save those who are lost—lost just like you and lost just like me. If we are sorry for our sins and call upon Jesus, he will come and find us and wash us clean. And Jesus will take away your shame, Blythe. All of it.'"

Sarah had to stop; she could not go on. She sobbed onto the bedclothes, reliving that moment, that beautiful moment when Blythe leaned against her, turned her trusting eyes to her, and said, "Please, Sarah, I want to call upon Jesus."

When she looked up, minutes later, Lola's sunken eyes were moist. Sarah had not thought it possible, given how dehydrated Lola's body had to be.

"What is it, Lola? Do you wish me to finish?"

"Y-y . . ."

Sarah brought the straw to Lola's mouth, and she was able to swallow twice. Then she looked at Sarah, willing her to continue.

"Blythe said then, 'Please, Sarah, I want to call upon Jesus.' We prayed together. She asked Jesus to save her, to forgive her, to take away her shame."

Swallowing down another bout of tears, Sarah said, "Some weeks later, Blythe became sick. We thought it a simple stomach influenza. It was not; it was her appendix. We called Dr. Croft in the middle of the night. He came and knew immediately how serious her condition was. We left for the hospital in his motor car. I sat in the back seat with Blythe's head in my lap.

"The pain was unbearable, and she was crying and screaming. Then . . . then she became calm and the pain eased momentarily. Dr. Croft said her appendix had ruptured. He took her into surgery and did all he could to save her, but he said . . . he said she could not fight off the sepsis. Her body was already dreadfully fragile, and the infection overwhelmed her. She died just as morning dawned."

Lola stared at Sarah, heartbreak in her sunken eyes.

"It was what Blythe said in the motor car, during the lull in her pain, that has never left me. She said, 'I am so glad you told me Jesus would find me, Sarah. I am not lost anymore.'"

Sarah tried to smile. "*I am not lost anymore*—those were Blythe's last words to me. I know that today she is in heaven, safe from all pain and sorrow, washed clean of shame. I shall see her again, at the Resurrection."

Lola slowly blinked, and Sarah knew that this moment was all the time she had left to press the claims of Jesus upon her.

"Lola, are you lost, as Blythe was? Do you wish Jesus to find you and take you to heaven?"

To Sarah's great wonder, Lola licked her cracked lips and gasped, "C-can he?"

"Oh, yes! Jesus has been seeking for you all your life. It is not too late to confess your sins and surrender to the mastery of Christ. Will you, Lola?"

With a slight but deliberate movement, Lola ducked her chin.

"Are you . . . are you ready to surrender your feelings for me to the Lord and give them up?"

Lola's eyes turned toward Sarah, and Sarah saw in their depths an anguish she comprehended—the agony of imminent crucifixion, the impending sacrifice and death of what was most dear.

"I . . . am."

Sarah fought back the moisture that sprang to her eyes. *How I thank you for hearing the cry of my heart, Lord! Thank you! Thank you!*

In slow, painstaking steps, Sarah led Lola to confess her sins before God and call upon Jesus for forgiveness.

Sarah paused often as Lola struggled to pull air into her diseased and failing lungs. She used up every bit of her waning strength to speak—in short, gasping phrases—her declaration of faith.

When Sarah ended with, "O Jesus! Thank you for saving me!" Lola could only move her fingers within Sarah's hands to affirm her gratitude.

Soon after, Lola began to pant, her chest rising and falling in rapid, insufficient breaths. Her fingers no longer moved, and her eyes became fixed on something Sarah could not see.

Lola continued so—until her shallow breaths stuttered, faltered . . . and ceased.

"Oh, Lola! You are lost no more," Sarah whispered.

"Thanks be to God."

# CHAPTER 25

Sarah did not know how long she stayed with Lola, holding her lifeless hand. She was still thanking God for showing her how to reach Lola in her final hour when Croft found her that way. He disentangled Lola's fingers from Sarah's and drew the sheet over Lola's body.

"Come with me, Miss Ellinger. You need to come away."

"She is with Jesus now," Sarah murmured, unwilling—unable—to stand.

"Is she? You were able to lead her to the Savior?"

"Yes. The Lord answered my prayer."

"Then he answered mine, also."

Croft lifted Sarah up and placed his arm around her. "Come, now. Get your feet beneath you."

"So . . . tired."

"You are weak from lack of sleep and nourishment. Please try," he urged her. Somehow, he got her from the room and onto the cot in his office. He went at once and fetched hot water, disinfectant soap, and clean washcloths.

"You must eat, but not before I wash your hands and face." He brought a hot, wet cloth to her hands and, one at a time, washed and rinsed them.

"I know you meant well; I know you felt the need for Lola to see your face as you shared Jesus, but you have put yourself in jeopardy doing so."

"If my jeopardy bought Lola's salvation, I am happy to bear the consequences."

One corner of his mouth quirked upward. "How did I know you would answer so?"

Then he lifted a steaming cloth to her face and began to clean it. The heat of the soapy cloth stroking her face was too gentle, too comforting, and she was too weary to resist. She closed her eyes and gave herself over to Croft's ministrations. As he rinsed her face with another warm cloth, she sighed.

When he finished, she opened her eyes, surprised to see him bending close, studying her.

"I pray you have realized by now that you need not fear me, Miss Ellinger. If anything, you have found the one man in this world who was as broken as yourself. I respect you more than you can imagine, and I promise you: I would never intentionally harm you."

*An enormous gulf lies between 'hurt' and 'harm,' Sarah, and not all that hurts us, harms us. Faithful are the wounds of a friend.*

With no little measure of wonder, Sarah admitted to herself that she was not anxious or agitated at his nearness; she felt neither threatened nor the urge to flee.

"If you allow me, I shall help you grieve for your friend, Miss Ellinger. You may lean upon me, and I shall offer you my consolation in Christ."

Unlike how Sarah had reacted before the Lord healed her heart, the thought of a man offering his strength to her no longer rankled: It calmed and comforted her.

Sarah stared back, curious, peering into the brown-flecked depths of his eyes for the first time, surprised at what she found there—not merely another man, but a kindred soul, a fellow sufferer like herself. Redeemed by grace.

*I have nothing to hide from him. He knows the truth about me. All of it. And he has entrusted me with his own failings and pain.*

"Thank you . . . Bryan."

He smiled—a rare occurrence for him. Sarah decided she might like his smile.

"Good," he murmured. "Now, then, let me get you something to eat." He smiled again. "Sarah."

# The End

MY DEAR READERS,

I have included, on the following pages, an appendix titled, *More on the Subject*, and a series of discussion questions suitable for a book club or Bible study group. I pray these resources will further your enjoyment of and benefit from *Sarah Redeemed*.

The Lord's blessings on you,
Vikki Kestell

# $\mathcal{A}$PPENDIX:

## MORE ON THE SUBJECT

Although I hold an earned Ph.D., my doctoral degree is not in a field relating to psychology, therapy, or counselling, nor do I approach this topic from that vantage point. I offer this appendix as a student of God's word who has studied homosexuality through the dual lenses of Scripture and personal observation.

Parts of this appendix are my opinion. You may agree or not agree with me. That is your right. As I respect your rights, I expect the same consideration. I wrote this book, not to persuade anyone who does not want to be persuaded, but *to hold out hope for those who want to be freed.*

I would not deny freedom to anyone who asks for it.

—Vikki Kestell

## INTRODUCTION

IN THE LAST FIFTY YEARS, our society has reversed its view of homosexuality. Until 1973, the American Psychiatric Association (APA) categorized homosexuality as a form of mental illness and recognized that sexual orientation could be changed. Today, the APA views homosexuality as a normal and positive variation of human sexuality.

God has not changed. His word has not changed. The findings of science and the medical community have not changed. So, what has changed? Only society's tolerance for what the Bible calls sin has changed.

Like other addictive sins, homosexuality is the external behavior and symptom of what lies within. It is not, however, as many believe, a biological condition an individual is born with. Proponents of the "born that way" view cite science and "studies"—but what have they found? *Categorically*, no scientific studies exist that prove or even suggest a biological link to sexual preference or behavior. Not one. The APA, while a leading advocate in normalizing homosexuality, confirms this:

"There is no consensus among scientists about the exact reasons that an individual develops a heterosexual, bisexual, gay, or lesbian orientation. Although much research has examined the possible genetic, hormonal, developmental, social, and cultural influences on sexual orientation, no findings have emerged that permit scientists to conclude that sexual orientation is determined by any particular factor or factors."[1]

The APA states, "no findings have emerged," because no study can support the "born that way" premise or provide any evidence that it is true. The APA states that the causes of human sexuality, whether it be heterosexual, homosexual, or bisexual, are unknown. What is known (as reported above) is that *no scientific evidence exists to support the claim that homosexuality is biological.*

In fact, a comparative study of adoptive and biological brothers reported in *Science* magazine (Vol. 262, page 2063, December 24, 1993) suggests that family environment plays a larger role in sexual development than genetics:

"Research into the issue of the origins of homosexuality suggests that adoptive brothers are more likely to both be homosexuals than biological brothers, who share half their genes, which suggests that homosexuality is not genetically caused."

**This finding prompted *Science* magazine to report, "This [study's outcome] suggests that there is no genetic component, but rather an environmental component shared in families."**

Despite considerable research to the contrary, the media does not report on this topic objectively. *Born or Bred: Science Does Not Support the Claim That Homosexuality Is Genetic,*[2] by Robert Knight, is a well-researched and well-documented article. A summary of research into homosexuality, from both sides of the issue, can be found online.[3]

The book, *My Genes Made Me Do It! Homosexuality and the Scientific Evidence,*[4] a scientific look at sexual orientation, can be ordered or downloaded free as a PDF file. Another biblical resource is found on Conservapedia.com.[5]

---

[1] http://www.apa.org/topics/lgbt/orientation.aspx. (See subheading, "What causes a person to have a particular sexual orientation.")

[2] http://www.cwfa.org/images/content/bornorbred.pdf

[3] http://www.mygenes.co.nz/summary.html

[4] http://www.mygenes.co.nz/download.htm

[5] https://www.conservapedia.com/index.php?title=Causes_of_Homosexuality

We also know, from the position of natural selection, that since gay procreation is not possible, it is also not possible for homosexuality to be genetically encoded. Because gay procreation is not possible, genes that create homosexuality cannot be passed down, particularly not at the rate of homosexual increase observed in modern societies. In genetic terms, a gay gene would have been "selected out."

## THE BIBLICAL PERSPECTIVE

HUMAN BEINGS ARE SEXUAL beings, and God meant sex to be a lifelong blessing. However, like everything in this fallen world, sex has been hijacked by sin.

Human sexuality is also a complex topic, not to be exhausted in this short appendix. *Sarah Redeemed* addresses only a fraction of the complexities found in homosexual tendencies, but it does provide the only sure solution: Jesus. I am not talking about "reparative therapy." I am speaking of transformation: the miraculous, internal changes only a believer in Christ can experience through complete surrender to him.

One of the most hopeful passages found in the Bible—for all of us, not just those who struggle with homosexuality—is 1 Corinthians 6:9-11:

> *Or do you not know that wrongdoers*
> *will not inherit the kingdom of God?*
> *Do not be deceived:*
> *Neither the sexually immoral*
> *nor idolaters nor adulterers*
> *nor men who have sex with men*
> *nor thieves nor the greedy nor drunkards*
> *nor slanderers nor swindlers*
> *will inherit the kingdom of God.*
> *And that is what some of you were.*
> *But you were washed, you were sanctified,*
> *you were justified*
> *in the name of the Lord Jesus Christ*
> *and by the Spirit of our God.*

That is what some of you *were.*

Not what some of you *are* but what some of you *were.*

Homosexuality and other sexual sins are nothing new. In every culture, children have been exploited for the gratification of sinful, unredeemed, unsanctified men (and women). Men, women, and children have been (and continue to be) trafficked and prostituted for the same.

During the genesis of the church, this was no different, yet Paul held out hope: "That is what some of you *were.*"

**Note:** Just so we are clear on this passage, the NIV has a footnote that reads, "The phrase, *nor men who have sex with men*, is translated from two Greek words that refer to the passive and active participants in (male) homosexual acts." I have studied this passage in the Greek for myself and found the footnote to be accurate.

## BREAKING IT DOWN

IN MY OPINION, HOMOSEXUALITY can be broken into at least three primary issues: 1) same-sex attraction, 2) emotional need/attachment, and 3) gender confusion/rejection.

### SAME-SEX ATTRACTION

"Same-Sex Attraction" is a term used to describe an individual who finds other individuals of the same gender sexually attractive and arousing. It is important to understand that sexual arousal itself is, in great part, a learned response.

**Learned Responses.** Every happily married couple knows what "floats their partner's boat." Over time, your intimacy grows sweeter because you know each other's wants and needs so well. You have "learned" each other sexually.

People can engage in damaging behavior—or can have damaging acts perpetrated on them—that become part of what they have learned sexually. Males, in particular, are aroused by what they see, what they touch, and what touches them, but females are, too, to a lesser degree.

Children who are sexually molested can become aroused because they are being touched, even while being victimized. The child may feel guilt for the experience, but it is the first step in "learning" arousal. Repeated encounters reinforce that arousal until it becomes a learned response. Once a response is learned, it is often difficult to unlearn.

This is why pedophilia is a plague upon any society: Innocent children, boys and girls, are damaged in their childhood and struggle for years to overcome the guilt, shame, and *learned responses* of those encounters.

We see the same effect with pornography. First, a spouse who "indulges" in pornography commits a form of adultery by replacing their husband or wife with another person's image or video and by performing sexual acts in response to those stimuli, acts that are outside the sanctity of marriage.

Second, the image that arouses him or her is "better" than his wife or her husband. Men who view pictures of model-perfect women become aroused by their physical and sexual perfection and then find it difficult to respond sexually to their real-life wives who carry stretch marks and a few extra pounds. Similarly, women who view male porn stars find their overweight husbands unattractive or repulsive in comparison.

Men and women who watch pornography have acquired a learned response to a fantasy and have lost their taste for reality. The result is that that their spouse can no longer arouse in them the same sexual gratification they receive from the pornography.

(Pornography is a sin that defrauds a wife of her husband and a husband of his wife, and the spouse who uses pornography commits adultery. The only solution to pornography addiction is deep repentance and sexual abstinence until husband-wife sexual relations can be relearned and trust rebuilt.)

In addition, depictions of and participation in sadomasochistic sexual acts can arouse both men and women and cause them to no longer desire normal, caring, monogamous sex. This is another type of abnormal learned response.

**Sexual Abuse.** We all know that sexual abuse is devastating to a child. It steals their innocence, warps their concepts of sex, and damages their emotional and sexual development. Even the early sexual encounters that seem so common in our culture are very damaging. God in his wisdom wants us to wait, marry one person, and enjoy sex *only* within that precious intimacy.

In the gay world, monogamous sex is nearly unheard of, and many gays had very early encounters, sometimes as victims seduced by experienced gay partners, sometimes in mutual sexual experimentation. These experiences all have damaging impacts on learned sexual response, how people perceive themselves and their gender, and on their emotional needs. God will need to reach deeply into these areas to heal them—but he *is* able to heal them.

Whatever we do sexually in our lives becomes part of our sexual library. This is one reason God tells us to keep ourselves pure, because a marriage is happiest sexually when the husband and wife only "know" *each other*. They are not competing with memories or learned responses from other sexual encounters, fantasies, or deviances.

## EMOTIONAL ATTACHMENT AND NEED

The intact family is the building block of society and the church. It is the depiction to children of the Fatherhood of God and his union with his Bride, the church. Children who grow up in a godly, intact family (I am not talking about a dysfunctional religious family) have a basis for relating to God. Children see, in action, godly role models for both genders.

Emotional attachment to someone of the same gender is most often the result of damaged or unmet emotional needs in childhood. People are never perfect, so families are never perfect. As we grow up, even in some very good homes, emotional needs are sometimes not met, and gender validation is sometimes damaged.

**Personality matters.** Some children have a more sensitive personality or nature, too. What is shrugged off by a sibling may be devastating to the sensitive child.

If I am a young girl and I do not receive an appropriate amount of my father's love and care, I could grow up to be sexually promiscuous, "looking for love in all the wrong places." We don't have any difficulty seeing the connection here.

In the same way, a young girl who receives the *wrong* kind of male attention at a young age (from someone sexually or physically abusive to herself, her mother, and/or her brothers and sisters) may reject her femininity because it is not a safe or desirable state. She may reject her female gender for a male or "other" role. If she adopts a male or an "other" gender identity, she will likely seek emotional validation from a woman who needs her in her "other" or male identity.

In the same scenario, the girl might keep her female gender identity but seek out a female partner who has adopted a male or an "other" gender identity. The girl would feel "safe" with this partner in every way: sexually, physically, and emotionally.

## GENDER CONFUSION AND REJECTION

Gender confusion and transgenderism are labeled gender dysphoria,[6] "a conflict between a person's physical or assigned gender and the gender with which he/she/they identify. People with gender dysphoria may be very uncomfortable with the gender they were assigned, sometimes described as being uncomfortable with their body (particularly developments during puberty) or being uncomfortable with the expected roles of their assigned gender."

---

[6]https://www.psychiatry.org/patients-families/gender-dysphoria/what-is-gender-dysphoria

Seems like only yesterday that gender dysphoria was a psychiatric illness. Oh, wait. It *was* just "yesterday." While the American Psychiatric Association still uses the term and definition of gender dysphoria, they have moved off the premise that the condition is something to be treated and "fixed." Treatment now consists of resolving the stress, discomfort, stigmatization, and discrimination related to the patient's preferred method of coping with gender dysphoria, whether it be medically transitioning, socially transitioning, cross-dressing, or other preferred methods.

If ever Pastor Carmichael's message on "delusion" was timely, it is now.

## EXAMPLES OF THE COMPLEXITY OF HOMOSEXUALITY

None of the three areas I very briefly described operates on its own. They overlap and reinforce each other. What is important to acknowledge is that an individual struggling in these areas operates from a position of unmet need. The lie, the deception they embrace, can be identified in the claim that the only solution to that need is an improper relationship. Yes, "we are all broken in one kind or another," but the answer is to call upon God to fix what is broken, not to seek solace in sin.

**Example 1.** A woman I know shared with me her struggle with gender identity. This wife, mother, and grandmother said that throughout her childhood and through her teen years, she wanted to be a boy, so she dressed like a boy and acted like a boy.

She did so, she said, "Because I felt that I would be safer from the abuse if I were a boy."

Her sentiments echo exactly one of the points I am making here: She did not feel safe as a woman, so she *rejected* her female identity and determined to be something else. Thankfully, later in her life she found the safety she needed and learned to embrace the woman God had made her to be.

**Example 2.** A boy with a tender personality may have a father who is "a man's man" and who belittles, criticizes, or in some way expresses disappointment at his son's tenderness, when he should bring his son alongside him to learn godly manhood. A boy who experiences male rejection (real or perceived) may relate to his mother's gender rather than his father's and may a) adopt his mother's feminine traits, b) experience anger, resentment, and hostility toward his father, c) long for the male affection and acceptance his father did not give him, and d) seek for that acceptance and love from older male sexual partners.

A boy with extreme anger toward his father, particularly if there is male violence in the home, may reject the male role model altogether and, thus, reject his own maleness. He may embrace a female gender or an "other" gender.

**Fathers Are Essential.** A child growing up in a single-parent home can struggle with the same issues listed above. Both boys and girls need a safe male role model and a father's love and acceptance. Absent a father in the home, children may look to find a father's attention elsewhere. Girls may seek a man's love "in all the wrong places" and become promiscuous; boys may seek male affection through male sexual encounters.

The varied "pieces and parts" of a bad or missing father relationship (absent any godly male role model) can wreak havoc on an adolescent youth's sexual and gender identity.

## CONCLUSION

AGAIN, THIS BRIEF APPENDIX is not intended to be an exhaustive treatment of homosexuality, but I would like to conclude with two observations. First, childhood and sexual development are complex, intertwined processes, but the family has everything to do with producing well-developed, well-rounded adults.

Second, no single experience or set of circumstances produces homosexuality. Family dynamics and dysfunction; how children perceive (translate) and internalize those dynamics; emotional attachment and bonding; how children observe gender roles played out; whether they identify with, are accepted into, or reject their biological gender role; early sexual trauma or experiences—desired/undesired/abusive (heterosexual or homosexual); and individual personality all impact sexual development and personal maturation.

Due to humanity's fallen nature and the influence of sin upon the world around us, not one of us has a perfect childhood or is a perfect parent. **Life manages to break all of us in some manner or fashion.**

The answer to every kind of brokenness is, and always will be, Jesus.

# GROUP DISCUSSION QUESTIONS

Your group's discussion may have more depth to it if those participating in the discussion have read, in addition to *Sarah Redeemed*, the Appendix, *More on the Subject,* before approaching this set of questions. Blessings!

—Vikki

1) "What is inside a person shows up on the outside" is a theme *Sarah Redeemed* presents in at least three ways within Chapters 3, 7, and 9. Discuss this concept and what it means with regards to a Christian's behavior and growth.

2) Pastor Carmichael, in Chapter 17, said the following about judgments: "You refused these men forgiveness, not realizing that your unforgiveness gave Satan a foothold in your heart. Your wounds festered over years of abuse, and you became angry, filled with rage—an uncontrollable of rage that erupted whenever you were offended . . . And when your anger fed upon new transgressions—both real and perceived—Satan's hold on you grew stronger. Your anger strengthened to the point that you passed judgment upon an entire class of people, upon all men."

   ▪ What kinds of judgments (as defined by Pastor Carmichael) against classes or categories of people do we see in society and the church today? (You may wish the group to make a list to study and discuss.)

   ▪ Do you observe any commonalities between the roots of Sarah's judgments and the roots of judgments in society and the church today?

3) What are some of the results of judgments we see in our society today? What about in the church today?

4) In Chapter 16, Minister Liáng said, "Deception, if we allow it entrance into our hearts and minds, is not static or inactive. Deception grows; it progresses. If we allow deception to develop unchallenged, its mature state is delusion."

   ▪ Discuss what Liáng teaches about delusion and error.

   ▪ What examples of delusion do we see in churches today? What about in our society?

5) How important was Pastor Carmichael's advice to Sarah (regarding ongoing forgiveness) when he likened forgiveness to the layers of an onion? (Read Sarah's recollection of this advice in Chapter 18.)

6) What did you think of Pastor Carmichael repenting and asking Sarah's forgiveness? How do you think it affected her ability to forgive the men who had abused her? (Chapter 17)

7) Universal brokenness is another central theme of Sarah Redeemed. For example, Sarah found common ground with Dr. Croft when he shared his brokenness; his vulnerability helped Sarah feel safe and able to connect with him. How does realizing that we are all broken free us to seek freedom from our own particular brand of brokenness?

8) In Chapter 20, Rose answers Lola with, "Despise you? No, quite the opposite, Lola. I wish only God's best for you."

   ▪ How does Rose's response show how we can bring the Lord into our conversations with individuals trapped in the gay lifestyle?

   ▪ When we "wish only God's best" for someone, are we agreeing with their sin? What is God's best for them?

9) After reading the Appendix, *More on the Subject*, how are you now better able to

   ▪ Have compassion upon those who struggle with same-sex sin?

   ▪ Pray for those who struggle with same-sex sin?

   ▪ Discern the difference between the truth of God's word and the gay community's agenda?

   ▪ Discern a gay individual's real pain and its undergirding lie and, lovingly, speak truth to that pain?

10) What is your most important "takeaway" from Sarah Redeemed?

_____

_____

_____

_____

_____

# ABOUT THE AUTHOR

Vikki Kestell's passion for people and their stories is evident in her readers' affection for her characters and unusual plotlines. Two often-repeated sentiments are, "I feel like I know these people" and "I'm right there, in the book, experiencing what the characters experience."

Vikki holds a Ph.D. in Organizational Learning and Instructional Technologies. She left a career of twenty-plus years in government, academia, and corporate life to pursue writing full time. "Writing is the best job ever," she admits, "and the most demanding."

Also an accomplished speaker and teacher, Vikki and her husband Conrad Smith make their home in Albuquerque, New Mexico.

To keep abreast of new book releases, visit her website at **http://www.vikkikestell.com/** or connect with her on Facebook at **http://www.facebook.com/TheWritingOfVikkiKestell**.

Faith-Filled Fiction™

www.faith-filledfiction.com | www.vikkikestell.com